HAWTHORN ACADEMY

HAWTHORN ACADEMY

YEAR THREE

D.R. PERRY

DISRUPTIVE IMAGINATION

LMBPN Publishing
PMB 196, 2540 South Maryland Pkwy
Las Vegas, NV 89109

First US edition, December 2020

ebook ISBN: 978-1-64971-355-1
Print ISBN: 978-1-64971-356-8

THE HAWTHORN ACADEMY YEAR THREE TEAM

Thanks to our JIT Readers

Rachel Beckford
Dave Hicks
Veronica Stephan-Miller

Editor
SkyHunter Editing Team

CHAPTER ONE

"This is creepier than I thought it would be."

"Peep!"

At least my dragonet agreed. The stairs down to the basement in the apartment in The Point were musty, damp, bare concrete.

"I wonder if they'll let us put a rug down here or something." Logan shrugged. "It echoes an awful lot. Hurts the ears don't you think?"

"I hoped it'd be a little, you know, homier." I sighed.

"I like it." Noah snorted. "Fits my new vampiness. Complements it, actually. Maybe even makes a fashion statement, like Dorian's wardrobe."

"Noah, honestly." Elanor held up her key ring, jangling the bobs of metal against each other. "Don't be so melodramatic. It's not like vampires are new. Or that you're the first one to get turned as a teenager either."

"Technically, I'm an adult." He held his hand out and gazed at his maroon-painted fingernails.

"I'm about to catch up to you." I chuckled.

"Nope." Noah shook his head. "Can't catch me; I'm the ginger fang man."

"Thought that was your boyfriend." Logan grinned. "Because Jonah's a redhead. Get it?"

After a moment absent of the laughter Logan expected, he slapped his hand over his mouth.

"No, no, I get it." Noah shrugged. "Or maybe I'm not getting any with Jonah in jail. Open the door already, El."

Elanor stuck the key in the lock and tried turning. Nothing happened.

"I just picked these up this morning." She blinked. "I don't understand."

"Peep!"

"Meow?"

"What is it, Doris?" Logan called after his mercat as she ran up the stairs.

The door at the top opened and briefly let in light. Thankfully artificial. It got blocked by the bulk of the person standing in the doorway.

"Trouble with the key?" The voice was a warm tenor, but gravelly somehow, as though the speaker had swallowed water down the wrong pipe a minute ago.

"Yeah, I'm afraid so, Mr. Micello." Elanor pushed past us, heading up the stairs to meet the man coming down it halfway.

He reached out, flipped a switch, and a bare bulb went on over her head. His face was broad and round, with a physique to match. He clung to both handrails as he descended, which I noticed were reinforced.

I narrowed my eyes, almost closing them, trying to get in touch with my sense of the magic around me. Something about Paolo Micello felt familiar, but I couldn't place from where. If he was an extrahuman of some sort, I wanted to know what kind.

He's a troll, of course. Like your friend. What's his name? Begins with a b and ends with an r. Oh, you know, from Gallows Hill.

"Bartholomew!"

"No, that's my nephew. But you've met him along with others I call kin." He nodded. "Which is one reason I agreed to rent this apartment in the first place."

"Oh." Elanor blinked and backed down the stairs.

"I'm sorry about the key. It goes to the apartment on the third floor, which is also for rent but unsuitable for a vampire. If you happen to know anyone else looking for a place," he glanced at Logan and me. "A nice young couple perhaps, please inform me."

He reached for a ring of keys on his belt and removed a set, then held them up while squinting. "My eyesight isn't what used to be. I mistook the B for three." He chuckled. "Let's switch, and you'll be all set."

"Thanks." Elanor exchanged keyrings with Mr. Micello.

"If you need help moving, that's Bartholomew's summer job. Let me know, and I'll send him over with the truck."

"That'd be super helpful," Noah said. "My hours are...limited, Mr. Micello."

"Understood. And call me Paolo."

He turned and headed back up the steps with a painfully stiff gait. Either Paolo Micello feared stairs or had trouble with his legs.

Why not both?

I narrowed my eyes and tried to visualize what my inside voice, which maybe wasn't so much evil as terrifyingly pragmatic, meant. Tiny flecks of reddish-gold dazzled me, collected somewhere around Paolo's knees. What that signified, I didn't know. Once the door closed behind him, Logan elbowed me.

"Write it down." He held my phone, which he'd managed to take out of my bag without my noticing. "Or type. And sorry about picking your pocket."

I glanced up, wondering whether Noah and Elanor had noticed this exchange. They were too busy opening the door. We followed them inside, me tapping out a memo on my phone about Paolo's spark-infested legs for later.

"Wow." Logan stopped so suddenly that I bumped into him.

"Whoa!"

We tumbled to the floor together, his arm caught in the strap on my bag. Ember swooped out of nowhere and caught my phone a hair before it fell on the floor. She landed while holding the electronic device against her scaly little face.

"Peep?"

Doris sauntered up to stand beside Ember, where she sat with her tail curled around her legs. The look she gave us reminded me of Professor Luciano, who died protecting us only a short span of weeks ago. I burst into tears, my awkward tangle with Logan suddenly transformed. I clung to him like a rock in the rapids.

Ember's eyes widened. She headbutted the mercat, knocking her off-center and breaking the impression. As though in apology, Doris ran to my side, rubbed against my shoulder, and purred.

"Hey." Logan touched my face and wiped away tears. "Hey, Aliyah. You're gonna be okay."

"He won't. Not ever again." I sniffled.

"Hawkins said this is normal." Tears stained his face too.

"I'm tired of feeling like this." I shuddered and leaned back. "Like any minute I'll go to pieces."

"Me too." Logan sat across from me now, our hands still clasped.

"I don't know what to do."

"Me neither."

Fabric rustled beside us.

"You're not alone." Noah's hand felt cool and soothing against my cheek.

"Yeah." Elanor hugged her brother. "That's why we rented this flophouse in the first place."

"You never gave us the ten-cent tour." I used my sleeve to dab under my eyes.

"As you can see, we've got this lovely linoleum, circa nineteen eighty-five."

"You doofus." Elanor rolled her eyes. "This design is clearly from the early nineties."

Just like that, we all laughed. For Logan and me, it was wet and snotty, with something sharp inside that still threatened. However, I was a fire magus and he was water. Both of us were accustomed to volatility, only not so emotional.

"Let's show them the bathroom first," Elanor said.

"Yeah. Don't want literally snot-nosed whippersnappers in my bedroom." Noah's attempted snort had a little too much sniffle in it. So he shared this grief also, but in a less obvious way.

The bathroom was right behind us. When Noah pushed the door inward, I expected a tiny room. Instead, it opened to my left into a decently sized space, decorated in Pepto-Bismol pink. The shower-head side of the bathtub sat behind it, the bar hanging bare without even rings for a curtain. A sizeable cabinet supported the sink, which stood between the tub/shower and toilet.

Logan stepped up to it and splashed his face several times. Then he turned, hands and face dripping. No towel hung from the ring by the sink or the hooks on the wall to my right.

"Oops." He blinked.

"Here." I reached into my bag and brought out a pack of tissues.

"Nah, this is better." Elanor held out a dishtowel.

"Oh." Logan reached for it but paused. "You were never this nice when I made mistakes back ho—I mean in Vegas."

"I don't have to pretend anymore." She shook the towel. "Go on."

He dried his face, then folded the towel and hung it neatly beside the sink. He gazed down at the damp pink porcelain, unmoving.

All those fine manners of his. Which of those were written in blood, do you think?

Angry red and orange lines in trails like the ones that come from staring at a light for too long crossed his back, superimposed over his clothes. I swallowed around a sudden lump in my throat.

"Let's call Bar." Elanor tugged her brother's sleeve. "And get out of here so Aliyah can wash up."

He nodded and scooted past me, not looking up, which was normal for Logan some of the time. But not for now. I could tell by the way his shoulders stood high like they reached for his ears.

"We're going to be okay." I squared my jaw and reached for the faucet. "All of us."

I felt Noah's presence in the doorway behind me although he didn't speak. Somehow, I sensed his abject disagreement. Instead of responding to that, I splashed my face thoroughly. Once the tight sting of tearstains eased, I closed the tap and made use of the towel.

"Let's finish that tour, then." Noah turned on his heel and led me out of the bathroom.

Elanor and Logan joined, having finished their call in the kitchen. There was plenty of room in there for a table and chairs. A set of wooden pocket doors slid aside to reveal a windowless living room. It had a bricked-over fireplace with a marble mantel. One of those faux flame lights squatted on the hearth. Noah sauntered over toward it, chuckling.

"This is what sold me on the place."

"Fun."

"It gets better." Elanor grinned. She headed for a door to the right of the fireplace, which I couldn't imagine led to anything bigger than a closet.

I was wrong.

It opened out into a room padded with thick noise-canceling tiles. A mic stand, an amp, a keyboard, and a stand holding an electric bass and an acoustic guitar filled most of the floor space.

"Welcome to Piercing Whispers central."

"Has Dylan seen this?" Logan asked.

"Later. He's still on shift at the Lyceum."

"So, where are your rooms?" I leaned against the mantel.

"Off that hall." Noah paced toward me, then linked his arm through mine. "Check it out."

Two doors led off the hallway, and each already had a sign on it, indicating whose room was whose. Noah's was a collage of construction paper decorated in rainbows. Elanor's sign was painted plywood decorated with FiFi's molted feathers.

"Luckily, the closets are the same size." She pushed her door open. The only thing in her room was a perch for her phoenix. "We'll be redecorating, obvs."

"Yeah." I nodded. "You got a great space here. How much did it run you?"

"Not much." Noah shrugged. "Some of it's barter. We're playing one free gig per month for Paolo. Did you know the Micellos own The Baybridge?"

"No, I didn't." I gave him a side-eye Izzy would have been proud of. "You're getting a job though, right?"

"Security." Noah nodded. "For the Ambersmiths, overnight."

"What about you?" Logan asked Elanor.

"Nothing yet. I applied all over town, though."

"Well, Paolo must think Piercing Whispers is something else." Logan picked at his thumbnail. "Renting to someone without a job. Or he's got some ulterior motive."

"You worry too much, Lo."

"Think I've earned the right."

I reached out, grabbed Logan's hand and squeezed, like he'd done for me the day after Professor Luciano died saving Noah and me. He glanced at me, eyes wide for a moment before nodding.

"Shouldn't someone be at Hawthorne Street when Bar gets there?" I asked.

"Yeah." Noah nodded. "Team kid siblings, you're on moving truck duty. El, we should check out that *bodega* across the street, see what they've got. I'm borderline hangry."

"Mood." Elanor patted her stomach. "There's nothing in the fridge."

We said goodbye at the door on the side of the house, where the basement stairs let out. For a moment, I watched them crossing Palmer Street toward Tropica Mart. Then, I turned and headed up the sidewalk with Logan.

"Should we text Cadence?" he asked. "Doesn't she live near here?"

"Yeah, she does. But she said something about going to Boston today."

"Oh." We walked all the way up Lafayette in silence. "Hey, look!" He pointed at the window for Engine House.

Brianna stood at the register inside.

"That's some good news." I sighed.

"Yeah. After getting laid off from Walgreen's, she was so worried. Should we go in and say hi?"

"I don't think there's time. The line in there is huge."

We caught her eye and waved enthusiastically before turning to walk up Derby Street toward Hawthorne.

Bar's truck was already in the driveway, and he stood shuffling his feet on the stoop outside as though he wasn't sure which bell to ring.

"Hey, Bar."

He turned, raising his eyebrows. "Oh. Hey, Aliyah. Logan."

"It's the one on the right." I reached into my bag and got my keys. "But no need to ring."

"How much stuff do they got?"

"Suitcases, a table and chairs, a futon." I opened the door and let the guys through. "That's all I'm sure about. My folks were in the basement when I left. Who knows what else they unearthed?"

In the living room at the top of the stairs, we found all the luggage and boxes. Bar hefted the entire stack of boxes with a suitcase balanced on top and carried them down the stairs without even pausing to catch his breath. Logan and I dragged the rest of the cases plus Noah's old knapsack, which he'd filled with adult coloring books and colored pencils.

Mom and Dad stood beside the truck, trying to offer Bar help putting everything in the back. He didn't need it. By the time Logan and I set the luggage down, the boxes were safely stowed.

"We've got furniture out back," Dad said.

"Kitchen stuff and some linens too," Mom added.

We made something like an assembly line, passing bags and boxes along the path that Bar navigated with the futon, table, chairs, and a pair of bed frames that looked like they could be bunked if desired.

"What about mattresses?" I shook my head. "Those frames aren't any good without them."

"That was my housewarming gift." Bubbe emerged from her office carrying a pair of handled grocery bags, sides bulging. "Ordered them yesterday. They're arriving on Palmer Street in about an hour."

"What are those for, then?" Logan stared at the bags, which smelled heavenly.

"Everyone helping out, of course." Bubbe grinned. "Rugelach and three kinds of babka. And a treat for Noah along with the recipe."

"'Scuse me for asking but is he gonna be able to eat at all?" Bar cleared his throat. "On account of being, well, a vampire."

"A dear friend recommended it." Bubbe nodded. "There are very few things vampires can eat, but she's got nearly two centuries of experience sampling them."

"Doctor Elizabeth!" I smiled. "How's she doing?"

"Well. She'll be up for the masquerade ball in October and staying with me."

"Cool." Logan elbowed me. "Third-years are allowed to go to that."

"We'd better tell Grace, then. And make sure you've got extra shoes."

"Not so fast, you two." Mom shook her head. "They haven't selected a new headmaster yet. The rules might change."

"Bummer." Bar sighed. "I hope you all can go. Our whole class from Gallows Hill will be there. Anyway, is there anything else going in the truck? There's still room."

"That's all." Dad nodded. "Thanks, Bartholomew."

"Hey!"

Everyone turned to see who had called down the driveway. A figure ran up it in the dark. As it drew nearer, I recognized Dylan Khan.

"Dylan!" Logan darted out to meet him, and they hugged.

"Is this all going to Noah's new place?"

"Yeah."

"Can I go with?"

"They're expecting you." I nodded.

"Cool." He smiled. "I've got news too. Mom's coming to work at Hawthorn."

"Whoa!" Logan clapped his hands. "Awesome! What's she doing?"

"School counselor." Dylan shrugged, clearly less excited than his roommate. "Trustees don't want Hawkins doing that while teaching full time."

"Oh." I blinked. "Hmm."

"What's wrong?" Logan stopped bouncing and glanced at Dylan.

"Could get awkward." Dylan sighed. "Like, if I ever happen to need help or whatever."

"Well, my door's always open." Bubbe handed me two bags of food, then set the third one in the cab of the truck with Bar.

"Wow, thanks." The corners of Dylan's mouth turned up.

"Now, you kids ought to get going if Elanor and Noah want to get those bed frames set up before the mattresses arrive." Bubbe went back up the steps in front of her office.

"Yes, and remember that Aliyah and Logan still have curfews to meet."

"Right, eleven-thirty." Logan nodded. "Which gives us two hours."

"Thanks, Morgensterns!" Bar waved out the window. "See half of you back on Palmer Street."

After he pulled away, Logan, Dylan, and I headed back toward The Point on foot.

I sat with Noah in his room and tried to put the bed frame together, which would only have been more frustrating if it had come from IKEA.

"Gimme the monkey wrench."

I slapped a length of metal into his waiting hand.

"No, wait. The Allen wrench."

I replaced it.

"Almost done?" I peered apprehensively at the contraption sagging around him.

Noah threw his head back and let out a laugh that almost sounded like a howl.

"Need help?" Logan stood in the doorway.

"Go help El." Noah waved him away.

"We're done with hers."

"Then have at it, gadget man." Noah stood and stepped out of the rickety-looking excuse for a bed frame.

"That's not bad. Like, for a parody." Dylan strummed the acoustic guitar in the corner and sang. "Gadget man, fixing up his furniture alone. And it isn't gonna take a long, long time. To get this bed set up in here. I'm not the man that's gonna sleep in it, but the one who does is gonna sleep alone. But Noah, he's not a gadget man. Gadget man, top of the class at the place I call home."

"That's pretty good, Dyl." Noah grinned. "Figure out how to make it less derivative, and we've got a new number, I think."

"You really want him writing songs about you sleeping alone?" Elanor chuckled.

"No. But at least he's honest." Noah sighed.

"Got it." Logan stood while dropping the slide wrench into the tool bucket. "Just in time, too."

A truck horn sounded outside.

We all got out of the way as the delivery staff brought in two mattresses and box springs. They left in a hurry, making me think at least one of them was a little weirded out by being in an apartment designed for vampires. We unwrapped the plastic and set the beds on the frames ourselves with little trouble.

"How was that Tropica Mart?" I opened the fridge, looking for drinks to go with the babka, but only saw bottled blood. "Nothing much there besides this?"

"Not true." Elanor shook her head. "I drank all the pineapple Faygo."

"Cadence swears by that stuff." I chuckled. "Is it still open?"

"All night. It's a twenty-four-hour sort of place," Noah answered. "Come on." Dylan leaned the guitar against the wall and headed for the door with us.

"Are you guys coming?" I glanced back at Logan and Elanor.

"Nah." He shook his head. "Can you get me some ginger ale if they have it?"

"Sure."

The Tropica Mart had a sign out front with the picture of a palm tree underneath a crescent moon. The brown-skinned man sitting under it exhibited a fangy smile. I understood why Noah was so enthused to go back to the clearly vamp-friendly establishment.

Inside, the shelves were close together and packed with a variety of grocery and household goods. A fresh fruit and vegetable stand sat at the back, near coolers filled with frosty beverages. I saw plantains, coconuts, papaya, jicama, yucca, tomatillos, and avocados along with apples, oranges, and pears.

"Oh, is this your *hermana*?"

"Yeah, it is." Noah nodded at the man behind the counter, who might have modeled for the figure on the sign. "Jefe, this is my sister Aliyah. Aliyah, Jefe."

"Jefe DelSangre. This is my store." He held his hand out, and I shook it. "Welcome."

"Thank you." I smiled. "Nice to meet you."

We gathered soda, which was mostly the Faygo brand. They had all the flavors, including ginger ale. After paying and wishing Jefe a good evening, we headed back across the street. At the apartment, we drank soda while unpacking linens and making beds. Logan and I had to go after that, but Dylan stuck around to get the drums set up in the practice room.

"Who's going to play them?" I asked. "Arick went back to Bergen."

"His parents own an airline. So he's coming and going a lot this summer."

"How's that going to work for your monthly gigs at the Baybridge?" Logan blinked.

"Maybe you'll fill in if he's not around?" Elanor shuffled her feet. "I meant to ask more nicely than that."

"No." He planted his feet. "No performing. Not anymore."

"Okay." She nodded. "I understand."

She doesn't.

The voice was right, but I wasn't going to start an argument and miss curfew.

"I'll ask Azrael tomorrow. His dad knows most of the musicians in this town." I shrugged. "For now, we've got to get home."

We left. Out on Lafayette Street, Logan spoke.

"Thanks."

"What did I do?"

"You backed me up." He turned, walking backward like Dorian did last year before Mercy died. In true Logan Pierce fashion, he looked at my face without meeting my gaze. "She would have kept asking if you hadn't mentioned Az. Eventually, I would have been their drummer. Whether I liked it or not."

"Hey, this is what friends do for each other."

"No. Dylan didn't say anything, and he's my friend. We're close." He cleared his throat. "But you're my best friend, Aliyah. Ever."

We stopped to hug on the corner of Lafayette and Derby, then held hands the rest of the way home. He walked me up the stoop in front of my parent's apartment.

"See you tomorrow morning for waffles?" He grinned.

"Yeah. I promise not to try passing ketchup off as syrup. Goodnight, Logan."

"Goodnight, Aliyah."

I ran up the front stairs as fast as I could, peered out the window, and was rewarded for my effort as I watched Logan walk through the door at Bubbe's office, Doris pacing in beside him.

"Peep." Ember nuzzled my cheek, cooing. Then she yawned.

"Yeah, girl. Let's get some sleep."

I only paused by Mom's office to wave at her before heading to my room for pajamas, the toothbrush, and bed.

CHAPTER TWO

The week before I turned eighteen, I stood in the kitchen.

"Mom, I have to take the extramagus test." I crossed my arms over my chest. "What are we doing about that?"

"Bubbe's still hammering out the details with the Director-General." She poured coffee. "There are still five days before your birthday."

"She's not still trying to get me out of it?" I tapped my foot. "You know how I feel about that."

"I know." Mom toppled a splash of cream into her cup. "And yes, she is trying to make the process easier."

"How does that work, exactly? If I'm an adult, she doesn't get to make that kind of decision for me."

"Which is why she's making arrangements now, while you're still a minor." Mom clinked a spoon in the clouded coffee and stirred.

"You know, Aliyah," Dad interrupted. "It has to happen after you turn eighteen, but there's no requirement for you to have it on your birthday."

"I didn't ask you, Dad." My arms dropped to my sides as the implications of what he said hit me. "Oh. Oh!"

"Aaron!" The air around my mother got warmer.

"I want things to be fair, Angie." Dad sighed. "For Aliyah and everyone else."

"That's why Bubbe's having those talks, so it'll be different this time." Mom said.

"Different only for me?" I narrowed my eyes. "It needs to change for every extramagus. Or else none of us. If Bubbe's planning to get me some special waiver, I'm going to say no."

"I don't want anyone else tortured either." Mom held her coffee in front of her like a shield. "Bubbe thinks you shouldn't have to put yourself through the full ordeal. She's using the summer to your advantage."

"What do you mean?"

"Available space and facilities give her an excuse to request a truncated process." Mom sighed. "Your recent acts of heroism are under consideration, too."

"Hawthorn had all the space and facility they needed for Dylan." I leaned against the counter. "And me."

"There's still no headmaster at Hawthorn. So until the trustees select and appoint one, the test can't happen on campus."

"Do I still get a witness?" I raised an eyebrow.

"That depends."

"That's bullshit." I glared, nostrils flaring, practically daring her to jump on my case for language. Instead, she sighed.

"You can postpone the test until proper facilities are available, but you've got to put it in writing and hand it directly to the Director-General. In person."

"Great. Where is he?"

"Bubbe mentioned the Hawthorne Hotel," Dad offered. "I'd wait until after the dinner hour to see him, though."

"Aliyah—"

"You can't talk me out of this, Mom."

"I know." She pushed the door to her office open. "You can use the guest account on my computer to write your request. I'll print it while you're out. Hold on."

Mom sat at her desk and switched accounts to the one Noah and I used on occasion.

"Thanks."

It took a few moments to compose my thoughts. Then I wrote something more formal than I might have managed without that pause.

Fix it. You don't want to sound...unhinged.

"Never turn in the first draft."

"Hmm?" Dad said from the kitchen.

"Something Logan says at school."

I finished after a few more minutes of work, but something was missing. I stood and paced while trying to remember how letters Mom sent to schools always looked.

"It needs addresses," Mom said. "I'll fix it. You were due down at Bubbe's to help out."

"Right." I nodded. "Thanks, Mom."

She sat at the desk and nodded without looking up. I left, heading out in the kitchen to let her work. More frustration must have shown on my face than I'd intended.

"Hey, Aliyah." Dad put his hand on my shoulder. "You know she's only trying to protect you, right?"

"I know, but she's not an extramagus. I have to do this my way or not at all."

"I get it. I'm proud of you for standing up. But you have to jump through the hoops first. You understand?"

"Yeah, Dad. I do. Thanks for reminding me of that."

I headed down the back stairs, and knocked at the bottom instead of barging in.

"Come in!"

I walked into Bubbe's office and closed the door. Ember swooped through the air above my head, flying up and down the hall. She peered into each room at the boarders and critters there for checkups. I went straight to the small kitchen in the middle of the hall, turning the corner to find Logan sitting over a bunch of patient files and paperwork. My grandmother bustled at the stove, boiling water.

17

"What's that there?" I peered over Logan's shoulder.

"They're about Doris." Logan tapped one of the papers. "We're trying to figure out what type of mercat she is. These are genetic tests."

"That's advanced work. Must be exciting for you." I sat beside him.

"Exciting for Doris too." He grinned. "She wants to know where she came from."

"Meow." Doris jumped up on the table and paced back and forth. She peered at the files, then bumped her head against my hand while purring.

"I guess that means she's doesn't mind me seeing them." I smiled.

"Yeah. Doris really likes you. I mean, you did save her life."

"That's not how I remember it."

"You carried her down the street to here."

"Oh, yeah. I barely remember that. But you gave her water."

"That's the part I forget." He chuckled.

"I'm bringing this decoction to the opossum in room two," Bubbe said. "I'll be back in about five minutes."

"Okay." Logan nodded.

I waited until I heard Bubbe crooning in the treatment room.

"I need your help." I drew a deep breath before letting the hard part out. "They're making me take an extramagus test. I want you to be my witness."

"What?" Logan blinked. "Extramagus test?" His voice cracked.

"Anyone with more than one element has to. I wasn't allowed to tell anybody, but I guess I'm telling you they exist because otherwise, I can't ask you to be there with me."

"They test every extramagus? But why? And how?"

"I'll tell you another time." I glanced at the open door. "It's a secret."

"It must be horrible if it's unspoken." He picked at the ragged skin by his thumbnail, a habit when something disturbed him.

"I found out when Dylan went through it last year. He chose me."

"Okay, then."

"Are you sure? You can change your mi—"

"It's utterly horrible?"

18

"Terrifying. Been dreading it all year."

"You don't need to tell me more. I'll be there, no matter what. Like I promised."

Doris jumped into my lap, purring. Ember landed on my shoulder, gazed down at the mercat, *peeped* once, then hopped on Logan's shoulder where she curled herself around his neck in a familiar fashion.

"She hasn't done that in a long time." Logan nodded at Doris.

I glanced at Ember. "Likewise." I rested my chin on one hand while petting Doris with the other. "So what's this about a genetics test?"

Logan launched into a lecture about chromosomes, alleles, and genetic markers commonly found in mercats. His enthusiasm for the subject made it more interesting than it would've been if I'd read it or even if Bubbe had explained it.

I spent the rest of the day in the extraveterinary office with Logan after going over the file. We fed and watered the boarded animals and took some to the backyard for exercise. After that, it was time for lunch.

We headed down the driveway. Izzy sat on her porch with Lee. After a brief conversation, they both joined us at Engine House for pizza.

It's hard enough to keep secrets from a clairvoyant. When Cadence the gossipy mermaid plopped down beside us, my privacy was a lost cause.

"Aliyah, you look off." Cadence peered at my face. "Iz, pull a card for her."

Izzy reached for the bag with her cards.

"Don't." I shook my head. "I've got kind of a big ask. Just Cadence and Izzy, but I trust you to keep this on the down-low, Lee." I picked a bit of cheese off the crust on my plate.

Izzy narrowed her eyes. "I don't like this, Aliyah."

"It's worse than that." Logan patted my shoulder.

"Oh?" Cadence raised her eyebrow while glancing from Logan to me.

"I'm serious. This is some 'never again' level stuff. Are you sure you want to hear it? Because I can't unsay any of this."

"Go on." Cadence leaned forward, elbows on the table.

"Spill it," Izzy ordered.

Lee nodded.

"After I turn eighteen, I've got to take a test because I'm an extramagus. I saw one happen last year, to Dylan. It's absolutely inhumane, like being tortured with every kind of elemental magic that exists. If enough people knew, maybe they'd find another way. So I want to record mine and leak it to the public, but I need your help."

Logan covered my hand with his. Cadence's eyes widened. Izzy nodded, and chewed on the inside of her cheek. Lee leaned back in his chair, lips pressed into a thin, flat line. He surprised me by speaking first.

"That's why he was off all last year." It wasn't a question but a statement of fact.

"I wish he'd said something." Cadence sighed. "Everyone assumed all his drama came from breaking up with Grace."

"He wasn't allowed to talk about it." I narrowed my eyes, trying to keep tears out of them. "I get one witness who has to be a magus. I chose Logan. The rest of you aren't supposed to know this. Or even be there when it happens."

Izzy's thrummed her fingers against the table. "So, how do we help?"

"With press coverage, of course." Cadence smirked. "At least that's my best guess. If you want to blow this thing wide open, my mom can make it happen."

"You've got it, Cadence."

"What's the other part?" Izzy tugged at the strap on the satchel she carried her cards in. "All I've got to offer is my skill with my cards."

"No. Like it or not, you're the most popular girl at Messing, Izzy. You've got connections. What I need is some way to pull the entire experience out of my head and share it. Are there psychics who can do anything like that?"

"Usually, that's a telepath." Izzy shook her head. "I don't know any, but Jacinda might be able to help you."

"She's Messing's cheer squad captain." Logan nodded. "A memory psychic, right?"

"Exactly." Izzy nodded. "If there's something you need to make sure somebody sees, a memory psychic is what you want. They can put your memory into an item, and anyone who activates it will see what happened from your point of view."

"Wow. Do you think she'd help us, though?"

"No idea," Izzy said. "She's kind of an introvert."

"She mentioned that Bar's her cousin." Logan traced shapes in the condensation on his soda cup. "Maybe he can help."

"I don't want him involved." I shook my head.

"Why? Because it's dangerous?" Cadence grinned. "Bar's a big boy, with powers to match."

I opened my mouth, about to say exactly what I thought.

Don't tell her it's because he's still hung up on her.

"Last year, danger got my professor killed." I made a fist and crushed the paper plate in the middle of it, pizza crust and all.

"You act like a sponge, not a mermaid." Izzy glanced at a card in her hand. She put it away without showing us. "You soak up every bad attitude your edgelord boyfriend puts on."

"Are you sure Crow's her boyfriend? Because that's subject to change." Logan's catty question made my mouth drop open.

"Why, Mr. Pierce. I never would've dreamed you had it in you." Cadence shrugged. "It's complicated. He's on thin ice."

"Good." Logan put his palms flat on the table, actually looking her in the eye. "I'm sick of people getting hurt. I'm not letting it happen this year."

"I'd love to chat with you about calculated risk." Cadence nodded, her auburn curls bobbing. "This isn't about one evil person. One of our best friends is facing off against persecution. The danger here isn't my fault, or Crow's." She raised an eyebrow at me. "Right, Aliyah?"

"I don't know." I sighed. "Both of you are right, but we should be more careful, not less."

Silence stretched. Eventually, I felt a presence nearby. I looked up to find Brianna Collins holding a pitcher of soda.

"Sorry. I guess I walked in on something?"

"Just talking about last year."

"Are you all okay?"

"Yeah," Logan answered.

"Thanks for the soda," Cadence said.

Brianna looked like she was about to say more when the bell above the door jingled. Elanor sauntered in with Noah, Dylan, and someone I didn't expect to see today.

"Is that Arick Magnuson?" Lee blinked. "From Norway?"

"His parents own an airline," Logan said.

The bandmates sat at the next table and leaned across to chat after giving their order to Brianna. Nobody mentioned the extramagus test. But the conversation about the future didn't stop there.

"So I hear your mom's the new counselor," Lee said. "It's going to be cool, finally meeting Dylan's parents."

"Parent. No Dad, just Mom."

"Why?" Cadence blinked.

"They split up."

"That's pretty heavy," Logan said. "Are you okay?"

"I guess." Dylan shrugged, worrying the napkin with his fingers. "They started arguing last fall. Think I've got something to do with it."

There's an elephant in this room.

I walked up and punched it in the trunk.

"Because you're an extramagus?"

"Probably. Mom filed divorce papers before I came out to them." Dylan sighed.

"I bet it's not about you." Noah patted his shoulder.

"Either way, it sucks." Izzy shook her head. "Let me know if you want a reading."

"Some other time." Dylan waved a hand. "We've got all summer."

"Are you sure you're okay?" I asked.

"Mom told me last month. Besides, I talked about it already." He glanced at Noah, then Elanor. "Bandmates are mates."

"Right." Noah elbowed him.

"Speaking of mates." Cadence glanced at Noah. "Have you seen Jonah?"

"They're only letting family visit. I've sent letters. He hasn't written back. I don't know why."

"Maybe he can't send anything out. Or his lawyer advised against it," Elanor said. "You'll talk sooner or later."

"I don't know." Izzy's brow furrowed. "Hang on." She pulled out a card. "Crap on a crap cracker."

"Share with the class?" Dylan said.

"It ain't nothing nice." Izzy slapped the card on the table.

It was The Chariot reversed, which meant something wrong with communication, usually deliberate.

"Let's hope any ban on letters out is prison-wide," Logan said. "Nobody wants Temperance sending out manifestos while she's locked up."

"She's not in the same place." Noah shook his head. "They put her in some white-collar juvie hall down in New York. It's totally unfair."

"But she's a murderer." Logan blinked.

"Her parents are saying she was duped, led down a dark path." Noah snorted. "By Alex Onassis."

"Weren't you calling him the prince of darkness last year?" Cadence raised an eyebrow.

"I can't stand the guy." Noah shook his head. "But Aliyah and I wouldn't be sitting here if he hadn't done the right thing at the last minute."

"Are you sure?" Izzy asked. "Because he definitely bought into all that magisupremacy."

"Temperance was worse." Arick snorted. "She handed out honest-to-gods fascist pamphlets. And blaming it on Alex? The guy who showed up bruised after their alone time?"

"I noticed." I shook my head. "Anyway, Coach Ives was her real boyfriend."

"What?" Cadence's mouth dropped open.

"The two of them were, um, intimate." I grimaced.

"Where did you hear that?" Izzy blinked.

"I overheard Mom," I answered. "He resigned when they got caught, and the state revoked his teaching license."

"I believe it." Arick nodded. "Nazis suck."

"Spoken like a true punk." Noah chuckled. "I mean that in the nicest possible way of course."

"Thanks." Arick grinned.

"Has she had her trial?" Logan asked.

"No." Noah shook his head. "There's a hearing, something about whether Jonah's coerced turning case is part of her murder charges. Her family's contesting his plea."

Elanor blew a raspberry. I nodded.

"When?" Logan pulled a pencil stub and a small notebook from his pocket.

"July," Noah answered. "I'm giving a statement. I'd appreciate some moral support."

"Can I give one, too?" I asked.

"I'm not sure, Aliyah." Noah shook his head. "You can offer, but they might not accept it because you're an extramagus."

I sighed. "Do they have that horrible device at least?"

"Yes. And the autopsy reports." Noah sipped his soda. "But it's a hearing, remember? They still have to decide whether me getting turned has anything to do with all that."

"If only Lotan could talk." Elanor glanced at the serpent sleeping on Noah's shoulder. "But what can you do?"

"Translate." Logan chuckled. "You know I can understand what they say, right?"

"No. I did not know that." Noah blinked.

"How long have you been able to do that?" Elanor narrowed her eyes at her brother.

"In my first year. Thought it was only Doris at first. But I under-stand all of them." He stared at his hands, his right one twitching as he tried to refrain from pulling a scab off his left thumb.

"Of course he kept it secret." I came to his rescue. "If your parents knew, what would they have done?"

"Had him committed." She paled. "That's the plan if he sets foot in Nevada ever again. They would've done it last summer if they'd known. Saw some nasty paperwork over winter break and that's why I moved out."

"Yeah." Logan stared at his uneaten pizza. "I figured. Feels like we're in a Grimm story. The kind where the parents end up eating their kids."

"What if they come to Parent's Night?" Elanor shuddered.

I looked around the table at all the wide-eyed faces. Dylan broke the silence.

"If they try anything funny, I'll conjure a tornado and drop a house on them."

Everybody chuckled a little, but nobody outright laughed. This humor was drier than a desert and twice as harsh. But as long as my friends could keep laughing, we could get through anything. Right?

―――――

That night, I leaned against the fence between the driveway and my backyard, gathering the courage to cross the street and head into the Hawthorne Hotel with my postponement letter. Could I face the Director-General? Would he accept my request if I stood there, visibly shaking? After watching him test Dylan, I feared him.

It's worse. The man terrifies you, with good reason.

Because I was alone, I answered my inside voice, which wasn't acting particularly evil.

"Thanks for understanding. But I don't know what to do."

Hand him the letter at your grandmother's appointment, perhaps?

"I don't want to risk her stopping me."

So go. Quake in your sandals if you must. You're not alone.

"That's right." I nodded at Ember, who sat on my left shoulder. "You'll help me be brave, right girl?"

"Brave for what?"

Don't be alarmed.

I turned slowly. The voice was right because Logan stood peering over the fence from the backyard.

"I didn't know you were out here."

"Likewise. What's going on?"

I told him.

"I'll go with you if you want."

"I do. But you're busy."

He jerked a thumb over his shoulder. "It's time for the opossums to go back inside, anyway."

"I'll help."

I strode through the gate Logan held open. The simple yet challenging task of wrangling baby opossums onto their mother's back and escorting them back to their room lifted my spirits. Maybe it was Logan's enthusiasm. Or both.

Absolutely both.

"Yeah."

Logan noticed my gaffe but said nothing. Did he not care about my habit of replying to nobody? Or did he think I communicated with Ember the way he did with Doris? At least he didn't seem to judge me for it.

Sooner or later you have to tell somebody about me.

I ignored the voice this time.

"Where are you headed?" Logan walked beside me down the driveway.

"I've got to hand a letter to an, um, intimidating person."

"This is about that test." Logan sighed. "How can I help?"

"Do you remember the first Parents Night dance?"

"Yeah. We hid your solar. But he knows you're an extramagus."

"It's not magic I need to hide, Logan." I sighed. "It's fear."

"Oh." He blinked. "Maybe you want someone braver than me."

"You've got plenty of courage."

"He's in the hotel?" Logan changed the subject.

"Yeah. Mom put the room number right on the letter."

"Let's cross the street then."

"Meow." Doris walked ahead of us, like a standard-bearer.

The front door at the Hawthorne Hotel was still open after dinner, the likeliest time for Director-General Rockport to be in his room. We turned left toward the bank of elevators. My finger trembled over the up button, but I managed to press it. The elevator opened immediately. Inside, my hands shook too much to select the floor.

Logan stilled the paper flapping in my grasp and glanced at the address on top. I let him take it from me. When he selected the fourth floor, the elevator closed its doors.

The pit of my stomach would've sunk anyway, but the elevator felt like it sent my guts straight to hell. That's an atypical thought for a Jewish girl like me, but that entire evening felt less normal by the minute. When the elevator opened, the hallway yawned in front of me like a gullet, the red paisley carpet and maroon striped wallpaper enhancing that impression.

Logan took my hand and led me down, glancing at the room numbers as we went. I followed, unable to do much more than measure my steps to match his pace. Doris brought up the rear this time.

"Peep." Ember nuzzled my cheek and wrapped her tail over my shoulder like a hug.

We stopped in front of his room. I didn't notice much about the door except that the knob was free and clear of the Do Not Disturb sign. At least I wouldn't feel like I was imposing.

"Hold this." Logan handed me the paper, the entire reason for my visit. "If you need, I'll do the talking. Formal introductions are like dancing for me."

He knocked solidly, four times. Muffled footsteps sounded on the other side. The door opened inward, revealing the man who'd haunted my nightmares since last autumn. He probably figured more frequently in Dylan's than mine now.

"Good evening, Director-General Rockport." Logan inclined his head in a gesture of respect. "Miss Aliyah Morgenstern is here to deliver a document concerning an appointment later this week."

Logan didn't look in the Director-General's eyes, but Rockport seemed to take Logan's mannerisms in stride.

He knows all the trustees, including Logan's father.

I almost replied to the voice. Instead, I addressed Director-General Rockport.

"I'm requesting a postponement of my test to a date and time when proper facilities and equipment are available at Hawthorn Academy." I held the letter out to him. "All the details are in the body of the letter, sir."

Good show, calling him sir.

"This is against the wishes of your grandmother." He raised an eyebrow as he perused the paper. "Nevertheless, as you must be an adult at the time of testing, it's not her decision. As unconventional as your choice may be, I'm inclined to honor it."

"Thank you, sir. I—"

"Conditionally. Give me a reason to postpone. The letter does not specify one." He looked me in the eye, no allowance for avoidance given the way he done with Logan.

"My experience should be fair. My knowledge of the process makes me think a modified test isn't equitable."

"Your knowledge?"

"I was the peer witness for Dylan Khan."

"Interesting." He tilted his head. "You will receive notice of your rescheduled date in August. Good evening."

He took one step back and closed the door. That's when my knees gave out.

"Whoa, Aliyah." Logan hooked his arm under mine, supporting my weight on one side as Ember flapped her wings on the other. Doris squeaked a few times.

"Right, Doris." Logan nodded. "Time to go."

He helped me down the hall and out of the Hawthorne Hotel. I'd carry the burden of the test all summer. I hadn't realized that before, but it wouldn't have stopped me anyway.

I stood on the back porch in the mist at six the next morning, peering through the haze at Ember flying from branch to branch in the mulberry tree. The door opened behind me. My grandmother leaned against the railing on my left, mug of tea in one hand, hair red as an autumn maple. The other held a postcard, which she slapped down on the railing between us.

"This arrived late last night. Read it."

"Your appointment has been postponed until further notice, per written request of one Aliyah Sarah Morgenstern. Director-General Walter Rockport, BEA."

"Aliyah, what have you done?"

"The right thing, Bubbe." I turned my head and met her gaze.

"I hope so."

"You know how I feel."

"Yes." She sighed and bowed her head. "You're not the only one with big emotions here. The first step on this path is the only easy one."

"The second one's the hardest." I put my hand over hers. "I know."

"You don't. That's what scares me, Bissel." She looked back up at me, eyes rimmed with red.

"Why do you keep acting like I didn't think this through, Bubbe?"

"Because that's impossible. You don't have enough information."

"So why didn't you give it to me?"

"I don't have it. Nobody possibly could." Her hands curled around warm ceramic. "Not even your mother, with all of her theory work."

"What about Logan?"

"Maybe he could have figured it out. Given more training than Hawthorn offers."

"Well, he helped me. Last night, delivering the letter. I was too scared to do it alone." I blinked, eyes suddenly damp. I glanced up, but despite the misty morning, it wasn't drizzling.

"At least that level of fear matches the danger." She shook her head. "I only wanted to spare you pain. Because I love you."

"I know, Bubbe. I love you too." I sniffled. "I care how you feel, so much. But since Dylan's test, I think about every other extramagus that doesn't have someone like you on their side."

"You're only eighteen. You can't save the world, Aliyah."

"I'm not trying to." I shook my head. "I want to spare them pain."

"It's unclear how your suffering will accomplish that." She set the tea down on the railing, covering the postcard. "But it's too late for me to change that now."

"I've got a plan. And help."

She opened her arms, and we hugged.

"All the same, I can't stop worrying."

"Why?"

"There's an old saying that when you have children, part of your heart lives outside your chest."

"That's harsh."

"Yes. And it doesn't soften for grandchildren."

"I'll be as careful as I can be, Bubbe. Because I love you."

She let go.

"And I you, Bissel. Forever and always."

CHAPTER THREE

In July, I stood in the exam room beside Logan, watching Bubbe remove a thorn from a moon hare's flank. It wasn't Grace's familiar Lune, thank goodness. Azrael's father found the poor critter under the bandstand on Salem Common.

"Once everything's sterilized, we must take extreme care," Bubbe explained. "If we touch anything but this shaved area, we'll need another tweezer."

"It's okay. She's helping." I tried comforting the poor hare, but she didn't seem particularly soothed by my words.

Logan stepped to my left, made eye contact with the frightened creature, and wiggled his nose. We saw the effects instantly. The hare lay back and extended her leg toward my grandmother. She took it in her gloved hand and brandished the tweezer over the puncture. The animal looked away from my grandmother but sat like a stone.

"Brave girl." Bubbe stepped away and tossed the thorn in the trash. "Now we'll patch it up."

The hare didn't need stitches, just a butterfly closure. Once Bubbe did that, she discarded her gloves and washed her hands. I brought the tray of soiled instruments to the sterilizer while Logan gathered the hare in his arms, humming as he carried her to a recovery room. He set her down, wiggled his nose a few more times, then let her rest on a cushion. He closed the Dutch door's bottom and joined me by the sterilizer.

His care for animals was miraculous as if he was born to help them. He had no ego at all about it, either. The longer I knew Logan, the more amazing I thought he was.

Tell him then.

The last time my inside voice encouraged me to express feelings like that, it went wrong. The moment passed, as they always had before.

"I would've had a much harder time without you Logan," Bubbe said behind us. "I hope you intend to visit frequently during the school year."

"Maybe I'll be in town." Logan sighed. "If I don't manage to get a scholarship, I'll ask to stay with Elanor. Maybe I can get a GED at the community college."

"Scholarship letters come in July. Have you checked with Mom?" I asked.

"Guess I spaced on the date." Logan shrugged. "I'll talk to her when we've finished."

"Okay." I closed the sanitizer and set the dial, then we washed our hands and headed upstairs.

It was about time for a snack anyway. Bubbe hadn't baked anything that day, and all the treats were upstairs until she went shopping that evening. I opened the cabinet for chips and salsa. Logan knocked on my mother's office. She emerged, closing the door behind her.

"How can I help you?"

"I wondered if my scholarship letter came in from Hawthorn." Logan lifted his hand and scratched the back of his head. "I don't want to be a pain, but my entire next year kind of depends on it."

"Hold on." Mom stepped back into her office.

I glimpsed someone inside but couldn't tell who. My father laughed in the living room at something on television.

"Who's in there?" I asked.

Doris chirped.

"Grace," Logan answered. "What if it's bad news?"

"Oh." I drew a deep breath. "I bet—"

"No, it's okay. You don't have to comfort me ahead of time." He pressed his lips together. "I'll be eighteen next month."

"Can't help it. I care."

He blinked and opened his mouth.

The door opened, and Mom emerged with Grace at her side. My mother raised an eyebrow at the chips. Grace gave them a longing look.

"Snacks for everyone." I grabbed the bag and poured more into the bowl, then pushed it toward them.

Everyone munched chips except for Logan, who rocked back and forth on his toes. When Mom noticed, she immediately brushed the crumbs off her hands.

"Logan and Grace have both received scholarships this year."

"How?" I blinked. "I thought they only gave one."

"What about Dylan?" Logan asked.

"Hawthorn didn't give any scholarships this year, just one work study. Dylan's mother works there now, so he gets tuition, room, and board as her family member."

"Mine's from Byers Beauty." Grace smiled. "I designed a makeup case and won my tuition. Ambersmith Fashions gave me a raise that more than covers my room and board."

"What about me?"

"A trustee's covering your third year."

"A trustee?" Logan blinked. "Not my father."

"No. Your benefactor is Hank Thurston. His offer is contingent, however. You must submit an early admissions application to Providence Paranormal College."

"No way." Logan's eyes widened. "That's my dream school."

"I'll give Mr. Thurston the good news." Mom smiled. "We'll work on your application over the rest of the summer."

"I never heard of a trustee handing out scholarships before." Grace shook her head. "And I've checked just about every scholarship opportunity in extrahuman society."

"Maybe the trustees aren't all like Mr. Fairbanks and—" I censored Logan's dad out of my musings. "And Mrs. Onassis."

"Oh, no." Logan glanced at me. "Sorry, Aliyah."

"Why?"

"PPC was your dream school too."

"I'm still applying." I grinned. "I think I'll make it."

"Oh, I almost forgot to tell you." Logan crunched chips. "Dorian has an app—"

The phone in Mom's office rang. She poked her head out and spoke. "Bubbe called. She says your friend's at her office."

We headed down the back stairs.

"Is it okay for me to be there?" Grace asked.

"Should be fine," I said.

We walked up the hall toward the lobby. Lune twitched his whiskers by the door where the stray moon hare slept but ultimately followed Grace. Dorian Spanos stood in the waiting room, signing in with Julia the strix on his shoulder. A married couple older than my parents sat behind him. She stared at nothing while he gazed at *Captivating Creatures Weekly* without touching it. I wondered if their unusual behavior came from their psychic abilities. They were only here because their magus son loved magical critters.

"Hey, Dorian." Logan waved.

"Hey yourself." He smiled, but less brightly than on the day we met last year.

"Come on back." Bubbe held the door.

Dorian followed her. We trailed behind him. I glanced over my shoulder to see his parents still sitting. Dorian's dad held the unopened magazine, his face wearing a bemused expression, as though reading an article without even flipping the cover over.

We went into the same exam room where Dylan bonded with Gale almost two years before. Bubbe opened the cabinet above the sink and pulled down a plastic container full of black and gold collars.

"Yeah." Dorian nodded. "We're formalizing a bond here. Plus the school paperwork stuff."

"Oh." Grace blinked. "It's okay that I'm here, right?"

"Sure. I'm glad you guys showed up. Mom and Dad mean well but don't get all this magus stuff."

"Does your dad do psychometry?"

"Yeah. He got a surprise the first time Julia said hello." Dorian grinned. "Said he always wanted to visit northern Italy, but in person, not through his hands."

"All right, let's see how Julia's doing." Bubbe bent her arm while smiling at the strix.

Julia hooted and hopped from Dorian's shoulder to Bubbe's forearm. She shook her feathers, then turned her head around before letting my grandma check her wings and examine her talons.

Julia had a sober personality, unlike Dorian's late familiar Mercy. She'd been ten pounds of mischief in a five-pound bag. The strix had always been stately and dignified. Since Professor Luciano died, she'd grown somber, too.

I watched Dorian sit through the examination, staring at everything and nothing at the same time. I didn't know how he felt. Losing a familiar was inevitable for most magi who bonded with them. Only a handful of magical creatures had comparable lifespans. Ember might even live longer than me.

Logan held Doris while studying Bubbe's examination process. Grace stood by the door, shifting her weight from one foot to the other as she stared down at Lune. Being unlikely to endure the same tragedy was no reason to neglect a friend in pain. I crossed the room and sat beside him.

"You okay?" I murmured.

"No." He sighed. "This is nothing nice."

"Can I help?"

"This does help." He closed his eyes and leaned against the wall. "Thanks."

Grace elbowed Logan, and they also sat by Dorian through the rest of Julia's physical. When he saw us there his shoulders eased slightly. We hadn't lifted his burden but maybe shared some of the weight.

"She's got a clean bill of health." Julia took off from her forearm and flew to Dorian's shoulder.

"Hello again, old bird." Dorian stroked her head, and she hooted.

"Are you both ready?" Bubbe held an unclasped black and gold bonding collar.

"Yeah." Dorian nodded. Logan peered at Julia, then nodded at Bubbe.

My grandmother handed the chain to Dorian. Purple, white, and gold lit around their hands. Bubbe had channeled her solar magic, and the ice came from Dorian. But what about the purple?

Julia, of course.

"Of course." I slapped my hand over my mouth.

"Inside voice," Grace murmured.

"Shh." Logan put a finger to his lips.

Dorian fastened the collar, and the magic surged again, this time without Bubbe's solar. The purple and white brought it all back like a blow to my chest, the same as that night in the locker room. Tears drenched my face.

You're not alone.

Dorian wept too. Julia comforted him by preening his hair. Ember roused from her slumber on my neck, *peeping* and nuzzling my cheek. The heat of her scales dried my tears, but they kept coming.

Grace is five foot nothing. Somehow she pulled us all into a group hug while murmuring about how we'd get through this. She knew all about grief from losing her parents. I wanted to rely on her experience, but my heart felt like it beat on the outside of my chest, raw and painful.

A few minutes later the teakettle whistled. Bubbe escorted us to the kitchen and poured boiling water over dried leaves. The aroma of tea had a universal and almost magical power.

Dorian sniffled, wiped his nose with the back of his hand, then grimaced and turned to wash them in the sink.

"Where's the Kleenex?" Logan glanced at the empty counter.

Bubbe set a box of tissues beside the tea tray. We blew our noses and dried our tears. Grace stopped crying first, then Logan, then me. Dorian ran out of tears last.

"Sorry." He blew his nose at the sink. "Mom said this was gonna hurt. Didn't want to believe her. But, well."

"Don't apologize for grief," Grace said.

"Thanks, then." Dorian sat down and poured tea. "It would have been worse if you all hadn't been here."

"Do you want to hear some good news?" Logan put sugar in his tea.

"Absotively."

He told Dorian all about the scholarship situation, with Grace adding a few details.

"Awesome." Dorian grinned. "I worried we'd be missing folks next year."

"We won't," Grace said. "Unless a certain situation goes sideways."

"What situation?" Logan blinked.

"Hal's."

Dorian cleared his throat. "Jonah's hearing is tomorrow, and I'm giving a statement. So we're staying at the hotel. Anything fun going on in town tonight?"

"There's a Piercing Whispers show at Dodge Street Café," I offered.

"How do we get there?" Dorian asked.

"We walk." Grace pulled her phone out and tapped out directions. "It's around the corner from Walgreens."

"Cool." Dorian checked his phone after it beeped. "I'll see you there. For now, we've got to check in at the hotel. Thanks again, you guys." He stood.

We left our tea behind and walked him out. His parents waited at the counter holding a check in the exact amount before Bubbe tallied their charge. Being clairvoyant had its perks.

The Dodge Street venue wasn't really a café. It was also a bar. The stage sat between the baristas and the bartenders, enough division for an all-ages gathering place. The bouncer checked our IDs and gave us wristbands at the door.

"This ruins my whole aesthetic." Dorian flicked the strip of neon green plastic.

"Looks cyber-goth to me." Grace snorted. "Neon green goes with black anyway."

"What do you know, K-pop Stan?" He chuckled.

Their banter was good-natured with no hard feelings, which couldn't be said about Dorian and Dylan. They had a sort of truce but still didn't like each other. Not even after last year.

They're jealous of each other. It's untenable.

I imagined why Dorian and Dylan needed to bury the hatchet. I hoped this next year would be easier, all things considered. However, the inside voice might be how my brain interpreted patterns of magic and coincidence. With practically his last breath, Professor Luciano said listen to the magic, even if it's harsh. Ignoring that would dishonor him.

"Is this it?" Logan glanced at empty seats.

"Don't worry," Grace said. "I think your sister's got that covered."

Brianna Collins walked through the door. She held it for an entourage. Brianna was one of Cadence's classmates at Gallows Hill, and she'd brought the entire extramural team, including Bar, Cadence, and Crow. After the last wolf shifter entered, she stayed put. Izzy led Lee, Hal, Faith, and Jacinda inside.

"Oh, that's good," Logan said. "You still need to talk to her about the thing."

"Is this the best time, though?"

"No. But maybe she'll meet you another day."

"What's this about?" Grace watched the door.

"Oh, I wanted some memory psychic help."

She's distracted.

"Cool." Grace stood on her tiptoes, trying to see over Crow's head. "Out of the way, featherbrain."

"Are you talking to me?" Crow narrowed his eyes.

Cadence put her hand on his arm. "Let her through."

Crow stepped aside.

Grace squealed and took off, dashing toward the door where a familiar face showed through the crowd.

Honestly, are you surprised?

"No. It makes sense."

"What?" Logan scratched his head.

"Grace and Azrael." I still hadn't told Logan about the inside voice.

"Is she trying to eat his face?" Logan grimaced. "He should watch his hands." He looked away.

"Found the virgin." Crow rolled his eyes.

"You found two." I glared, making fists. "You got a problem with that?"

Shut that fire off.

I banished the flames around my knuckles, but he'd seen them already.

"Um, no. It's fine, whatever, uh, doesn't float your boat. " He swallowed and edged away.

"Edgelords are so last year. You okay?" I patted Logan's shoulder.

"Yeah. I shouldn't have said that about Grace and Az. It was rude." He sighed. "They're the normal ones."

"I know what you mean." I nodded. "It's awkward for me too, watching public displays of affection."

Logan blinked as his mouth dropped open. For a moment, the muddled sound of several conversations acted like a white noise machine. Our eyes met. Had we ever locked gazes like this?

The first time you met. Last summer. And here you are again.

"Aliyah, are you a—"

"Hey." Izzy waved at us from the line at the coffee counter. "Come on, before they get swamped."

In line, we talked about the show, wondering what they'd play. Noah said they mostly did covers, but Logan mentioned they'd been practicing original stuff the last time he visited Elanor. Drinks in hand, we looked for seats. By that time, the place was packed. Most folks on the bar side were college kids from Salem State.

All mundane.

"I don't care."

"What?" Izzy blinked.

"Inside-outside voice problems again." I let out a nervous laugh.

"Did you want me to bring Jacinda over here?" Logan nodded toward where she stood by the door.

"No, they're about to start. I'll catch her after their set."

Piercing Whispers chose that moment to step onstage. Elanor switched her keyboard on. Dylan slung his Paul Reed Smith over his shoulder. Noah adjusted the mic stand. Arick sat behind the drum set. Some of the college kids snickered, probably because Arick had such a baby face.

"We're Piercing Whispers. Two, three, four." Noah cut the laughter off. Arick kicked off the beat as Dylan popped a riff, starting their first song.

At first, I didn't recognize the melody. That made sense because I'd never been a fan of The Cure. Piercing Whispers changed my mind about the post-punk band. *Push* had a long, uplifting introduction that showcased the band's teamwork. Logan got up and danced. People on both sides of the Dodge Street Café joined in.

Nobody snickered at Arick after such a strong open. As their set continued, so did the dancing. Even the bartender and baristas rocked out while pouring and brewing.

Their last song was *Nine In The Afternoon* by Panic! At The Disco. Logan dragged me up to dance with him. We weren't formal like at Hawthorn, but I found myself able to keep up. Somehow, he'd taught me to dance without really trying.

At the end of the set, most everyone cheered. As the crowd quieted, I headed straight toward the door, where Jacinda still stood. As I approached, her eyes widened.

"Hi there, I'm—"

"Yeah, Aliyah Morgenstern. I know." She blinked. "Why are you here?"

"I recognized you from extramurals. You led the Messing cheer squad, right?"

"Yeah, but what do you want with me?" She leaned against the wall like she wanted to merge with it.

You're scaring her. You know that, right?

My heart didn't feel it, but my mind shouldn't forget that I scared some people.

"Logan says a lot of nice things about you."

"I thought you were classmates." Her shoulders eased a little. "Didn't realize you guys were a thing."

"He's one of my best friends. Anyway, it was nice to meet you. Sorry if I spooked you."

"I'm okay. Talk to you some other time, I guess."

"Yeah, don't be a stranger."

I sat back down at the table I shared with Logan, Izzy, and Lee, shaking my head.

"I told you to let me introduce you." Izzy sighed. "Jacinda's jumpy around strangers to begin with, and you were the tough gal on campus last year."

"I didn't feel tough."

"The rumors say you fought Tempe in a room full of vampires, saved Dorian, and survived a lethal attack." Izzy sighed again. "I know what really happened and still think you're a badass."

"I'll reintroduce you," Logan said.

By that time, Jacinda was nowhere in sight.

I stood outside the courthouse on Federal Street with Noah the next night, along with Dad, Logan, and Dorian with his parents. Because Jonah was a vampire, the Night Court handled this case.

"It's only a hearing." Mr. Spanos said.

"But it's important." Noah sighed. "This is where they decide whether the cases are connected."

"That's not right." I swallowed the urge to conjure fire. "They are. All three of us were there."

"The judge doesn't know that." Mrs. Spanos said. "The bones gave me no sure answer, and my auguries were unclear."

"The truth will out." Dorian nodded. "At least that's what I keep telling myself."

"Hoo." Julia preened his hair.

Our group was the first inside the courthouse's expensive lobby. We walked through the second set of thick wooden doors on the left. The bailiff already stood beside the judge's chambers. The court reporter tapped her device with a wand. I watched raptly. Wand magic was college-level work.

Minutes later, a diminutive white-haired man with twinkling brown eyes and beige skin walked through the door. He set a briefcase on the defendant's side, opened it, then sat. He must be Jonah's lawyer.

"That's Yoshi Ichiro, from Providence," Dad murmured. "Your mother met him in Providence two years ago."

"Is he any good?" Noah asked.

"One of the best." Dorian sighed. "The other guy's better."

The man sauntering toward the prosecutor's table had a grin like a thousand knives. I read the name on his ID badge, which also stated his registry status and legal credentials. Slade Sharpe was a shark shifter and had alphabet soup after his name.

I hope the defense has more witnesses.

Another bailiff escorted Jonah to sit with Mr. Ichiro. I glanced over my shoulder and spotted familiar faces. Alex Onassis wore a suit with a bow tie, not his usual choice of attire, but appropriate if he meant to give a statement. He sat beside a man about Bubbe's age, who I'd never seen before.

Behind them sat Arick Magnuson, alone and also wearing a tie and jacket.

So, he came to town for more than a gig.

"All rise."

The judge entered, and everyone stood. Before she sat, the door opened once again behind me, and Temperance Fairbanks walked through, flanked by her father and her older sister Charity. Faith was nowhere in sight. I hoped she was still at Hawthorn with Hal.

"Be seated," the bailiff directed.

The hearing started. From what I understood, they were trying to determine whether Jonah wanted to turn Noah or if there was a chance he'd been coerced. The judge took a written statement from Temperance.

Of course, she denies it all.

Arick handed over a magisupremacist pamphlet against vampires and anyone who accepted them, stating she'd given it to him last fall.

The judge perused it with a raised eyebrow and set it on top of Temperance's statement. I crossed my fingers in my lap, hoping that meant she considered it more important.

Dorian handed over his account next. He hadn't seen much, only a little before he got knocked out. I saw the page as he carried it up. It referred to Alex, which explained why he was here.

When Alex rose to give his statement, his hands were empty. The man with him stood at his side, holding a magipsychic device I recognized as a lie detector. The judge shook her head.

"Only written statements at this time, Mr. Onassis. You have two hours to compose remarks. "

"Miss Fairbanks, your statement please."

She spoke to Charity, who stepped forward with an entire folder full of papers.

Once again, the judge shook her head.

"This is excessive. Statements must be no more than three pages. You also have two hours. I suggest you edit them." The judge tapped her gavel. "Two-hour recess." She rose and exited through the door to her chambers.

The man with Alex sat, shaking his head. Dad stood and spoke to him.

"It must be confusing, navigating a whole new legal system."

"Yes." He nodded. "Is different." His voice was heavily accented.

"The most important thing to do is summarize, highlight incidents related to the specific charge."

"Hmm." The man sighed.

I wondered where Alex's parents were.

They sided with the Fairbanks. He's here against their wishes.

"I've got this." Dorian strode down the aisle toward them.

Alex widened his eyes and dropped his pen. Julia swooped down to retrieve it and held the writing implement out to him in one talon. Then something unexpected happened.

Dorian explained everything in Greek. His parents grinned approvingly at their son.

The man smiled. "This makes sense now." He rattled off several points in his native tongue, using his fingers to count. Alex nodded and began writing his statement.

"That's Alex's cousin, Konstantin. Did you know Alex's father is an earl?" Dorian whispered from his seat after he'd returned.

"No." I blinked.

Bet Alex's mother married him for the title.

"He needed more information." Dorian smirked. "Neither of them understood the legalese."

"My son, the future lawyer." Mrs. Spanos smiled.

"Who can argue with a clairvoyant?" Everyone chuckled at Dad's joke.

"Looks like the other side's having a harder time."

Temperance and Charity squabbled over her statements as their mother ignored them. Unsurprising considering everything Faith had said about her family.

They finished before the two hours were up, so the bailiff informed the judge, who emerged a few minutes later. After they handed over their documents, the judge announced that she'd make her decision tomorrow at sunset.

The hearing ended. Noah leaned forward before the bailiff came to lead Jonah away.

"We'll get through this," he said.

"We?" Jonah kept his back turned. "There is no we, Noah."

"What?" My brother clutched the lapel over his heart. "You can't mean that."

"I advise you to discontinue this conversation, Mr. Arnold," Mr. Ichiro said.

"Come on Arnold, back to your cell." The bailiff clipped a chain around the shackles on Jonah's wrist, then yanked it.

Without another word, the bailiff led him from the room.

"Can I stay in my old room, Dad?" Noah asked. "Just for tonight?"

"Sure." Dad put his arm around him. "It's still sunproof."

The entire walk home, Noah was silent. Once inside, he headed immediately toward his room and shut the door. I followed, but he didn't answer when I knocked. Later, when I got in bed to sleep, my brother still sobbed on the other side of the wall.

The next day, Noah stayed until we heard the news, which was good. The judge considered Jonah's case to be part of Tempe's and sent him home to await the trial in the winter.

But no matter how many times Noah called or texted, Jonah didn't answer.

CHAPTER FOUR

"What do you want to do for your birthday, Logan?" Dad asked.

"Oh, I almost forgot it was August." He smiled down at Doris, who purred in his lap on the sofa in the living room. "I'm not sure. Nothing big, though. Maybe pizza with friends."

"I can round everyone up," I offered.

"Yeah, let's do that." He glanced up. For one brief shining moment, our eyes met. His smile nearly broke my heart. I wasn't sure why.

You care for him. Deeply.

That truth was like the back of Bar's truck on the day Noah moved. Full of stuff that needed unpacking. Eventually.

I texted Izzy, Cadence, Brianna, Noah—everyone who wasn't on Hawthorn's campus. Gathering everyone from campus meant I had to go out since they didn't have phone service. I left him with the *Encyclopedia of Magical Creatures*, Bubbe's birthday present. Which reminded me, I ought to do some shopping. I'd managed to save enough for what I hoped was the perfect gift.

On the street, I turned down Essex, searching for the door to Hawthorn Academy. This year I wasn't on probation or banned from entering campus, but I hadn't had much time to visit there. I'd only gone once to swim in the baths with Faith and Izzy back in June.

The door was beside the bank this time. In summer, you had to knock unless you were living on campus. Penelope answered. She gave out to-go bags at dinnertime. My smile faded, and my excitement leaked away. Her face looked stretched and weary.

This does not bode well. Find out what's rotten.

"Penelope, what's wrong?"

"There's been an unexpected—" she started.

"Aliyah." Hal peered over her shoulder. I hadn't seen him since June, and he'd grown. He'd been shorter than her a few months ago. "Come in. I've got this, Mrs. Andros."

They stepped aside to let me through, but neither spoke. Hal led me to the stairs and called out our floor, leaving Penelope behind.

"Hal, what's going—"

"In a minute." He held a finger over his lips and leaned on the banister.

"You grew." I changed the subject.

"Yeah, up mostly, but a little out." He grinned but not with his eyes. "Wouldn't call it a glow-up but square's a better shape than round, am I right?"

He was. Hal Hawkins had always been husky, but the added height had transformed him from bulky to imposing.

"You could be Bar's stunt double." I waved a hand at his shoulders. "You're almost as tall as me now. Is it from your magiglobular anemia?"

"The air's super thin up here." He deflected. "Why didn't you warn me?" His banter was a band-aid on a bullet wound.

We walked down the hall to the room he shared with Lee, who wasn't inside when he opened the door. Hal's father sat at the foot of his bed. Instead of a suit, he wore the teacher's version of the school blazer over khakis and a polo shirt.

"Miss Morgenstern." He stood and straightened the blazer. "You may as well hear it straight for me."

"Hear what?"

"The trustees found a loophole in my terms." He paced. "They didn't choose a replacement from my list. Instead, they reinstated a former headmaster. My father, to be exact."

His face wore the grimmest expression I'd seen on it since Hal's diagnosis. This wasn't good news.

It's bad. But not as awful as it could've been, I suppose.

"How can I help, Professor?"

"By minding his rules, even the ones that seem absurd." He sighed. "My father's tenure was well-established by the time your parents attended Hawthorn. They likely have stories. However, there's something you specifically should know."

"What is it?"

"I became headmaster because my father was under suspicion of aiding and abetting your uncle, Richard Hopewell." He faced Hal. "Furthermore, my mother was also involved."

"Nana?" Hal tilted his head. "Why?"

"She's a djinn, pledged to her lamp not long after you started kindergarten. You'll learn this in class, but all lamp-bound djinn serve three terms with three wishes each. On her first term, Richard held her lamp."

"She's done horrible things, then." Hal's hands curled into fists. "Murderous things."

"She couldn't help it, I thought?" I put a hand on Hal's shoulder. "Djinn have to obey."

"There's no way to ascertain whether she was reluctant." Professor Hawkins sighed. "Although I'd love to think she was. The court only ordered a list of wishes, not her opinions on them."

"I get why you want *me* to know this, but Aliyah?"

"Because her lamp's recently arrived on campus. I don't know who brought it." He leaned against the wall by the door. "If it's the wrong person, there will be trouble."

"What if Grandpa's got it, though?" Hal asked.

"That's not so bad but still dangerous." Professor Hawkins sighed. "He's holding an enormous grudge against Richard for exploiting my mother's lamp. Which extends to Aliyah."

We watched Nin chase Ember across the floor.

"You both should be on guard. I'd advise against anyone in her family attending school events in the near future, including Parent's Night."

"What if someone else has the lamp?" I hugged myself, shivering all of a sudden. "Do we have to worry about Temperance-level problems, I mean?"

"Headmaster Hawkins will stick to the official rules of the school, no matter who breaks them. And his space magic is far stronger than mine. He'll respond to threats much faster than I was able to."

Did he just refer to his father as Headmaster Hawkins? Family drama on display isn't his usual look.

"I still don't understand." I shook my head. "Why tell me all this?"

"I'm telling you both." He sighed. "Our families built this school together, connected to it by generations of magic. You've each helped defend it in your ways. You might have to step up again."

"I'm not afraid to fight." Hal pressed his lips together.

"I am. But that hasn't stopped me before."

"That's all I can reasonably expect. Thank you both." Professor Hawkins strode toward the door, opened it, and left. The tension went out of the room with him.

"Well, that was intense." I blinked. "Are you okay?"

"I will be. Anyway, you had your reasons for coming to campus, and I totally hijacked you."

"I'm on a mission." I sighed. "It's Logan's birthday."

"Oh my God, I almost forgot." Hal chuckled. "Are you throwing him a party?"

"Some covert shopping and taking him to Engine House at eight. He wanted me to invite you and Faith. Everyone on campus and our friends in town, is what he said."

"Are you sure he meant everybody?"

"I think so?"

"Because Alex is on campus. Has been since July."

"Really?"

"Yeah." He nodded. "Cousin Konstantin went back to Greece last week, and he moved in here. By the way, is Noah okay? I haven't seen him since that hearing."

"The first night he took it really hard. Came back to our house instead of going to his apartment. He's ghosting me now."

"Dylan says Noah's throwing himself into music. He's worried."

"I'm here for him. If only he'd say something."

"It's hard." Hal nodded. "Faith spent almost every day in the gym and the baths. I've never seen her this angry."

"Is she okay?"

"She's bringing Seth to Bubbe's for his check-up later. Working out helps her cope. Her father sent her a letter. He's moving into the faculty wing in September."

"Why?"

"Trustees have the right to take residence while school's in session. Almost all of them have moved things in already."

"Wow." I blinked.

"I hope Grandpa gives them strict guidelines."

"So he's a rules guy?"

"Major disciplinarian, letter of the law. No wonder he married a Seelie djinn. Anyway, you said you're shopping?"

"Yeah, for Logan."

"What are you getting him?"

"No idea." I shrugged. "Are you up for a stroll through town?"

"Yeah, actually." He grinned. "Nice thing about this growth spurt, I cover more ground with less effort. I need to drop the invites in the tubes on the way out."

Before I could ask how he'd managed to make invitations while sitting there chatting, he pulled them from under the device on his desk.

"Is that what you've been doing all summer? Making that?" I jerked my thumb at the squat wood and metal box.

"It's a perpetual printer. Never runs out of ink. Lee and Faith helped me enchant it."

"Where's the manual?"

"There isn't one outside my head." He beamed while holding one of the invitations toward me. "I invented it."

I stood and peered at the paper. It had all the information about Logan's birthday, printed in a purple so dark it was almost black. I glanced back at the unassuming device.

"Wow, this is amazing. Does it work with computers? Magipsychic displays?"

"Yes and yes." Hal chuckled. "Dad hated trying to order ink in here. Mail order is tricky because the front door's always moving. So, I figured at least Grandpa won't have the same problem."

"Butter him up, is that it?"

"I can neither confirm nor deny that." He winked. "But kindness never hurts."

Except when it does.

"Anyway, let's go." I grinned while swallowing the voice's naysaying. "Logan's gift isn't going to pick itself."

Out in town, Hal kept up with me easily. I could pretend he wasn't sick, never had magiglobular anemia. Almost. Because he paused a little too long in front of some of the windows and leaned more heavily against counters and walls than I might have.

Nothing in the shops along the walking-only section of Essex Street felt special enough for Logan's birthday gift. That's why we crossed Washington Street, Crombie, and Summer Street toward the Salem Athenaeum.

It was the oldest book repository in town. To mundane society, it was a treasure trove of genealogical, trade, and city records. For extrahumans, it was more. The basement catacombs contained the area's magical histories. Even Boston couldn't boast this comprehensive a collection, in large part because the Salem Athenaeum's records predated colonial times.

We only planned to stop for a break from the heat in a building with climate control, but we walked right into their semi-annual antique fundraiser.

I sifted halfheartedly through jewelry and knickknacks, then moved on to a small shelf of books. I ran my fingers along the spines but stopped after feeling a brief jolt of energy. I pulled the item under my hand from the shelf. I mistook it for a book at first since it was bound in pebbled leather until Hal pointed out the clasps along the top and bottom.

"Is that a box?" Hal blinked. "What's inside?"

"I don't know." I opened the clasps.

When I lifted the lid, time seemed to stop. A lustrously bristled brush rested between pots of color, unfaded and still full despite the wooden housing's obvious age.

"This is it."

"You've seen paints in five other shops already today though," Hal countered.

This is no ordinary paint set. You know it.

"This one's an antique." I swallowed, suddenly reluctant to mention the jolt I'd gotten. "It's got history. Logan loves that kind of thing."

"I'm rooting for you." Hal held his hands up, crossing fingers on both hands. "It might be more than you can afford, though."

It wasn't. When I brought the box of paints to the woman sitting at the table with the cash box, she declared its price as eighty-five dollars, almost exactly what I'd saved over the summer.

"Are you an artist?" she asked.

"No, it's for a friend." I scrounged in my bag for the last few bits of change. "It's his birthday."

"Your boyfriend?" She winked at Hal.

"My best friend," I confirmed. "It's a surprise."

She put the gift in a brown paper bag, and that was that.

Once outside the Athenaeum, we headed back down toward the center of town.

"I thought Izzy was your bestie." Hal elbowed me.

"Um." Despite the August heat, my cheeks blazed.

"Logan's a special guy," he agreed. "Best friend isn't an absolute anyway. You can have more than one."

"Do you want to see if Faith's still at Bubbe's?" I studied his face, checking for signs of fatigue. "Or maybe go back to campus and rest?"

"Bubbe's sounds great."

I blinked and stopped in the middle of the sidewalk. He glanced over his shoulder, then paced back toward me.

"Look, I didn't feel up to leaving campus for months. Ever since this growth spurt, I feel downright normal." Hal gave me a lopsided grin. "I don't know if that makes sense."

"It does." I nodded. "I'm happy for you."

We continued down Essex to the door of the school. I nodded at it, but Hal shook his head. He wasn't even winded. Ember swooped off my shoulder. Hal chuckled as Nin scampered down his arm, then hopped on her back. My dragonet flew with her passenger the rest of the way down Essex, around the corner, along Hawthorne Street, and up our driveway.

She landed on the front step in front of Bubbe's office, where Nin jumped off and excitedly squeaked while waving her front paws in circles. She hopped up and down a few times while chattering excitedly at Hal. He smiled and scooped her up into his arms, then stroked the top of her head.

"This is a good day." Hal beamed.

"With any luck, it'll only get better." I smiled back.

"I'm going to see how Faith is doing."

"This needs wrapping upstairs." I shook the paper bag. "I'll be down soon."

He entered the veterinary office while I headed into my apartment. I ran up both flights of stairs, gulping down air like I ran laps at the school gym. I huffed and puffed, struggling to wrap Logan's gift in brightly colored paper. I debated putting a bow on it, but then someone knocked at my bedroom door.

"Just a sec!" I jumped up, swept the gift under my bed, and threw the empty bag into my closet before closing the door.

"Aliyah?"

"Come in, Mom."

"Is everything okay?"

"I was wrapping a, um, birthday present." I chuckled. "For Logan."

"Oh?" Mom raised an eyebrow.

"I'm not breathing a word about what's in it. Doris hears everything, and it's a surprise."

"I understand." Mom nodded. "The letter came from—"

"Hiram Hawkins. He's the new headmaster. Hal told me. We hung out today."

"Oh. Well, that's a relief." She sighed. "Did he say anything about what Hiram is like?"

"No, but his father did." I told her everything I remembered about my conversation with Hal's dad.

"Interesting." Mom leaned in the doorway and pondered her next words. "I suppose there are pros and cons to having him back. Although, I had hoped Nancy Gauthier would have been their choice."

"Gauthier? Why does that name sound familiar?"

"Nancy's got long experience on staff at Weir Academy up in Niagara. Her presence might have proved restorative. Especially with Andre Gauthier on the Board of Trustees here. They're siblings."

"That would have been nice, I guess. But for now, everything's a mess."

"Perhaps so. It gets better, I promise."

"I'm not sure it will." I told her what Hal said about Faith's father living on campus.

"I need to make some calls, Aliyah. Don't be alarmed."

"You rush off to make phone calls and tell me not to be alarmed?"

"Yes. What I discover in those phone calls is more important than the fact I'm making them. If you've got cause to worry, I'll let you know."

"Okay."

I trusted her but knew nothing about her sources. My mother's back retreated down the hall. Once she turned the corner and descended the stairs, I followed slowly. By the time I reached the first floor of our apartment, she was already in her office with the door closed.

While heading down to Bubbe's, I decided not to tell my friends about Mom's concerns until I had the whole story.

CHAPTER FIVE

Logan opened the door, placed one finger over his lips, then pointed at the kitchen entrance. I nodded, jerked my thumb over my shoulder toward the stairs, and raised my eyebrow. Logan nodded so we headed back upstairs and sat on stools at the kitchen counter.

"Seth's checkup is over. Faith's having counseling. Hal's in there, but we shouldn't be." Logan got a banana from the fruit basket and peeled it.

"Makes sense." I took an apple, held it, and stared instead of taking a bite. I put it back, suddenly not hungry.

Those unknown phone calls are spoiling your appetite. Go and insist on listening in.

"I'll talk to her again."

"Faith?"

"Sorry, inside voice came out." I grimaced. "Mom."

"About school stuff?" He blinked.

"Maybe."

"She told you about Hal's grandfather, didn't she?"

"Yes. But there's something else. Something harder to deal with."

"Do you need a test run?" He broke off a banana chunk and popped it into his mouth, where it comically muffled his voice. "I can talk just fine."

He looked like a hamster with his cheeks full of fruit, so I giggled.

"What?" He blinked, then widened his eyes and puffed his cheeks out even more.

I held my sides, laughing too much for speech, reveling in the broken tension. In typical Logan fashion, he made things better by being himself.

There's a typical Logan fashion now? How interesting.

I recovered from my mirth enough to pat his shoulder, but I was still too breathless to speak. Or sit up straight. He set the banana on the counter and caught me as I toppled from the stool. We ended up hugging.

His longer than usual hair brushed against my cheek, soft and ticklish, like Doris's whiskers. All my worry about Mom's covert conversations in the other room melted away.

"Thanks, Logan." I leaned back. "Maybe I needed a hug."

"Hugging works for Elanor." Logan glanced down and to the side.

You've seen that before.

I kept my mouth shut, thinking my question at the voice. *When?*

All the time.

"Would you mind if I finished that?" Logan nodded at the half-eaten fruit.

"Not a bit." I let go of him, grinning.

After that, I went to the fridge for lemonade. He followed, so I poured a glass for us both. By the time we finished our drinks, Bubbe had opened the door from the stairs and beckoned.

We followed her down and into the kitchen, where Faith and Hal sat with the remains of their tea in front of them, Nin and Seth curled up in the corner. Logan stopped in the doorway, staring at Hal with his mouth open. Apparently, he hadn't seen him come in. They had a conversation off in the corner about the amazing growth spurt.

"Are you coming to Engine House? I asked Faith.

"Wouldn't miss it." She nodded. "It'll be good to get off campus and do something."

"You haven't come out for Piercing Whispers, though."

"Hal wasn't feeling up to it. But over the last couple of weeks, he's had way more energy."

"More energy?" Bubbe tilted her head. "Was that before or after the growth spurt?"

"Hmm." Faith stacked teacups and saucers on the tray as she thought. "I think just after. He was still tired when I noticed I could put my head on his shoulder without leaning. After that, he started running in the gym with me. He's still slower than Coach Chen's tortoise, though."

"Noted," Bubbe said.

I didn't like her flat expression or the appraising glance she gave Hal on her way to the sink with the tea things. Surely she'd noticed his height already, but his newfound energy concerned my grandmother enough for her to mask her reaction.

"I've got another appointment coming in, so you kids ought to head out. Enjoy your special day, Logan."

We nodded, smiled, and bid her farewell on the way out the door. Standing around in the driveway, we tried to decide how to kill time.

In the end, we knocked on Izzy's door, but she wasn't there. Her *abuela* said she'd gone to Hawthorn with Lee. We found the entry on Essex Street and went inside. Hal went upstairs to find Lee. The rest of us went into the café, ordered lattes, and sat drinking them in the lounge together.

"Morgenstern. What are you doing here?" The voice was more haughty than hostile. I turned to find my ex-boyfriend standing over us, his basilisk hissing at us from his shoulder.

"Hey, Alex." Logan spoke to the magus but looked at his familiar instead. "I'm going out for my birthday. Want to come along?"

"You're not seriously asking me to some boring nerd party?" Alex blinked.

"It's just pizza. But yeah. I am." Doris chirped at his feet for good measure.

"I'm busy. But I guess it's a nice thought." Alex walked up to the counter, then around it, where he pulled an apron off the hook and tied it on. He narrowed his eyes. "Don't act like you've never seen work-study."

None of us knew how to react. Alex Onassis was the last person anyone expected to need financial aid. His mother was a trustee, his father nobility. He'd also disparaged Dylan for standing behind that same counter.

However, Faith, Hal, and Logan hadn't been at the hearing. They didn't know only his barely bilingual cousin had accompanied him.

He's had trouble at home.

Should I tell them? I thought at the inside voice.

It's not your story.

Hal returned.

"They're here but doing, um, some projects right now." His eyes moved from the floor to the table to the wall and the ceiling before settling on the floor again. "Anyway, we've got some time to kill before Engine House."

"I wonder if Creatives is open?" Logan pondered. "I haven't painted at all this summer."

"It is, but I haven't gone." Faith shrugged.

"Maybe we should make some art," I suggested.

Logan led us all down to the academic wing and into the Creatives room, where we spent time engaged in arts and craft projects. Our familiars played in the corner.

I'd arrived at Engine House before everyone else last summer. This year, we walked in to find the section in the back entirely marked off and halfway occupied. Elanor waved us over and ushered Logan toward a seat decorated with balloons.

"Peep!"

Ember flew in circles around the floating rubber orbs, careful not to touch them. Gale warbled and took off from Dylan's shoulder to join her.

"Wow." He blinked. "Thanks. I would have been happy with plain old pizza."

"You only turn eighteen once." She shrugged. "Anyway, Brianna made assistant manager last week. So she helped me with this whole birthday scheme."

"Scheme?" I raised an eyebrow.

"The second she knew the location, El made a plan," Noah said.

We shuffled around and searched for seats, which wasn't easy. The section was packed. Cadence sat with Crow and Bar in one corner, laughing over one of her mom's newspaper articles. Lee had his familiar Scratch on his lap, where the sumxu sat up, flopping his lop ears while twitching his whiskers. Izzy filmed the critter's antics with her phone.

Grace sat nearby, oblivious to just about everything besides Azrael. In moments, she climbed into his lap, and they put their arms around each other. He whispered something in her ear that made her blush.

I let Hal and Faith sit together, which meant I got stuck in a corner, wedged between Crow and Lee, who both had bony shoulders. My comfort didn't matter. This was Logan's day.

Brianna brought pizzas and pitchers out, assisted by a coworker I'd never met. We ate, drank, and socialized. Logan made it a point to grin at me from across the table more than once. The third time, I noticed something outside the window behind him.

No, someone.

Sure enough, it was Jonah Arnold out there, walking with a redheaded woman who closely resembled him, which made sense. After the hearing, the bailiff hadn't led him back to jail.

He glanced over his shoulder, eyes widening when he spotted Noah. Who, thankfully, didn't see him. The woman with him shook her head and tugged his arm. She looked to be my parents' age. Was that his mom?

Jonah caught me looking. He made a zipping motion across his lips and walked on. I nodded, agreeing with what I thought he meant. That it'd be better for Noah not to know he'd been there.

You're taking on an awful lot of burdens for other people lately. After literally saving lives so recently. What exactly do you think you owe them?

"Nothing."

"Huh?" Crow glanced over his shoulder. "You talkin' to me?"

"Um, no."

"Good."

"She's cool." Bar snorted. "Hey, Aliyah."

"Hey, yourself." I snorted back to stay in the spirit of things.

"What are we now, kelpies?"

I laughed, deliberately making it sound like a whinny.

"Cornball troll." Crow rolled his eyes.

"That's Mr. Cornball to you, pal." I raised an eyebrow. "And don't you forget it."

Cadence threw back her head and laughed. Crow sighed and shook his head. Then he looked at his watch. I blinked.

"Gotta go." He twisted his shoulders somehow, then untangled himself from the row of seats.

"Aww." Cadence pouted. "All work and no play makes Crow a boring boyfriend."

"So dump me again." He smirked.

"I'd rather do this." She stood and kissed him, wrapping her arms around him under the trench coat he wore even on the sultry August night.

Her response utterly confused me. Not because I couldn't recognize Crow's sarcasm. But because I couldn't imagine anything like it being endearing in a romantic context.

"Thinks he's Han Solo." Bar shook his head. "Maybe he's not wrong."

"What do you mean?" I was glad to have a distraction from Cadence's long goodbye.

"He's a Merlini."

"Hmm." I nodded and closed my eyes around the sting of tears as I remembered one of Professor Luciano's more memorable lectures about Salem. "Rum runners. Prohibition, right?"

"Hey. You okay?"

"I'll live." I opened my eyes. "I guess you've got a point. Families have room for variety."

Like the birthday boy. And Faith.

Being reminded of my friends and how they'd survived boosted my mood.

"Yeah. His kid sister's their straight and narrow." Bar sighed. "Wish I'd rubbed off on him more, though."

"I hear you." I thought of Alex.

"Look, more root beer."

Bar pointed, nearly clunking his elbow into the side of my head. Ember swooped down from where she'd been perched beside Gale and *peeped* at him scoldingly. I laughed into my hands while Bar guffawed and slapped his knees. Ember hovered in the air, blinking at us. Then she circled back and landed next to Gale again. Their tails hung down and waved momentarily before twisting together.

They're holding hands, essentially.

"Cute." Bar jerked his chin at the dragonets.

"Yeah." I nodded, my throat suddenly tight.

"How'd it go, by the way? With that guy last year?"

"Nowhere, but we're cool being friends." I realized where Bar was trying to go with this. "I'm cool being friends with everyone, pretty much."

"Oh." He reached across the table and tipped the root beer pitcher over his cup. "So, who's pretty much?"

"Um." My face felt like I'd run ten laps around the gym. "I mean I can't imagine myself doing anything like that."

I glanced at Grace and Azrael, still intertwined together on one seat, their pizza entirely ignored. Cadence chose that moment to sit back down and lean in front of Bar while raising her eyebrow.

"What in the world did you say to my friend, Bartholomew?"

"Don't look at me." He shrugged. "It's Ambersmith's fault."

"I suppose their PDA pushes the bounds of R-rated." Cadence shook her head. "Seriously, Aliyah. You go to boarding school. Surely you've seen stuff like that before."

I ignored her and focused on finishing my now tepid pizza. At least the Sprite in my cup was still cold and fizzy. Bar followed suit. Cadence's banter was usually harmless, but it had never made me feel this uncomfortable before.

By the time I set my pizza crust down, the lights had dimmed. I glanced at Logan, who looked a little lost at the head of the table. Almost like he was alone in the crowd. The lighting change must have surprised him but not too much. A moment later, Elanor started singing Happy Birthday and Brianna came out of the back carrying a large sheet cake, decorated with the words "Happy Birthday, Logan" and eighteen candles on top.

Logan looked at Elanor, smiling. Right then, I thought he wished for peace in his family. When he turned to blow the candles out, he glanced at me, and I wasn't sure. After putting the candles aside, Brianna used one of the semicircular pizza slicers to cut the cake. Inside it was vanilla with vanilla frosting, Logan's favorite. I ended up with a piece that had half his name on it.

After the cake, Brianna shooed us out because Engine House was closing. Outside, friends exchanged hugs along with promises we'd see each other again soon. They trailed away in small groups or pairs. Elanor, Noah, Logan, and I lingered. At first, I thought they stalled to invite us over. When Brianna shut the lights off inside the restaurant and came out, I realized something else was going on.

"Okay, I'm ready to hear that new song." Brianna stepped beside Elanor and grabbed her hand. She glanced over her shoulder before crossing Derby Street. "Happy birthday again, Logan."

"Thanks." He scooped a sleepy Doris up in his arms. "Can we go, Aliyah? I'm tired."

"Sure."

I started down Derby with him. Ember landed on my shoulder and curled around my neck, also exhausted. Was I the only one with any energy left?

You're nervous.

I couldn't imagine why.

The gift. And me. You were going to tell him.

"Do you think you could stay up a little longer? After we get back, I mean."

"Maybe." He glanced at me. "Why?"

"I've got something for you."

"Oh, you shouldn't have. I didn't get you anything back in June, and that's bad manners."

"Logan." I stopped and stepped in front of him. "In my family, we give gifts because we care, not to get something back."

"Wow." He blinked. "Well, lead on then."

I did. After another minute, we stood in front of my house.

"Do you want to come up?"

"Um—" He swallowed and stared at the entrance to Bubbe's office.

"Never mind. I have to go upstairs to get it. Can we meet on the back porch?"

"Oh, okay." He nodded, shoulders easing.

We went through separate doors. After climbing up two flights of stairs, swapping a sleepy Ember for the package, and descending again, I still wasn't tired. My legs burned slightly with the exertion, though. Out on the back porch, Logan stood staring up at the moon.

"Hi." I stepped toward him. "Where's Doris?"

"Wouldn't budge after camping out on my pillow." He grinned while glancing sideways and down again. "Is it a laser pointer?"

"Hmm?"

"The, um, gift?" He sighed, turned toward the porch railing, and gripped it as though he needed support.

"Well, no." I blinked. "You don't have to answer, but what made you guess that?"

"Just how stuff like that usually is." His knuckles whitened in the moonlight. "Bubbe's the only person who gave me something, well, for me. Must be some kind of world record for that, huh? Being given stuff someone else would want for seventeen years."

"I don't know about that." I brought the hastily-wrapped package out from behind my back. "Maybe you get to break a personal record because I saw this and instantly knew it belonged with you." I held it out. "Happy birthday, Logan."

When his hands let go of the railing, they shook. Not in a trembling way, either. He was flapping them, what Mom referred to as a self-stimulatory behavior. While I'd heard him hum through tests and schoolwork, I hadn't seen him do one physically before.

You have with his nails. Anyway, you know what to do.

I nodded, waiting. I wish I could say Logan took it in stride, but his face reddened, jaw dropped and eyes wide and feral. Tears gathered at their corners. Mine stung, too. Mom always said this is a natural response to excitement for folks on the spectrum. The Pierces either hadn't gotten that memo or knew and shamed him for it.

The latter. They're horrible.

Afterward, he turned his back. "I'm sorry. You can go if you want to."

"I'm not going anywhere."

"Why?"

"This is your normal, Logan. Like the fire and solar are mine. You accepted that about me the minute you saw it. Why shouldn't I do the same?"

"You saved my life that day." He turned his head enough for me to see him in profile. "I did...that...in the middle of you doing me a favor."

"Eighteen's a big deal, especially away from home. It's an exodus of sorts, nothing to sneeze at."

"I'm ashamed."

"Whatever happens, I'm here."

"Okay." He sniffled and drew his sleeve across his face under his eyes.

When he turned, tears still silvered parts of his face. He looked strange and fae in the moonlight, but not alarmingly so.

Some people have a hard streak, like tinfoil wedged into the heel of a loaf of babka. Inside Logan Pierce lived a profound gentleness, one that wouldn't have survived if he hadn't encased it in a lumpy and sometimes awkward shell.

I silently thanked God that he'd spent an entire year thriving here instead of withering in Las Vegas. When I held the parcel out this time, he took it.

Instead of ripping the paper, Logan peeled the tape on the edges and along the seam. He managed to unwrap it without making a single tear, grinning the entire time. Some of my schoolmates were defenders, like Faith and I. Others were creators, like Grace and Hal. Logan was something else entirely. "A conservator."

"No, it's a book." He stared down at the leather-bound box. "Wait. No, it's not."

I memorized his face, trying to imprint every detail of his expression as his fingers traced the spine, navigated the corner, and found the first latch.

"A box that looks like a book!" He smiled. "I always wanted one of these. Thank you!"

"There's something inside."

He opened it, the contents striking him speechless.

"Oh, Aliyah." His voice dropped half an octave in pitch. "This is too beautiful. I almost can't—" He sniffled again, closed the box, and set it on the railing.

My shoulders felt tingly all of a sudden. My lip trembled, vision doubling then blurring over. Before I knew it, we were both in tears and in each other's arms, exactly like that night in Noah's apartment three months earlier.

"I gave what I thought you'd want," I said behind his ear.

"You do too much for me, Aliyah." His hands pressed flat against my back, different from how they did every other time we'd hugged.

"You deserve it."

"If you say so."

"I know so."

We disengaged, studied each other's tear-stained faces for scant moments, then walked inside. He parted from me in the stairwell, his free hand a silhouette waving shyly in the light of Bubbe's hallway.

I'd forgotten something but couldn't think of what. When I ascended the stairs, barely feeling them under my feet, I couldn't imagine why. Despite my attempts to ask my inside voice, it didn't respond.

CHAPTER SIX

It should have felt all wrong, walking to Hawthorn without Noah. But Logan's presence made it better, if not exactly right. We began making our goodbyes to my parents and to Bubbe, who'd come with us. She handed me an old medical case, not large.

"What's this?" I studied its battered nylon surface.

"A brooding box."

"Whoa!" Logan beamed. "I'll help you set it up if you want. This is awesome! Do you think Ember's going to lay eggs?"

"Peep?"

My dragonet craned her neck down, flaring her nostrils at the case. Then, she turned her head and started preening my hair. Or at least that's what I thought she was doing at first.

"Ow!" I winced, reflexively ducking my head. Anyone would have if they'd had several strands of hair yanked out. "I have a hairbrush I always forget to clean, you know."

"That's a nesting behavior, so I'd say she's either ready or will be in a few months." Bubbe nodded. "She'll be on campus with a male about her age, too. I want you to be prepared."

"Okay." I nodded, trying to keep my expression neutral. I'd heard rumors. The prospect of feeling amorous via my familiar bond was pretty close to horrifying. "Thanks, Bubbe."

"Do you need help carrying that?" Logan gestured at all my luggage.

"I'll manage." I jerked my chin at his baggage. "You've got more than me."

"Oh." He chuckled. "I guess I do."

In the end, we made it because Dad handled the doors.

"Call us if you need. Remember, you can come home on week-nights this year too, Logan."

"Home?" He blinked.

"Yes." Dad nodded. "If you're not too busy studying, smartypants."

"That's Mr. Smartypants, Dad." I smiled.

"Gotcha." He winked.

With that, we walked through the interior door he'd held open and into the Hawthorn Academy lobby.

"This is...different." Logan stopped in his tracks.

"Do you need a minute? Because I sure do."

The changes were subtle, considering the way everyone else milled around the lobby. However, a person sometimes overwhelmed by his surroundings and a solar magus could not ignore this. The entire lighting system had changed.

"It's awfully harsh." Logan glanced up at the ornate magical chandelier. "Poor Zeke."

"I was going to say the same thing." I sighed. "Last time, it was like an autumn afternoon, but this is desert mirage levels of sunshine here."

"No kidding." Dorian brushed past us on his way through the door at our backs. "Good thing I've got built-in AC." Julia hooted sleepily on his shoulder.

"I'm beige and getting a sunburn," Dylan chimed in while sauntering over from the stairs.

"What's up, Jerk!" Dorian smirked.

"Nothing much, Coward." Dylan rolled his eyes.

I froze, waiting for the inevitable showdown I'd have to stop.

They'd had enough of those last year for me to recognize when one was imminent. But they didn't start fighting. Instead, they did some kind of secret handshake.

"I don't get it," Logan said.

"Different strokes, man." Dorian shrugged. "Anyway, race you to the stairs!"

I got there first but went up a few steps and waited for the others to get on before calling out our floor. The steps moved upward like a magical escalator, which was always nice at the beginning and end of terms when everyone had luggage.

Gale, Dylan's dragonet, did the same nostril-flare at Bubbe's case that Ember made earlier. Then he peered at my hair, looking for her. She'd hidden pretty effectively. He tugged Dylan's ear, chirping.

"He's in a state over that thing. What is it?"

I swallowed and tugged my collar as my face blazed like the stupid chandelier.

"Brooding box." Logan clapped his hands, almost losing the bag draped over his shoulder. "Bubbe thinks Ember might nest this year. Isn't it exciting?"

"Wow." Dylan blinked.

Before we could say more, the stairs stopped, and we had to part ways to get to our rooms. Dorian followed me because the room he shared with Eston was on the way to mine.

"You're worried about Ember mating. Why?"

"I thought maybe she's a little young. And she hasn't ever met any other dragonets."

"Bullshit, Aliyah." He lowered his voice. "With the changes on campus, we should be straight with each other. Well, in a manner of speaking, anyway."

"Can we talk about this somewhere more private than the hallway?"

"Sure."

He dropped his luggage off in his room, told Eston he'd be back in a while, then waited until we were inside my room.

"Go on."

I opened the suitcase with my hanging clothes and started unpacking it so I'd have something to do with my hands.

"I think something's wrong with me." I turned my back, hanging a pair of blazers. "I'm not comfortable. With sex. Like, at all."

"Okay." I turned to find him nodding. "There's nothing wrong with you."

"But, like, everyone else." I glanced at the still-empty bed across the room. "Noah figured out he was gay in middle school. Grace has been all over Az this summer." I closed my eyes. "I don't know anyone like me."

"Maybe you do. We'll get to that in a minute." He sat on Grace's bed, then patted the spot beside him. I hesitated.

You saved his life. Let him help.

I nodded and sat.

"There aren't only hetero, homo, and bisexual people. Some people aren't sexual at all."

"Wait; what?" I blinked. "Like, they never fall in love or what?"

"No. Some fall in love, even get married and have families. But they don't get attracted to other people in a having sex way."

"Not ever?" I blinked.

"I don't know." He shrugged. "Still, you're not alone. Not by a long shot."

"Anyone can be like this? Like, not just us?"

"Absotively." He nodded. "Mundanes and all kinds of extrahumans."

I sighed. "It's a relief, knowing it's not a, um, weird extramagus thing."

I was about to ask him exactly what he meant about me not being alone. Was there someone else, maybe even a person I knew, who felt the same way I did? But the latch clicked, and the door opened, revealing Grace. She held it and let Lune hop inside, then walked in.

"We're all running late. It's almost time for the headmaster's welcome assembly."

"Wait; what?" Dorian pulled out his pocket watch and checked the time. "That's way earlier than last year's."

"Yeah. New headmaster, new rules." Grace set her bags down and jerked her thumb over her shoulder. "It's in five minutes."

We got up and followed her out into the hall.

"Oh, I should warn you about Hiram."

"Do it while we walk."

I gave them the basic gist of Professor Hawkins' explanation.

"This is gonna suck." Dorian sighed. "Oh well. So much for fun this year."

Grace snorted. "If the kid who transferred from The Academy is this worried, we're screwed."

We had no idea until after the assembly how much.

I sat in the front row at the end of the aisle. Grace sat beside me, and Logan directly behind. Dorian sat across the aisle. The clock on the wall behind the empty podium stood at scant seconds to ten in the morning although the lights made it feel like high noon. The squeak of rubber-soled shoes made me turn my head, expecting Dylan, late from a shift at the cafe.

He doesn't work there anymore, remember?

"Can I—"

A *crack* and rush of air interrupted Alex, who stood like a deer in headlights, holding his green apron in one hand. I nudged Grace, and we both scooted over. As Alex was about to take the seat, he vanished in another one of those whooshing *cracks*.

"Mr. Onassis." The voice boomed through the room but was somehow raspy with a slight quaver. "I don't tolerate tardiness. If it happens again, there will be consequences."

Alex stared out at the audience. Yes, the bunch of us felt more like a group watching a staged performance than a gaggle of assorted students at their first day of boarding school, because that's what Hiram Hawkins intended, of course.

Astute. Your new headmaster is, as you say, "old school" and will employ methods your parents are more accustomed to. Consult them, and there's hope for you yet.

I wasn't the only one who noticed, either. It wasn't much of a surprise that the kid from the school for delinquents knew that to do next.

"Sorry, sir," Dorian whispered from across the aisle.

Unbelievably, Alex took his advice. Sort of.

"I'm deeply sorry, Headmaster." He bowed so sharply his jet curls bounced.

"Purchase a timepiece." Hiram Hawkins narrowed his eyes, and Alex vanished again, reappearing at my side in the seat, head over knees.

"Sit up." I elbowed him.

He did.

"For the First-Years, welcome. It's my hope that you'll thrive in the structure I've built since my arrival." The new headmaster grinned. "As for the upperclassmen, you'll have some changes to get used to. First, some faculty arithmetic. Ezekiel Brown is working elsewhere. Nurse Smith will be assisted this year by an Emergency Medical Magus. We have another new addition to staff, Ms. Rupi Khan, our school counselor."

A smattering of applause covered Grace's question.

"Ms.?" She nudged me.

"Divorced. Ask Dylan."

"Additionally, all seven of the trustees on our board will live on campus this year. You'll get the chance to meet them at the mixer this evening. They'll be auditing your classes, so take the chance to get to know them sooner rather than later."

This time, whispers and gasps sounded throughout the lobby.

"However, their quarters in the Faculty Annex are strictly off-limits to students. Likewise, they are restricted from entering your dormitories. Including those who are family members. I demand professional levels of decorum from both the trustees and you students."

"Relief city." Alex leaned back in his seat but shot me an intense glance. "You'd better avoid my mother, Morgenstern."

Easier said than done, but nice of him to warn you, I suppose.

Warn me? I thought.

Yes. I imagine learning to speak Prince of Darkness will be useful this year.

"Finally, I welcome you all to get familiar with the common areas and your roommates.. Dismissed."

He grinned, then vanished with a *smacking* sound.

"That's some seriously strong space magic." Grace shook her head.

"He's the most powerful one on the planet." Alex shook his head. "Watch what you say in here."

"Um, thanks, I guess."

"Look, I'm serious. About him and the woman who birthed me." On his shoulder, Asceco hissed.

"Okay. I hear you. Why the help?"

Before he could answer, Ember screeched and took off from my shoulder. She winged into the air, banking toward Gale, who'd soared by. They circled each other while flying off together into the shadows of the rafters.

I blinked, crossed my legs, then pressed my hand against the middle of my chest where my heart threatened to break ribs.

"You're in for it, Morgenstern." Alex stood and slung his apron over his free shoulder.

"What?" Grace stood and put her hands on her hips. "You did not threaten my friend, Onassis."

"It's a warning. Asceco mated three years ago." Alex shrugged. "Good luck with that."

He sauntered off.

"Oh no." I hung my head, hiding in my hair. However, my tresses couldn't protect me from the implications. My familiar's desires could impact my emotions, no matter what I did.

Hopefully not your actions. Because he slept with Noah's boyfriend back then.

The voice didn't console me, but Grace's hand on my shoulder managed to.

"Don't pay attention to him. Let's go get beverage roulette."

I nodded and followed her into the cafeteria, but once I'd had some food and drink, I couldn't focus on the conversation. Or much of anything else. My face felt flushed and my pulse racy. I excused myself and headed for the infirmary. By the time I made it down the ramp, I practically collapsed into one of the chairs in the waiting area.

"Whoa!" The guy trotting toward me wasn't Nurse Smith. He had curly hair and held a wand, which he used to tap his spectacles, then pointed at my forehead. I didn't notice any hint of a familiar anywhere. "You're running a slight fever. Any other symptoms?"

"Um, my heart."

"Hmm." He pointed the wand at me again. "Yeah, looks elevated. And your blood pressure's high. Let me help you into—"

"Ian, what are you doing?"

"Uh, helping, um, what was your name, Miss?"

"Aliyah." I gasped, my heart fluttering. "Morgenstern."

"I see that, but you haven't checked for her familiar." Nurse Smith glanced around the room, then upward. "Where's Ember?"

I mumbled something about her and Gale going off together.

"This sometimes happens to bonded magi, Ian. You've got a lot to learn about the way that works. Still, it can't hurt to let her rest." Nurse Smith sighed. "Set her up in room one if you think company will help."

"But there's a patient—"

"She's on his list of permitted people."

I wasn't sure what he meant and wasn't in the right mindset to reliably ask without it coming out weird, like when Ian asked my name. So, I let Ian lead me into room one, where I sat on the bed beside Hal's. Ian waved his wand, and the foot elevated.

"To help your blood pressure," he explained.

"You didn't forget to hydrate and collapse again, Aliyah?" Hal asked once Ian had gone.

"No." I turned my head away. "How are you?"

"It's infusion time again." He chuckled. "Dad insists, although I still have mostly good days."

"Is that why Faith's not here?"

"She wanted to help Kitty unpack."

"Cool."

"How'd it go with Logan?"

"Um."

"That bad, huh? Sorry."

"No. It started awkward but ended up good."

"So you're together?" Hal grinned.

"I didn't go there." I stared down at my hands. "I don't want to end up in a situation. With everyone assuming. Again."

"Logan's not Alex. But you're the only one who can figure out what you feel."

"How did you do it?"

He took his time answering. I looked back at him. Hal's skin was bright instead of ashy, and the area under his eyes wasn't puffy like it had been last year. Something about his cheeks, how they'd lost their roundness, bothered me. He might not feel stretched too thin, but Harold Hawkins looked that way to me.

"I read Faith's essay. Like I read everyone's our first year. It told me about her circumstances. The second I laid eyes on her, I knew she was constantly angry, in pain. But underneath it was this strength. I thought, we need her on our side." The corners of his mouth tilted up. "You saw it too."

"Yeah." I nodded. "I knew as soon as school started that Faith needed some real friends. I tried so hard, but nothing worked until you talked to her. What happened?"

"It was that day in the cafeteria before you tangled with Charity. She ran off."

"You went after her."

"Right. Because it was my duty. We talked. And changed each other's lives."

"I mean, I saw some of that. But when did you know? Like, what was going through your head at that exact moment?"

"I held out my hand. She took it, and honest-to-God magic happened. When she let go, it was still there." He sighed and beamed.

"That's one of the most beautiful things I've ever heard, Hal." I shook my head.

"But?"

"There's not really a but here. I wish something like that could happen to me."

"Nobody ever does it the same way."

"For Bubbe, it was like you." I sighed. "Her brother introduced them and instant magic. Figurative on his part. He was mundane."

"Oh." He reached across the space between the two beds and patted my hand. His arms were long enough to do that now. "Your story doesn't have to match your family's. Mine doesn't."

"What do you mean?"

"Grandpa and Grandma had an arranged marriage. Dad chased my mother for months. She was totally afraid of commitment. Faith and I are totally in love since that first day."

"I'm having a hard time figuring out what anything means. Romantically, anyway."

"Well, we have a counselor now. Maybe talk to her?"

"Good point." I nodded. "Any other ideas, though? I mean, in case that doesn't work out."

"Grace."

"Oh."

"What's wrong?"

"I'm not sure we share a, um, perspective."

"Ask her about Azrael sometime."

"I think she'll talk about, uh, sexytimes if I do that. Like Cadence does."

"Hmm." Hal lifted his arm to scratch his head, but the tube connected to it hindered his movement. "What about Izzy?"

"Only for a reading."

He nodded. "Logan himself? I mean, he's one of your best friends. And it's efficient."

"I don't know. He's in a state because his mother's a trustee."

"That entire thing is an accident waiting to happen if you ask me."

"Their wing's off-limits. And our dorms are to them."

"I'm not sure that'll make a difference."

"You think they'll barge in?"

"No. Only that there's ample opportunity for them to interfere with us despite that." He sighed. "Grandpa's rules are hard, but they're limited until someone blatantly violates them."

"That doesn't bode well."

"I'll do my best to head off that kind of crap."

"Are you sure that's safe?" I blinked. "I only mean that you're mostly okay until you conjure. I still want you to survive and have a gaggle of kids someday."

"Conjuring space and moving through it is totally different from keeping tabs on where certain people are. I only have to worry about the three trustees we know are bad actors. No need to track Masters, Gauthier, Thurston, or Dunstable. They mean us no harm."

"Thurston? Like the headmistress at Providence Paranormal?"

"Yeah. He's her dad. The worst he'll do is encourage us to apply there."

"So you're planning to keep tabs on the other three?"

"When class isn't in session. They have to submit forms to Grandpa before auditing classes."

"You still have access to the records with him here?"

"Yes. He's a stickler for the way things have always been. Nepotism is one of those. I'm going to use it to our advantage."

"I'm glad you're on our side, Hal."

"Ditto."

A chime sounded from the wall. Ian and the nurse entered the room, took Hal's vitals, and unhooked him from the tube in the wall. I knew it led into the Under and was a way to funnel raw magic into his system. The medical professionals thought he still needed that, despite his positive attitude.

Hal's not out of the woods, not by a long shot. Be careful.

I nodded but refused to give that idea any more room in my headspace that day. We still had a mixer to attend before we could rest, after all.

For the first time in three years, I got to try the punch. As I sipped from my cup, tasting coconut, cherry, and something like citrus, Alex tiptoed over. He pulled a metal flask from his blazer.

"Um, no." I wagged my finger at him.

"You're not in the shitty parents club, Morgenstern. Don't judge." He sneered at someone behind me. "Goes double for you, Spanos."

"Let her get a refill then," Dorian said behind me.

"Fine."

I ladled enough punch to refill my cup. Then he upended the flask over the bowl. Grace sidled up, stirred, and poured for herself.

"What is this for, exactly?"

"Spiking punch." Alex smirked. "And spiting trustees."

"Cool." Grace raised her glass.

"What about the younger students?" I elbowed her.

"The first-years aren't sticking around after their introductions. Most of us are legal in our own countries. Anyway, loose lips sink ships." Grace glanced toward where Mrs. Pierce sat with Mr. Fairbanks. "I want theirs to go down like the Titanic."

"Sentiments." Alex dipped a fresh cup in, not bothering with the ladle. "Exactly."

"I can't believe the two of you agree."

"Get used to it." Grace sighed. "The dogs of war can't be picky. Besides, Dorian trusts him. At least this far."

"War?"

"You expect peace after last year?" Grace gestured vaguely behind us. "With the enemy on campus like this?"

"No way," Dorian agreed.

"I'd kind of hoped we could have a normal year, yeah." I sighed.

"You can try. I mean, we all could." Dorian shook his head. "But we'd get swallowed up."

I opened my mouth, about to say something, anything, to try and prove them wrong. But the magipsychic screen lit up and the presentation introducing the new students started.

I sipped my punch, standing in the shadows to one side as I watched faculty and other adults come and get their drinks. Alex was right, the three untrustworthy trustees all had multiple servings of spiked punch. They didn't notice, either. I watched Nurse Smith and Coach Pickman spill their drinks into a potted plant near the door.

Professor DeBeer sipped, blinked, then chugged hers. She had five more, too. I wasn't entirely sure what kind of effect that might have on a stressed-out professor who'd seen her colleague dead on the floor less than six months earlier. Tears stung my eyes as I considered it.

Minutes later, she paced from the room, eyes on her feet and hand on one wall, treading unsteadily. Professor Hawkins followed her after glancing over his shoulder long enough to catch me looking.

"Hey, Aliyah. There's someone I want you to meet. My mom."

I turned to find Dylan standing beside a woman who looked a lot like him. Her skin was the same deep beige and her curls twisted in the same ringlets although she hadn't dyed them blue.

"Um, hello." I held out my hand. "I'm Aliyah Morgenstern."

"Dylan's told me so much about you. And your brother, Noah." She clasped my hand. "I wish I could have seen the two of you play Bishop's Row last year."

"Oh." I blinked. "You're a fan?"

"I played first defense for seven entire years between prep and uni." She grinned. "From what Dylan tells me, you have enough talent to go pro."

"That's what I'd say about him." I glanced aside. "I'm decent, but he's the real star."

"Don't sell yourself short," Dylan advised. "Or I'll tell Bubbe."

"Back at you." I smirked. "It's nice to meet you, Mrs. Khan."

"That's Ms. now. Likewise. I'll see you and the rest of your classmates around this year. I'm excited to work with the third-year students. I bet you all have excellent college prospects."

"I guess."

"Aliyah's totally a shoo-in for PPC." Dylan grinned.

"There's a college and career event at the Hawthorne Hotel this weekend for seniors from all the area schools," she said. "They'll have a table."

"I'll mark my calendar." I nodded.

"Oh, Mom, there's Logan!" Dylan pointed. "Sorry, Aliyah, but I've got to introduce them."

I nodded and looked away, letting them monopolize my best friend's attention. It made my escape that much easier. As I ascended the moving stairway alone, I breathed a sigh of relief.

You can't run from Logan forever. Or Bubbe. Or that test coming in October. Or college applications.

"One day at a time for now, imaginary friend."

The voice protested as I made my preparations for bed. Despite the fact that I hadn't fully unpacked, I went to sleep. All night, I dreamed of tests. Thankfully, the type taken at desks and lab benches and not in isolation behind magical glass.

CHAPTER SEVEN

The classroom was the same one we'd sat in with Professor Luciano for almost two years. Part of the difference came from the drawings on the magipsychic screen, done in a different hand and style. Mostly, it was the desk placement.

Instead of rows, Professor Hawkins had our seats arranged in a circle. Dorian sat on my right and Faith on my left, closest to the professor. Hal sat between Logan and Dylan directly across from us. The fact that Faith was basically up front surprised me. Until I realized she was making more of an effort at academics this year than the last two combined.

Normally, Logan was first to raise his hand. This year, Faith preempted him nearly every time. Dorian gave her the side-eye more than a few times. Dylan raised his eyebrow almost every five minutes.

Professor Hawkins took it all in stride. Despite the fact that he'd had us at our normal dynamic at the end of spring last semester, he went with the flow. I couldn't imagine that was good for Logan, whose academic primacy had become something of a routine. When we broke for Creatives, he told me otherwise.

"It's kind of a relief." Logan sketched out a horizon on the canvas with a length of charcoal from his art set. "Faith wrote to me all summer and told me about her plans. She wants to do well enough for a scholarship."

"Aren't you worried?"

"About what?" He reached for a thicker piece of charcoal.

"No longer being valedictorian?"

"I already have a full ride at PPC if I keep it above 3.5 this year." He grinned at my chin. "That's the rest of the news that came with my Hawthorn scholarship. College is the most important thing about grades for me."

"Good point." I smiled back. "Guess I'd better get to work."

"Why?"

"Well, because I always wanted to be—"

"You need to work on something, Miss Morgenstern."

"Yes sir, Professor Hawkins." I nodded. "See you later, Logan."

I wandered around unable to settle on a creative project. Clay was okay but nothing exciting. Woodworking reminded me too much of last year. Grace was teaching Hailey how to sew knits.

"Want to make scented candles?" Kitty gestured at a shelf full of wax and essential oils.

"Hmm. Yeah. That sounds good."

We worked with wax for the rest of the time. Then my class headed off to gym while DeBeer's went to the library. Kitty and I said goodbye. Once inside the gym, I headed directly toward the locker room. Coach Pickman blasted her whistle at me.

"Morgenstern! Front and center!"

"What's up, Coach?"

"You're captain this year for the school's Bishop's Row team."

"What? We haven't had—"

"Tryouts, I know. Those are next Tuesday. You and Khan are on the team already. He's still reverse point."

"Shouldn't he be captain, then?"

"He said if you weren't in charge, he wasn't playing. So, we made a deal."

"Oh. Well, what do I have to do?"

"You'll be at tryouts, with veto power. And running conjuring drills, strategies, and focus exercises every time we practice."

"Is it really that big a deal though? Compared to last year, I mean."

"We're trying to work out a way to play the other schools. Off-campus this time. Colleges are interested."

"Like, with scouts?" I blinked.

"Yeah." She nodded. "Providence Paranormal's starting a national college Bishop's Row team next year. You'd better apply there."

"Wow." I grinned, despite my fear they'd never accept me. "Thanks, Coach."

"Don't thank me yet." She nodded. "Captain's harder than it looks. Keep the off-campus plans secret for the time being. Half the trustees don't like the idea. Now get changed, Morgenstern."

I did, quickly. We ran laps, put on our equipment, and did drills. Hal even participated after showing the coach a note from the nurse. Was he thinking of trying out for the team? Was this what Coach meant about it being hard to captain a team?

You'll find out.

After our drills, Logan spoke with the coach. Right before dismissing us to change and shower, she blew the whistle and waved us toward the bleachers.

"Bishop's Row tryouts are next week on Tuesday afternoon. We'll have cheer squad again this year, too. Those tryouts are the same day."

"Why so early?" Faith blinked.

"Because extra practice makes extra perfect."

"Okay." She nodded.

On the way to Lab, Faith stopped me in the hall.

"Should I bother trying out?"

"That depends." I chewed my bottom lip, trying not to blurt the news to her.

"On?"

"How serious you are about all the academic work."

"It's that obvious?"

"Logan filled me in. What's the deal?"

"I'm applying for Alternative Therapies at PPC."

Of course, she wants to be a doctor. Good on her.

"Yeah." I nodded. "I can see you doing that."

"You're not going to advise against it?"

"No way. Go for it."

"Thanks, Aliyah."

We headed into the lab, where I waved her toward a momentarily confused Logan. They sat together at the bench in front while I partnered with Dorian.

"Team Miscreant?" His grin was too shallow.

"Nah." I gestured at Ember, swooping lazily toward the perch Julia already sat on. "I don't aim to misbehave this year. Let's be Team Airborne."

"Okay." He nodded. "I don't want trouble, either."

This year, there wasn't anything so simple as a lab safety tour. Instead, we got right to our first experiment, one where we had to slow the growth process of a fungus from the Under.

"Usually, I'm the first to say I love a fun guy." Dorian raised an eyebrow, conjuring ice at the bottom of the flask containing the gray mushroom. "But this is ridiculous."

"Ha." I held a hand over the container, thinking of the mid-morning sun in autumn. I didn't want to sauté our specimen, merely inhibit its growth. Overall, we were doing pretty well. Hal and Dylan had chosen a similar tactic, but they had trouble heating their air.

"Wait a minute." Hal glanced at me, then narrowed his eyes.

My inside voice giggled as if someone had goosed it. I blinked and almost dropped my beaker.

Tickles!

I laughed.

"Aliyah?" Dylan stared at the space between my conjuring hand and the top of the beaker. "What just happened?"

"My bad." Hal shrugged. "Just used my space to borrow us a little sunshine."

"Never mind." Dylan shook his head.

I thought that was the end of it, but after Lab, I tried heading to the infirmary to see if any first-years had Familiar Bonding. I wanted to keep track of them in case they needed help. Before I turned the corner toward the ramp down, someone tapped my shoulder. I turned to find Dylan.

"Hey."

"What's up with you?" He scratched his head.

"Huh?" I played dumb. Because I was pretty sure whatever he'd noticed had something to do with the inside voice.

Not him. You're supposed to tell Logan first.

"It just happened again." He narrowed his eyes. "I'm taking you to see my mom."

"Wait, no." I shook my head. "I'm okay."

"Then why is there," he waved a hand at the top of my head. "All this?"

"I don't know what you mean."

Overhead, Gale warbled out a melody. Ember responded by peeping and launching off my shoulder to follow him.

"Is it that?" He jerked a thumb at the dragonets. "Ember going broody and taking Gale with her?"

"I don't know." I shrugged. "Maybe you can explain exactly what it is that's worrying you?"

"Um." This time he blinked. "No. Actually, I can't."

"How about we talk after you figure that out?"

"Okay, I guess." He nodded.

"Let me know when."

We parted, and I headed down the ramp, not bothering to call Ember. I stared down at my feet, sighing. Should I find Logan instead? Or maybe Dylan had a point and I should talk to his mom. We had a school counselor for a reason.

"Whoa!"

I didn't get out of the way in time and ended up on the floor.

"Sorry, Aliyah." Logan stood over me, holding a hand out to help me up. I took it.

"It's okay. I was thinking about you."

"You were?" His mouth dropped open.

"Can we talk?"

"Yeah. Dinner?"

"It's not a public subject. Can we drop my bag off in my room, talk, then get food?"

"Sure."

We walked through the lobby in a tense sort of silence. I was relieved to find my room empty. Doris jumped up on the bed, chirping at the empty headboard, where Ember often perched.

"Where's Ember?" Logan asked.

"Probably with Gale."

Definitely.

I sat, closing my eyes. When I opened them, Logan had stepped back, eyes wide and one hand over his mouth.

"What's wrong?"

"You didn't ask me in here because—" He dropped his hand and cleared his throat. "Um, because of the dragonets?"

"No." I shook my head. "I need to tell you something. Should have done it over the summer. Maybe even last year. I'm sorry."

"All right." He stepped over like the floor was twenty stories off the ground and made of glass. He sat by the foot of the bed, facing the other side of the room.

Just say it.

"Ever since that fire in the lab, I've heard a voice in my head."

"Wait." Logan turned, eyes narrowed. "That's...different."

"You don't think I'm crazy?"

"No way. It's mysterious, though."

"Believe me. I know that feeling." I swallowed, my throat suddenly tight. "I never told anyone before. Professor Luciano—" I sniffled, eyes stinging. "He figured it out." My voice broke, but I continued anyway. "Some extramagus thing. Said he'd teach me about it. But then he—he never got to."

"Oh no." He slid over and pulled my head on to his shoulder. "It's okay."

"It's not." I sobbed. "Everyone will think I'm evil again."

"I don't. You're different. Maybe it's a talent, like mine. We can learn about it."

We rocked back and forth for a while. The motion reminded me of being out on the harbor with Dad, in the outrigger canoe that used to belong to Grandpa. The salt on my cheeks and those sunlit seafaring memories soothed me enough to speak again, finally.

"How?"

"There's got to be research, books the professor studied." He stroked my hair. "If he checked things out, maybe the Ashfords have records."

"I hadn't thought of that." I pulled away enough to look at his face. He'd been crying too. "Not since first year, when I found some articles about extramagi. They didn't have much. Then I forgot to look any further."

"You get distracted sometimes. That's okay." He squared his jaw. "I won't. Consider this my new special interest."

My stomach growled.

"Speaking of distractions." I tried to chuckle, but the sound reminded me of a fish out of water.

"Dinner."

"Yeah." I gestured at my face. "I should clean up a little."

"Me too."

We let go and met up again by the stairs after using the bathrooms. Downstairs in the cafeteria, Dylan joined us but refrained from his earlier line of questioning. Toward the end of the meal, his entire demeanor seemed more relaxed. He smiled an awful lot at Logan, too. When I dropped off my dishes, I turned to see him off in a corner, whispering something to Grace. They giggled but hushed up as I passed by.

I had no idea what they were up to but decided to let it go. Ember was still cavorting with Gale in the rafters. The feelings bleeding through our bond made me hot, cold, giddy, and uneasy all at the same time and I wanted to put some physical distance between us. My dragonet found me in the hall returning from my evening shower. She perched drowsily on my shoulder and fell asleep before my head hit the pillow.

The week passed, full of scheduled classes and extra time running in the gym on Tuesday and Thursday. Faith joined me, and I swam with her on Wednesday and Friday. A third person followed. Lena was still as silent as last year but more stoic than shy around us. On Thursday, as we left the gym, we saw Alex beginning a set of laps.

"It's lights out in an hour!" Faith called to him.

He rolled his eyes and ran faster.

"He's trying out?" Lena asked.

"We'll see, I guess." I shrugged. "Are you?"

She nodded.

"Good." Faith nodded.

"Seriously?" Lena blinked.

"Yeah." I winked. "Can't wait to see what you can do on the court."

She blushed, then pushed through the doors to the lobby.

I went home on Saturday morning with Logan, where we both helped out at Bubbe's. Ember sulked all day while Doris kept trying to cuddle up with her. Eventually, my dragonet warmed up to the idea of friend time. They sat on the back porch together and watched a litter of poodles frolic in the yard.

"Will she always be like this?" I sighed.

"They don't mate for life, so probably not," Logan said. "But until any eggs she lays hatch, she'll miss Gale when they're not together."

"At least she'll have her clutch before college. Can you imagine how she'd be if I brought her to some school on the other side of the country?"

"You're not thinking of leaving New England?" Logan blinked.

"I don't want to. But if I can't get in at PPC—"

"You will."

"Please don't say that." I looked away. "In October, after the, you know. Things might be different. I might be—"

"I get it." He rubbed his thumbnails with his index fingers, a precursor to mangling them. "This is your home. You shouldn't have to go so far away."

"It's your home too."

He put his hands flat on the wooden railing. "Not really. Most days, it almost feels like that. I'm mostly like that poor woman in the play that's not really about a streetcar. Depending on the kindness of strangers."

Bubbe called us in then before I got the chance to tell Logan in no uncertain terms that he wasn't a stranger. He was special, important, part of the landscape of my life. At the time, I didn't think I had to put it into words because while working with the animals and relaxing upstairs, we acted otherwise.

Like a family.

CHAPTER EIGHT

The waffle iron was broken so Dad ladled the batter he'd mixed into a hot pan and made flapjacks. Logan insisted on syrup, saying that's the only way he'd eat them. He fed Ember all his strawberries. I spooned his whipped cream into a saucer for Doris, then sat with my now ostentatious looking stack of cakes off the griddle.

"I told you it's odd, topping pancakes with fruit."

"Hmm?"

"Isn't that why you're not eating?" he asked.

"I'm nervous."

"Me too." He nodded. "I'm in, but this is meeting new people. Academics, not showbiz people."

"Is there a big difference?"

"Yeah." He nodded. "Elanor says showbiz has more room for eccentricity."

"You're not meeting professors, though." Mom sat with her plate. "Each school sends seniors or graduate students. They figure you already know about their academic programs. They want you to learn about student life."

"I feel a lot better now." Logan grinned, then attacked his pancakes.

"Me too." I nodded, breaking my fast at a slower pace.

At one point, Logan looked up and smiled at me, syrup smeared across one cheek. My heart felt so full, my eyes stung. At first, I thought my breath caught in my throat too, but unfortunately, that wasn't the case.

You're choking.

I put my hands to my throat. Ember shrieked while rising into the air. Mom dropped her utensils.

Dad was behind me, lifting me out of the chair and attempting abdominal thrusts. Doris stood staring at me, her tail straight up, back arched, all her hair standing on end.

Logan dashed over, kicking my chair out of the way. Finally, Dad got a good grip on me. A burning sensation came with the pressure, but it didn't matter.

A chunk of flapjack flew across the room. Ember batted it with her tail and sent it sailing into the trash. I could breathe again.

"Ow." I winced, clutching my left side. Mom kneeled beside me, as if she could see my ribs through my hand.

"Is it broken, Angie?" Dad peered at her.

"I'm an educator, not a doctor, Aaron."

Logan reached out.

"Can I check?"

I had no idea what he meant, but I nodded because I trusted him. He put his hand on mine, moved it aside, and held it. With the other, he touched the spot that burned and closed his eyes. Doris rubbed her head against his leg, meowing.

"No. It's strained, though." He opened his eyes. "You should take it easy today."

"How do you know?"

"One advantage of being a water magus is that people are mostly water." He glanced at his mercat. "Isn't that right, Doris?"

She purred.

"That's an advanced technique." Dad raised an eyebrow. "Where'd you learn it?"

"Nurse Smith." Logan shrugged. "I asked him to teach me some water-based first aid. After last year, I think it's important."

"I agree." Dad nodded. "Aliyah, do you want me to tape that before the college thing?"

"Nah." I shook my head. "I'll do it myself. Logan's not the only one learning first aid."

I gave up on breakfast after that and went upstairs to change out of my pajamas. Ember followed, staying closer than she had for the past week. I grabbed the tape from the bathroom and washed my face before heading into my room.

Thanks to my reading, I had a good idea of how to tape a strained muscle. However, the book was back on Hawthorn campus. I got my phone and looked it up. While following the diagram I'd found, a message came through.

From Blaine Harcourt, no less. Hoity-toity.

"Hush, you."

"I didn't say—" Logan turned away as I pulled my shirt back down. "Oh. The thing you talked about on campus."

"Yeah. I'm decent. Come in." I held my phone up after he turned around again. "Got a message here."

"What's LORA?"

"An acronym, I forget what it stands for. Blaine asked me some questions last year and put a bunch of information into it. He wants to talk about something at the event today. I guess that means he'll be at the PPC table."

"Makes sense." He glanced up at me. "What's it about, do you think?"

"No idea. Meeting him feels like it happened a million years ago."

"Well then, let's go and find out. Among other things."

"Not in my pajamas, though."

We laughed, and he left the room to let me change.

I hadn't been in the Hawthorne Hotel since that night delivering the letter postponing my extramagus test. I was almost afraid to step inside, but Logan held my hand as we crossed the threshold. The lobby had an entirely different feel in the middle of the afternoon than it had after nine at night. The crowds of students and parents milling around near the ballroom entrance helped, too.

We strolled together along the rows of tables, looking for Providence Paranormal.

"Should have grabbed a program." I jerked my chin at a man reading one.

"It's okay. It's nice to walk."

"Hey!" Cadence flagged us down from a table at the end of that row.

We headed over. She sprang from her seat and hurried around to give us hugs before I got a chance to read the banner hanging from the tablecloth.

"What are you doing working here?"

"Helping my boyfriend's family."

She stepped to one side, posing and making a gesture worthy of a game show hostess featuring a prize. The banner was white with a large black bird emblazoned on it and words below. Logan read them aloud.

"Corvid Couriers: Delivering since 1919." He scratched his head. "You're not a bird. And a delivery company isn't a college."

"Of course not. This is also a career fair and I've got the gift of gab." She winked. "Anyway, they're looking to hire seasonally. And beyond, for an international expansion next year."

"Good luck," Logan said. "Oh no. I didn't mean it that way."

"You usually don't mean any harm." Cadence glanced over her shoulder, then sighed. "But don't let Mrs. Merlini hear you say anything like that. She's a tough customer."

"We'll keep that in mind."

"She's a bitch."

"Mavis!" Cadence blinked slowly and pivoted slightly to reveal the girl behind her. "Language. And honestly, talking about your mother that way isn't ladylike."

"It's true, though." Mavis flipped a lock of jet black hair over one shoulder, looking right at me. "And well-behaved women rarely make history."

"Um, did I miss something here?"

"Your reputation." Logan patted my shoulder. "I think she knows who you are."

I peered at the girl, trying to figure out what was so familiar about her. She might be old enough to go to high school next year, so she'd have been at my grade school if she was local. However, I hadn't met her. Her name gave me the information I needed to place her.

"Hi, I'm Mavis Merlini." She stuck out her hand, which was pale and freckled. "Big fan."

"You must be Crow's sister. I'm Aliyah Morgenstern." I took it. "Do you follow Bishop's Row or something?"

"All of the above." She smiled.

"I don't get it." We shook.

"That's okay." Mavis nodded and let go of my hand. "You're humble."

"She's talking about your heroism, of course." Cadence grinned. "Standing up to someone like Temperance is a big deal in some circles. Even if magi don't make a fuss about it."

"Well, thanks, I guess." I tried to hide in my hair. "Anyway—"

"Look, Aliyah, it's Blaine." Logan pointed across the room. "We're supposed to talk to him. Sorry, but we've got to go."

"See you later, Aliyah," Cadence said.

"Bye." I let Logan drag me away.

"She wasn't kidding about the career part of this." Logan pointed out a table for the Federal Bureau of Extrahumans, where a man with honey-colored hair paced behind a woman with brown curly hair deliberately unfocusing her gaze at passersby. "She seems spacey for a federal agent."

"Probably a psychic, maybe checking auras."

"Look, the Coast Guard." Logan grinned at the purple-haired man behind that table, who had conjured some water into an empty glass.

"Are you interested in some pamphlets?" he asked.

"That depends on three things." I answered. Logan stared at me, mouth open. "Is it the New England Coast Guard? Can we serve either before or after college, and do you have any use for fire magi?"

"We're recruiting for Portsmouth, Salem, Boston, Providence, and Groton. I joined up after college myself but before works too." He ducked under the table to retrieve a box of pamphlets. "We absolutely take fire magi. My commanding officer tells stories about this one guy, a huge hero who was fire and also—" His eyes widened as Ember landed on my shoulder. "Is that your dragonet?"

"Yes."

"This is totally fate." He almost dropped the pamphlets. "Because that guy I mentioned—"

"Must have been my great-uncle Noah Morgenstern." I grinned. "He had a dragonet too."

"Wow!" He chuckled and handed me the glossy folded papers. "Well, look everything over. There's a recruitment bonus that can go toward either tuition or student loans. Plus you get to help people, which is my favorite part."

"Thanks."

As we walked away, Logan asked, "Why the Coast Guard?"

"What you said last night about not going too far away. You were right. If I don't get into PPC right after Hawthorn, I want to be nearby." I cleared my throat. "Near you."

"Really?"

"Yes. Because you're—"

"Ow!" A sharp bark and a series of squeaks followed the exclamation.

"Sorry, Faith." I winced.

She turned, eyes narrowed and gleaming with anger. But they softened almost instantly. Nin and Seth quieted too while peering at me from her oversized tote.

"It's okay, you were busy." She glanced at Logan, then dropped me a wink.

"Um, what—"

"I'm waiting for Hal. He's getting recruited by MIT, I think."

"For that new magitech program?" Logan beamed. "That's amazing!"

"It is." Hal peered over Faith's shoulder. "Last year, I would have stayed on campus and not thought much about the future. It's like life gave me a second chance."

We all smiled at that, but Logan and I excused ourselves because we had to get to the PPC table, which Faith had already visited. Finally, we made it, but Dylan stood in front of it, staring past us at our friends.

"Like a train wreck," he said.

"What's that?" Logan blinked.

"Nothing." Dylan turned his head and dabbed his eyes with a sleeve. I would have thought he'd been about to cry, but then he ran it across his brow, and I wasn't so sure.

Don't fall for that. He's upset.

"We're talking later."

"Yes, we are." He stared at a spot near my right shoulder. Ember was perched on my left, agitatedly looking for Gale. After a moment, he noticed her. "He's outside. Nature called."

"Go on, girl." I gestured toward the door leading outside. She *peeped* and took off. "For now, I'm supposed to talk to Blaine Harcourt."

"Oh, right." Dylan sighed. "Sorry, got in your way, then distracted. Where are you headed, Logan?"

"I don't need to visit any tables." He grinned. "Did you want to take a spin around the room?"

"Sure thing, mate."

"See you, Aliyah!" Logan waved, and they left me standing in front of the table.

"Hi," I said to the burly but friendly-looking fellow on the other side. "I'm looking for—"

"Trogdor!" A short woman I almost hadn't noticed called from the chair beside the man. She had glossy, light brown stick-straight hair held away from her face with a headband.

"No need to holler, Lynn." The big guy pointed across the room. "He's on the way, see?"

"I'm vertically challenged, so no, I don't see." She shrugged, nose still in a book on faerie anatomy. "But I believe you, sleepy bear."

I watched them hold hands, squeezing. It reminded me of something.

You hold hands like that with Logan.

"Let's walk, Aliyah," Blaine said. Then he took off without waiting for my agreement.

"Was that Lynn Frampton?"

"Yeah, my brainiac friend. Yours went off with the British athlete, didn't he?" Blaine strode into the lobby, where the din of a hundred separate conversations couldn't distract us.

"They're roommates."

"Like Bobby and me." He gestured at a pair of tufted chairs near the entrance, then sat in one.

"That's what she meant by sleepy bear? Was he the hibernator? At the beginning of all the, um, trouble at PPC."

"You know an awful lot about my friends." Blaine narrowed his eyes as a puff of smoke rose from his nostrils.

"I mean, said trouble was my blood relative." I sighed and leaned back against the chair, which turned out to be way less comfy than it looked. "Sorry."

"True, and accepted."

"So, what did you message me for?"

"Your test."

"Excuse me?" I stood. "You shouldn't know about that. I don't have to talk about it either."

"You don't, and it was unfair of me to spring that on you. I'm no good at tact. It's part of the fire element. I'm sure you understand."

"Yeah." I sat again. "I get that."

"So. The reason I know about your test started when your uncle called my mother in as peer witness for his extramagus test."

The words that came out of my mouth were ones Faith said last year about her sister. I would have been embarrassed if Blaine hadn't sat there nodding a reaction.

"How dare he?" I finished.

"Somehow, he thought only the *de facto* queen of the dragons could be his peer." Blaine studied his fingernails, then made a dismissive flicking motion. "Anyway, Mother's invited him to all her soirees since then. He went to the latest one and it gave me an opportunity. I might have peeked at the Director-General's schedule."

"You remembered?"

"Kim put all of your information into LORA last year, and it gave me an alert. He's due in Salem on October fifteenth although they don't send letters until the week before. Anyway, we want to help, like we did for Dylan."

"You know what would be better?" I leaned forward.

"Do tell." More smoke streamed out of his mouth with the words.

"Find me a way to record it."

He shook his head. "Can't help with that. You need a memory psychic, and the only one I know is on a job for the next three months at Weir Academy in Niagara Falls."

"Logan knows one." I sighed. "Jacinda Flores. She was at extramurals last year. Everyone swears she's super nice, but it's like she's got a problem with me specifically or something."

"Hmm." He tapped a finger against the arm of the chair, opened his mouth, then closed it while shaking his head. He cleared his throat and spoke again. "You'll have to try harder because the heinous device they use interferes with communication orbs. Even LORA can't record it." He glanced toward the doors leading from the ballroom. "The only way is a memory charm. So you have to make nice with this psychic if—"

Blaine cut his eyes away, focusing on me. He even leaned to one side as though trying to block my view. I narrowed my eyes, frowned, and leaned farther. Which maybe wasn't the best idea.

Logan and Jacinda stood framed by the ballroom doors like a Norman Rockwell painting, him with his hands up and her on tiptoe, leaning in for what could only be a kiss. On the lips.

My hands smoldered against the chair's arms. The light streaming through the glass doors behind me brightened. When Blaine's mouth dropped open, and he stood, I realized it wasn't the sun.

You're going nuclear.

"I'm jealous, okay?"

"It's okay." Blaine nodded, stretching his arms out to the sides. "But I'm not a magus and can't banish your conjures. And burning down historic hotels is not a good look."

"Whoa." Dylan ran toward me from the hallway by the elevator, Ember and Gale flying past him. An icy blast pushed back against my heatwave. "Chill out. What happened?"

The sudden cold shocked my rage. I shook my head because I had no answer. I shouldn't be angry at Jacinda. Logan wasn't my boyfriend. We'd declared our feelings platonic back in first year, and I'd said nothing since.

Dylan's tapping foot practically demanded an answer. Blaine's face creased with concern.

"I need to go cool off I guess." I sighed. "Anyway, that's the memory psychic over there."

I jerked a thumb in Jacinda's direction but didn't dare look. My mind kept conjuring images of them making out in the middle of the lobby.

I wish it would stop, I thought at the inside voice.

Granted.

My mind's eye switched to a memory of Piercing Whispers practicing *Hey Jealousy* by The Gin Blossoms. I snorted.

"Are you sure you're all right?" Blaine asked. "Because I could swear you almost puffed a smoke ring just now."

"I need to cool off. Outside, I think."

"Good idea." Dylan nodded.

"Can you introduce me to that psychic, please?" Blaine nodded.

"For what?" Dylan asked.

"A job. With pay."

"I'll go get her, then."

"Thanks," I said.

Dylan glanced at me one more time before walking away, eyebrow raised. I stared at the floor, hands clenched. I had to go but didn't want to leave without being sure about the memory charm.

"Scram, kid. I've got this."

"What?"

"I know tons about memory charms, including what you'll need in October. If she's got a crush on your boyfriend—" Blaine shook a finger, decapitating my protests on that. "I'm no whelp. I'll handle this. Go bank that furnace."

I did as he asked, stepping outside into the breeze coming off the harbor. Well, indirectly. The Hawthorne Hotel was three blocks inland, but it still got plenty of ocean air when the wind came from the east.

Someone stood against the wall in the shade nearby, but I paid them no mind.

"Morgenstern, you're on fire."

"Go away, Alex."

"No. You're burning for real." He batted at my blazer with one hand, wincing.

"Oh." I waved a hand and banished the embers from my smoldering sleeve. "Guess I need a new one of these."

"I saw you react to something in there. What happened?"

"It was stupid. And not your business."

"Fire safety is everyone's business."

"Afraid I'll burn the place down?"

"Yourself, actually." He gestured at the sooty streaks on my garment.

Dorian walked through the door to my left. He froze and stared, a sheaf of folders and pamphlets in the crook of one arm.

"Like you care."

"I owe—"

"No, you don't. Whatever honor code you're following, I'm not on it."

"Fine." Alex walked past me but turned his head to look me in the eye. "Talk to somebody."

"I will if you leave me alone."

He joined Dorian. I watched them cross the street together, heading back toward campus.

A few minutes later, Faith emerged. She insisted on bringing me back to the Providence Paranormal College table to request an application, singed blazer and all. Bobby said I should expect a package at Bubbe's office by the beginning of October, from Blaine.

As we left, I noticed Logan sitting at a table with Lynn Frampton, going over one of his notebooks. She pointed excitedly at something on the page, and he nodded. He glanced up at us and waved.

The flare of heat in my face and around my hands made me walk even faster, snagging Faith by the arm as she slowed.

"Why'd you ignore Logan?" Faith asked.

"It's weird."

"Try me."

I told her all about Jacinda.

"I'd be angry too."

"Why would you care about who kisses Logan Pierce?"

"Because you do. I'd be jealous if someone up and kissed Hal."

"He's your boyfriend. Logan's only a friend."

"There's no *only* about you two, Aliyah. Maybe in first year, but not anymore."

We walked in silence because I wasn't sure what to say. I'd spent the better part of two years with an enormously uncomfortable crush on Dylan. My feelings for Logan weren't like that at all. I couldn't decipher them beyond my certainty that he was important to me.

"Sorry if that came out bitchy." Faith sighed.

"It's me, not you." I shook my head. "Maybe I'm too confused."

"Okay." She nodded. "If you want to talk about it later, I'm around."

"Thanks, Faith. That means a lot."

I walked her back to campus, then headed back home to pack up my things for the coming week. It'd be busy with tryouts. Maybe the routine of athletics and academics would distract me from this seemingly unsolvable problem.

CHAPTER NINE

Truth Sharper Than Fangs
Noah

The Hawthorne Hotel's ballroom was sun proofed with umbral wards over each of the doors, and I'd used the underground entrance. I stood in the lee of the door anyway, away from the cracks. Unless I'd conjured it myself, any glimpse of sunlight scared me, despite signs clearly marking the wards. If an anti-vamp toe-rag decided to mess with them, I wouldn't know until it was too late.

I waited until Grace DuBois turned around. I caught her eye, gestured at the sign, then the ward. She nodded and gave me a thumbs-up. Being a vampire sucked, but at least I knew an umbral magus I could trust.

Even without any effort toward getting my GED, I'd attended the college and career fair with one fervent hope. That I'd get even one precious glimpse of Jonah Arnold, but he hadn't shown up.

Instead, I witnessed that awful kiss and my sister's anguish over it. She was gone before I could rush to her rescue, and Blaine Harcourt dragged Jacinda away moments later. So I did the next best thing.

"Logan Pierce, how could you?"

"I—what?" He pulled a pack of tissues from his blazer's pocket, got one out, and scrubbed his mouth with it. "What did I do?"

"Oh." I nodded. "I get it now."

"She ambushed me." He wrinkled his nose, curled his lip, and swallowed with a grimace like he'd taken bitter medicine. "I don't get it. All I said was hello."

It sounded more like an assault to me, but I didn't want to traumatize my bestie's kid brother. So I invited him to sit down at an unoccupied table in the corner, away from the doors.

"Are you okay?"

"I don't know. Why did she do that?"

"Maybe she has a crush on you, Logan." I sighed. "But she shouldn't have kissed you without asking first."

"Getting, um, physical freaks me out." He hung his head. "So I'm not gay. Or straight."

"Some people need time and being really close to the right person first. Or to be the one doing the kissing." I patted his hand. "Some people never get into displaying affection."

"Another way I'm built all wrong."

"You're not." I didn't try to look him in the eye although I had some idea what he was going through.

"This can't be normal. I can't be."

"You can be different and still be normal, Logan." I opened my mouth and pointed at my fangs. "All vampy. Still Noah. Same person, only a little different from other people."

"Changing rules is hard."

"Right. But you're not changing. You're discovering. Like a new subject to learn, but about yourself instead of a magipsych lab or history."

"So more like going from dance to cheer?"

"Yeah, something like that." I nodded. "What do you do when you have to study a new topic?"

"I ask a lot of questions and take notes." He rummaged in his satchel. "Oh! I can take notes about this. Like writing down how I feel."

"Exactly."

I watched him set his notebook on the table, take out a pencil, and start writing. Not bullet points or a numbered list, but an academic outline. He wasn't valedictorian for nothing. After a few moments, I realized the project totally absorbed him so I said goodbye, stood, and paced away, hoping to find Jonah eventually.

"Hey." Faith Fairbanks stood in my way.

"Hey?"

"Aliyah's outside. I'm going to see how she is. Do you want me to tell her anything for you?"

"No." Lotan hissed in my ear. "Oh! Remind her to request an application packet from Providence Paranormal. Don't tell her it was my idea."

"Why?" She crossed her arms and looked at me sideways.

"She doesn't always take me seriously."

"Whatever works for you, Noah." Faith shrugged.

"Thanks, Faith."

She waved and sauntered off. I decided to make myself scarce, or better yet, find a decent vantage point to catch Jonah's arrival if he showed up. Even if his lawyer didn't want us talking, I still wanted to see his face. Almost had to.

I worried maybe I'd started to forget him. I couldn't possibly. I loved him, right?

Nobody was at the PPC table when I passed it. When I glanced over my shoulder, I saw the brunette who'd been sitting there earlier chatting with Logan. Not in a flirtatious way, thank goodness. She wore a big sparkly engagement ring and had her notebook out. She seemed to be comparing something in it to Logan's notes. I left them to it and kept walking.

Doctor Elizabeth had been down to see me over the spring. Mostly, she helped me cope with the physical changes. She also educated me about where our powers came from. Vampiric instincts and reflexes weren't designed to help vampires hunt extrahumans or even mundane folk.

Ages ago, our role in extrahuman society was to bring in large and swift game over the long winters or eliminate threats like giant cats or bears. We took blood from our kills in exchange for the meat, bone, and furs. That became the basis for our alliance with the werewolves, whose stamina and resistance to the harsh conditions complemented ours.

Unless we were starved to the point of Rage, a vampire's instincts were to guard our found families against harm.

They didn't teach that in schools like Hawthorn Academy, no matter how progressive a headmaster Hector Hawkins tried to be. Even integrated schools like Providence Paranormal only included that in its more obscure curricula. So it fell to older vampires to remember and pass that knowledge on to whoever would listen.

All of this had a point.

I saw a chair in an alcove with a direct line of sight to the door from the tunnel. As I made my way toward it, a swift movement at the corner of my eye triggered my reflexes and diverted my attention. *Why did I feel predatory in a room full of extrahumans?*

Jacinda walked along the wall that ran parallel to the street. My instincts tracked her as a threat and Logan as family.

Solar magi have bad tempers. Vampires even more so. Experience with one helped manage the other. I strode toward her instead of dashing but ended up cornering her only paces away from the exit to the street. I needed to train my instincts to consider her neutral from now on.

"Jacinda Flores, how could you?"

"I know. I'm horrible."

"That's not—"

"The reaction you expected?" She sighed. "Ditto. Anyway, I'd better go home."

"Don't you still need to check some colleges out?" I blinked. "Or, um, careers?"

"I came for one reason, and he's in the corner recovering from my crap decision."

"Oh."

I watched Jacinda turn as if to leave, but after a few steps, she stopped and looked back over her shoulder.

"What about your colleges and careers?"

"Well, I came here for, uh, a not academic reason too."

"Jonah's not coming. I'm sorry." With that, she continued her trajectory and left through a side exit to the street. Also umbrally warded, thank goodness.

I started a snort that I tried turning into a chuckle. That failed, and it went all the way to a sob. A hand fell on my shoulder, cool but firm. For a moment, I hoped Jacinda had either made a sick joke or lied.

I turned, expecting to look up into the pale, freckled face I wanted to see more than anything else in the entire world. Instead of blue eyes and lips pouty with the fangs behind them, I beheld dark blue curls framing a dusky-skinned and square-jawed face.

"Dylan. Of course, your hands are cold."

"Part of ice magic, I guess." He let go of my shoulder. "Are you okay?"

"I spent most of last year asking you the same question, and now you want to turn this dynamic around?" I raised an eyebrow and sniffed like I meant to quip instead of hiding my heartbreak.

"I mean it, if you don't behave, that's what I'll do, mister." He tried making a stern line with his lips, but they twisted instead into a lopsided grin. "So, which schools are you applying to?"

"None."

"Come on. At least one. Practically every one of these want Bishop's Row players—"

"I won't get in."

"I bet a whole lot of them take GEDs. Especially the nocturnal program ones."

"I don't qualify."

"Wait." He blinked. "You didn't finish?"

"Did the courses, but not the test."

"Why not?"

"Because I don't want a GED, Dylan. I want my Hawthorn diploma. I worked too hard." I swallowed, unable to continue. Why was I saying any of this to him? Because he cared and he was there? He deserved better than me dumping on him. I started to walk away, but he stopped me again.

"Have you tried an appeal?"

"The trustees voted last year against letting me finish, even by distance learning."

"Bollocks." He clenched his jaw, then glanced behind me and waved someone over.

"Hey." Lee waved, joining us along with Hal and Izzy. "What's this about?"

"Getting Noah his diploma from Hawthorn."

"Is that possible though?" Izzy asked.

"There's a new headmaster, so yeah." Hal nodded. "Either once per year or with a leadership change, you can appeal that decision."

"They voted four to three against me the last time." I shook my head. "What makes a new hearing any different when it's still the same board?"

"The trustees are on campus with all of us." Lee grinned. "You know, your friends?"

"Exactly." Hal nodded. "We only have to change one mind. I can figure out which way they voted pretty easily. Dad's not headmaster anymore, but I can still play the family card to get into the office. Give Grandpa the old puppy dog eyes."

Hal's demonstration made almost everyone laugh. I abstained.

"Seriously though, you shouldn't bother." I waved a hand at them as if I could make them all vanish. Or myself, maybe. "It'll never work."

"Let the cards be the judge of that." Izzy patted her bag.

Before I could protest a second time, they practically herded me toward one of the two chairs flanking a cocktail table. I sat and let Izzy shuffle the cards, cutting the deck when prompted. I'd known that drill since she started reading tarot on her seventh birthday.

Nothing could have prepared me for The Wheel of Fortune

reversed, right in the middle of my spread. In fact, I couldn't even bring myself to look at the other ones she flipped over because I'd gotten that card in this position exactly one other time in my entire life.

The reading before coming out to, well, everyone. It was the first time I truly took my life into my hands and tried to steer my destiny. If I hadn't, I'd have lived a miserable lie all these years.

"So Noah, these cards say—"

"No need, Iz." I stood.

"Are you sure?" Hal blinked.

"He is." Izzy gazed at the cards, reading them anyway. After a moment, she began to clear them but paused when she came to two Knights, one of swords and the other cups reversed. "Hmm."

"Was it that reversed Wheel of Fortune?" Lee scratched his head. "Has he gotten it before or something?"

"Yes." She nodded. "Tell them what it means, Noah."

"It's time to wrestle with destiny. Unexpected changes are coming for me, and if I sit by, they won't go my way. It's time to do something, try to improve my situation. So if you all are still willing to help—"

The chorus of voices saying yes nearly had me in tears again. But I'm a curmudgeon prone to fits of drama, not a softie. I held them back. A vampire crying is not a good look.

"I trust you guys." I grinned at them, hoping it touched my eyes. "Go ahead and do the thing. Check the decision, sway opinions. I'll write an appeal letter as needed. Just tell me when to send it in."

Dylan seemed relieved. Hal nodded. Lee smiled. Izzy opened her mouth, then closed it again.

The exhibitors had started packing up their tables, which meant this event was pretty much over. Dylan waved goodbye and went to collect Logan, who was still engrossed in his notebook but alone now. Hal trailed after them. Izzy elbowed Lee, who stood aside and turned his back as she approached me.

"What's up?" I asked.

"Those Knights in your reading gave me such a strong vibe, I've got to mention them. But you might not like what they mean."

"I'll put on my big vampire pants."

"I'm serious."

"I know. May bravado be my armor and quips my sword."

"That's what I sometimes call the Rolling Stones formation of suit cards."

"Which is?"

"You can't always get what you want. You already know what Knights signify, Noah."

"Suitors. Of the young and male variety." I sighed, then asked her a stupid question on purpose because I already knew the answer would cut deeply. "Which was reversed again? The Sword Knight?"

"No." She shook her head, reached out, and put a hand on my arm. "Cups. I'm sorry."

"Thanks for being honest anyway." This time, I did dab at the corner of one eye.

"It doesn't mean you should give up, though. Remember that the Wheel of Fortune has the most influence here. Everything's still up to chance and subject to change. The other cards give a difficulty level. Maybe."

"How hard will it be, do you think? Wooing Jonah again, I mean."

"It's going to be brutal. Because I think you have to give Jonah time and space to handle this on his own. Noah, wooing him wasn't in your cards."

"But I can't—" I sighed. "Sorry. You read what's there, so I'm not arguing."

"I wish I'd seen something different, if it helps."

"Thanks for that. See you around."

She linked arms with Lee on her way to the lobby. I headed for the tunnel. As I descended the stairs, my spirits sank even lower. Trust had escaped me since Darren's cheating incident. It wasn't right to judge Jonah's future over my past. But there I was, doing it.

My inability to let go was like my left fang. Something sharp that caused me injury if I wasn't careful. The fang on the other side was impatience, and it had an even keener point.

I'd never been able to wait. So far, I'd been unable to temper it with my new vampiric extended lifetime. It was one reason I never wanted to go into extraveterinary medicine.

Izzy's readings hadn't steered me wrong before. But I couldn't bring myself to accept them.

If I did, it meant that Jonah Arnold wasn't my destiny.

I could try doing everything in my power to prove those cards wrong. But the outlook was not so good.

CHAPTER TEN

Aliyah

Logan said nothing about Jacinda on Monday, and I didn't dare ask. The last thing I wanted was a repeat of my first year when I almost burned the cafeteria down. If I brought it up without figuring out what my problem was, it wouldn't be fair to either of us.

He spent most of his free time at Monday lunch and in Creatives with Dorian, which was typical, although without their notes, which wasn't. I tried joining him and Lee for a to-go dinner in the cafe.

"Oh, Aliyah," Lee twirled his fork in some pasta. "This is important and kind of private. Sorry."

"That's okay." I nodded. "See you guys later."

Logan gazed into his chamomile tea the entire time, only looking up to wave shyly as I left to sit with Faith and Hal.

"What's that about?" she asked. "Are Lee and Izzy okay?"

"I don't know." I shrugged.

"Probably. It's college stuff." Hal added. "Lee's going for early acceptance at four different schools."

"Wow." I blinked.

After that, Ember got a ball out of Faith's bag, and we got

distracted by the adorable game of keep-away she played with Seth and Nin.

On Tuesday, the tryouts usurped every conversation I was involved in, including the one at lunch.

"What if people try out for your team and my squad and we both want them?" Logan finished his grilled cheese sandwich.

"The coaches talk about it and decide what they both want," Dylan said.

"Yeah, compromise is important." I nodded.

"Nobody has to fight over me, anyway." Dorian chuckled. "I'm not going out for either team. Maybe people will stick to one thing."

"I'm going for both." Faith twirled her spoon in the dregs of her soup. "I need whatever I can get on my college applications."

"I hear you," Hal said. "That stuff's important."

"Says the gadgetry genius." Dorian shook his cup. "I'm all out of beverage roulette."

"Bell's about to ring, though."

It did. We managed to pay attention in Lab. Right afterward, I got food to go from Penelope. After a hasty meal, I headed toward the gym to change and do some warmups. The locker room was empty. I stood in the doorway, staring at the arch over the gender-neutral bathrooms, unable to enter.

The yellow tape had been gone since last spring, but my mind's eye supplied plenty of memories about the crime scene, including how it looked before the authorities arrived.

I must have been there for a long time because after the squeak of shoes on wood startled me, my arm had a red mark from leaning in the doorway. I turned around to find my roommate.

"I knew I should have come over here earlier." Grace put her hand on my shoulder. "Are you okay?"

"Not really. There's a lot in my head."

"Let's get changed and run some laps. If you think that'll help?"

"Yeah."

Running occupied my body out on the track, but my mind wandered. Fortunately, away from the life-changing catastrophe last year. However, my thoughts strayed to something still ominous. The almost-overheard conversation between some of the trustees, whose presence on campus hadn't made us miserable yet.

After the third time around the track, I stopped. Grace ran by for a moment but turned and came back.

"What's up? You look like you've seen a ghost."

"I was thinking about last year."

Grace's jaw and shoulder eased as I explained what I meant. She must have been more worried than I thought. Having a target, whether an objective or a person, put Grace in her element.

"I knew we should have followed up on that more." She chewed her lower lip. "Well, we didn't have the opportunity last year like we do now. Maybe they made a mistake, invading campus. Leave it to the umbral magus. I'll find some clues, and we can brainstorm what to do with them. If your parents are okay with some sleepovers, that is."

"Should be fine." I sighed. "But I want you to be extra careful. Hiram's no slouch with the space magic and this is his school now."

"Understood."

A crowd of students came into the gym, heading for the locker room. I didn't bother looking to see who since both tryouts were happening.

Coach Pickman ran Bishop's Row tryouts, and Coach Chen ran cheer squad's. Faith went between both groups as I expected, which must have been taxing. Her main athletic strength was endurance so she managed.

Hailey and Bailey Overton also did dual tryouts. Both of them looked exhausted about halfway through, but Hailey kept her chin up while her twin glared and snapped at everyone.

Grace and Dylan were both brilliant at Bishop's Row, with Lee showing his usual competence. Nothing unexpected there. However, we had a couple of surprises.

Hal tried out. His space magic was nothing to sneeze at and a distinct advantage in the game. I could tell he'd been practicing over the summer, too. Coach Pickman's enthusiastic note-taking during his tryout made me nervous, but she'd given me veto power. If she tried putting Hal on the team, I'd block her. Sure, he'd be disappointed, but both Nurse Smith and Bubbe still seemed too concerned about his health for my comfort.

Lena Zanelli might be the quietest girl at school, but she was practically a force of nature on the court. Her endurance needed work, but she conjured almost as fast as Lee and matched me for speed. She even tagged Dylan out.

"Wow!" Grace clapped. "You're awesome!"

"Thanks," Lena mumbled.

I realized I could make up for vetoing Hal with Lena, no problem. With that all but decided, I relaxed.

Here comes trouble.

"If it's not too late, I'd like to try out."

"Onassis." Coach Pickman blew her whistle. "Morgenstern, swap with Khan! Onassis, there's no time for you to change, but drop the apron and let's see how rusty you are."

He wasn't. In fact, he'd improved since first year—while playing in steel-toed work shoes and cafeteria whites.

"He helps me practice," Lena said to Grace.

He conjured faster than he used to and made a throw I barely dodged. I tossed underhand and almost tagged him, but he smirked and spun out of the way. I burned his next orb with mine, then ran behind him to conjure again. He turned and ducked, so I jumped. It was a fakeout, and he threw high, tagging me squarely in the middle.

Coach blew her whistle, and we stopped. Dylan stood on the sidelines wide-eyed. I crossed to him and passed Alex on the bleachers. Logan stood nearby.

"No cheer squad?"

"Sorry." Alex shrugged. "Got here too late."

The coaches blew their whistles, and everyone headed out besides Logan and me. We sat on the bench together.

"There's no question DuBois is in. The same goes for Zanelli. They'll make our defense amazing."

"That's fair." Coach Chen nodded. "I want both Overtons on cheer squad."

"No problem. I want Fairbanks on second mid. Undeath rounds out Morgenstern's fire and solar to counter vamp and unseelie players from the other schools." Coach Pickman checked her notes. "For reserves, Hawkins and Onassis."

"Veto."

"Who?"

I closed my eyes. Life or death was more important than tolerating a jerk.

"Hal Hawkins." I sighed. "I know he looks better, but I'm not sure he'll be able to keep up."

"Not even with accommodations?" Coach Pickman raised her eyebrow.

"What do you mean?" I blinked. "Does he have a doctor's note or something? Because I think he's got better team synergy than Alex, but I worry. He's my friend."

"I was thinking of leaving him on the bench unless we need an ace up our sleeve. I can replace him with Young."

"I don't know." Coach Chen shook his head. "I'll miss having Fairbanks on squad. I had ideas for Faith's sha and Kitty's sphinx. What do you think, Logan?"

"I think we can use any of the familiars for that idea, except the pigeons. Skinner can do the same tricks, and I want Arick on the squad. He's got the best rhythm out of all the second-years, and he only tried out for cheer."

"What's your opinion on Hawkins then, Pierce?" Coach Pickman asked.

"Aliyah's right. Unless he has a note from his doctor, he shouldn't be doing athletics."

"Hold on." She stood, walked away, and took out her wand. She spoke into it like a phone, which made me even more eager to learn that type of magic in college. If I ever got in.

You will. Somewhere.

"Thanks."

"We both have to do the right thing for Hal, Aliyah. Even if it hurts his feelings."

"Oh." I blinked.

"Was that, um, the thing?" He glanced at Coach Chen, who seemed to be tuning us out.

"Yeah." I nodded.

Coach Pickman returned.

"That was Nurse Smith. He agrees with you on Hawkins." She sighed. "As much as I love an underdog story, you've got your team, Morgenstern."

"Thanks, Coach."

"Chen and I still have to hash things out. Lists post tomorrow morning before breakfast. Dual practice every Tuesday and Thursday. Now scram."

She blew her whistle instead of shooing us away like other faculty.

I headed toward the exit instead of the locker room. Logan looked over his shoulder, then trotted to catch up with me.

"No shower?"

"Upstairs for me." I sighed.

"Oh, right." He nodded. "Me too, then."

We walked together in a silence I hoped wasn't too uncomfortable. I thought I could make my escape and continue avoiding the topic of my bizarre jealousy. He stopped me in front of the stained glass doors.

"Wait a minute." He turned and faced me.

"Okay?" I looked at the mural done in glass. Shadows of other students passing by in the lobby made the shadows on the Unseelie side look like ghosts.

"Aliyah?"

"What?"

I turned my head toward him again and found him impossibly close. Our eyes met, and everything stopped. All the burning rage about Jacinda snuffed itself out, and my worries over Hal faded into evanescence.

"This year, we have three dances. I want you with me at all of them." The corners of his mouth tilted up but his eyes widened almost fearfully. "As my—um."

I blinked.

"Date?" The word seemed to steal all his breath, and he gasped afterward. "Maybe like Lee and Izzy."

"Oh!"

The world seemed to shatter into tiny bits, like the glass beside us must have looked before it got framed up and soldered together. Finally, it resolved into something more cohesive, a pattern of colors and shapes that felt right although I couldn't have described them if my life depended on it.

"But still a date?" I managed. "Because they always say it's not."

"Right. Maybe not exactly like them but—"

"Yes." I nodded as my hands fumbled toward his.

He didn't take my hands. Instead, he caught me up in a hug and lifted me off the floor for a heartbeat before setting me down. I still felt weightless in his arms, the same as every time we'd danced together.

I'm not sure how long we stood hugging like that, but when we broke it off, my eyes were misty. We held hands and pushed through the doors together.

For the first time since starting at Hawthorn, I crossed the lobby without the excruciating awareness of everyone else there and the suspicion they judged my every move. Although people noticed us, it felt different. Like nobody waited for disaster to follow me.

Ember peeped and dove through the air, landing on my shoulder but wrapping her tail around Logan's arm. Doris trotted over and walked between us.

We parted at my door. Grace sat at her desk in her pajamas already. I paced through the room, gathering my shower things.

"Are you humming?" Grace turned in her seat and raised her eyebrows.

"Sorry."

"Don't apologize. You're glowing in a non-fire kind of way. What happened?"

"I'm giving things a shot with Logan."

"Get out!" She jumped up, knocking her homework helter-skelter across her desk. Lune hopped and capered all over the room. "No, I mean don't like, literally get out. Leaping Luna, this is awesome!"

"It is?"

"Wait. Are you happy about it?"

"Yes." I nodded. "Why are you so excited?"

"I know it's a little weird to ship real-life people, but I always hoped you two would get together." She squealed. "Can we hug?"

"I'm still kinda sweaty from tryouts but okay."

We hugged. Grace wrinkled her nose.

"Yeah, you're stinky. Go shower. I'm so excited!"

I headed out and down the hall while chuckling. Life would be a million times harder without the people I cared about in it. They made it better, interesting. Weird too, sometimes.

How else do you learn?

"Right," I said into the empty bathroom.

I regretted having missed Faith and wondered how her reaction might have differed from Grace's. There'd be plenty of time to chat with my friends in the morning. I took my shower and went to bed, more tired than I'd realized.

Before breakfast, I headed to the gym to see the teams. Hal was already there and when I approached he turned toward me, glaring.

"I can't believe Dylan did this to me." His nostrils flared, and his cheeks deepened in color.

"Did what?" I blinked.

"He's reverse point, so he's captain. Must have used his veto to keep me off the team."

"No, Hal."

"There's no other way I didn't make it." His hands balled into fists.

"I'm captain." I sighed. "It's not Dylan's fault."

"*You* wouldn't." He blinked, eyes wide and edged with impending tears. "You *didn't.*"

"I did. Your health—"

"Fuck my health!" Hal briefly flickered like he'd lost control of his space magic. "This was my shot. The only way I'll leave a mark on this school. Maybe even the world."

"That's not true. Hal, you can still—"

"No." He crossed his arms over his chest. "You *know* I'm dying. This is the last good spell I'll ever get. You took this from me. *You*, of all people!"

"I backed her up." Logan stepped between us. "Because she's right."

"You don't know any better."

Logan swayed back, face red as if Hal had slapped him. The air around us grew heavy with moisture. Hal uncrossed his arms and put his dukes up, fists flickering, this time on purpose.

A *pop* and a rush of drier air blew us all backward as Headmaster Hiram appeared out of nowhere.

"No fighting on campus." The water coalescing around Logan's hands vanished, and Hal's fists stabilized. "Even my grandson must follow the rules. If you insist on settling your differences physically, you may opt for a faculty-mediated duel at an appointed time as per the student handbook."

"That's not needed, Headmaster." Logan hung his head. "I'm sorry, Hal. I don't want to waste our third year as enemies."

"Me too," I said. "I'm sorry."

"Harold?" Hiram raised his eyebrow.

"I'm going to see Ms. Khan." He turned and stalked away but paused and turned his head. "I'll decide about dueling later."

We stood together in mortified silence and watched him go. Once the door closed behind him, the headmaster vanished again. Logan put his arms around me.

You've got an awful lot to think about.

I told him what the voice said.

"Me too, Aliyah." He patted my back. "Maybe together. Can I come with you on Yom Kippur?"

"You're not Jewish." I sniffled.

"Is that not okay?"

"It's okay if you want to." I pulled back and studied his face. "We can bring people. Check with Bubbe first."

"I do." He nodded. "I will."

"Are you all right, Logan? What Hal said—"

"I didn't expect it, and yeah, it hurt. But we hurt him too when he literally trusted us with his life. Can we go to breakfast now?"

We held hands all the way to the cafeteria, in an entirely different mood from the night before. We'd both made a horrible mistake, but we could try to make up for it together.

That opportunity didn't come until after Yom Kippur.

CHAPTER ELEVEN

"I can't believe they tried to vote down the town's Bishop's Row tournament!" Dylan slapped a hand on the table, almost overturning my juice.

"Failed, though." Lee sprinkled salt on his eggs.

"Thank the gods." Alex held out a carafe. "Coffee?"

"Um, they never made me do that." Dylan blinked. "Pour tableside, I mean."

"That was under Hector. This is Hiram's school now so you get beverage service." He shrugged.

"I'll have some, thanks." Grace held her cup out.

"So it goes." Alex sighed as he poured.

"Vonnegut rocks," Dorian said.

"You got that reference?" Alex raised an eyebrow while withdrawing the carafe.

"He's my favorite." Dorian grinned.

"Thanks." Grace raised an eyebrow. "Aren't you going to give your fellow fanboy a refill?"

"If he wants."

"Nah. Breakfast beverage roulette is a rare and special animal."

Dorian stood and waggled his empty cup. "I'm hunting it. Come on, Aliyah."

"Um, okay?"

I had no idea why Dorian wanted my company but obliging him couldn't hurt. He elbowed me as we walked toward the section with the cereal, toaster, and drink dispensers.

"So. You and Logan are leaving campus early together?"

"For Yom Kippur."

"He's not Jewish."

"Doesn't matter."

"That's cool." He held his cup under the apple juice dispenser for a moment, then switched to orange. "How are you? With him?"

"Platonic. We talked. When he mentioned Izzy and Lee, it completely changed...well, everything."

"Hmm." Dorian added cranberry juice, sloshed some of his over-flowing blended juice down the drain, then added grape.

"Hmm?" I got water because I fasted from Rosh Hashanah to Yom Kippur.

"Our, um, talk on the first day ended kind of abruptly."

"Ah." I grinned and sipped my water as he added a little more apple juice. "I'm still sorting myself out. The plan includes talking to Noah later."

"Good call." Dorian turned his head and met my eyes. "Remember when I said you're not alone if you're asex—"

"Miss Morgenstern." Mrs. Pierce strutted toward us, eyes on me.

"Mrs. Pierce." I resisted the urge to curtsy.

"Happy Yom Kippur." She cradled her teacup in both hands.

"Um."

This holiday isn't happy, and she knows it. Call her bluff.

I didn't.

"Thanks?" I blinked.

Julia hooted and ruffled her feathers while glaring balefully at Logan's mother.

"No." Dorian shook his head. "You don't get to swing your privilege and insult my friend." He put his hands on his hips.

"Excuse me?" She raised her head and looked down her nose at him.

"It's a solemn holiday," he retorted. "Self-reflection time."

"Is this true, Miss Morgenstern?"

"Yes, ma'am."

You gave her an inch. Keep your eye on her, or she'll take a million miles.

"Well, then. May you have a meaningful day." She turned and clicked away on high-heeled shoes, her bouffant bleached blond hairdo not even bobbing as she went.

"Dylan says she reminds him of Margaret Thatcher." Dorian snorted. "Let's get back."

We went to the table. Grace was gone by then, and Logan sat in her place with only a glass of water in front of him. I blinked, wondering why he'd bothered with fasting.

"When in the High Holy Days, do as the Jewish do." He grinned.

"Okay." I sat beside him.

Lee chewed extra crispy toast and grinned. Dylan followed suit with his third breakfast sandwich. Ember took off, launching from the back of the booth to meet Gale, who'd shown up late again. As they cavorted in midair, Dylan glanced across the table at Dorian, who seemed oblivious.

Although I'd leave after lunch, it seemed like this would be a long day.

I left with Logan as soon as Creatives ended. He said he saw no point in sticking around with glasses of water while everyone else ate lunch and I agreed. Ember soared into the late summer air. I almost ran into the Polaroid cart. Azrael wasn't driving it this time, though.

"Um, hi?" I peered around to look at the person on the bicycle end of the contraption.

"Hello!" Mr. Ambersmith smiled. "Let's capture this moment."

He held up one of the cameras. Before he snapped a picture, Logan held my hand. Fortunately, there was no flash. He hated those.

"On the house." Mr. Ambersmith handed Logan the piece of plastic the camera produced.

"Thanks," I said.

We walked along Essex street as the balmy air developed the picture. Logan peered down at it.

"Wow. That's an amazing smile. Too bad mine looks like cardboard."

I snatched the photo from him and had a look.

"I think it's perfect."

Logan squeezed my hand. We continued quietly but comfortably. Logan went directly to Bubbe's as I headed upstairs.

All the curtains were drawn inside the house because Noah had shown up the night before. He hung around the kitchen, sipping from a cup of blood, and helping Dad with the baking. As soon as we arrived, Mom came out of her office and chatted reassuringly with Logan, who was concerned about being dressed appropriately.

"I remember Angie's first time. It was our third year, too," Dad mused as he pressed dough between his fingers.

"Really?" I blinked.

"Oh, come on." Noah rolled his eyes. "Don't tell me you didn't know Mom converted?"

I shuffled my feet.

"With a name like Hopewell? Really?"

"Shh," Dad said. "She doesn't talk much about it, but yes, that's what happened."

"After you started dating?" I asked.

"Pretty much." Dad's smile was faint but genuine. "She officially started the process of joining this family after graduation." He shrugged, his smile now in full bloom. "Unofficially, it started the first time she visited."

"So romantic." Noah sprinkled the last of the flour over the lump of dough.

"Last year, you would have rolled your eyes." Dad chuckled.

"Sorry." Noah sighed. "I got better."

"Can we talk?" I nudged my brother.

"I can handle kneading this for the next fifteen minutes," Dad said.

Noah followed me upstairs but shook his head when I reached for the door to my room. He opened his and waved me inside, where the windows were sun proofed.

"Sorry about that." I sighed.

"Last time we talked in here, this was hot cocoa." He held up his mug of blood, downed the dregs, then set it aside. "The only thing certain in this world is that everything changes. Anyway."

"I'm sorry—" We both said at the same time.

"Jinx. You owe me O negative."

We laughed.

"Seriously." He smirked. "What's up?"

I told him about my conversation with Dorian on the first day back at school.

"So, I did some searches on days off-campus. Do you think I'm asexual, Noah?"

"Maybe." He sighed. "At the end of the day, all you can know is how you feel and what you want."

"Well, I don't want sex. Love? Yes, please."

"Unsurprising." He grinned gently.

"How?"

"The look on your face every time Cadence talks about cute boys. Or Elanor about pretty girls." He took my hand. "Their opinions aren't relevant. Logan's are. What does he want?"

"A relationship. Something like Lee and Izzy, he says." I sighed. "Which made more sense to me than anything else I've seen, but it worries me."

"About?"

"Whether it's love. How do you know?"

"Imagine your life without him in it."

"That's awful."

"Okay, now imagine the world without him. Would you give up the first to stop the second?"

"God, Noah." I closed my eyes, tears running down my cheeks. "That's horrible either way, but I'd do it in a heartbeat."

"You love him, then." He handed me a tissue. "I know this firsthand."

"What about being in love?" I wiped my face. "And his feelings."

"You have to have a serious talk with Logan about that last part. I don't know about the other." He sighed. "For me, love's all tangled up with sex. Maybe you should talk to Bubbe about that."

"Bubbe?" I blinked. "She had Dad. So—"

"She wasn't totally celibate because she wanted a child." He took the tissue and tossed it into the wastebasket by his bed. "When I came out, she said a few things... Talk to her. I mean it."

"Yes, sir." I gave him the weakest salute ever.

"Are you okay now?"

"There's one more thing."

I told him about Hal.

"Oh, no." Noah's eyes widened. "You apologized, though."

"Maybe that's not enough."

"I've gripped grudges enough to know one thing, Aliyah." Noah chuckled but dabbed the corner of his eye. "It's up to the holder to let them go. I pray he finds peace."

"Me, too."

Dad called from downstairs. We headed downstairs and out.

Logan sat between Bubbe and me at the service. At first, I thought he meant to be a buffer. I'd felt more distant from my grandmother since June than at any other time in my life. After the first few minutes, it became clear that this wasn't about her or me. It was for Logan.

He took all his cues from her, nodding and following along like he was on a dance floor instead of inside an unfamiliar temple. Although he clutched a weathered old stenographer's notebook, she must have described everything ahead of time, too.

Mom saw me glance at the notebook.

"I used it," she murmured. "Years ago."

When the Shofar blew, I closed my eyes. In my mind's eye, I saw

Filberto Luciano sitting here between Great Uncle Noah and Bubbe in grade school. That scene faded, replaced by what I thought were Noah and me. However, my hair was too short and permed, and Noah wouldn't ever wear acid wash jeans. I realized it was Bubbe again, this time with my grandfather. It was impossible for magi to be psychic, but those visions felt real.

Coincidence is a series of patterns woven by the magic we use. Of course, they are.

When I opened my eyes, Logan was touching my cheek. He wiped away a tear there. When he lowered it, I reached out and twined my fingers with his. I knew immediately that Bubbe and Grandpa went through similar motions decades ago.

On the way out, we walked together behind everyone else.

"You should talk to her after dinner. Bubbe, I mean."

"I will." I squeezed his hand. "What about you?"

"Your mom asked me for my study guides from the first two years."

"Makes sense."

"It does?"

"I bet she thinks they'll help students in the future."

"If that's the case, I'll give her the one from this year, too. Once it's finished."

"You're amazing, Logan Pierce."

He blushed as we got in the car.

At dinner, Logan tried a little of everything, which surprised me. He'd always been a picky eater at school. That trait followed him to a degree because he made a face after sampling the whitefish salad and only took second helpings of challah and noodle kugel. Noah beamed.

"If you ever want me to make that for you, let me know." He jerked a thumb at the half-empty casserole dish, then refilled his cup with blood from the refrigerator. "Vicarious eating isn't the same, but I'll take it."

"Thanks, Noah."

The rest of us practically pigged out. The fast before Yom Kippur was the longest one we observed. Eventually, we all sat back and patted full bellies. After coffee, Bubbe headed downstairs. I waved to

Logan as he got his notes out for Mom, then I followed my grandmother.

"Bissel." She turned, standing in the hall to face me.

"Bubbe." I sighed. "Can we talk?"

"I need to make my rounds, but yes." She raised an eyebrow. "Is this a topic for working or teatime?"

"Maybe both."

"Then start with the part you can manage while we work."

Love or fear. Choose wisely.

"How did you know you loved Grandpa?"

"I'm a serious person by nature, like you, Aliyah. I spent a lot of time worrying. He let me share my burdens. That's how it started."

"So it wasn't right when you met, like how Dad tells it?"

"That only happens in movies and to people like your father, who lean into the physical side of things." She chuckled while refilling a water dish for a sleeping fox. "My first meeting with Morris was a little awkward."

"How?"

"He told me he liked my shirt. Which was covered with fewmets at the time."

I put my hand over my mouth to stifle my giggle until we reached the next room, where a wood owl roosted. He was awake, of course.

"Hoo?"

"Just me." Bubbe grinned at the bird, then swept the pellet it had regurgitated into the dustbin.

This time, we laughed together, but she put a finger to her lips as we approached the final overnight guest. A puffin nested in a box on the floor, beak under her wing.

"Wait." I blinked. "That bird looks familiar."

"Oona's with one of the trustees. He thinks she strained a leg."

"He mentioned that while auditing our lab yesterday." I sighed. "He was nice, but I forget his name."

"Justin Glen from New Hampshire, a family friend of your class-mate Eston." Bubbe refilled the small plastic temporary pool with water. "That's his familiar."

132

"Are all three of them—"

"Shh." She led me back into the hallway. "Yes, the fox and the owl are companions to trustees as well."

"They're all injured?"

"Not that I could tell. Only Oona. But their magi wanted them seen as a matter of routine."

As Bubbe led me toward the kitchen, I checked the doors. The owl's name was Smokey, and the fox was called Zephyr. I'd have to ask around at school, find out more about their magi. Logan would help. I gasped.

Burden sharing, table for two.

Bubbe set the kettle on the stove while I got mugs and tea out of the cupboard. Once we sat with cups steaming in front of us, I drew a deep breath, inhaling the herbal aromas.

"I'll go first," Bubbe said. "I'm sorry for trying to make the choice about your testing for you."

"Why?" I stared at her hands, how only the fingertips touched the ceramic. "You were as adamant as, well, adamantine."

"They called me that in high school." She sighed. "Shiny, but hard-headed. And hearted."

"How?" I blinked. "You're a caregiver."

"It's no easy thing to be, especially for animals, who can't speak for themselves. I choose for them, most of the time. Sometimes, that means wearing armor around my heart. Like I tried doing with you last fall and this summer, although you were willing and able to tell me what you wanted and needed for yourself."

"Wow. I thought you'd been angry with me all this time for going to Rockport behind your back."

"I was, but only for a moment and unfairly." She reached across the table. "Can you forgive me?"

"This isn't what I expected." I took her hands. "Yes."

"Thank you."

"I'm afraid, Bubbe." I looked down at our hands, joined together in the middle of the table. "Of the test."

"That's natural."

"Not normal?"

"Nothing about the way extramagi get treated is normal. Who's your witness?"

"Logan."

"Good." She nodded. "I wonder why you chose him."

"He offered the moment he found out about it." I glanced up at her face. "I realized he would have been my first choice anyway."

"Ah." She let go of my hands, reached for her tea, and sipped. "Will you be afraid still, with him there?"

"Yes." I nodded. "Because the test doesn't make me fear for my physical safety."

"You worry that taking it damages mental health."

"Everything went sideways for Dylan after his. Do you know he almost went home with Temperance last year over winter break?" I shuddered while gazing into my tea. "Then there's Richard."

"Richard's childhood environment was more toxic than a nest of basilisks. He hid what he was for decades and avoided the test until he got arrested. Neither of them had the kind of help and support you do."

"He should have asked someone else to be his witness."

"The school should have had a counselor besides the headmaster." She sipped her tea again. "But running that school's not my business."

"You think I'll be okay, then?"

"If you do the work on self-care before and after, yes."

"What work, exactly?"

"Start seeing Ms. Khan now, and make it regularly. Talk to Logan about what you fear and what he can expect. Then afterward, take time and small steps. With help, from them and your other friends and family."

"I'm not supposed to talk about it though."

"You've got a lot of people who care about you, Aliyah. Most of them are brilliant. I think you'll figure out how."

"Especially Logan."

"You two are exceptionally close since last spring. Is this why you asked me about your grandpa?"

"Partly. Noah had something to do with it too."

"Oh?"

"I tried talking to him about love. We think maybe we're too different when it comes to that."

She raised an eyebrow.

"There's no, um, sex in it for me." I winced. "He said he thought you might understand better than him."

"He's right." Bubbe nodded. "It's never been about pretty faces for me. Maybe I'm not wired like the majority of people. There's no shame in that. I experience love a little differently; that's all."

"So what did that mean for you and Grandpa?"

"When we were together, the world felt kinder. Friendlier. A more joyful place. Does Logan make you happy?"

"Not all the time, no." I sighed. "There's been too much misery going around, stuff not our fault."

"Then what's it like when you're unhappy together?"

"We've done an awful lot of crying on each other's shoulders. Over his parents. The test. Professor Luciano."

"Would those times have been harder if you'd cried alone? Or with a different person, even?"

"Absolutely." I looked up. "Bubbe. Crying with Logan is almost like crying with one of you. Like he's part of the family but not another brother. Is that love?"

"I think you're well on the way to an answer." She nodded. "It's your decision, what your feelings mean."

As we finished our tea, Logan came downstairs yawning. Bubbe cleaned up the tea things, leaving him to walk me to the stairs. Although I had a potential name for the place he held in my heart, I didn't dare say it aloud until I was sure.

CHAPTER TWELVE

The next morning, I went to the office before breakfast and requested an appointment with Ms. Khan, saying it was urgent. All through class, I figured she'd be too busy to see me, but on my way to the library, she stopped me in the hall.

"If you're not doing any critical research, I can squeeze you in, Aliyah."

"I've got time."

I followed her down the hall and out of the academic wing. Instead of the office, she brought me down the ramp toward the infirmary. A door I hadn't previously noticed opened off on the wall to the left of the infirmary's entrance.

The door wasn't here until this year.

The voice was right. I could feel it as I opened the door. As I passed through, I deliberately brushed against the frame and felt a tickling sensation like I had in Lab when Hal used space magic to borrow some sunlight. Inside, the room wasn't much larger than the one Logan used at Bubbe's. Except there wasn't a bed or even a desk.

Ms. Khan sat in a chair similar to the coveted comfy ones in the lounge. There were six more in a circle only incomplete to leave room for the door to open. While the one Ms. Khan sat in was neutral beige, the rest were each different colors, all vibrant instead of the pastel I'd so often seen in offices. Red, blue, yellow, green, white, purple. I sat in the blue one and spent a moment glancing around the room.

Instead of motivational posters or medical diagrams, these walls were hung with tapestries, again in multiple colors and geometric patterns. It gave a soothing effect without the blandness that usually came from more formal decor.

"They let me choose my trappings." She smiled. "How would you have decorated, Aliyah?"

"That's an interesting question." I sat up straight and thought about it. "The ocean. With sailboats and a wharf, like in town."

"Ah, the seaside is certainly a popular favorite." She nodded.

"What's another? Popular one, I mean."

"Well, mine's a frozen lake with skaters. That's unsurprising for an ice magus like me."

"So the ocean is a surprise from a fire or solar magus?"

"After twenty years' worth of answers, none quite surprise me." She sat back in her chair. "So, what brings you here?"

"First, I have to ask you a question to be sure I can speak freely." I paused, unable to properly phrase everything at first. "It's tricky."

"Okay."

"Last year, Dylan asked me to witness something for him. And this year. Well, if there'd been a counselor here, could he have come to them about it?"

"No." She shook her head. "Unless it was me. As his mother, I already knew about the test. I was under the impression you'd done yours over the summer, however."

"No, I asked to postpone it. It's coming up in a few weeks." I cleared my throat. "My grandmother said I ought to get into a routine to prepare, including counseling."

"She sounds wise."

"I left things a bit to the last minute though. Or maybe this is too soon. I'm sorry."

"Don't be. It's never too late to ask for help. Or too early. Especially when you know harsh terrain lies ahead."

"That's a relief." I leaned back in the chair and let the back of my head rest against the cushion. "Maybe the second one since my birthday. The test is brutal, and I'm afraid I might not come out, well, healthy on the other side of it."

"I've done some reading on the subject, and you're right to worry."

"Really?" I blinked. "That's not what I expected a counselor to say."

"I'd be doing you a disservice to dismiss a true concern, especially about a clearly risky ordeal." She shook her head. "Constant positivity isn't counseling. We're getting short on time, so I want you to make some lists. The things that worry you most for getting through the test, your biggest fears about what might happen afterward, and one list of things you're happy with about yourself now."

"That last one doesn't seem like it fits."

"Think of your version of soothing decor, Aliyah. The ships on the ocean. Don't they go out and encounter storms at sea?"

"Yeah."

"You included a wharf with your seaside. Why?"

"Because it's part of Salem, my home." I gasped. "Oh! The sailors need to know where home is."

"Exactly. So, work on those lists. I'll see you back here again tomorrow. Is there a better time than your library period?"

We figured out a schedule, with visits four days per week. By the time I headed back in time for Lab, I knew I'd made the right choice.

Mrs. Onassis showed up to Bishop's Row practice. Her familiar was a basilisk, but otherwise unlike Alex's in every way. Instead of green like Asceco, this one was purple and much larger, with fangs that protruded slightly past her lip scales. While Mrs. Onassis feigned indifference from the top of the bleachers, the basilisk watched me so intently that I shuddered a few times.

"Ignore Pharmaka, Morgenstern." Alex said while retrieving his ballistae from the equipment chest.

"A basilisk named remedy?" I blinked. "That's ironic."

"It's not." Alex adjusted the Velcro on his left wrist. "Double meaning, like a lot of Old Greek."

"What's the other one, then?" Dylan raised an eyebrow.

"Poison, of course." Alex rolled his eyes. "Anyway, like I said. Ignore her. She only gets worse if you pay attention to her."

"Like your mom." Grace snorted.

"Exactly." Alex cinched his cestus.

Grace blinked. Lena caught her eye and slowly nodded. When Grace opened her mouth, Lee put a finger over his lips.

"She sucks. Might as well own that." He shrugged. "Anyway, see you on the court."

He turned and jogged away, beginning a warm-up lap. Grace looked about as shell-shocked as I felt. Dylan patted the top of her head, then elbowed me.

"I think that's the most pleasant conversation our lot's ever had with the prince of darkness."

"Earl, not prince." Lena fished her equipment out of the chest.

"Same difference to this blue-collar boy." Dylan shrugged.

"His collar looks more cerulean every day." Faith stood from where she'd been leaning on the bottom bench. "If he's nobility and his mother's loaded, why's he working in the cafe?"

"He said it was none of my business when I asked," Lee offered.

"I think there's family trouble." I told them about the hearing, how Konstantin Onassis showed up with Alex to help him testify against Temperance.

"I bet it's one of those situations where the titled family went broke and married money." Faith took a casual glance over her shoulder and aimed a lazy grin at Alex's mother. "She knows my mom from way back. Logan's too. Debutantes all. So my guess is, he rebelled and she's cut him off to retaliate."

"Yeah." Lena nodded, then took off for her laps.

"Whoa." Dylan shook his head. "Like the evil version of you three." He indicated Faith, Grace, and me.

"Don't forget obscenely wealthy." Grace chuckled. "Because the three of us sure aren't."

"Two out of three," I corrected.

"Don't look at me." Faith did a few side stretches. "If all goes well, they'll write me out of the will."

"How does that mean going well?" Dylan asked.

"Wait and see." Her grin reminded me of a locked diary.

Coach Pickman ended our conversation with a blast on her whistle. We jogged out to run laps with Alex, doing our best to ignore his mother and her creepy basilisk.

"No Azrael?" Soda overflowed and splashed Dorian's sleeve. "Are you two okay, Grace?"

"We're fine." She handed Dorian a wad of napkins. "Gallows Hill has a craft fair that runs right over Parent's Night so I'm going stag. We'll meet up the next day off-campus."

"That's good." He dabbed at the spill, then mopped it up off the counter after he'd saved his blazer. "What about you, Aliyah? Who are you going with?"

"Hoo?" said Julia.

"Logan." My face heated up so I grabbed the sodden napkins and turned to toss them in the trash. "We've got, er, an agreement. About all the dances and stuff."

"Peep!" Ember stood up on my shoulder and flapped. Then she groomed the hair she'd blown out of place.

"Oh, right." Dorian chewed his lower lip, then opened his mouth and closed it again.

"Were you looking for a date?" I asked. "How about Dylan? He's not going with anyone."

"Not for me." Dorian shook his head. "I'm the DJ."

"Whoa! Congratulations!" Grace held out her knuckles for a fist-bump.

"Thanks. I've got some big shoes to fill, though." He sighed. "And someone to find a date for at the last minute."

"Right." I nodded. "Zeke's still staying in town."

"I know. I met up with him at your grandma's office to get his music files. Anyway, for a centuries-old vampire, he knows a lot about audio technology."

"Who are you playing matchmaker for, then?" Grace scratched her head.

"I'd rather keep that to myself for now." He set the fresh cup of beverage roulette on his tray and waved as he strolled away.

Grace let out a frustrated growl, and Lune stamped his foot.

"What's wrong?"

"Not knowing's going to bug me the rest of the week. Whoever it is, they were going with Dorian until he got tapped as DJ."

"We'll find out soon enough, I guess." I shrugged.

"Do you think it's Arick?"

"He's going with Hailey again." I grinned. "I think they're a couple."

"Lena?"

"A first-year guy asked her."

"Coach Pickman?" Grace wrinkled her nose. "Ew. Didn't mean to remind you of you know who."

"It's okay if we don't know, Grace. It's only a date."

"I want to help, is all." She sat, stirring her soup. "And see Dorian happy."

"I know. Look at it as a break. Social maneuvering's so last year."

"So's you and Logan being just friends, apparently."

"We are friends, though. In a bigger way."

"Really?" She raised an eyebrow.

"It's like Izzy says. There's no *just* about this friendship."

"I don't understand it, but if that's how you two want to do things, I'm in your corner."

"Thanks, Grace."

After lunch, I headed straight to Lab. We had time in the library, but I wanted to check on the plants we had growing for the end of the semester. They were a big part of the mid-term practical, where we'd use their roots to concoct a sleeping draught for familiars.

Inside at the teacher's bench stood a man I didn't recognize. The creature on the table was a different story. He sat on his haunches and tilted his head, bright blue eyes peering at me from a mask of red and white fur. He glanced at my shoulder and yipped. Ember flew off to join him, *peeping* good-naturedly.

"Hello, Zephyr."

"Hmm." The man closed Professor Hawkins' lab binder with one gnarled hand. "Miss Morgenstern, is it?"

"How did you know?"

"How else would you know my critter's name?"

"Good point."

"You're an overachiever, is that it?"

"No. Just interested in plants." I headed toward the trough that held my specimen, beside Dorian's. "I'm Aliyah."

"I'm informal." He grinned and shuffled toward the experimental garden in the window. "I'd like you to call me Hank, but that's not flying in here. So call me Mr. Thurston."

"Okay, Mr. Thurston."

"Aren't you surprised to see a trustee here?"

"Not really." I shrugged and examined a mottled leaf on the plant. "After last year... Look, I was in the room when magic with the power of a solar flare almost ashed the school. It's hard to believe it could be worse."

"A threat exists whether you believe in it or not." He shook his head, grin fading like blooms in frost. "Be prepared."

"Why?"

"You don't get to be my age by letting your guard down."

"Great." I sighed. "More danger. Exactly what we wanted."

"Keep your ears and eyes open, Miss Morgenstern."

"If it's so bad and you know about it, can't you say more? Or do something?"

"The people you've got to worry about are good at keeping their secrets. All this old air magus can do is show up. I'd rather be back on Block Island taking in the sea air."

"Okay." I nodded. "Anyone in particular I should watch—"

"Miss Morgenstern, please return to the library." Professor Hawkins stood at my elbow. "I've got to prepare the lab for class later."

"Yes, sir."

I collected Ember, who seemed dismayed about leaving her new friend, and headed down the hall where I sat with a botanical book until the bell rang. By the time Lab started, there was no sign of Mr. Thurston or Zephyr.

All week, I waited for Grace to bring outfits around like she had the year before. It never happened. She had the dresses and suits, but on Thursday she invited people to the room for them instead of dragging a rack through the hallways. Which was a good plan because there was no way she could have gotten it on the stairs. Somehow, she'd made garments for Lena and Arick too.

And Alex. She gave me ten minutes' warning before he arrived.

"Why him?" I asked with my back to her as I buried my nose in history notes.

"He's trying. I know what it's like, not being able to afford something decent to wear." She poked my shoulder and waited until I looked up at her before continuing. "Remember that dress you lent me our first year?"

"Yeah, but—"

"No buts. This is how I pay it forward."

"You're no moneybags."

"Neither were you. Didn't stop you. Anyway, I gave you the heads-up. You can take your homework to the cafe if you want to."

You don't.

"Whatever." I shrugged. "Mean people suck, nice people rule. Queen Grace forever."

"Thanks."

I couldn't fault Grace for paying it forward. Last year, doing the right thing had felt like an act of rebellion. Supporting a friend, doubly so. The main reason I stuck around was curiosity. I wanted to see what she'd made for him.

When Alex arrived, he mostly ignored me. His nonchalance was a relief. However, it didn't stick. He didn't indulge my curiosity either. Grace handed him the garment bag, which he unzipped only enough to reveal velvety purple fabric.

"It's beautiful."

"Thanks."

"You shouldn't have."

"I did for everyone else. Why not you?"

"Because." His voice cracked and his breath hitched. Then he said something too softly for me to make out.

"I don't care whether you wear it or not, but take it with you when you go. I don't have the room for it."

He walked toward the door, back stiff but shoulders shaking. He paused, and the tremors stopped. Alex turned his head and glared at me, but addressed my roommate.

"Not a word about this, DuBois."

"About the suit?" Grace raised an eyebrow.

"No, that's fine. Everything else, keep your mouth shut. Especially you, Morgenstern. Or else."

"Mum's the word." I narrowed my eyes.

"Nice double entendre. Remember it."

He pushed the door open and stalked out.

"Did you threaten him, Aliyah?"

"Back. He did it first."

"Oh yeah, he did." Grace sighed. "So much for mending fences. Anyway, did you want to see your gown?"

"I peeked in the bag already." I grinned. "Blue's an interesting choice."

"That's the overlay. Are you sure you don't want to try it on?"

"Nah. Your dressmaking is at epic levels. I trust you."

I finished studying while she left to shower. When she got back, I went to get cleaned up. By the time I'd done that, Grace had gone to sleep.

CHAPTER THIRTEEN

"Why can't we go down whenever?" Dylan shuffled his feet.

"We have to wait for the third-year music." Logan sighed.

"Meet the new rules, same as the old rules," Faith said. "That's all the headmaster cares about this year."

"Shh." Hal tilted his head toward the stairs. "It's starting."

"How you can hear the difference is beyond me." Faith sniffed. "I miss Zeke's pop waltzes."

"It's Voices of Spring, duh." Bailey rolled her eyes. "We get the fun stuff later, after introductions. Or don't you remember all those debutante balls?"

"Move it." Grace shooed her toward the stairs.

We got on two to a step with one in between, and Grace called for the lobby. The stairs moved more slowly than usual, and as we descended, Dorian announced us over the music through the PA under festive amber lighting.

"Feels like time travel," Logan murmured. "You look like a Gilded Age film star."

"Oh?" I blinked. "Like Marilyn Monroe?"

"Nah. She was only pretty."

I blushed, unsure what to say to that.

Fortunately, it was appropriate not to speak. We paraded across the dance floor in measured steps, like a procession or a living display. I would have felt embarrassed with all those eyes on me, but it was easy enough to imagine everyone gazed at Grace's handiwork.

Most of the third-years walked singly, with Hal and Faith and me and Logan the exceptions. The rest had dates, but not with each other and trailed off to meet them by the chairs at the sides of the dance floor.

Lee walked directly in front of us, his eyes glued to the door. When Izzy walked through it, he almost stopped in place. I didn't blame him. Grace had outfitted her, too.

Izzy's dress was sleek and red, a shade that complemented her deep bronze complexion. Instead of her usual braids or pigtails, she'd gathered her voluminous natural ringlets to one side, with a bright red hibiscus accenting a finishing touch. The moment he stepped off the parquet, Lee hurried to her side. Logan and I followed.

Bad idea.

At first, the inside voice's statement made no sense. A phoenix dove through the air like a comet toward Izzy. But Fifi was Elanor's familiar and friendly. As Ember launched from my shoulder and Doris hissed at Logan's heels, I realized my mistake. The plumes on the tail were blue instead of yellow, indicating this phoenix was older than the one I knew.

"Brand. Pattern eight."

The voice was brisk and clipped, exuding authority. The bird turned, inches from crashing into Izzy. He assumed a tight spiral over her head, and although no attack seemed imminent, the air shimmered above Izzy. Her hibiscus began wilting.

Banish some of that.

I clenched a fist and focused on damping down the heat. Logan tightened his grip on my other hand and the air immediately around us grew heavy with humidity. Lee put his hand on Izzy's shoulder. A moment later, the flower in her hair perked up, opening in full bloom. Scratch shook his head, loppy ears flopping from side to side as he sat on his haunches, whiskers twitching.

Logan gasped, still gripping my hand as he stepped slightly behind me, eyes averted. His posture reminded me of something. My mind shuffled through memories, but the train of thought derailed a moment later when Logan's father stepped into the middle of our group.

"Mister Young." He tilted his head back and glared down his nose. "You know outside guests aren't allowed at formal school functions."

"I got permission," he insisted.

"Yeah, I've got a letter and everything." Izzy reached in her bag and pulled out a bright yellow paper. Mr. Pierce took one glance at it and barked out something not quite a laugh.

"The headmaster hasn't informed us of any such request." Mr. Pierce narrowed his eyes.

"Does he have to?" Logan's voice shook and cracked like a sandcastle under a rising tide.

"Read the new handbook. And look a man in the eyes when speaking. You're such a disappointment. Like you were raised by wolves. As an Omega."

"Or dragons, perhaps." Professor DeBeer stepped between Mr. Pierce and us. "Have a closer look at that document."

Mr. Pierce glared at the paper as if he'd incinerate it.

"Why? Is it a forgery?"

"Nope. I signed it with the headmaster late this afternoon. Would you like to see my copy?" The bird on her shoulder opened and closed his beak, sending off blue sparks of lightning. "I'll gladly escort you to my office if so."

"No need." A man with chestnut hair gone gray at the temples stepped out of the shadows by the doorway. "Back down, Leo. It's authentic. At least precognitive psychics aren't undesirables."

"Thanks, Trustee Fairbanks." Professor DeBeer shot us a glance over her shoulder. "Anyway, this is a dance. Why not let the children go enjoy themselves?"

"Don't drench the ladies, son." Mr. Pierce glared at Logan, then snapped his fingers. Brand the phoenix swooped down to his shoulder, and the temperature cooled so suddenly it got foggy around Izzy's head. "Or you'll never get anywhere with them."

"Sorry," Logan mumbled. I felt him rein in the water he'd been conjuring.

"No worries." Izzy fluffed her hair. "Humidity's amazing for curls."

"Shall we?" Lee offered her his arm, and she took it.

We stepped onto the dance floor although Dorian was in mid-transition between the last song and the next. I didn't recognize what we danced to.

"What's this one?" I asked.

"*Perfect Day*." Logan sighed. "By Lou Reed. Ironic."

"How?"

"Wait until the end."

The song was short, and he was right. It faded out on a dark promise of reaping what's sown, and made me shiver. Logan gripped my hand and my waist tighter while leading us through the steps.

"Here's *Return to Serenity* by Testament." Zeke never announced songs, so I wasn't sure why Dorian did it now. "For everyone who needs it."

And they do.

The building magical tension on the dance floor palpably eased. Shoulders lowered, stances widened, and brows smoothed over. I felt bad for Dorian, though. Headmaster Hawkins appeared beside him a moment later, wagging one wrinkled finger in his face. Apparently, he'd violated some rule with those two sentences. The reprimand ended long before the song. Logan kept on dancing through the opening bars of *Black Letter Day* by The Cardigans, which Elanor had practiced almost all summer.

"Can we cut in?" Faith tapped my shoulder.

"Is that okay, Logan?"

"Um." He glanced at her, then Hal. "Okay."

I expected Faith to step in, but Hal did instead. We shuffled along somewhat in time with the music. Although my dancing had improved over the last couple of years, it was hard to get past my shock. Hal seemed more tired than I'd seen him all summer.

"You were right." He sighed down at me. Somehow, he'd grown again in the last week. At tryouts, he'd been a hair shorter.

"No. Not about how I did it." I shook my head. "Should have talked to you."

"Couldn't have. You had to decide right after tryouts."

"I could have given you a heads-up that night." I squeezed his hand. "I'm—"

"Don't apologize again." He squared his jaw. "Everybody does that now. The doctors down in Boston. Nurse Smith. Even Dad."

"I won't, then."

"Good. I'm sick, and it's nobody's fault except my cells. And bloody coincidence." He grinned. "I'm trying out UK cussing. The f-bomb felt too mundane, and I shouldn't have said it to you in the first place. So it's my turn to apologize. Sorry."

"It happens." I grinned back. "I'm glad you and Faith cut in."

"It was her idea. I wanted to corner you by the punch bowl."

"Don't look now, but Alex is spiking it again."

"Joy."

"I wonder if Logan can fix that." I glanced over my shoulder at Alex, who tucked the flask back in his purple velvet jacket and waved. "Detox it, I mean."

"Not until I've tried it." Hal dropped a wink. "I was serious about joy."

Oh. So it's like that?

"Why?" I asked my voice and my friend.

Bucket list.

No, I thought back.

Wait and see.

"I've never tried it. I'd like to, at least once."

"Well, okay then." I let him escort me off the dance floor. "I'm your designated driver."

"Thanks." He filled a cup, then raised it to me.

My eyes stung as he drained it and got another. Someone poked me in the back. I turned slowly so as not to attract any unwanted parental attention to Hal's underage drinking.

"Don't say a word, Morgenstern."

"Way ahead of you there, Prince Poison."

"Are we going to do this all the time?"

"Are we?" I raised an eyebrow.

"I'm trying to be...decent here."

"Spiked punch and ominous warnings aren't exactly normal overtures of friendship."

"What's normal, anyway? How you do it, or is variety allowed?"

"No. I mean yes." I took a step back.

"You don't even know." He shook his head. "Or believe me."

Is it so hard to imagine he's clueless?

"I believe you, Xan." Dorian tipped a ladle of punch into a cup. "Thanks for the drinky-drink. I've gotta go before the song changes."

"Xan?" I blinked. Dorian only rushed off without answering.

"Yeah, it's a nickname. Dorian's idea." Alex sighed. "Starting fresh, he says."

Xan. Try it.

"Why?"

"Never mind." He turned toward a stretch of empty wall, then strode away from us.

"Worked for Dorian." Hal hiccupped. "Different reason. But that's why."

"How many cups did you drink?"

"Dunno. It's good." Hal's grin was goofily lopsided. He finished the dregs.

"Okay, time to get you back to Faith."

"No. Water first, okay?" He glanced at the dance floor, where she and Logan glided around gracefully. "I couldn't keep up with her before."

"Let's sit, then."

I filled cups from the water cooler and sat with him, sipping.

"Wow." Hal chuckled. "It hurts less now."

"What hurts less?"

"Everything." He held his free hand out, opening and closing it. "Along with the mad energy I had aches, growing pains, all summer.

"Even on Logan's birthday?"

"Yeah. They got worse this week. Even with all the magic in here."

"Hey, have you talked to Bubbe lately?"

"No. Should I?"

"Remember what happened after we went to her office on Logan's birthday?"

"Oh!" His eyes widened. "She made phone calls."

"Right. Maybe she's heard something back by now."

"I might not want to know what, though."

I sat silent, trying not to make assumptions and screw up as I had with Alex. Or maybe Xan. Life on campus got more confusing by the minute. Curiouser, like I'd fallen through a looking glass.

"Hey, I want my future husband back on the dance floor." Faith held a hand out to Hal.

He took it, and they were off. He seemed more limber out there, despite his weariness. Maybe there was something to be said for removing pain from the complicated equation of his illness. "Wish I could do more to help him."

"Me too." Logan took my hand. "He drank punch by Alex, didn't he?"

"Yeah." I leaned my head on his shoulder.

"Good for him."

"I wanted to ask you to detoxify it, but he said no."

"Wouldn't have anyway." He leaned his head on mine. "Unless Hal asked me himself."

"He's like our leader this year, how Grace was last time."

"You think?"

"You don't?"

"No, I can't argue with your logic." Logan sighed. "I wish everything were easier for him, is all."

"Wish!" I sat up so fast our heads clunked together.

We both turned to face each other, checking for sore spots. He took both my hands in his once we verified we were unharmed.

"What's your eureka?"

"Wishes." I smiled. "Magic ones. You know the stained glass on the entrance to Academics?"

"Yeah. *Long Division*," he recited. "By Gamila Haddad-Hawk—" His eyes widened.

"His grandmother. In August, I found out she's a djinn. She's been gone, divided from the family. But someone on campus right now has her lamp. And after that, she's got one more turn left in it."

Logan gasped.

"Aliyah, you're a genius. If we find that lamp and get Hal mastery, he can wish away his illness."

"Doesn't work that way."

We looked up to see a woman who looked older than Bubbe standing over us. She was taller than me, but without the gangliness of my frame. Her plaited hair was entirely white, and her skin lightly dusted with amber freckles. A small brown bird with the same delicate carriage perched on the wide-brimmed hat she wore. I would have thought it a decoration if it hadn't let out three throaty chirring calls.

"Lamps can't cure disease?" He spoke to the bird, then put a hand over his mouth. "Oops. That was bad manners, talking to your familiar like you aren't even there."

"You must be Logan Pierce."

"Yes, ma'am." He stood and bowed. "And you're Duchess Georgina Dunstable, of the Queen's court. From Marblehead."

"Duchess no longer, but the rest is true." She nodded.

I stood.

"Marquess?" he asked. A *faux pas* when talking to full-fledged Faeries, retired or not.

"I can't imagine why he's so interested, Miss."

"I'm Aliyah Morgenstern." Now I curtsied. "Aaron's and Angela's daughter. Mildred's granddaughter. Noah's great-niece." I kept my head bowed. "Richard Hopewell is my uncle."

"You may call me Georgia. One could say I'm retired."

"You can't retire from being a Faerie, I thought." I made it a statement instead of a question. Once changelings became Faeries, answering and asking them questions got tricky. Favors could come into play if we weren't careful.

"I was a magus first and graduated from Hawthorn Academy before the other side of my heritage made itself known. Under certain circumstances, mantles come and go. I completed my duties to Her Majesty and together with the king, she released me from court obligations to meet others."

"That's amazing!" Logan smiled. "You've got a rare set of circumstances. And a rare bird as well. Nightjars aren't usually magical."

"You are as well-educated as I've heard, Mr. Pierce. Your talents aren't exactly common either."

"Thanks." His smile faded. "So it's true that a lamp can't help Hal."

"Fern said it couldn't cure his specific illness, not that it can't help." The left corner of Georgia's mouth turned up. "Lamps are unpredictable and gaining mastery is no easy feat."

"If only someone knew where we should start," I commented.

"If only one were at liberty to say." She nodded. "I'm a wood magus. The walls have ears, among other things."

"I understand, Georgia." I grinned. "Thank you."

"Oh?" Logan blinked, then followed along. "Yes. Thanks for the chat. I kind of filled Aliyah's dance card for the evening and—"

"Say no more. I might be more of a recluse than the other trustees, but if the other students are as charming as the two of you, my habits may be due for some alteration. Perhaps I will entertain the idea of audits in the future, as time and space allow. Good evening."

We left her, stepping out on the dance floor as *Hallelujah* by Leonard Cohen played.

"What did all that mean?" Logan asked as we stepped along with the music.

"We have to talk about it off campus." I glanced to one side, where Mr. Fairbanks stood staring at me. "Too many enemies."

"Why can't people just be kind?"

"I don't know." I sighed. "Wouldn't the world be paradise if they were?"

We spent the rest of the evening dancing. As we ascended the moving staircase, we slipped our shoes off with sighs of relief. At least Logan's didn't have holes in them this time.

We said goodnight in the hall, halfway between our rooms. The hug was only awkward because of the shoes in our hands.

A large envelope, a legal-sized letter, and a package sat on my bed. The former was the application for Providence Paranormal College. The package had a return address from Harcourt Manor in Newport. The memory charm, which was an oval locket on a long chain. I tucked them both in my desk drawer.

I left the letter on my bed, waiting until I'd gotten into pajamas, used the restroom, and returned with a freshly scrubbed face to open it.

The stiffly formal text on the crisp beige page informed me that my extramagus test would take place on October fifteenth in the Hawthorn Academy Auditorium promptly at half past noon. I tucked the paper under my pillow, curled up under my comforter, and silently wept until I fell asleep.

CHAPTER FOURTEEN

Logan got a red marker and circled October fifteenth on the calendar he kept in his room, and in his planner. He even wrote it in the margins of his notebook. Every time I was in his quarters or studied with him elsewhere, the number fifteen stared at me like a baleful eye.

I kept waiting for my inside voice to admonish me, point out that I could have done this the easy way. It didn't. A few days before the test, as I ran laps in the gym by myself, I asked it why.

Because you're doing the right thing. This can't continue, and Hopewells have always been catalysts to change.

"Didn't Richard hate the Reveal?" I gasped.

I didn't say they all like that feature of their coincidental landscape, but you must admit, he changed the world. So will you.

Why does it have to hurt so much, though? I thought my question this time instead of speaking to pace my run better.

Growth hurts.

I remembered the summer before my first year when I discovered I'd outgrown my bathing suit. The frantic sense of shame, the almost painful relief when Mom showed up with a new one. And bumping my head, elbows, and knees on everything for eighteen months before getting used to my height. *This will be worse. I'm submitting to torture. Then sending out a recording of it.*

Yes. It's the right thing.

Some people will laugh. Or worse. Say I deserved it.

Maybe more will rally against such cruelty.

Maybe I should leave the memory charm under my pillow. Let someone else do this.

That's your choice, but nobody has so far, not for centuries. Not even dragons, who live for eons.

I stopped running and leaned over with one hand on my knee and the other on my gut. I struggled to stay on my feet as dry heaves wracked my body. Staggering, I made my way to the bleachers, sat, and sobbed with my head in my hands.

Nobody came to my rescue. The gym remained empty and silent. The solitude felt like a blessing, time and space to recover from the enormity of what I meant to do. A pause, if not a moment of peace exactly.

I stood and went upstairs to my room, then the baths. Faith swam, and we greeted each other briefly. Ember played with Seth as I showered and prepared for bed. Back in my room, Grace studied. Our syllabi finally aligned this year, so I took some time to discuss the reading on Faerie courts with her.

"I get that the Monarchs only reconciled recently, but how did they ever maintain balance between their courts when she had the only navy?" Grace tapped her pencil against her textbook.

"The King had practically an armada of pirates, mostly trolls. I thought you knew about that since you spent two summers in town and the Pirate Festival happens every August right here on Essex Street."

"Guess I'm more of a workaholic than you knew, eh?" She grinned. "So, pirates. Were they organized like in mundane Elizabethan times?"

"Yeah. They have ranks and everything. Az says they were like a militia with ships."

"Oh! I should pick his brain on this subject over coffee. Maybe in a couple of days. Want to bring Logan and make it a double study date?"

"Oh, I'm not sure." I turned down my bed, a reasonable excuse to put my back to her. "I have to ask. Don't remember cheer squad's practice schedule."

"Okay. You okay? This is early for you to turn in."

"Hard workout at the gym."

"Okay, I'll finish studying in the lounge." She scooped up her text and notebook and tucked her pencil behind her ear. "See you later."

"Yeah. Goodnight, Grace."

After the door closed, I turned out the light and lay in bed trembling. Sleep eluded me until Ember curled up in the crook of my neck and crooned softly in my ear.

The hardest part wasn't watching Nurse Smith come in and take Ember away to be sedated. It wasn't walking down the hall toward the auditorium. Or remembering to activate the memory charm outside the door. It wasn't even Director-General Rockport standing like a stone as I entered that glass and metal box or hearing his monotone incantation of the elements.

Leaving my friends in the cafeteria, called on and teleported away by Professor Hawkins was hardest. They all assumed I'd gotten myself into trouble, something I'd kept to myself. The last mind's-eye image of the people I counted on included disbelief, shock, and even suspicion. If Dylan realized what was going on, his face didn't show it.

That indignity only amplified the entire ordeal because I couldn't lean on remembering Grace's kindness, Faith's resilience, Dorian's sass, or Hal's righteousness. Instead, after the darkness that compelled me to conjure light and the arctic blast that invoked my fire, I had nothing to lean on.

Oh, but you do. Front and center.

I looked out and found my candle on the water.

Logan Pierce sat in the front row. I couldn't tell you who sat beside him because they didn't matter to me. Only he stood out, clutching his notebook to his chest with tears glowing on his cheeks as though he'd conjured instead of shed them. A sharp spike of guilt made me gasp. He'd broken before I had.

No.

I looked again and realized my error. Logan wasn't breaking. When he started rocking in his seat, I understood. His tears were a valve, releasing pressure. While the trustees looked at him sideways, especially his father, the rocking helped him cope with what he saw.

Which was me, stuck in a cage while it filled with water I couldn't banish or conjure air to counter. I clutched my throat, willing myself not to scream and lose precious air. Or worse, let water into my lungs. The last thing I wanted to do was vomit on film. Or the next best thing.

The water vanished, replaced by nothing. Not even air. That's when I realized my test was different than Dylan's, more comprehensive. I stood in a vacuum, spots of gray invading my field of vision.

Good. Let them do their worst for everyone to see.

They did. I was on my knees, barely able to get back up when I felt my arms and legs displace themselves. Not like dislocation, which I'd done to my shoulder when I was eight and fell out of the mulberry tree in the backyard. They flickered, like Hal's fists when we almost fought over Bishop's Row.

They're using space on you.

I screamed, knowing Logan, the faculty, and the trustees couldn't hear. The sensation of flickering in and out of existence was so horrifying I'd nearly forgotten the memory charm. How could Hal stand it?

Just a moment more.

The phasing stopped, and I shivered uncontrollably until a disturbingly familiar swooning sensation came over me.

Poison. You know what to do.

I burned it out of myself easily, hands flaring with flames as my magic did its work. Now, that grin felt a million times more genuine.

It vanished a moment later when my head filled with a cacophony of traffic noise, fire alarms, and air raid sirens. I held my hands to my ears, shaking my head, but could find no relief. I didn't understand. Sound manipulation was a psychic power. I almost panicked, thinking they were trying everything on me, beyond the limits of even extramagi.

It's mind magic.

I wish I could have relaxed with that knowledge, but too much noise, even inside my head, was impossible to ignore. And it got worse. A voice joined in. An outside one.

Save the world.

I did not say that.

Kill yourself.

Don't.

You almost did last year. Don't give up on giving up.

No!

I dropped to my knees, screaming, my head feeling like it had been impaled on an iron spike, that it'd split open any moment. With palms to temples, I tried to banish that other harsher voice and the noise that must have let it in.

Dylan endured. You can too.

Ram the glass, nose-first.

Be still.

And you'll die.

Live.

And never have to hear any of this again.

"Get out of my head!"

No.

I was never only in your head. Keep fighting.

I'd either lost the ability to form words or had nothing left to say, but I listened to the voice. My voice, the one with me through my entire time at Hawthorn. The one that helped me save Logan and Noah. I felt worn out, spread thin, practically flattened. My voice was like a live wire, a conduit, my connection to something bigger.

Hold on.

The image of a rope hanging down from a cliff face came unbidden to my mind's eye. I imagined myself grasping it and clinging, but I didn't move up or out of the miasma that filled my senses. Not until I tugged.

Let go.

"No. Get out!"

I kept pulling. That imaginary rock face moved. No, I did. Until it blurred beside me and air moved in the wake of my passage. I opened my eyes to find that nothing like that was actually happening.

The noise cut off mid-wail.

Director-General Rockport stood staring at me. One glance at the audience confirmed my suspicions. I'd shocked them all, especially Mr. Fairbanks, whose face was an alarming shade of crimson. Except for Logan whose lips tilted up, hinting at a grin. His eyes glanced to one side. I finally recognized where I'd seen that before.

Azrael's chess set, I thought. He—he was the King. And I—

The chamber opened behind me, and I passed out.

"—no idea she—"

"—as rare as mind—"

"—couldn't have known—"

"—could be null instead—"

I tried banishing those voices like I had the one advocating suicide. It didn't work. Moments later, I understood why. They were in my ears, not my head. My hand didn't move when I tried lifting it because it was tangled up with someone else's.

My eyes opened on Logan, the light around the back of his head like a halo.

"Angel." The voice croaked.

"I'm Logan." He blinked. "You're alive, not in heaven."

Explaining was impossible until he held a cup of water with a straw in front of my mouth. I sipped, swallowed, repeated.

"You look like one."

"Oh." He blushed. "Same. Except you're, uh, lying down."

Something soft that vibrated rubbed against my hand. I glanced down to see Doris, tail slightly twitching as she purred on my stomach. I looked around for Ember and saw her asleep in a basket on the bedside table, her side rising and falling in time with her tiny snores.

"What happened?" I glanced at my other side and saw the headmaster sitting there with Nurse Smith.

"The official answer is fire, solar, and an as yet unknown ability. Inconclusive." He raised an eyebrow. "Perhaps you can tell me."

"I don't know." I groaned. "I'm exhausted."

"It'll be at least a week before she fully recovers, sir." Nurse Smith took my wrist in his hand, checking my pulse. "Maybe two."

"You'll have to figure it out by All Saint's Day and have proof you're telling the truth." The headmaster's lips pressed together in a bloodless line. "Or go through a second round of testing next month."

My eyes teared up immediately, and I wept. I'd never experienced such a hat-drop emotional reaction before in my life. But then, I'd never been through anything as harrowing as that last round of the test.

"Hiram! How could you?"

I blinked and looked around. The owner of the distinctly feminine voice wasn't in the room. Hal stood in the doorway, looking about as confused and worn out as I felt. Faith stood on his other side, her arm out in case he needed it. On her other, Seth and Nin rode in a tote bag.

"Grandpa. You're too harsh." He shuffled over and sat on the bed across from mine.

"It is, however unfortunately, true." He sniffed. "You shouldn't be here, Harold."

"Infusion time, Gramps." Hal smirked. "By appointment. Check the schedule."

"Miss Morgenstern, you know what I require." The headmaster straightened his tie. "Report to my office with it on November first." He turned and left the room.

All three of us waited until the tap of leather-soled shoes on tile faded away. Faith sat in the chair at Hal's bedside while Nurse Smith started the IV line leading from the wall. Once he finished, he closed the door as he left to give us all privacy.

"You didn't start up last winter's exercise regimen again, Aliyah?" Faith raised an eyebrow. "You look like—well. Like you tangled with my sister again."

"No." I patted my shirt just over the breastbone and found the memory charm still there. The next time I went home, it'd be going in the postage-paid box back to Blaine and Kim in Rhode Island, where they'd extract the psychic impressions. "I can't say exactly, but you'll find out soon."

"Okay?" Faith blinked.

"She tangled all right." Hal shook his head. "Alone but with an audience, somehow. I can't figure out how or why, though."

"You used your magic to spy on us?" Logan's nostrils flared.

"I've known something was up for a week now." Hal sighed. "The same thing that I couldn't figure out last fall with Dylan."

"Why?" I cleared my throat. "I mean, why go to all that trouble, checking on me?"

"We're friends, aren't we?"

"Plus, he's nosy." Faith snorted. "Always has been."

"You love me anyway." He grinned.

"You might not be perfect." She took his hand in both of hers. "But you're perfect for me."

Someone knocked on the door. Seth barked and wagged his tail. Logan grinned at the sha.

"It's Dylan. Do you guys want him here?"

We all nodded, and Logan let him in.

"Hey." His hands were full with a tray of beverages so Logan closed the door behind him. "Smoothies don't fix everything, but they definitely help. So I figured I'd bring some."

"Thanks." I looked him in the eyes as he handed me a purple concoction. "Is this what you drank?"

"Last year, yeah." He nodded. "Ginger and elderberry for you. Hal's is orange coconut." Each cup was marked with a name in silver sharpie, but not Dylan's handwriting.

"How did you know what I drink on infusion day?" Hal asked after a sip of his orange-tinted smoothie. "Did you make these?"

"No." Dylan had his back to us, trying to coax Gale away from Ember's basket. He was trying to get in with her, but there wasn't much room. "I went to order something, and they were already there."

"Let him stay," Logan said. "She's still zonked from the sleeping draught."

"Yeah." Dylan let the dragonets be and paced the room. "It took Gale over an hour to wake up from that."

"So the same thing *did* happen last year." Hal sighed. "I knew it."

"You're not supposed to know." Dylan handed Logan a vanilla smoothie and took the green tea one for himself. "Nobody but us chickens." He gestured at Logan and me with his beverage.

"It's got to be because you're both extramagi, but I can't figure Logan's part in it." Hal glanced at each of us in turn.

We sat silently.

"Look, somebody important gave me an ominous warning recently." Logan leaned back in his seat. He pointed at the wall, then his ears.

"Let's go out this weekend." Faith nodded. "It's been a while since we all hung out in town, and Halloween stuff is everywhere right now. It'll be fun."

"I've got a gig on Friday night," Dylan said.

"That's good." I grinned. "It'll be nice to see everyone. Where are you playing?"

"Out on the Common. Part of Haunted Happenings, thanks to our Ambersmith connections. We're going to want food afterward. Engine House?"

"I'd like someplace quieter. Um." I cleared my throat and made a show of rubbing my temples. "In case this headache isn't totally gone."

"I'll talk to the band. We'll figure it out." Dylan nodded.

"Peep?" Ember lifted her head and bumped it against Gale's.

"Broo?" Gale thumped his tail against the outside of the basket and put a wing over her.

"Peep." She settled back down.

We all did too, drinking our smoothies and letting Faith point the conversation at cheer squad and Bishop's Row. We'd discuss the serious business over the weekend.

CHAPTER FIFTEEN

Piercing Whispers played mostly covers, classic spooky numbers like *This Is Halloween* and *Strange Magic*. However, they closed out their set with their hyped-up version of *Groovy Kind of Love*. They'd turned it into *Spooky Kind Of Love* and doubled the pace. The crowd loved it. After the opening number, I wasn't part of the throng that made me feel claustrophobic despite the outdoor venue. Hal sat with me on the swings at the playground in the far corner of the small park.

"I don't have the spoons for that." He gestured.

"Spoons?"

"Sorry. I learned it a while back, but it hasn't slipped out around you all until now. It's a way to measure energy. How much you have left to use once whatever ailment takes its share."

"How does that work?"

"Well, think of it this way. When you wake up in the morning, you're pretty much rested. For people like me, that's not a sure thing."

"So it's like choosing your battles?"

"I wish." Hal sighed. "More like choosing whether to go all the way to the bathroom to wash my face or use the grooming station in my room."

"It's that bad?"

"It was worse last year than it is now, but not way worse." He hung his head. "Faith grooms Nin every week now because I never have the spoons."

"How can I help?"

"Well, there's one thing." He looked up. "I invented a device that'd help me, but I'll never get it done alone."

"Whatever you need for that, consider it done." I grinned. "Even if it's other people enchanting things. I'll herd those cats."

"Thanks. I'm making myself a magipsychic moving chair. One that fits on the stairs." He chuckled. "Match my rhyming if you dare."

"Strong enough to lift a bear?" I snickered. "Perhaps a pair?"

We sat there rocking in the swings and laughing so hard I feared we'd fall out of them. Almost.

"Are you done?"

I stood immediately and turned as Hal tried to catch his breath. My hands held out in front of me, dukes up, glowed enough to reveal the speaker's identity.

"Crow?"

"Get out of here." Something sharp gleamed in his hand and he took a step toward me.

"This is a public place."

"It's also my turf, and I've got business here. Scram." He held the object up, leaving no doubt it was a knife. A punch dagger, to be specific, a nasty sort of weapon. I'd seen Bubbe care for critters wounded by those.

"He needs a minute." I jerked my chin at Hal, not daring to lower my hands.

"He's got ten seconds."

"Or you'll do what?" My hands glowed brighter. "Make me melt that blade?"

"Think you can flame hot enough to melt Damascus, extranutcase?"

"If that's Damascus, I'm the Goblin King." Hal snorted. "Anyway, we're gone. Come on, Aliyah. He's not worth it."

I saw him stumble and almost turned away from the knife-brandishing shifter to catch him. However, someone else did—a girl, short but strong enough to support Hal's new and improved bulk alone. With one arm, I noticed as she gave me a thumbs up with the other.

"Cadence will hear about this, Crow." The girl spoke airily, as though this was a game to her. Or routine.

I backed away, somehow following Hal and his rescuer again without looking at them.

"Like she'll believe you, kid." He stepped into the shadows under the slide.

Although punch daggers weren't balanced for it, I waited until we were out of throwing range before turning around. I banished the fire and got a better look at the girl helping Hal, who looked familiar but I couldn't recall her name. She was about Grace's height with black hair falling in untidy waves around her face. Her clothing was a strange mix of too big for her and too small. While her ankles stuck out awkwardly from the hem of ragged jeans, she practically swam in her pullover sweatshirt.

"Where'd you come from?" Hal asked.

"Around. I'm local, like you. You've got the biggest balls I've ever seen. Figuratively. I'm still only allowed to watch PG-13 movies if there's sex in them."

"I'm Hal. What's your name?"

"Mavis." She sighed and I remembered. I'd met her at the college fair. "Merlini. Sorry about my brother. He's jerkier than an entire case of Slim-Jims."

"Crow's your brother?" Hal blinked.

"Misfortune is my birthright, yes." She nodded. "And I'm an enormous tattletale. The best, in fact." She patted the pocket on the hooded sweatshirt she wore. It chimed. "Cadence already knows about these shenanigans. That's my read alert."

"Red alert?" I blinked.

"No, read like a book, not roses." She giggled. "Danger, Cadence DelMar."

"I get that reference." Hal chuckled.

"For a dude challenged by walking, you've got a good sense of humor, Hal."

"Where are you taking us anyway?" I didn't exactly trust Mavis Merlini, even if she was Cadence's pal and momentarily helpful.

Good call. She has an agenda. Maybe if you pushed you'd discover it. Or something about yourself that you need to know next week.

I swallowed, unsure whether to follow the voice's advice this time. It had been correct usually, and mostly on my side, but I refused to experiment with mind magic on an unwitting and unwilling person. That was the point of meeting with my friends, after all. To ask for help. If I did this, I could harm an innocent girl and worry my friends for no reason.

Thanks but no thanks, I thought at the voice.

"That gate there." She pointed.

We reached it a moment later. Mavis waved and jogged away from us. Not toward the crowd, but not the playground either.

"Isn't she a little young to be out here by herself?" Hal asked. "Maybe you should go after her."

"She said PG-13, not PG." I shrugged. "If you want me to ask, I will."

"Please." He clung to the fencing with both hands. "I'd do it myself, but—"

"Say no more."

Mavis wasn't anywhere near as fast as me. I caught up with her easily, and she stopped.

"What's up?"

"We wondered if you needed someone to, I don't know, walk you home?"

"I'm fifteen. Didn't your parents let you wander around town in October at that age?" She tilted her head while peering at my *Shema Yisrael* necklace. "Ooh, that's pretty."

"Yes they did, but with friends. Thanks. It was my great-uncle's."

"I don't have friends."

"Other siblings then? They made me go around with Noah a lot."

170

"Look, Aliyah, I get what you're saying." She nodded. "I'm a lone wolf."

"We're people, not islands, Mavis. Do you want me to walk you home or not?"

"You really are as white-hat as Cadence says." She smiled. "Like a unicorn."

"They're mythological." I shrugged. "Which direction?"

"I'm not going home yet." She pointed toward Irzyk Park. "Take me to the tank. People are there who won't let anything bad happen to me, I swear."

"Okay." I pulled my phone out and sent a group message to everyone I'd come out with that night. "Let's go."

"What's it like, being an extramagus?"

"It kind of sucks most of the time. I scare people but don't like that at all."

"I get that." She sighed. "It's hard making friends when people are scared of you. How'd you do it?"

"It wasn't easy. The first day of school, I almost burned the cafeteria down."

"Get out!"

"It's true. But that guy you helped, Hal, he wanted to be my friend anyway."

"Is he your boyfriend?"

"No. That's Logan." I blushed. "Hal ended up with Faith Fairbanks."

"Then he's super courageous. Fairbanks." She snorted. "They're almost as scary as—well, as some people even I'm afraid of. So basically, when you're scary you have to let the brave people come to you?"

"No. Sometimes, it's laughing at the same things." I told her about Grace, how we shared a joke at the beginning, and that bond stuck.

"Well, I'm good at humor at least." She shrugged.

"Plus you're a shifter. That's always got a coolness factor."

"How did you know?"

"Lucky guess."

"Can you guess what kind?"

"A crow?"

"Wrong!" She blew a raspberry. "But you're close."

"Raven then."

"Damn, you're good."

"We're here." I jerked my chin at the defunct tank that made up the war memorial. A familiar pickup truck pulled up, and the window rolled down.

"Aliyah?" Bar stuck his head out the open window. "Oh, hi Mavis."

"Bartholomew Michael Angelino Micello!" She ran up to the truck's passenger side and tugged on the handle. "I said your true name! Now you have to drive me anywhere I ask."

"For the millionth time, that's not how changelings work."

"IHOP, pronto!" She got in the cab.

"No pancakes." He looked back at me. "What's going on?"

"Mavis helped Hal so I offered to walk her home. She said to take her here instead."

"Makes sense."

It didn't to me, but I was mature enough to understand that normal varied.

"Is Hal okay? Do you guys need a ride?" he asked.

"No, we were with more friends over on the Common. Piercing Whispers had a gig."

"Oh, cool. Are you all going for afters or anything? I'd love to see my pals from Hawthorn."

I didn't want to leave a friend stuck babysitting but couldn't invite him. Extramagus business was still secret business.

"No. But we'll all be at the masquerade ball on actual Halloween. Are Gallows Hill kids going?"

"Yeah, the whole crew from extramurals and then some." He grinned.

"So, we'll see you then. And at whatever afters happen."

"Sounds good."

We said goodbye, and I sprinted back to the gate on the Common. By the time I got there, Faith, Logan, and Piercing Whispers were all with Hal. Grace and Azrael had just walked up too. They'd already worked out a location. All I had to do was follow.

Elanor brought Arick and Azrael across the street with her, leaving the rest of us relatively alone in the apartment Noah shared with her.

"Get in." Noah opened the door to the soundproofed studio. "This is as private as it gets, but it might be a little crowded."

"It's not that bad. Just stay put." Hal sat on the bench behind the keyboard with Faith.

"So, what's this about?" Dylan raised an eyebrow at Hal.

"Don't ask me." He waved his hand. "This is not the fearless leader you're looking for."

"Dammit Hal, you're a space magus, not a Jedi mind trick." Grace chuckled. "Anyway, is this like an intervention or a support group or something? Because we're all in a circle and stuff."

I let go of Logan's hand and stepped away from the wall into the middle of the room.

"No. I'm coming clean to you all about something because you're my friends and you should know." Dylan opened his mouth so I spoke before he did. "Yeah, Dylan. A few of you already know some of this."

"Dish," Noah ordered. "Elanor can't stall forever."

I told them about the extramagus test, which entirely shocked Faith and Grace. Hal sat with his jaw clenched and his nostrils flaring. Noah and Dylan nodded through most of it, but even their mouths dropped open at the end.

"So, either I have to show proof of mind or null magic by All Saint's Day, or do the whole test again." I sighed. "And I don't know how."

"That's bullshit." Hal narrowed his eyes.

"It is. They should have checked her medical history." Faith twirled a strand of her hair between her fingers. "Especially to rule out null. Aliyah doesn't get migraines, and everybody knows null magi are practically plagued with them." She cleared her throat. "I might have studied a little too much on magical maladies." She mumbled something about alternative therapies and Providence Paranormal College.

"That makes sense." Logan nodded. "There are no documented extramagi in recorded history who had null magic. It might be impossible."

"So, how do we prove she's got mind magic, then?" Dylan asked.

"Mind works on line of sight." Grace grinned. "Aliyah has to be able to see us without knowing who's who. So how about a game of reverse hide and seek?"

"What's that now?" I blinked.

"We'll all be in costume at the masquerade ball, right? So, we keep our costumes a secret. That night, I hide myself and Aliyah with shadow magic. Then she tries to find you using her mind. Since she's hidden, nobody can give her unconscious clues. We should probably include some non-magi Aliyah can trust with this topic, like Izzy and Cadence."

"If we each start recording on our phones after Grace does her shadow thing, that's all the proof she needs." Logan clapped his hands.

"Okay, let's do this. I'll talk to Izzy and Cadence about it tomorrow." I looked around the room and watched everybody nod.

"One other thing." Noah drew a deep breath. "I might need your help, Aliyah. About my diploma."

"Sure. Anything."

"Hal?" Noah gestured at him. "You've got the info."

"So, a trustee named Andre Gauthier made the vote that expelled Noah last year. We want to talk to him, but he's a total recluse on campus. So, if this mind magic exercise is successful at the dance, do you think you could help us find him?"

"I'll do my best." I nodded.

After that, we all went back into the living room and hung around playing Mario Kart while eating convenience store snacks, saying nothing more about tests, games, or proof for the time being.

I slept at home that night and messaged Izzy and Cadence on Sunday. Only Izzy replied. We talked on a walk around the wharf, with liberal use of inside jokes and obscure references we'd shared since kindergarten. She agreed with Faith and was all in for the game, and said she'd get Cadence on board.

"How's she been?"

"A mess, to be honest." Izzy sighed. "She's not speaking to Crow. Says she never will after what happened on the common last night. How Crow threatened you and Hal. I flipped a few cards." She stared into her half-full cup of cider, then tossed it into the nearest trash bin without another sip.

"That bad, huh?"

"It's awful. He's worse than anyone could have guessed. Even with that stuff you and Grace overheard in the Lyceum kitchen last year."

"At least Hal and I can avoid him. What about Cadence? I'm worried he'll do something to her."

"Me too. The cards agree with us. But she says she's got it handled."

"Because of her mermaid's voice?"

Izzy nodded. "She didn't want to hear my reading."

"I learned way more than I wanted to last year about cruel people. They don't wait for people to defend themselves."

"Maybe she'll listen to a warning, coming from you. Want to take a spin by her place for a chat?"

"Yeah, let's do that." I tossed my cider too and we headed out of downtown toward The Point.

Nobody was home at the DelMar's apartment. Cadence didn't answer my calls or messages that day or any other I stepped off campus to make during the week. The following Saturday, Cadence sent me a picture of her folks doing an event at The Willows, along with the words "I'm in." After that, I didn't hear from her until the masquerade ball.

CHAPTER SIXTEEN

No matter how many times I asked Grace about her costume for the masquerade ball, she gave me no straight answer. The only thing I knew for sure was that her outfit took up half her closet and that she used a box from a pair of boots to hold the accessories. I couldn't imagine anything as cool as the dragon costume she'd worn in the contest our first year, but she seemed far more excited about this one.

Grace didn't get dressed for the ball on campus. Instead, she brought everything to Azrael's and said she'd meet me there. That was fine with me. I wanted to mentally prepare for the reverse hide and seek game we'd be doing during the ball. Putting my costume on alone proved more challenging than I'd expected, however. I ended up trotting down the hall to find some help, but I was late.

Nobody was home at Faith's and Kitty's room, or Hal's and Lee's. Dylan and Arick were at Noah's because they were the opening act. I headed to Logan's, although the last thing I wanted to do was ask him to help me dress in case he thought I wanted something else. Talking with Bubbe had helped, but sexuality still confused me, and the inconclusive extramagus test results had distracted me from thinking more about it. That's why when I knocked on his door, I prayed that he wasn't there.

You know he's not.

He wasn't. I took a long shot and headed to the only other room on this floor that housed students and knocked.

"Just a minute!" Dorian called.

"Okay."

The door opened almost immediately after I spoke.

"Oh, you can come in." He grinned. "Thought you were Xan."

"Um." I stepped inside.

"We're walking over together." He closed the door. "For reasons."

"Are you two dating?"

"No. But there are reasons of a non-dating variety. Anyway, what's up with the bathrobe?"

I opened it and revealed the dark blue fabric, which sagged in ways it wasn't supposed to around my shoulders.

"Elsa? Not what I expected but cool. What's the problem?"

I turned and moved the white faux-fur trimmed hood and long braid away from the zipper. It ended in the middle of my back, between the tops of my shoulder blades, exactly where I couldn't reach.

"I can't fasten this by myself, and Grace went to Azrael's. I should have dressed at Bubbe's. Have you seen Logan?"

"He left with Hal and company." Dorian sighed. "His dad was looking for him, Faith said."

"Wow." I wrinkled my nose. "It's hard to get my brain around their families."

"Ditto. My parents are awesome. Kind of like yours, but without a kick-ass grandma downstairs. My Nonna's way older than Bubbe. She lives in a nursing home."

"Sorry."

"Thanks." He patted my shoulder. "Voila, you're a queen! Have a look."

He went to his wardrobe, opened it, and tilted the mirror on the inside of the door toward me. I loved how the nearly indigo blue looked with my hair and the way the silver diamond-shaped rhine-stones glittered in the light. The shimmering mesh cape made me feel extra pretty. I did a little twirl and smiled until I noticed something missing from Dorian's reflection.

"Where's your costume?"

"I'm going, well sort of as myself, but wearing a mask." He crossed the room and opened the hatbox on his desk. "Check it out."

Before I got the chance, someone pounded on the door.

"Spanos, we gotta go!"

"That's my cue." Dorian gave me a sheepish grin.

Out in the hall, Alex glanced at me once and nodded. "Backup. Good idea."

I blinked, but both of them acted accustomed to this sort of talk. If that was the case, why did the two of them seem so nervous and in such a hurry? For all I knew, it was the regular dynamic in their strange friendship.

Not that strange.

I pondered the voice's opinion and decided to accept it. Hadn't I concluded last week that normal varied? I trotted to catch up with them again, not wanting to be the lone third-year student left on campus. Plus, I had business at the masquerade ball. Sitting it out wasn't an option. Alex practically jogged once I caught up. He couldn't run as fast as me, but it was a near thing. Poor Dorian struggled to keep up, breath chugging like a steam engine.

Once out the door, Alex grabbed our wrists and pulled us around the corner and into a shadowy alcove.

"Wait," he said, then let go of Dorian to put a finger over his lips.

I almost protested but started shivering instead. Ironic, given the character I'd dressed as. However, it wasn't the cold bothering me. Despite my confusion, I felt a clear and present fear. It struck me so unexpectedly that I didn't bother pulling out of Alex's grip. The urge to conjure an inferno or flee Hawthorn's entrance at top speed didn't feel natural, like this wasn't my idea.

It's not.

Dorian, who'd called himself a coward last year, stood in front of us with his mask under one arm. He pointed with his other hand at the cobblestone five feet from us, like he aimed a weapon. No, his magic. I couldn't figure out why until Alex whimpered beside me and I looked up. He'd grabbed Dorian's jacket and clung like it was a rope over a cliff.

Mrs. Onassis walked briskly away down Essex Street. She blended into the crowd a moment later, but Dorian and Alex waited, still uneasy.

"She's gone. We can—"

"No." Dorian shook his head. "Not yet. *He's* still coming."

"Think nothing," Alex whispered.

I blinked, considering that next-door to impossible. Especially after he told me not to.

Think Halloween.

Now that I could do. The sounds of excited costumed tourists, the aroma of cotton candy and popcorn wafting from food trucks, and the rich loamy scent of crisp autumn leaves underfoot already filled my senses. A childhood in Salem experiencing these every year let me magnify the experience until it drowned everything else out, even oddly-heroic Dorian and unexpectedly-cowering Alex.

I barely noticed when Mr. Fairbanks dragged Mr. Pierce along after him away from the door and into the crowd. He thought so loudly that I immediately knew he sought Alex, trying to pay back some sort of favor. A mind magus of his age and experience should have had no trouble, especially with how distraught Alex was. But he seemed entirely ignorant of our presence. I watched the back of his head grow smaller as he continued down the street.

Mental camouflage. You're doing it.

"What did you do, Morgenstern?" Alex whispered.

"I'm not sure."

"So you did do something." He let go of me and turned his head. "Uh, thanks. He found me every other time I tried going out."

"Wait, you haven't been off campus this whole time?" I blinked.

"His mom." Dorian shook his head. "But this is a masquerade. We thought, with costumes everywhere, nobody would know."

"Speaking of that." Alex pointed at the box. "We should mask up."

Dorian opened the box and handed a mask to Alex, who put it on and turned around. It gave him a grotesque visage, human but twisted so hideously I took a step back. That's when I saw Dorian's mask, a placid and beautiful but somehow masculine representation of a face. They were opposite but somehow similar although I couldn't determine how.

"We're Dorian Gray and the portrait of same." Dorian chuckled. "Cool, huh?"

"Wow. Well, nobody will recognize you, that's for sure." I nodded.

"Even so, would you happen to know an alternate route to the Hawthorne Hotel? Just to sort of make sure we avoid trustees."

"No problem."

I took them down Washington Street to Front Street, where we had to skirt the line for the Salem Wax Museum but otherwise walked without incident. At the door, we handed over our tickets. I noticed Alex's wasn't one given by the school, which meant he'd shelled out over a hundred dollars for it. At first, I wondered why but then realized only the third-years got school passes. Then I thought he'd worked for it in the cafe.

"Thanks again." He cleared his throat and nudged Dorian.

"See, that wasn't so hard." Dorian elbowed him back.

Once inside, I parted ways with them, looking for a familiar face. I found Grace and Azrael almost immediately. They were the center of attention because of their costumes, which crossed the line from cosplay over into cinematic quality territory.

"Do you like them?" She grinned and flourished her hands along with the mesh fabric draped between them and the skirts of the black and silver dress. The collar towered over her head, pointed on either side like horns. The neckline plunged to her waist, clearly held in place with dress tape.

"It's amazing, but I don't recognize it."

"Dark Lilli from *Legend*. Az is Jack. I chose them because they sort of rescue each other."

"While saving the world too." Azrael chuckled.

"And wearing lots of glitter." I grinned while peering at his face, which looked practically iridescent. Whatever makeup they'd used matched the finish on the combination plate and scale armor he wore. "How are you going to dance in that?"

"It's pretty light, glamoured to look heavier than it is."

"Let's take it for a spin a little later." Grace jerked a thumb at the stage where Piercing Whispers had finished tuning up. "This dress might not hold up to their first few numbers."

"How about some punch?" Az asked.

"Sure!" Grace grinned. "Thanks." She stood on her tiptoes and kissed him on the cheek, which didn't leave a single mark despite her jet black lipstick.

"That's unsmudgable." I pointed at my lips.

"The new Eternal Glamour line. It's not officially out yet, but I've got connections." She chuckled. "Anyway, let's play that game. Everyone else is ready to go."

"Really?" I blinked.

"It's better to try it when you're off-guard and don't know what everyone's wearing yet."

"Okay." I nodded. "Let's go."

Dylan struck the opening chords of *Doing the Unstuck*, a song they'd practiced at their apartment on my last visit. At least half the crowd hit the dance floor, but not us. Grace led me into a corner, sent a group text, put her phone on record in front of us, and conjured shadows. I knew from experience that her magic would make people fail to notice us, not make us look like a purple blob moving through the crowd. However, we couldn't interact with our surroundings. There wasn't much point in wandering so I stopped Grace, and we stood still. I tried looking for Logan, frustrated. Searching without my eyes was an effort in futility.

It's not, really. Can't you sense him, of all people?

Mind magic worked on line of sight. This search reminded me of wearing headphones on a train. The scenery goes by only generally seen because music is more present in those moments. So I tried thinking like that, attempting to hear and see without ears or eyes. I imagined sensing minds in terms of surface thoughts, vaguely whispered.

That idea might as well have been on the moon.

I'd opened myself to a cacophony nobody else in the room endured. Like being in an electronics store with televisions and radios and music players turned up as high as they'd go except with hundreds of devices, not just forty or fifty. I didn't see the inside of people's heads or hear thoughts. That was telepathy, something only psychics did. Without a device or cooperation, mind magic was vague and sensory, a random collection of humming frequencies. Our textbooks explained that brains have energy, a low-grade electrical impulse, that mind magi could conjure and manipulate.

And banish. The books won't tell you that, though.

I shuddered. At least my inside voice came in loud and clear over that din. Now that I remembered it shouldn't be verbally coherent, the wall of sound began to make more sense. I remembered untangling a box of Bubbe's old costume jewelry, where feeling the knots in silverplated chains was as important as watching my fingers while undoing them.

Two threads of frequency stood out, off in the corner near the stage. They felt familiar so I walked toward them. A glance at Grace revealed nothing about my guess. Her poker face was on point that night. A pair of costumed superheroes with full-face masks leaned against the wall holding their phones, one in red and black and the other in pink and white, both with spiderweb designs.

I hadn't noticed this anywhere else in the room yet, but something besides the clearly related costumes connected the pair above their hearts, a harmonious frequency that made me think of Beethoven's *Ode to Joy*. And that made it all too obvious.

"It's them."

"Bingo." Grace dropped the umbral magic. "Who are these masked friends?"

"Hal." I pointed at the one in red and black. "And Faith."

"Dammit. I wanted everyone to think I was Miles."

"You're even more heroic, I think. Anyway, she's got more spidersense than us." Faith pulled hers off too, and they both stepped away from the wall. "Go find the rest. We're hitting the dance floor."

"Just a sec." Hal removed his mask, then tapped the screen on his phone a few times. "Sent it to the group text."

My phone beeped. Grace took me into the corner and activated her magic again. I had to repeat this process three more times. Each would send the video they'd taken of me finding them. Those, along with Grace's recording, would be my proof for the headmaster.

This time, it was easier to sort through, and I found the next pair in a few moments. The thread led me to the bar, toward a knight in wooden armor and a veiled priestess who could have walked off a Tarot card except for the phone in her hand. They had a connection too, loud and clear as the one between Hal and Faith but it made me think of that old Beatles song about friends. I nudged Grace, and she dropped the shadows.

"Hi, Iz. And Lee."

"How did you know it was me?" He lifted the visor on his helmet. "Everyone else from school was clueless."

"Knight of Wands hanging out with the High Priestess?" Izzy winked. When she finished tapping her phone, mine beeped again. "Aliyah's been my divination guinea pig since we were five. Of course, she knows it's us. Let's dance, knight in wooden armor." She grinned at Lee.

"Cool." He nodded. "Are you guys coming?"

"Nah, I've got to find Cadence and Logan."

After they left, Grace hid us again. By then, the wall of sound had reared its indecipherable head again. At first, I couldn't imagine why this exercise had suddenly gotten harder.

This isn't fire or solar magic. Mind is harder to sustain without practice.

I sighed, hoping for a miracle to get through the rest of this strange game. I needed the proof, especially now that I was sure I had mind magic. It came on golden wings.

"Peep?" Ember soared through the air over the dance floor, searching for me.

I'd forgotten she wasn't with me when Grace started this because I always tried to block out her alone time with Gale. Now she wanted to hang out with me. Homing in on the familiar bond was a eureka moment. I tried thinking of Cadence and Logan, picturing their faces in my mind and how I felt with them. I followed the first familiar frequency, trailing it to the door.

I found a pair of women wearing the same green and gold costume, accented with fans. Identical makeup instead of masks hid their faces. One wore her ash brown hair in a bob, but the other's was a wig. That's the one I knew. I didn't hear a bond between them although they laughed together, holding a phone. I nudged Grace, who did the thing with the shadows.

"Cadence!" I chuckled. "Nice *Last Airbender* cosplay! Are you Kenoshi or Suki?"

"Wow!" She blinked. "How did you know it was me? With the wig and everything? Brianna's Kenoshi. I'm too short." Cadence handled her phone, then tucked it away as mine beeped.

"Hi!" Brianna waved.

"What are you doing at the door?"

"Waiting for Piercing Whispers to finish their set because Brelanor is a thing." Cadence sniffed. "Also, Arick's my date."

"No Crow?" Grace blinked.

"Never again." She shook her head.

"I'm sorry." Brianna patted Cadence's shoulder. "What happened?"

"Ask Aliyah." She glanced at Grace's phone, which was still recording. "Or Hal, later. I don't want to talk about it."

Brianna's forehead crinkled. Grace led us away from the door and set up her shadows again.

"One more. How are you holding up?"

"I'm tired, but let's finish this."

Of course, Grace didn't have much more to do. I focused again, expecting difficulty. But it wasn't. Not once I realized that I didn't hear Logan's frequency like I'd done with everyone else's. Instead, it sang in my chest.

"You're humming," Grace said.

"Oh?"

"Yeah. *You're My Best Friend.*"

"I think you're awesome too, Grace."

"No, the song. By Queen."

"Oh!"

Grace dropped the shadows because she had to hurry to keep up with me as I rushed toward a figure in white hooded robes with a pair of wings at the side of the dance floor. He turned while holding his phone in front of him. His head was down, the hood's shadow obscuring his face. I would have known him anywhere, though.

He pushed the hood back, his smile saying more than two year's worth of words. Logan had put something in his hair, making it almost white instead of his usual ashy blond. I knew the character too because we'd watched the Good Omens miniseries over the summer.

"Aziraphale!" I clapped. "Those wings are amazing. You must have put a lot of work into that."

"Not really." He grinned. "I borrowed these from Azrael. That's my favorite of Elsa's dresses, by the way."

"I know." I blushed.

We stood staring at each other. I smiled so much my cheeks ached. Ember sat up on my shoulder, *peeping* at us.

Grace reached out and plucked Logan's phone out of his hands to shut off his camera. Then she did the same with hers. My phone beeped twice in a row.

"You're way too cute." Grace chuckled. "Angel and ice queen."

Azrael sauntered over with cups of punch. He handed them out. "Never would have shipped Elsa and Aziraphale. Aliyah and Logan is another story."

Logan blushed. I gulped down the punch. All that work had made me thirsty. Once I set the cup down on an empty table, he held out his hand. I took it, and we danced through the rest of the Piercing Whispers set. The change between acts took about ten minutes, so we sat. I sent the videos in my messages to my school email to make things easier in the morning.

A man I'd never seen before sat beside me. He wore his black hair shoulder-length and it had ample amounts of silver at the temples. His face was largely unlined. Straight, even teeth smiled from his almost too pale complexion. His eyes didn't twinkle so much as glitter. He wore purple robes adorned with silver chains and skulls. The skeleton mask that went with it rested in his lap.

"Andre Gauthier. Charmed." He put his hand out as if for a handshake.

I focused on the minds in the room again, imagining them as guitar strings and pulling on the most familiar ones. Here was the man Noah wanted to meet, and this was the only way I could think of to call him over without alerting the trustee. If I ended up reeling more of my friends in than originally intended, so be it. I took the adults in charge of Hawthorn Academy seriously and as possible threats. Safety in numbers.

"Um, Aliyah. Morgenstern." I gave him mine, but he kissed it. I noticed he wore black gloves embossed with bones. "Aren't you a trustee for Hawthorn?"

"I know who you are, young lady. Yes, I am." He glad-handed like a salesman. Or a politician. But spookily, in an old "creature feature" way.

"What do you want?" Logan's bluntness surprised me, but I welcomed it.

"Logan Pierce." He grinned again. I realized what he was trying to do. Make everyone he met feel connected to him, somehow. "You were almost my nephew."

"How?" Logan went stony-faced.

"Leo's sister. We were supposed to get married, or didn't you know?"

"Dad never mentioned a sister."

Mr. Gauthier raised an eyebrow at Logan's blank expression. "Never mind that for now. You're both friends with my niece. The good one who takes after me."

Logan and I sat there blinking at him.

"Faith. My sister married her father, unfortunately." He shook his head.

I narrowed my eyes, heeding the inside voice instead of snaring myself in his social maneuvers.

"So you're an undeath magus."

"And you're the extramagus." He grinned again. "Already making a name for herself as something of a hero. We could use more like you."

"She's one of two here." Dylan sat, trapping Andre Gauthier between us. "I'm the other. So, tell me what you've got against Noah Morgenstern."

"Excuse me?" Mr. Gauthier blinked.

"A former student who got expelled last year." I raised my eyebrow. " My brother."

"He got turned through no fault of his own." Dylan pressed his lips into a flat line, and the temperature dropped a few degrees. "You were the swing vote. The one responsible for kicking him out in the first place."

"Ah, well." Mr. Gauthier sighed. "He was an exemplary student and a fine athlete. Talented musically, too. I wish I could have voted otherwise."

"So why?" Dylan asked before the words were out of my mouth.

"Rules. Thurston's arguments were morally correct but procedurally unsound, even if they swayed Dunstable and Glen."

"So change them." The air warmed as I spoke.

"That's...a delicate exercise." He shook his head. "Students whose natures pose a grievous threat to others aren't allowed admission."

"Extramagi are so dangerous that we go on a special registry like vampires." I tried smiling, but it felt more like a grimace. "So I should be expelled."

"And me," Dylan added.

A trio of figures stepped out of the crowd milling beside the dance floor.

"Me too." Dorian lifted his mask. "I came from The Academy. Got a record."

We all blinked. Everyone thought he'd only gone there because his overprotective parents wanted him to live in a fortress.

"Yes, Mr. Spanos." Mr. Gauthier nodded. "You do, but your sentence is over. Stealing an item from black market mobsters is hardly in the spirit of criminality."

"You have to tell us that story yesterday, Dorian." Noah grinned without showing his fangs. "This was all my idea. I only want my diploma, Mr. Gauthier. With you on campus, along with Faith, I don't see how I could be a threat. Please, bring my situation up at the next meeting."

"We don't have one until February."

"That's fine. I only need to study for and take the final exams. I can wait."

"The classrooms aren't sunproof."

"I get accommodations," Logan said. "My IEP says I can take tests in the library if needed, and there aren't windows in there. Why not Noah?"

"You certainly have some dedicated advocates, Mr. Morgenstern." Mr. Gauthier sighed. "I'll bring it up at the appropriate time, but no guarantees."

"Yeah, I know. Some of the trustees aren't so reasonable about vampires." Noah raised an eyebrow at Gauthier's costume. "Thanks for not being one of those."

"You'll each owe me a favor if I succeed."

"No." Noah shook his head. "Only one of us benefits so only one owes—"

"Then I choose Mr. Pierce."

"I ought to owe you." Noah blinked.

"It's okay." Logan nodded. "He says we're practically family."

"Then it's settled."

His phone beeped so he excused himself. The main performer didn't bother introducing himself. Everybody in eastern Massachusetts knew Aurelius Voltaire. He opened with the song *Vampire Club*, which packed the dance floor. I hoped it would give Noah good luck. Logan and I stayed out there for four entire songs.

"Can I cut in?" Dylan asked.

"Yeah, I wanted some water anyway," Logan nodded. "If that's okay with Aliyah?"

"Sure."

Dylan and I danced through the opening of *When You're Evil*. He shook his head, chuckling at the lyrics with a strange smirk.

"What?"

"The irony in this song. I wanted to ask you something. Extramagus stuff I don't want to say on campus."

"Go on."

"Do you, like, see things?" He glanced to his left. "Um, that other people don't see."

"No, can't say I have."

He gulped, hands trembling.

"You're not going crazy." I drew a deep breath. "I hear stuff other people don't. It's something that can happen to us. A way of sensing magic."

"How do you know?"

"Logan's been researching it." I sighed. "The records are super obscure, mostly written by an old green dragon in the sixth century who researched all kinds of rare extrahumans. He tested similarities between dragons and us. Extra magic sense happens to them, too."

"Dragons see colors when there's magic?"

"Colors? Not always, but mostly. Is that why you're such a beast at Bishop's Row now? You see everyone's conjures before they happen?"

"Yeah." He laughed. "It's useful that way. And a total relief to know I'm not losing my marbles. Thanks, Aliyah."

We danced through to the final verse before he spoke again.

"Your mind trick worked, you know."

"Hmm?"

"You called us all over there when Gauthier showed up."

"How'd you know it was magic?"

He pointed at his eye. "You looked like a spider, in the middle of a web."

"What color is it? The mind stuff, I mean."

"Blue. Almost like Professor DeBeer's lightning, but with more green in it."

"You should make a list sometime of all the magic colors. Keep track."

"So should you, with the sound." He chuckled. "Bet it'd make a unique research project at uni someday."

I had nothing positive to say to that, so I kept quiet. Logan returned at the end of the song, and Dylan left with a wave.

At the side of the dance floor, I noticed a flurry of movement. It was Noah, approaching Jonah with his face almost literally lit up. Then joy fled from my brother's face like a hind from a wolf. The reunion soured and he took to the dance floor alone, moving as if to a dirge instead of the spooky yet upbeat music. At first, I almost asked Logan for a break so I could comfort him. Before I could, I realized what was missing.

I hadn't been able to sense it as concretely over the summer, but back then, they still seemed bonded somehow. Like their care for each other was tangible.

Now, there was nothing at all that connected the two of them.

After an entire year nursing a broken heart over his ex Darren, Noah was back at square one. In a brutally ironic contrast, Ember and Gale wheeled overhead, in what every nature show on magical critters would describe as a courtship flight. The pit of my stomach sank along with Noah's, while simultaneous elation lightened my head. All the emotions felt too big for my body, so no wonder they leaked from my eyes.

I sniffled and put my head on Logan's shoulder. He patted my back and murmured in my ear.

"Whatever it is, I'm not going anywhere."

"Thank you." I lifted my head and looked at his face.

Instead of grim determination like the last time he'd said those words, his expression was almost impossibly tender. I heard it now—the song Grace said I'd been absently humming. If it hadn't been for everything we'd been through together, I might have chalked my feelings up to bleed from Ember's courtship. But no.

I'd gone and fallen in love with Logan Pierce. But was he interested in romance? Did I even feel that way, or was it more like Bubbe's relationship with Grandpa? Did big love always have to be cinematic romance?

"Logan?"

"Yeah?"

"Would you mind if… I mean. May I kiss you?"

"Oh!" He blinked. "Nobody's ever asked me that before."

"No?"

"They just did it." He grimaced. "Without asking. Like that's the normal thing to do. So I ran away both times."

"Wish I'd been as smart as you." I patted his back. "Should have kicked Alex in the shin and left."

"You couldn't, though." He sighed. "Doris said you smelled like poison that night."

"I wish I could get a do-over."

"Listen, Elanor didn't always know she was lesbian. She kissed a boy and didn't like it. When she kissed a girl, she called it her second chance at a first kiss." He cleared his throat, then leaned in close. "I want to try kissing you sometime. But not now. It's…too many people here. I'm sorry."

"Don't be. I get it."

We hugged, then kept right on dancing. The silence after the last song nearly startled us. When we looked around, everyone from Hawthorn had left already. Ember glided sleepily down from her perch on the crown molding and settled on my shoulder. We walked out into the night air together, crossed the street, headed up the driveway at 10-1/2 Hawthorne, then through the back gate. Ember took off up the back stairs inside, and that's where we nearly parted ways. Then Logan tugged my sleeve.

"Yes." His eyes shone bright blue in the faint light from the upstairs doorway. "If you still want to, let's try it.

I nodded, unable to think of any words, let alone the right ones. It didn't matter. We got our second chance.

Our first kiss was a little breathless but perfect all the same.

CHAPTER SEVENTEEN

"I don't generally check email on weekends, but since this is a matter of import beyond the walls of this campus, I shall make an exception."

I sat, waiting as Hiram Hawkins logged in on the computer his son had purchased the summer before my first year. Somehow, he looked out of place using the machine although Bubbe wasn't much younger than him. I'd never felt that way watching her keep medical records. For some reason, he flipped open a folder on his desk although he didn't look at it.

Maybe Mom was right, and Bubbe's generation was all over the place in terms of comfort with technology. Eventually, he stopped clicking and frowning. Sounds from the night before emitted tinnily from built-in speakers, giving me an unsurprising sense of déjà vu. I'd put them together in a playlist, so only brief pauses separated each video. Silence stretched after the last one finished. I didn't dare break it first.

"It seems you do have mind magic Miss Morgenstern."

I only nodded.

"It's as I expected. And rather unfortunate."

"How?" I blinked.

"Any other year, I'd have no choice but to expel you from school."

My mouth dropped open. I couldn't speak, could barely even breathe.

"Mind magic is risky and rife with potential for academic unfairness, accidental or otherwise."

"Aren't there accommodations?"

"Yes. Which is why you may be allowed to finish out the year and obtain your diploma. If you agree to them."

Say nothing.

"Anything."

Oh no.

"You will see a tutor twice per week, as a way to ensure you do not, inadvertently or otherwise, violate the minds of classmates, faculty, and staff. Additionally, Director-General Rockport will fit you with a device that you must wear during all athletic practices and events, lab practicals, and exams taking place on this campus."

"I'm already in counseling twice a week, sir."

"Then you will have extra obligations four days of the week. It's the only way to make things fair."

"That's bullshit, Gramps." Hal Hawkins stepped through the door, followed by Logan and Faith.

"Language, Harold."

He shrugged. "Aliyah's saved lives on this campus. It's unfair to treat her like this."

"I understand all the familiars in this place." Logan crossed his arms over his chest. "Are you making me wear a device in exams too?"

Faith only glared with her hands on her hips.

"The safety of everyone here is my direct responsibility, including Miss Morgenstern's. If I do nothing, she is at risk of persecution, Harold." The headmaster stood. "Even the most intelligent familiar in history can't dictate entire essays during exam periods, Mr. Pierce." He raised an eyebrow at Faith. "Before any of you say another word, this meeting is being officially transcribed."

Faith blinked. Logan paled. Hal's nostrils flared.

"I'm not afraid to go on record." Hal's lip curled. "Tell Aliyah who tutors mind magic before making her agree to this."

"Abraham Fairbanks." The headmaster sighed. "And technically, she verbally agreed before you walked in the room. To anything."

"Then I insist on auditing her lessons, Grandpa." Hal smirked.

"On what grounds?"

"To take notes regarding the family business. trustees aren't supposed to teach except in emergencies. I don't want us stuck without a mind magus on staff when I'm headmaster in the future."

"Future?" The headmaster's eyes widened. "Harold, you—"

"Are you disowning me?"

"No. But magiglobular anemia has no—"

"I've read all the literature." Faith's smile was pure saccharine. "Over fifty percent of patients with magiglobular anemia live through their twenties and over twenty percent into their thirties. Of course, there's no cure yet, but in ten years, who knows? He'll probably outlive you, sir."

Faith's bluffing. His case is more advanced than that. But say nothing.

"I'll allow it." He flipped open a folder on his desk. "But you must designate an alternate to take notes if you are too ill to audit."

"No." Hal shook his head. "If I'm ill, we move the session to the infirmary."

"And if you're in the hospital? What then?"

When Faith opened her mouth, the headmaster held a finger up to silence her.

"You'll be with him, Miss Fairbanks. And we must avoid conflicts of interest between you and your father."

"I'll do it." Logan glanced at Hal.

"Brilliant." Hal beamed. "Who wouldn't want the valedictorian to help out with tutoring?"

"Then we have a plan." The headmaster wrote on the paper inside the folder, then turned it toward me. "You begin on Monday."

I read the paper, which had automatically filled in all of our verbal agreements. He'd signed it, and there was also a space for my name. However, something was missing.

"What about Director-General Rockport, sir? The device?"

"He'll contact you soon. A copy of this exact agreement is on his desk at this moment. Remember, be on your most conscientious behavior while meeting the terms of this agreement. Violating code of conduct while in tutoring sessions may result in probation or even expulsion."

"Okay." I leaned forward, took a pen from the cup beside his name-plate, and signed.

I straightened, then turned my back to follow my friends out of the room. When I had one foot across the threshold, he cleared his throat. I turned.

You forgot to thank him.

"Thank you, Headmaster. I won't forget your advice."

"Same," Hal murmured as he closed the door on his grandfather.

"Well." Faith stooped to scoop Seth into her arms as Ember flew down from the perch across the hall. "How screwed are we?"

"Totally." Logan stared at Doris, who paced ahead of us the entire way out into the lobby.

Once out there, Dylan hurried over to us.

"Did you hear last night?"

"No, what?" I asked.

"I did." Faith sighed. "Tempe's guilty, but I didn't want to say anything. Too angry about it."

"Yeah." Dylan scowled. "Because she barely got a slap on the wrist."

"How?" Logan blinked.

"Wrongful death for bringing that device on campus, because of the professor." Dylan's lip curled up in a sneer. "That's it."

Hal opened his mouth, then shook his head and sat on a bench.

"What about Noah?" My throat felt too tight. "And Mercy?"

"Accidental." Faith kicked at the bench's leg. "They said one mistake shouldn't ruin her life."

"So much BS." I clenched my fists.

"More like so much money. The court fees for wrongful death and the accidents are enormous." Faith narrowed her eyes.

"She's not coming back here, is she?" Logan gulped.

"Nope." Hal looked up. "Expulsion is serious business. It wasn't just ineligibility, like with Noah."

"Dad said he's sending her to The Academy." Faith frowned. "She'll be on the long-term plan. That's when they stay past getting a diploma until the staff thinks they're rehabilitated. Better there than at home, I guess."

"How do we tell Noah?"

"Your brother already knows, Aliyah." Dylan sighed. "He's how I found out."

"Dorian, then?"

"I don't know." His stomach rumbled. "Let's think it through over breakfast."

We got our food but didn't talk any more about it. Later, on my way to the gym to run laps, I saw Dorian leaving the office. He was wiping his face on his sleeve. It'd be better for him to know, but maybe that's why he'd been in the headmaster's office. Perhaps I was too late.

Only one way to find out.

"Hey. Are you okay?"

"Not now, Aliyah." He shook his head. "Sorry. I need to be a wreck in my room."

"The trial?"

He nodded and hurried away without another word. Julia glided after him on silent wings. Later, I saw him in the café, shirtsleeves rolled up to the elbows, scrawling words in a notebook as though if he wrote fast enough, he could outrun the past. I took one step toward him, but Alex gave me a death glare. A hum in my head told me something was different between them, although I wasn't sure what or how.

What would Bubbe do?

I headed to the counter instead. "What?"

"You butt in too much." Alex shook his head. "He needs time and space."

"I believe you." I turned toward the door.

"You're backing off?" He blinked.

"Take good care of him."

"Or else what?"

"Or else nothing. I'll butt out."

"Maybe you shouldn't."

"What was it you said last spring? You owe Dorian your life?" I gave him a tiny grin. "You'll do the right thing for him."

I walked away finally. Once I'd fully turned my back, I smiled as tears welled in my eyes. Maybe this was Bubbe's wisdom proved right, that hurt didn't just come before healing. Sometimes it came in tandem. Maybe something decent could come from last spring's pain and anguish, after all.

The next day before dinner, I had my first tutoring session with Mr. Fairbanks.

"See you later." Logan hugged me. "Do you want me to make a to-go order for you? We're eating in the lounge."

"Yeah, thanks." I pulled back and smiled at him.

"Be careful." Faith studied her fingernails.

"We will." Hal grinned.

"If I had a magic lamp, I'd wish there was some other way." She crossed her arms over her chest. "It's not safe."

"I know," Hal said. "But the buddy system works."

"I'm not sure." Faith looked from him to me. "I hope you're stronger than him."

"Me too." I nodded. "I'm scared."

"That's good." She nodded. "Stay on guard. That goes for both of you."

"I've got insurance." Hal reached into his blazer pocket and scooped Nin out. "She'll literally squeal if something goes sideways."

"It's me." Logan grinned as Hal passed her over. "I'm safer than State Farm."

"*And* he doesn't wear tacky khakis." Dylan peered around the corner. "Or make sales calls at three in the morning."

We all chuckled.

"Come on, Ember." I tried coaxing her down from my shoulder, but she clung on.

"Doesn't she want a playdate with Gale?" Dylan raised an eyebrow.

The moment he spoke that name, my familiar launched into the air and flew in circles, peeping her lungs out.

"Well, there's your answer."

Everybody waved. I took one last look over my shoulder, then walked with Hal down the hall. Unfortunately, this tutoring session was in the same room Ms. Khan used for counseling.

"His tactics are so on the nose that it's almost insulting." Hal snorted, a habit he picked up from Faith.

"Hmm?"

"He wants you to let your guard down, sitting in here." He shook his head.

"Ugh." I rolled my eyes. "If I stay vigilant, I bet he hopes it means counseling's less of a help in the future. So, what do I do?"

"I vote for vigilant. If it's horrible, I play sick, and we're in the infirmary. Faith knows what she's talking about, so there's this, too." He patted the notebook he'd brought.

"What's that?"

"Double insurance." He tilted his head, then pointed at the door. "That's all for now."

He's inside.

I nodded as we crossed the last few feet before walking into the lion's den.

"Sit." Mr. Fairbanks gestured at a metal folding chair in front of the desk. The cozy chair Ms. Khan used sat in a corner.

I did, finding it cold and too slippery. He ignored Hal entirely, as though he wasn't there. So, Hal sat on the couch and put his feet up, shoes and all. He held the notebook on his lap with one hand, smiling as he gave a friendly wave. Mr. Fairbanks didn't even turn his head or glance in his direction. He also said nothing at all for an entire minute. I know because I watched the second hand moving around the clock behind him.

"Um, sir? Is this detention?"

"It's mind magic, Miss Fairbanks." He tapped the side of his head with one finger. "You'll have to show me you'll do it here. Focus. Or I'll tell the headmaster this isn't working. You're aware of the consequences?"

"I'm new at it, though." I blinked. "I mean, the first time it showed itself was in the test."

"I find that hard to believe." He narrowed his eyes.

"It's true, though."

"Prove it."

"How?"

"Either your videos misrepresented your abilities, or you're unwilling to meet the terms of your accommodations. I don't care which it is." He scoffed. "If you can't think of a way on your own, the headmaster will hear of this and will remove you from campus."

I needed help and Hal was only supposed to observe. Stumped, I consulted the inside voice in a desperate attempt to discover the problem.

You closed your mind off to him the night of the masquerade ball when you hid with Dorian and Alex. You're still blocking him.

Shouldn't I be? Faith flat-out said he's dangerous.

Not when it'll get you expelled. He's using this situation to get you out of his way. That's a danger, too.

I tried relaxing, but it was no use. Remembering the fear in my friends, how horrifying Temperance was as his favored child, made that impossible.

"I'll allow you to waste three more minutes of my time."

Don't think about him or the night in question, the voice pleaded. *Find something else.*

"No."

I couldn't, so I didn't. If Abraham Fairbanks, the architect of so much horror, wanted a display, he'd have it. I immersed myself in last year's memories of the locker room, awash in swampy ice-rimed water, blood on Jonah's face, and my brother's neck. The flat, metallic stench of old machinery. A fanatic's crazed glare framed by green and brown hair. I imagined the lighting board in the auditorium, with my hand on the follow-spot, aiming it at his eyes in what I hoped would be an arresting if not blinding display.

Well, you've got his attention now.

His face lit up momentarily. I'm not sure what reaction I expected, but it certainly wasn't what I got.

"Brava." He clapped, one corner of his mouth tilting up. His eyes remained sharp and hard, like a board riddled with rusty nails. "Clumsy, but powerful enough."

I sat blinking, wondering how he wasn't shaken. The memory that still tormented me and a handful of my friends made him feel, what exactly?

Happy. Proud. Vindicated.

"Of what?" I slapped my hand over my mouth as a wave of nausea pressed the remains of my lunch upward.

"To be formidable eventually." He'd misheard me. "Although I doubt you'll ever have the stomach to use mind magic to its fullest potential."

"Thank you, sir." I removed my hand.

"You may go." He waved a hand at the door.

I stood and hauled my satchel up to my shoulder.

"Aren't the sessions supposed to last forty-five minutes, Mr. Fairbanks?" Hal stretched, leaning back more firmly against the couch cushions. "I don't want Grandpa to get the wrong idea."

"Think of this first one as more of an evaluation, Hawkins." He scrawled something on a piece of paper. "The headmaster just got notice of this day's completion, along with my reasoning."

New words appeared on the page, in an untidy copperplate I recognized as Hiram Hawkins' handwriting. Hal rose, sauntered toward the desk, and had a look. He nodded and let me lead us out of the room.

In the lounge, I had almost no appetite but managed to choke down half a turkey sandwich. I fed Ember the rest as she sat in my lap. Nin draped herself around Hal's shoulders like a scarf.

"Let me see." Faith pointed at the notebook Hal had kept in his lap the entire time.

He handed it over, and she flipped through it, nostrils flaring and cheeks reddening.

"What did you show him, Aliyah?"

I told her. Logan held my hand. Dorian hunched over in his seat, pale and trembling. Hailey and Bailey Overton tried walking in the room, but Eston stopped them with a wagging finger. Bailey turned and left while Hailey leaned in the doorway, tugging Kitty's sleeve.

"It's okay."

"It's not." Hal sighed. "Or it won't be unless I do some work tonight and tomorrow. Do you mind if Aliyah and I partner up in lab tomorrow?"

"Knock yourselves out." Dorian looked up as Julia the strix landed on his shoulder, hooting softly. "But why?"

"Don't say anything." Faith shook her head. "Off-campus chatting only."

"That's right." Hal nodded.

"Okay." Dorian sighed. "See you all on Saturday, then."

We gathered up paper napkins and cups and brought them to the trash. Everyone headed upstairs, but Dorian lingered. Before putting my foot on the moving steps to let them carry me away, I looked over my shoulder. He stood, head bowed, leaning between the fluted column and the garbage can beside the lounge's doorway. Alex came with a cart full of bags from other cans around campus. I almost went back until I heard an unmistakable hum coming from their direction.

Alex tapped his knuckles against Dorian's shoulder, then stared at his feet as he spoke.

Dorian nodded and wiped under his eyes with the back of his hand.

Alex shrugged, then pointed at the cart and said something else.

Ice and poison. Like Professor Luciano.

The hum got stronger and more melodic until I knew what would happen almost before I saw it.

Dorian gazed up at Alex, eyes wide. Then he laughed. Fully, from the gut with the sort of smile I hadn't seen since before that horrible night last spring.

Somehow, Dorian Spanos navigated the rocky coast of tragedy, and Alex Onassis was along for the ride. No. They were in the same leaky boat together, taking turns with the paddle.

I got on the moving staircase and said a prayer, hoping it wouldn't strike them again.

On Friday afternoon, Director-General Rockport met me at Bubbe's office. My parents, Noah, Bubbe, and Logan sat in the kitchen with me. An army of classmates along with Izzy and Cadence waited in the backyard with hot cocoa. There wasn't room inside, but they all wanted to support me. Everyone at Hawthorn Academy had gotten a direct link to the video of my extramagus test before it posted on social media across multiple verified accounts. I wasn't sure whether it had gone viral yet.

"This range-limiting unit restricts mind magic. It activates when worn and means you'll be unable to sense or influence other minds unless you maintain physical contact with another individual. You are required to wear it during exams, quizzes, lab practicals, and competitive games. I'd suggest wearing it to practice as well, so you grow accustomed to playing without the use of this particular magic. Do you understand?"

"Yes, I do."

He handed over a small box, the kind gifts of jewelry come in. I half-expected to see a necklace inside, possibly with a locket or something.

"Ears?" I blinked. Because that's what they looked like, except made of pale gold metal instead of flesh.

"Ear cuffs, to be precise. Devices like this must be worn on either side of the head. Now, put them on."

Bubbe held up a mirror so I could see what I was doing. The ear cuffs hooked on the top of my ear and had tiny levers with rounded stoppers at the back to hold them in place. They felt so impossibly light I couldn't imagine how they'd stay on during Bishop's Row without getting crushed.

"Wow." Logan peered in the mirror over my shoulder. "You look like a Sidhe."

He was right. The tips of the cuffs had points and extended far enough above my natural ears to mimic Sidhe anatomy. They almost looked nice but didn't feel that way. The levered clamps pinched, and the metal tingled where it touched my skin. Even worse, they emitted a constant discordant hum nobody else seemed aware of. That made sense, considering my brain interpreted mind magic aurally.

"Are you comfortable?"

"Not really, no."

"In pain?"

"No. It's annoying and pinchy."

"Good."

Dad clenched his jaw so tightly I heard his teeth grind. Mom put her hand on his arm and shook her head. Noah bared his fangs. Ember and Doris both hissed. Logan rested his chin on my shoulder.

She's so brave. My hero.

I blinked. That wasn't the inside voice. It was Logan's. The ear cuffs didn't only decrease the range of mind magic. They seemed to compress it. Maybe I couldn't hear people and the connections between them with these ersatz torture devices on, but the thoughts came in more like telepathy, somehow. Had telepaths had a hand in making these? Was it only because Logan and I had a bond? My eyes stung.

"Are you sure there's no pain?" Rockport asked.

"No. Just my dignity."

"Hmm." His brow furrowed. "I had hoped the aesthetic design would help with that."

"You made them?"

"No." He shook his head. "But I selected them from the vault with you in mind."

"Thanks for that."

Before he could move too far away, I patted his hand.

A wordless wave of guilt and grief crashed around me as if I stood on a storm-swept shore of an ocean made from tears. Staring into the Director-General's eyes, I understood his profound despair. The man might have haunted several of Dylan's nightmares, and even a few of mine, but he was the one drowning. Had he known what this job would entail when he'd taken it? Considering how unprepared I felt for adult life, I thought it likely he didn't.

"I'm sorry, sir."

"Noted." He placed a card with a phone number and email address on the table. "Contact me if there are issues with the device. Are there further questions?"

I shook my head. My family followed suit. Bubbe escorted him out of the kitchen. Nobody spoke until we heard the front door close.

"That son of a bitch."

"Noah!"

"I'm a grown-ass adult, Mom. And he's a government-mandated sadist who's tortured two people I—care about."

"He's not a sadist."

Bubbe froze in the doorway. Everybody did like they'd been encased in ice. A moment later, everyone's voices overlapped.

"—can't possibly know his—"

"—trauma response—"

"—like a robot without feelings—"

"—reputation as a stoic—"

"She touched him," Logan finally said. "He said they work with physical contact. She must have felt something."

"Thanks." I nodded. "That's what happened. He's a wreck on the inside. Guilt, sadness."

"Sorry," Noah snarked. "Not sorry. However he feels about it, that test is evil. Everyone knows about it now. It's been all over the internet for the last two days."

"Did he mention anything about that?" I gulped and glanced at the door. "Before I got here I mean."

"No." Bubbe raised an eyebrow. "But a news brief on a viral memory charm video about extramagi aired this morning. They didn't show the content, but implied it's not a hoax. I can't imagine he hasn't heard."

"I wonder." Dad stroked his beard. "Why did you ask that particular question after you admitted to reading his mind?"

Mom tilted her head, appraising me. "Did you have something to do with this, Aliyah?"

I nodded and cleared my throat, then told them everything.

"That's why your friends are all outside." Bubbe put her hand to her chest. "You don't do anything by halves."

"Well, you're grounded." Mom narrowed her eyes. "Go upstairs and stay there for the weekend."

"Why?"

"You didn't lie when we asked, but you omitted big time. Smuggling a restricted item into a government test. Not asking for help in a dangerous situation."

"She did, though," Logan countered. "She asked me. I did the omission thing too."

"Then you're also grounded." Bubbe shook her head. "I know you're an adult, Logan. But if you're staying here this weekend, those are the rules. Otherwise, campus is the place to be."

"Yes, ma'am." He hung his head and paced out of the room. I followed him down the hall, holding the box the ear cuffs came in.

"Sorry for mixing you up in this."

"Mix happens. I'd do it all again a million times for you." He opened the door to his hidden room. "See you on Sunday?"

"Sunday." I nodded.

Once he closed the door behind him, I headed up the stairs.

"I'll tell your friends they'll see you after the weekend," Noah called from the bottom.

I didn't have the heart to thank him for that until much later.

CHAPTER EIGHTEEN

The whistle blasted so loudly I almost thought Coach Pickman broke it.

"Morgenstern! Front and center!" She pointed at Lee on the bench. "Fill in, Young!"

I jogged over, passing Faith as I left my teammates practicing on the court.

At first, Coach said nothing, which wasn't her usual method of ribbing. She glared directly at my ears as if her scrutiny could deactivate the devices clipped there. I hung my head, ashamed. With good reason. I'd fumbled five saves and missed every fakeout Dylan made.

"Take those off, Morgenstern."

"I'm not allowed to—"

"Practice with them off, I know." She nodded. "But we're off-court for now. You can put them back on in a minute."

I did it, letting the ear cuffs sit in the palm of my right hand.

"Now, look out there at them and tell me what you see."

I faced the court and watched.

"Grace dodged Dylan's ice, but he's following up with air. She's out."

"How long have you had it, do you think?"

"Coach?"

"The," she pointed at her head. "Whatchamacallit. Jedi mind tricks."

"I don't know." I shrugged.

"Seems to me, since before I met you."

"What?" I blinked.

"Morgenstern, your brother I mean, always said you cared too much." She twisted the whistle's lanyard. "He's not wrong, but it's because you pay attention to your teammates and opponents. Until today with those fracking things." She pointed at my hand.

"Wow, Coach. I never thought about it that way."

"Do extra practice off-campus. With alumni and those star players from Messing and Gallows Hills. Collins, Micello and Mendez. Bring Pierce the elder and your brother too."

"Why?"

"The only thing we mitigate in Bishop's Row is damage. The rest is twenty percent talent and sixty percent training. Experience." She wrinkled her nose at the cuffs. "Colleges don't require bull—uh, extreme stuff like those. The scouts are coming this spring. They should see you at your best."

I didn't know what to say to that. Coach must think I had scholarship potential at least.

"Thanks, Coach." I nodded. "I'll talk to my friends in town about practicing, but I'm not sure there's anywhere with space for it."

"I'll make a few calls to Salem State. I've got connections there. Let me know when you have a group together."

"Shouldn't I bring the rest of the team though?" I fastened the ear cuffs on again. "In the interests of being a good captain and all."

"Whoever's able. Don't bother asking Onassis though. He's confined to campus." Before I could ask why, she blew her whistle again and sent me back in, this time calling Dylan back.

Practice went better with me playing reverse point. Or maybe without Dylan and his famous fakeouts on the court. Eventually, we moved on to straight-up throw and block drills, where I partnered with Lee.

"I don't like those." He glanced at my ears, then blocked my solar orb.

"Same here, but they're required for this and tests." I conjured fire this time.

"Hmm." Lee faked right and tossed left. I managed to dodge but not block. "Double standard."

"How?" I threw, obliterating his half-conjured orb.

"A mind magus trustee is walking around without those." Lee brushed ashes off his hands and conjured again. "One with a grudge against you."

"Yeah, but who's going to call him on it?"

"I kind of hoped you would."

"I'm just trying to graduate, Lee." I sighed. "The headmaster says this is the only way to make sure things stay fair for everyone."

"Right." He tossed and tagged my arm. "What if it's unfair to you?"

"This magic just showed up." I reset my ballistae then conjured solar again. "I got by without it for two years here, right?"

"I don't think so." He tossed, tagging me in the middle this time. "If it's not new, then this is all wrong."

The whistle blew, ending practice. I sighed, canceled my conjure, and dropped my hands. I took the ear cuffs off again, finally for the rest of the evening. Izzy always said her favorite thing about Lee was his observant nature. He must have noticed stuff I didn't, as Coach had. I couldn't bring myself to agree with him out loud. In my heart, I knew he had a point.

The guy has an entire harpoon. If Fairbanks knew you had mind magic since Parent's Night in first year, he's exploiting this situation. And you.

I'd never know unless I could literally get a hand on him while wearing the ear cuffs. I didn't want to do that. What I'd seen in Director-General Rockport's head was bad enough. Abe Fairbanks' mind had to be an even worse place. It was probably impossible anyway since the tutoring sessions required me not to wear them.

See? More of a reason to think he's up to something.

"Maybe Rockport gave me a gift."

"Are you okay?" Grace put her hand on my arm.

She said something else about the locker room, but I missed exactly what. That palm against my biceps made Grace's concern feel like the weighted blankets Nurse Smith gave to Temperance's survivors last year. I still had one in my room for the bad nights. My eyes misted over. I shook my head.

"Practicing in that contraption must suck." She tugged my arm. "Let's get cocoa after we clean up. With the tiny marshmallows."

I nodded and went along with my roommate, telling her about the off-campus practice idea as we washed up and changed.

"Sounds awesome." She grinned. "Glad Coach is looking out for you. Because the tournament in spring is off-campus, and you can play in that without the emo faerie jewelry."

In her typical fashion, Grace drifted through the locker room's common area, getting almost everyone else on board for extra practice. Alex avoided her, but I expected that. He was in the café when we got there, alone with his notes from class. He turned his back to us, head down, which surprised me. I got up to put my mug in the dish bin, then lingered by his chair.

"Hey." I shuffled my feet. Ember lifted her head off my shoulder. He looked up when she *peeped* softly.

"What?"

"Sorry you can't come to the extra practices. You're a real asset on the team."

"You don't have to say things like that. Not after what I've done."

"I know, but it's true." I shrugged. "Anyway, maybe you can make it out sometime. Stranger things have happened, right?"

"No." He glanced at the doorway behind me. "I haven't been off campus since I got here from Greece, remember?"

"Right." I nodded. "Anyway, good job at practice."

I made the thumbs-up gesture at him before walking back toward Grace, who was getting ready to leave. Sure enough, Mrs. Onassis stood near the doorway, talking to her familiar. She spoke loudly and distinctly enough for me to hear every word.

"Every poison has a remedy, doesn't it, my pet? Even the ones that act on the mind. Some work slowly, but they're still effective."

Once we got into our room and were ready for bed, Grace asked the million-dollar question.

"Was that trustee threatening you?"

"I don't think I want to know."

"This is starting to feel like a case of same vulture, different liver."

"I'm no Prometheus, Grace."

"Could have fooled me, Aliyah Morgenstern. Fire, light, big ideas. You always bring it. And buzzards like her keep showing up."

"I give in. Here are my chains." I shook the box with my ear cuffs inside before I set it on my dresser and shuffled toward my bed. "Now I need Heracles to break them."

"Hmm." She yawned. "Soon, I hope. Goodnight, Aliyah."

"Goodnight, Grace."

I closed the blue book and set my pencil down on top of it a minute after Faith, fifteen after Hal, and twenty behind Logan. We sat, glancing at each other as we waited for Dylan and Dorian. The ear cuffs buzzed, which was pretty much the only difference between this day and the last time I'd taken a test. So, the dampening device didn't affect me here as much as it did on the court.

The inside voice didn't chime in about this. Had it spoken up any time I wore the cuffs? No, not that I could remember. Whether it came from mind magic or not, I had no clue. The only information I had about it was what Professor Luciano had said, that he thought it came with being an extramagus, an idea that Dylan's auras supported. We hadn't found anything further, no matter how many books Logan borrowed on interlibrary loan.

"Excellent." Professor Hawkins clapped his hands. "You've all finished ahead of the time allotted. Take a break in Creatives, and I'll see you all for the Lab practical after lunch."

"A round of applause for you, Prof." Dorian applauded back at our teacher, moving his hands in a circle. "This is the best I've felt after a test. Thanks!"

The professor cleared his throat a few times as he went around the room to collect the blue books. A tiny grin played at his lips, and I figured he held back laughter that might have been considered inappropriate. But why?

I turned my head. Mr. Pierce stood in the back of the room by the door with Brand the phoenix on a perch over his head. Both the magus and his familiar wore grim expressions, as though they'd watched a battle to the death instead of teenagers taking a test where everyone finished early and cheered the teacher.

After collecting my things, I stood. Dylan, Dorian, Faith, and Hal were already headed for the door. Logan still sat in his seat, his hand hovering over his pencil as though frozen in time. I strode across the row toward him.

"Come on, let's paint." I picked the pencil up and put it in his hand, making sure not to touch him. He knew the ear cuffs made me sense thoughts and I wanted to give him privacy.

"Um, yeah." He swallowed, then nodded. His shoulders shook but not with cold.

"What's wrong?"

"I can't say it." Logan stood, keeping his back to his father. He slung his backpack on as though it could stop him from shaking. He inhaled, then with a slow and deliberate motion, took my hand. I saw way too much. Including the first time Logan almost died.

The childhood memory flashed between my mind and his in an instant, but its events had helped shape his life since then. Of that I was sure, even if the circumstances were still a reeling blur from my perspective. It'd take time to sort through and piece them together. One thing was clear. Leo Pierce was every bit as horrible as Abe Fairbanks.

Professor Hawkins's voice connected me back to the present. I wasn't sure what he'd said but knew what I had to do.

"We're getting out." I squeezed Logan's hand. Although he still trembled, he nodded.

The entire way through the room and the doorway, he ignored his father and only had eyes for me.

"I'm sorry," he said while sitting in front of a blank canvas.

"Hmm?"

"The, um, hatching." He stared at the still-empty palette in his hand. "It was awful."

"You never spoke of it. If you ever do, I'm here."

"It's easier to express stuff like that without words." He nodded at the canvas. "But scary. Because once you put something on canvas, there's your life for everyone to judge. Even the people who wanted it kept secret."

"Hey." Dylan sat nearby with his guitar. "An awesome guy once told me if your art's amazing, it needs to be heard. Or seen, in your case. Your life is yours to depict. If people don't like their part in it, oh well. They should have treated you better."

"Aliyah?"

"He's right." I handed him the tubes of black and white paint. "Why not do a portrait of that giant cat hero?"

Dylan raised an eyebrow. When neither of us responded, he shrugged and strummed chords. Logan's eyes lit up, and he put paint on the palette, then went to work. I finally removed the ear cuffs and stashed them in the box in my blazer. Then I stayed near the door, watching in case Mr. Pierce tried to audit us in here. He stayed away the entire time.

We had an auditor for the Lab practical too, but it was Andre Gauthier. He kept quiet for the most part, his owl asleep on his shoulder. Their presence didn't disturb any of us. Unlike with the lecture final, the ear cuffs made everything harder for me.

We moved around the room individually, taking turns at the benches. They were set up as numbered stations each with an item we'd all seen before during the semester. And no instructions. We had to remember what to do with each of them. I'd studied, but trying to recall my notes only produced a faint buzz as I gazed at the watch glass and dropper bottle. Out of time, I moved to the next station and let Dorian take my place. I shook my head at the graduated cylinder and foiled metal.

Usually, the inside voice would have chimed in by now, at the very least to tell me I was an idiot. But it didn't. The ear cuffs had to be blocking it out. So I tried to imagine what it'd say.

"Do something," I mumbled.

"Shh." Professor Hawkins put his finger over his lips.

Right. Silence was mandatory. I reached out and picked up the cylinder. Then I remembered. We infused the metal before pouring the solution on it. If my mind wasn't working, at least it seemed I could get results with muscle memory. Or magic memory or whatever. I managed to get back to the station that stumped me before the end and do something with it.

My revelation didn't mean I aced the practical. My grade came back as a B minus, lower than usual for Lab. The professor called me to his office before dinner, which is why I knew about it before folks started leaving for break.

"What happened, Aliyah? You've been in the top three for practicals every other time." He cleared his throat. "I'm not the greatest instructor for magipsych lab, so if there are methods I didn't use that help you, please let me know."

"It's not you." I rummaged in my bag and produced the ear cuff box. "It's these."

"Ah." He shook his head. "I'll do some research over break and look for study methods you can try."

"You don't have to, Professor. It's probably a matter of practice. Bishop's Row was harder when I wore them, too. Since I put them on in gym every time, I'm adapting. I should have worn them in Lab every time, too."

"I don't like that idea." He sighed. "I'll look into it anyway if you don't mind. It's better to have more than one plan."

"I just didn't want you to go out of your way, is all."

"It's the least I can do."

I nodded.

As I headed out of his office, I noticed a photograph hanging on the wall. It was Professor Luciano, sitting at the desk that now belonged to Professor Hawkins. A wall of melancholy sound washed against my back, like a wave breaking while wading out of the ocean.

Guilt, shame, grief. Of course. What will you do about it?

"Thanks, Professor." I opened the door. "I can tell you care about all of us."

With that, the tide of his negativity receded.

Faith's parents had already left for Rhode Island to move Temperance into The Academy.

"They said they don't care what I do with myself." She watched the teaspoon make a whirlpool in her morning coffee. "Guess I can finally live the dream of getting pregnant and dropping out."

Hal had a coughing fit. Lee put a hand over his mouth. Dylan's mouth dropped open. Logan's face went beet red. Alex ran his coffee cart into a table.

"Come to wassail at the Ambersmith's," Grace said. "Az asked me to invite everyone. So all of you should. It's on Twelfth Night, which is January fifth." She looked over her shoulder at Alex. "It's a blast."

"Bollocks," Dylan said. "I'll be back from NYC by then, but Piercing Whispers has a gig that night."

"Aww." Grace pouted. "What about the rest of you?"

"I haven't been since grade school. So excited!" I clapped my hands.

"What's wassail?" Logan asked.

"It's where Christmas caroling comes from," Dylan said.

"In January?" Lee blinked.

"They do Yule caroling too, in town," Grace said. "On Twelfth Night, they sing to the trees at their orchards in Danvers first, before coming into town. And there's tons of hot cider."

"I'll try it." Logan nodded.

"What do you think, Hal?" Faith gripped his hand.

"I want you to go even if I can't, Faith. Make videos." He nodded. "I think it'll be ready in time, so you'll probably see me for the in-town part."

"What?" Dorian blinked.

"It's a surprise." Logan smiled. "You'll find out in a few weeks."

"Not me. I'm going home." Dorian glanced at Alex. "Maybe you'll send me a postcard, Xan."

"I can't."

"The post office is down the street."

"No. I mean I can't leave campus to mail it."

"Hmm." Grace stirred her coffee. "You know some people, just saying."

"No." Alex shook his head. "No magical sneaking hijinks. I'm only allowed to walk Dorian to the train. Or else."

Nobody knew what to say to that. After a moment, he remembered the cart and pushed it back through the cafeteria to finish his work.

I went upstairs to pack, and Logan to fetch his already prepared bags. We made it down to the lobby, where everyone else in third year waited. The familiars huddled together in a cuddle pile on a bench, all aware of what came next—a brief parting of ways for many of us.

Kitty was heading out to Portland, where she had a college interview. Eston would meet her before New Year's after seeing his great-grandmother in New Hampshire. Hailey and Bailey would leave the next morning on a train to New York City, traveling at the same time as Dylan and his mom, who'd go sightseeing and take in a Broadway show. Lee was staying at the Mendez's. Grace would visit the Ambersmith's extended family in Haverhill. Only Hal and Faith would remain on campus.

We turned on Washington Street toward the train station. The temperature was cold enough to nip our noses although the puddles still splashed in response to several sets of booted feet. I watched Alex and Dorian walk together, hands down between them but not touching.

"Are you sure you don't need me to stick around?" Logan asked. "To finish the project, I mean. My parents have shows in Vegas through New Year's so that's not stopping me."

"If so, I'll get a message out." Hal grinned. "I think we've got it."

Hal and Faith said goodbye at the top of the stairs. He looked worse than worn out, dim somehow, although not unkempt. Faith gave him her arm as they walked away. The rest of us descended behind Alex and Dorian.

"Slow down. You're not on the track." Grace elbowed me. "I think they want a little space."

"Oh, sorry." I hung back. "Are they—"

"Dating?" She raised an eyebrow. "No. I asked yesterday."

"Uh, that wasn't what I meant."

"What then?"

"Are they okay? They both look weighed down."

"I don't know."

At the bottom of the stairs, I jogged to catch up with them. Dylan and Grace bolted after me. Even Logan tried to keep up. Up on the platform, I realized I'd caught them mid-argument.

"So fight back." Dorian's eyes reminded me of icicles in March, almost liquid.

"You don't understand. I can't. Like, I freeze up." He shook his head, mouth a thin flat line.

"I totally get it. Cowardly ice man here, remember? You can do this. I believe in you."

"Maybe I shouldn't." He glanced at Grace and me, Logan and Dylan. "Maybe I deserve what I'm getting, after what I've done."

"Or what you've always gotten from her is the reason you screwed up." Grace crossed her arms over her chest. "Going against the grain is hard, but it's important."

"I don't know your story, DuBois." Alex sighed. "Probably should have asked instead of writing you off. Sorry."

"Hey, that's a step." She nodded. "Keep going."

"I'm trying, but she pulls me back every time."

Dorian put a hand on his shoulder.

The train squealed to a halt, brakes and engine hissing out plumes of steam. We waited it out and said goodbye. Dorian stopped in the doorway.

"Get on, Xan." He held out his hand.

"What?"

"I've got enough cash to get you a ticket on board. Come with me."

"I've got nothing with me. No clothes."

"I have three entire closets."

"But your parents—"

"Always ask when I'll bring friends over, already."

"She'll think I ran away." He hung his head.

"Run toward a welcome, then." Dorian smiled.

He stood, hands opening and closing, shoulders trembling.

"Go. It worked for me."

Alex looked at Logan like he'd just walked out of the Under.

The conductor called for all passengers to board.

Dorian stepped sideways, making room in the doorway, and beckoned.

And just like that, Alex Onassis escaped for the holidays.

CHAPTER NINETEEN

Only Hope For Me
Logan

The morning of the Ambersmith's annual wassail, I sat up, still awash in the worst of my nightmares. Doris headbutted my side, then went behind me and leaped up to my shoulder where she perched, purring in my ear. She always knew when it was worst and never left me alone in those times. I sobbed, head in my hands, because of how lucky I felt to have found her.

"Was it him again?" I heard in her purr. "On the mountain?"

I nodded, then told her the entire story for what had to be the thousandth time.

No decent parent puts small children in a territorial animal's nest. My father wasn't decent in any way. He was a stunning performer and a brilliant marketer, an iron-fisted trainer, and a demanding instructor. Decency only got in the way of talent, he said.

He barked orders at us from a much safer position, yards away, with a rock wall to his back as we sat in a feather-bedecked circle beside a clutch of ash-smeared eggs the size of my head. He expected both Elanor and me to bond with the phoenixes that were about to hatch right there in the nest. She'd used fire several months earlier, but my magic hadn't even come in yet.

When my sister picked up one of the eggs, it blazed. The one I tried stayed cool under my hand. Nothing happened after touching two more, so Father shooed me away. I followed his orders as obediently as the animals he commanded. Because I'd been able to understand them ages before I started talking, which was later than normal. I knew what happened behind the scenes, things my parents never mentioned. Not long after that, I saw it firsthand. So, I started back toward him, shuffling my clumsy feet over loose rocks and sloping terrain. I fell on my backside in stone and scree when something cracked behind me.

Elanor's eyes went wide as the shell burst into a million flaming pieces. Father ordered her to banish every one, but she wasn't strong enough. The nest she sat in caught fire and my big sister cowered in fear, clutching a tiny featherless and ashen hatchling in her arms. That's when it happened. My water came in like a tidal wave, although I'd never seen the ocean. It doused the entire nest. I cried because I might have harmed the eggs to save Elanor.

She hurried out of the nest and ran toward me. I tried to follow although my feet never moved well without a beat to guide them. Father grabbed me by the shoulders and shook me so hard my head snapped back and forth. He lifted me, too. Held me in the air at the side of that treacherous drop.

"That wasn't even the worst part, Doris."

She rubbed her head against my cheek, absorbing my tears into her glossy silver coat.

"It's what he said afterward." She meowed.

"Yeah." My voice hardened, imitating his. "Give me one reason not to toss you like garbage, retard."

Back on the mountain, I couldn't get a word out. Both the baby phoenix and Elanor shrieked at the top of their lungs, almost matching in volume and pitch. I understood the bird better than my sister. Both cried out for help.

It came on velveted paws.

An enormous black and white feline, larger than a tiger but not one on account of its scaled hindquarters, leaped down from the ridge above us. It roared, startling my father back from the edge.

I shook, unable to conclude the story because sometimes the dream had me landing on solid ground as it actually happened, sprawled with Elanor, watching our father flee.

In the dream last night, I went over the side, screaming at the rocks below as the mysterious hybrid cat-dragon tried in vain to catch me.

Doris didn't press again. I mumbled words of love and thanks while scratching behind her left ear where she always seemed to itch.

"We should go upstairs for breakfast soon," I muttered although my stomach felt like a washing machine. "And yeah, I'll wash up first."

The spare room had a tiny bathroom, with a shower I thankfully fit in. Once I was decent, I opened the door that separated my room at Bubbe's from the animals on the other side. Finally, I smiled at the din of their combined voices, comforting in a way that a room full of people talking wasn't. People mystified me, for the most part. They pushed in too much with their voices and bodies. It was different with magical creatures. I could listen to them all day long, stand in crowds of them for hours.

Nobody in my family, not even Elanor, understood that about me. I'd tried explaining, maybe a hundred times. That I felt out of place almost constantly, homesick while sitting at home. Until I wound up here, where the critters came for healing.

Bubbe got it. She couldn't hear them as I could, but she'd devoted her life to their care. Even the ones actively dying.

No wonder Aliyah wanted to be like her. I did too, which is why I paced up and down the hall, stopping at each Dutch door to say good morning to all the patients and boarders. I found Aliyah's grandmother in the room closest to the waiting room entrance, checking on a karkinos, her underside berried with a clutch of eggs. They weren't exactly like a regular crab's. Instead of thousands, the eggs numbered only ten. The mothers carried the baby crabs on their backs after hatching, too.

"I can't wait to see your children, waving with their little claws."

The mother karkinos clacked in response, saying it'd be a relief to have the weight on her back for a change.

"Good morning, Logan." Bubbe grinned.

"Hi, Bubbe." I smiled back while looking at the crustacean instead of her, which she'd never complained about. "Are you coming upstairs for breakfast?"

"In a while." Which meant she wasn't.

"Can I bring anything down for you?"

"You're so thoughtful, Logan. Some toast and marmalade if they've any to spare. Thank you."

"See you later." I waved at them both.

Every morning since I started staying here, she always gave me a kind word. The first two weeks, I'd been a wreck over it that she'd go out of her way to drop a compliment. I discovered it wasn't extra, only how the Morgensterns did things. Still awkward, but way better than my family's exacting demands.

Upstairs it was the same. Aliyah and her parents passed words of love and gratitude along with dishes of food, like sentiment was something sweet to sprinkle over life in general. I sat at the table, giving and receiving in the space they made for me. If only it could be like this forever. Someday, I'd have to move on even if I'd left Las Vegas for good. College. Extraveterinary school. Those places might be more like home than here. That scared me, almost enough to make me give up on my dream.

Then Aliyah smiled at me.

I grinned back and blinked. Not because her expression surprised me. All her smiles were like sunrises. Different every time but beautiful. Other guys at school called Aliyah Morgenstern pretty, and they had a point. That kind of thing wasn't important to me, though. The best thing about her was her heart. It was like the ocean, vast and powerful, a force of nature. She cared. Noah said too much, but there's no such thing. Caring is like oxygen. Everyone needs it, and it's a catalyst that lets amazing things happen.

By the time I remembered them, my eggs and toast were cold. Mr.

Morgenstern put my plate in the oven, which he always kept warm during breakfast.

"It's too easy for some of us to get distracted," he explained. He'd been talking about Aliyah's mom, but that habit he got into for her helped me too.

"Speaking of distraction." Aliyah rinsed her plate in the sink. "I totally forgot yesterday to mention it. That book we ordered on inter-library loan came in. We should go to campus and have a look."

"Right." I nodded. "That's the book we can't take off-campus. Maybe you don't want to spend half the day in the library."

"We're going out tonight. Plenty of excitement there." She put the plate in the dishwasher, then dried her hands. "I'm game if you are. Besides, who doesn't want to read the musings of medieval dragons?"

"Hmm. Probably Bailey Overton. She always says dragons are so last week."

Although she'd proved me wrong for over two years, I winced, expecting a reprimand for answering a question I only realized was rhetorical after the fact. But she smiled at me, followed up by a hug this time. I hugged back. Over her shoulder, I had a perfect view of her parents, framed by the doorway into the living room. Their relationship looked like a classic romance; something Aliyah probably wanted in her life someday.

Although we'd kissed three more times after the masquerade ball, the way I felt about her hadn't gotten any different. There wasn't a rush of blood away from the head like Eston described when he and Kitty had alone time. I didn't get all tingly like Hal said happened with him and Faith. I was comfortable with her, pleasantly warm like being under a blanket on an autumn afternoon before the heat kicked in. Or like the swimming pool at the penthouse in Vegas, bathwater temper-ature. That's the way it was since the first Parent's Night. Something everyone else I knew described as platonic.

I loved her more than I ever thought possible, but like almost everything else about me, the way I loved wasn't how everybody else did it.

Aliyah deserved a conversation about that, but we had to go to the library first. I headed out the door she held for me and started down the stairs.

"You need some shoes, Logan. Oh, and we need to grab Bubbe's toast and marmalade."

"Oh yeah, forgot." I chuckled, then went back up.

***

"Are you sure?" Aliyah gestured at the lexicon. "It's such a pain to translate those."

"It might be painful, but I've got my routine for it." I patted the cover. "I'll handle good old Ludovico's journals while you get our drinks. I mean, it's not like I've got to duel an actual green dragon or something."

"There's no way I'd leave you in actual danger, Logan." She planted a kiss on the top of my head. "You know that, right?"

I nodded. She headed out to get tea, which the Ashfords allowed in their library over breaks and exam weeks. Moments later, I got lost in a puzzle of Old Germanic. Languages were a special interest for me, and I'd discovered that dragon shifters also were by extension because most of them were polyglots, like the dragonets.

Most people wouldn't have realized that, but since I understood magical creatures, I had. Each species had its articulate way of communicating, along with a sort of common parlance conveyed physically. The entire idea of studying, possibly even classifying and recording these languages, fascinated me. So did each of Ludovico's tomes. However, we'd only been able to check them out one at a time from the Black Forest University library, and it took weeks to ship them over.

I went *tharn* to the rest of the world while translating. *Tharn* was an awesome word, as in awe-inspiring for real. I'd always imagined Richard Adams, the man who wrote *Watership Down*, was an extrahuman with an ability like mine, and that he'd chronicled the folklore and history of actual rabbits. Or maybe even moon hares. That made sense with all the Frith and Inle stories anyway.

Usually when I waxed oblivious in here like that, Aliyah kept watch. She said it was to make sure I didn't get interrupted, but it probably had something to do with my dad and his cruel friends. Fortunately, they didn't show up that day. Instead, someone else did.

"That's some heavy reading, young sir." The voice was low but musical, sort of sing-song. It reminded me of my old kindergarten teacher. I felt so comfortable listening to it that I didn't feel the need to look up.

"Uh, yeah. But it's pretty amazing." I didn't look up, merely pointed at the phrase I'd just translated. "Ludovico the Green was obsessed with extramagi. I don't blame him. He found out they have extra abilities, not only their elements. This part mentions dragonets. Did you know they almost went extinct during the Reveal? Ludovico thinks they're significant to extramagi. I haven't finished translating yet, but it looks super interesting."

"I suppose it's hard to compete with unearthing ancient history." A deep beige hand with rounded pearly fingernails set a much newer book beside the Old Germanic lexicon. "However, you should have a look through this. It's no less significant although much more recent."

I only intended to glance at the glossy cover, but the photo of a young woman with a mercat on the cover hooked me. I read the words above and below it.

"It's a yearbook. From Hawthorn. In my Dad's first year?"

"Take care, young sir. I'm not as benign as I seem."

Doris pressed her head against my hand. "No more questions. She's Fae."

Now I looked up. The woman reminded me of someone. I wasn't sure who. Forgetting faces was a weakness of mine, so maybe I'd seen her before. One look at her clothing told me no. She wore a robe. Not the kind people put on before and after a bath or even ones folks graduate in. A caftan. It was long and deep mauve with yellow paisley print. Mirrors decorated the neckline, sleeves, and hem. Grace would have gone nuts over this woman's clothes because they looked both vintage and magical.

"Do you not know who this is?" One of those rounded fingernails underlined the picture.

I shook my head, then turned back to my translation work.

"Do yourself a favor and check the yearbook out before you leave."

All of a sudden, it was too much. Her unexpected presence. The interruption. The mirrors flashing on her sleeves. Was she even allowed on campus? What if she worked for my father? She'd said right out that she wasn't what she seemed.

"You know, I didn't get your name." I looked up. Her face wasn't as young as I'd originally thought, forehead and the bridge of her nose etched with lines. Not the kind that came from smiling, either.

"Mila."

"There's aren't any Milas on the staff here."

"There were, once upon a time." She caressed the cover of the book, then pulled her hand away.

My mind parsed all the possibilities in an instant. She couldn't be a ghost. They couldn't come on campus and without a medium present, couldn't move books. And Doris said she was Fae. She didn't belong here, and adult guests weren't allowed without a legal or blood relation to a student. The Hawkins family saw to that with their space magic. So, there were only two possibilities.

Mila was related to a student. One currently present on campus. Or she was the djinn Aliyah and I had been looking for all semester. If the second was true, so was the first. Could Mila be short for Gamila, as in Haddad-Hawkins, maker of the stained glass mural? I couldn't ask because she was a full-fledged faerie and I'd naively asked her two questions already. I'd end up owing her a favor. I had to do something to get more of a clue. Or maybe let on that I wasn't entirely clueless.

The library's door opened.

"Please, I'm out of time. The yearbook is important."

"I wish I could take your word for it."

She flinched, confirming my theory. I turned my head, looking for Aliyah, hoping she could make sense of Mila's sudden presence. Instead, it was Faith walking toward me, not her.

"I'm making Aliyah take a lunch break, with solid food. You too, so come on." She stuck a scrap of paper in the lexicon, then pulled the ribbon over Ludovico's journal.

"Wait, I was talking to—"

When I looked up, my visitor had gone. My stomach rumbled like it was the underside of a thunderhead.

I went along with Faith and checked the old yearbook out of the library on the way.

Lunch was chicken nuggets with applesauce and mashed potatoes. Childish, people say. Comfort food, actually. Texture and flavor always as expected, without surprises. No matter where or how those three foods get prepared, they're universal. Like Swedish meatballs, but easier to find. I'd already had enough excitement for the morning and a new experience planned for later on. The last thing I wanted was an embarrassing stimming episode, like the night of my birthday. Or worse, a meltdown.

My friends cared. Hal did the right thing always, and I trusted Faith with my life. Those two were fierce and fair, and wouldn't ever hurt me on purpose. Grace went out of her way to include me, even when I couldn't keep up. They didn't understand all of it though. Not like Aliyah. That's why I pretended not to notice Grace's nudge and Faith's raised eyebrow. And why I answered Hal with a little white lie.

"You deserve a better lunch than that, Logan. Want me to ask Penelope what else she's got?"

"Translation fried my brain. It's all I could think of." I gestured at my plate. "Anyway, I'm almost full. Thanks for asking, though."

"So, Grace. Why aren't you at Azrael's?" Aliyah sipped chicken soup from a mug.

"Brought you all something." She grinned.

"Clothes." Hal grinned at Faith. "I bet anyone a cookie." He pointed at the last chocolate chip on the dessert plate.

"Sorry, Hal." Grace shrugged. "Textiles, but not technically garments."

I looked up, my jaw dropping with my eureka moment.

"Blankets!"

Grace pushed the plate toward me. I shook my head at the spoils. Hal shrugged, then gave the cookie to Faith, who broke it into pieces and shared it around to the familiars.

Nin fiddled with her hunk of cookie, trying to get Hal's attention. She had a point. Hal had thinned out a little during his summer growth spurt, but he hadn't ever looked this gaunt. I could see his cheekbones, and his temples had hollows. I crossed my fingers under the table, hoping it was five-o'clock shadow and a recent haircut. He'd started shaving this summer, too. Maybe it was good old rising testosterone and not magiglobular anemia trying to kill him.

Lune turned his nose up at it, insisting he was strictly vegan, then dropped it at Aliyah's feet. Seth and Doris gave their pieces to Ember.

"I wonder why he did that." Faith shook her head. "He never turns down a treat."

I blinked and stood, hearing the animals chatter.

"You guys, she's expecting!"

"No way!" Grace put her hands on her cheeks. "Did you know, Aliyah?"

"Um, well, I knew she'd mated. During exam week." She blushed.

Grace dropped me a wink. Now it was my turn to blush because I understood on an intellectual level what she thought. A familiar's emotions carried over through their bonds. It wasn't uncommon for magi with familiars to get amorous at the same time as a mating familiar. However, I knew for sure that wasn't the case with Aliyah because I'd been with her every night of exam week and we hadn't done anything but typical cuddling. Mostly, she'd been exhausted. Then there was me.

"I'm asexual."

I slapped one hand over my mouth and the other on the table. I was suddenly in my worst nightmare. The one where I *did* end up falling off that cliff in Tibet. My friends all sat staring in silence that stretched like Nevada afternoon shadows until one of them cleared her throat and broke it.

"What, like a sea sponge?"

"Grace!" Instead of rolling her eyes, Faith widened them. "Uncool. It's an orientation, like being bi or gay."

"Sorry." She hung her head. "I know. I meant it as a joke. It didn't come out right."

"Well, neither did I." I sighed.

"Hey, are you okay?"

There Aliyah Morgenstern went again. Caring about the aftermath of my inevitable blurt instead of however she must feel about it.

"Well, that depends. I mean, are you?" I looked up at the shallow bowl of her perpetual slight smile, unable to meet her eyes. "I understand if you want to stop dating."

"That's our cue, I think." Hal wobbled a little as he rose from his seat.

"No, you can stay." Aliyah put her other hand out. "I'm fine, Logan. Relieved." She drew a big breath. "Pretty sure I am too. Asexual, I mean."

I sat blinking at her, breathless. Was this happening right now, in the cafeteria? Coming out to my friends after keeping it secret for a whole year why it hadn't worked out with Dorian? Had I truly gotten entangled with a person who felt the same way I did? My father said that I'd spend my life settling because water wasn't flashy enough to be more than an opening act. Because I was too picky. Because I didn't ogle women or men. Because I was different. Which meant unlovable.

Doctor Morgenstern and her family, especially Aliyah, proved every day that those hadn't been facts, only my father's opinions. Here was more. All my friends sat quietly, giving me time to respond. Although I was slow with this, they didn't seem to mind. Aliyah took my hand. I looked up into her eyes for the few breaths I could manage. I had no idea what to say to her but opened my mouth anyway.

"Thanks for coming out with me." I squeezed her hand. She let go, then held her arms out. I nodded, and we hugged.

Everybody laughed, even the familiars. But with me, not at.

Lunch was over after that. Hal and Faith went back upstairs.

Aliyah and I promised to bring the blankets to them after finishing up in the library. Grace left campus. I put my bag over my shoulder, remembering why it was heavy—the yearbook. I'd missed the chance to talk to everyone about it. But not Aliyah. I filled her in on our way back down the hall.

"I agree." She nodded. "You saw Gamila Haddad-Hawkins. Which is pretty amazing."

"I feel bad though. Don't really have time to look into that yearbook with all the translating."

"I'll do it."

After we sat, I handed it over to her. Aliyah didn't even open the cover.

"This girl could have been a supermodel. She looks almost exactly like you."

"I don't see it." I winced. "Sorry."

"That's okay. I'll figure this out."

She pulled a notebook out of her knapsack and started flipping through glossy pages. I stuck to my alternately pulpy and oily ones. The lexicon was my bargain bin purchase from Wicked Good Books on Essex Street. The interlibrary loan copies of Ludovico's journals were so old they were on genuine parchment.

At some point, Aliyah put the pen down and sat back in her seat. I kept on working. We only had until the Ashfords closed the library and the stuff I'd discovered was essential. The old green dragon had started experimenting with blood. His methods were far from modern in a scientific sense but the magical methods tracked with much of common practice today. I'd be showing all of it to Bubbe as soon as possible.

"I'm sorry Mr. Pierce, Miss Morgenstern." Mr. Ashford bowed his head at each of us in turn, steely blue hair brushing both sides of his cheeks. "That's all the time for today."

I packed up my lexicon and notes, then headed toward the desk to hand the journal to Mrs. Ashford, who checked it back in. When I got back to the table, Aliyah had opened the yearbook to the page showing the name, quote, and plans of the young woman from the cover. Her name was Petra, but Aliyah's finger blocked her last name.

"I know what it says here, Mr. Ashford. What happened to her? Because I know for a fact she's not who this yearbook says she'd be."

"Sadly, it's not my story to tell. Perhaps Mr. Gauthier would take such liberties. Or Mr. Pierce."

I shuddered, fighting the urge to turn and leave.

"I've tried the former. The latter, I don't trust." Aliyah's lips twisted into the grin she always put on before a big Bishop's Row game. Her game face. The mask of defiance. "I'll find a way. Thanks, Mr. Ashford."

On the way out, we stopped in the Creatives room, where the lights were out. They didn't come on, so Aliyah conjured some. Grace's blankets were inside the textiles cabinet on the far wall. After retrieving them, we started toward the doors again. I reached to open them, but she stopped me. A moment later, I heard voices—my father's.

"Frankly, you should have done a better job controlling your son."

"Says the man whose offspring haven't been home in over a year." The woman snorted. I didn't recognize her voice. "You will help me find him. Or I'm spilling the beans on your little plan."

"I'm not sure how a fire magus can help in a missing persons case. Why not call the police?"

"You think I haven't tried? You know how public servants are since the Reveal chaos died down. All about doing the same for everyone, not treating families like ours with proper respect."

"You have a point, Lavinia. So what do you want from me?"

So, the woman was Alex's mother.

"Money, of course. To hire a private investigator. All of mine's tied up in trust at the moment. The holidays, you know."

"This month's dividend already gone?" He chuckled. "You're like a sailor on shore leave with money. How do I trust you to repay?"

"Oh, I promise you'll get paid back. And then some."

Doris and Ember wondered together how asking a friend for help could sound so sinister. They didn't know my father.

"How much?"

She dropped a figure she could have purchased a yacht with. He laughed, and they negotiated. My stomach churned. Finally, they wrapped it up.

"So in exchange for this sum, you will say nothing."

"About what, exactly?" She tittered.

"The conservatorship I've got drawn up. Or the plan we've got to thwart Gauthier and give me grounds to invoke it on him."

"As soon as the funds hit my account, I promise to stay mum on the matter of entrapping your son."

"I'm surprised you're not making a similar demand."

"Oh, Leo." She clicked her tongue. "Nobody likes my son. They don't care how I treat him, not after the things he's done. I understand the need with yours. He's surprisingly popular."

"Like the idiot mascot of the bleeding hearts." My father laughed. Doris hissed. "Elanor's fault entirely. I should have separated them after that incident in Tibet."

"You know what they say about hindsight."

Their voices got smaller, which meant they headed down the hall. I sat. Had to, or I would have fallen. And it would have been a disaster, clattering chairs and them barging in here.

Doris jumped into my lap. Ember, although she'd clung to Aliyah like a statically charged sweater since getting pregnant, draped herself over my shoulders. Trails of smoke curled up to my right. Doris put her paws on my shoulders, purring in my face. When Aliyah sat on the edge of the table beside me and smoothed my hair, it was all over. My self-control.

Tears rained down on my face, sudden and torrential as a thunderstorm but silent as the snow. I'd learned over the years, not just how to cry noiselessly, but how to sob without sound.

I'm not sure how long it went on. Thunder-boomer length, or hurricane? Was this the eye? Would an hour of peace pass, only to blow apart in the next storm surge?

"Sorry," I finally managed and wiped my eyes on my sleeves. It almost felt like a lost cause, but at least my nose wasn't running.

"No." She shook her head. "If Bubbe were here, what would she say?"

"Be quiet?" I glanced at the door.

"No, they're gone." She tapped her temple. "Mind magic says so. She'd say don't apologize for healing."

"Can't argue with Bubbe." I sighed and leaned my head against her side. "Guess it's going to take time. Should be used to that by now."

"Someday, you'll be free from this." She put her arm around my shoulders. "From them."

"How do you do it?"

"Hmm?"

"Be so. I don't know. Unsurprised? That my parents aren't like yours? Because yours shocked me."

"First year was when I started understanding. Nobody's got it the same at home as anyone else. It started with Grace."

"How?"

"I guess you don't know. In first year, Grace told me her parents had passed. Years ago. It hit her hard, and the only thing I could do was be there for her, without judging."

"So, it's like a bedside manner? Something I could learn maybe?"

"Wow." She got off the table and crouched in front of me. "Logan, you don't have to be blunder-free. Making mistakes won't stop your friends from caring."

"Okay." I stood and held my hand out. "I'm ready to go now."

We walked arm-in-arm through the hallway and into the lobby. Fortunately, Faith was there, so we handed the blankets off to her. While separating them off the bundle, we noticed one each for Izzy and Lee, which we delivered to her house. After that, we helped out in Bubbe's office before dinner. I left my translation notes on Ludovico's blood research with her before leaving for the evening.

We met the others in front of the Essex Street municipal parking lot, where we waited until Azrael showed up in a minivan with Grace. At first, I wondered what we'd do about Hal's wheelchair.

That's a misnomer because Hal's prototype didn't have wheels at all. It hovered instead, powered by fans underneath, like a hovercraft. But the fans were magipsychic. Dylan and I helped enchant those, and Lee helped make the frame as lightweight as possible with his wood magic. It was an enormous secret, and Hal couldn't handle all the walking and singing without it.

There was no way Grace or Az could have known we'd need a bigger vehicle. But he held his phone up and tapped something on it. Then he put the emergency lights on, and they got out.

"Do you want the good news or the bad news first?" he asked Aliyah.

"The good." She grinned.

"Bar's coming. He can fit Hal's contraption in his truck. And he's bringing Cadence."

"Okay, what's the bad news?"

"He's got Mavis coming too."

"How's that bad?" She scratched her head.

"She's a Merlini." He sighed. "You know how they are."

"Hold on there." Hal blinked. "Because it sounds like you're pushing bias on a middle school kid."

"It's more complicated than that." Tires crunched on the pavement. A door slammed.

"Complicated or not, she helped us out big time."

"The entire family's horrible."

Everybody stared at him, even Grace. Az shuffled his feet, face turning red. The pit of my stomach dropped. If Azrael felt this way about Mavis over her family, what did he think of me? I shivered. Aliyah put her arm around me. I looked up.

Bartholomew Micello kept right on approaching, but Cadence stopped walking toward us in mid-step. I'd never seen the dark-haired girl whose arm she held, but she looked sad, like a kid with no cake or presents on her birthday.

"We don't do the sins of the father thing here." Hal took Faith's hand. Right. Her family was awful too. "Everybody gets a chance."

"Okay then." Azrael nodded. He strode over toward Cadence and the girl. His entire manner changed like he'd stepped on stage, suddenly in character. "Miss Mavis Merlini, I do humbly apologize for my unkindness. I'm only a changeling, but I owe you one favor in exchange for my uncouth outburst."

"Um, okay?" She tugged Cadence's sleeve. "Like, now?"

"Any time." The mermaid nodded. "But it's simpler to call faerie favors in sooner rather than later. You don't want to forget that kind of debt."

"Okay then." Mavis grinned. "Azrael Ambersmith, I want you to hop on one leg and bark like a dog. Then we're square."

He looked ridiculous but didn't seem to mind acting so clownish. Grace clapped her hands once he finished, starting everyone else off. After the applause died down, we helped Hal into the minivan while Bar put his magic chair in the back of the truck. Mavis jumped up after and strapped it down with bungee cords. Then we were on our way to start the evening's festivities at the Ambersmith family apple orchards across the border in Danvers.

I kind of hoped wassailing would be like musical theatre. But it wasn't. No dancing at all, only singing, which I'm no good at. And lots of hot beverages, which made up for that. The adults had whiskey in theirs, except for Old Grandpa Ambersmith. Along the way, he walked with the younger crowd, regaling us with stories about the adult Ambersmiths. He spoke with a slight whistle, due to missing his front teeth. And he made epic dad jokes.

"My medication goes with booze like ugly Christmas sweaters and the Fourth of July." He dropped me a wink. "Get it?"

"Yeah." I chuckled. "Good one, sir."

"Call me Old Grandpa. Or OGP if you want, kiddo."

"Thanks, I will."

"You've got fine manners, for a Pierce." He elbowed Aliyah. "I approve."

"Oh, um, thanks OGP."

"Like he's a Morgenstern already. When's the wedding? You could double up with Az and Miss Gracie." He glanced at Hal and Faith. "Make it a triple, even."

Aliyah and Faith both blushed while Hal hid his face behind his blanket. Cadence smiled but sighed. Mavis rolled her eyes.

"OGP!" Azrael shook his finger at his grandfather. "Enough with the wedding talk, already."

"This is his usual schtick now, you know?" Grace rolled her eyes. "Time for some new jokes, Old Grandpa."

"Watch out for Miss Gracie. She'll rule the world someday." OGP nodded.

"Nah." She shrugged. "I only want to decorate it."

Everybody laughed.

Somewhere on the north end of Salem, near the bridge to Beverly, I overheard Aliyah and Cadence.

"Why hasn't it been in the papers, though?"

"Does that really matter? I mean, the video's internet famous."

"It was for about five minutes. Mostly, it got me in trouble with my parents. It's yesterday's news now. I thought you said your mom would want to interview me, Cadence."

"Now that I think of it, she hasn't mentioned you or the test video at all. That's strange for her. She's not the sort of adult who's oblivious to internet trends."

"Can you ask her, then?"

"It's tricky, but I'll try."

"Do you need help?"

"Nah. I'll ask her out for mother-daughter mimosas after I get home. I should know something before we go back to school."

"Yearbook." I nudged Aliyah.

"Oh, right!" She nodded. "Cadence, have you ever heard of Gamila Haddad-Hawkins?"

"Hal's grandmother? She's a djinn, works for the Sidhe Queen. She's lamp-bound. Typical djinn story—separated from her family for years because of the lamp."

"How does that work, exactly? The lamp thing?"

"They do three terms of service, for the first three people who activate the lamp. After that, they're bound to service forever unless someone willingly takes their place."

"Another djinn?"

"Preferred but not required. But they've got to be extrahuman and not a shifter. I don't know much else." She shrugged.

"Okay, more library time then." She nodded. "One more name to drop if that's okay?"

"Hit me up."

"Petra Pierce."

My mouth dropped open. So, the yearbook girl was my relative.

"Logan, she's your aunt. That sister Andre mentioned, remember?"

I couldn't speak, so I shook my head.

"Well, no wonder. It's a sad story." Cadence didn't know my father. "She graduated Hawthorn, top of her class. Went to Providence Paranormal for a semester and got engaged to her high school sweetheart. And then there was an accident. Her familiar passed and she got sick. Mental illness, like paranoia and hallucinations."

"What happened after that?" My voice cracked.

"Nobody knows. Her fiancé never married. Or dated anyone else either."

"I bet you five bucks I know his name." Aliyah sighed.

"Oh?" Cadence blinked. "Go on. I love easy money."

"Andre Gauthier."

"And, I'm broke." Cadence opened her handbag and paid her debt. "I think that's enough gossip for now. I'll talk to Mom tomorrow morning about the other thing."

On the way home, most of us were sleepy. I had my head on Aliyah's shoulder, struggling not to nod off.

"Will I see you tomorrow?" Aliyah asked. I almost told her of course when Hal answered.

"I think so." He hung his head. "After all the court business with Dad pushing Mom out of my medical care, I feel bad going over his head. They'll be angry."

"They'll be angrier if they find out this could have helped." Faith sighed. "Their issues aren't your fault."

"Yeah, I know. But I have to make sure they'll be okay, that I'm not burning bridges with Mom and Dad. I won't have time to fix it later."

I didn't know what decision about tomorrow Hal had to make, but I had too much experience walking on eggshells. So I sat up.

"Hal, it's not your job to fix your parents." I studied his face, half-lit from the orange streetlights outside. "You're trying to survive. Do that however you have to. They're the adults. If they have problems with whatever you're doing, that's on them."

Az turned on Washington Street, and we rode a few blocks in silence. Finally, Hal nodded.

"Okay, so I'll see you tomorrow."

We said goodnight and trudged back to our homes, temporary and otherwise. I kissed Aliyah goodnight at the bottom of the back stairs. Bubbe waved from her kitchen as I passed by, taking pictures of my notebook with her phone. Coming to live here the year before had seemed like my last resort at the time. The Morgensterns were my lifeline now. And Aliyah herself, nothing short of hope.

That night, the dream of the cliffs didn't visit me, and I slept in peace.

CHAPTER TWENTY

Aliyah

At sunset the day after the wassail, I helped Bubbe in her kitchen, setting two tea trays up on the table. I knew why even before she poured a bag of blood into the yellow teapot decorated with copper-plate letter Bs. She put it on a hotplate with a digital display instead of the stove and set it for 98.5 degrees Fahrenheit.

"Is Noah coming over?"

"No, but our guests are both vampires." Bubbe put our usual teakettle on. "They want to talk to Hal about his magiglobular anemia."

"Why am I here, then?" Dylan pulled his head and the carton of cream out of the refrigerator. "And Aliyah?"

"That's extramagus business."

"Can you explain?" My hands shook, and the china rattled. Up on top of the refrigerator, Ember peeped, and Gale chirped.

"Even I'm not clear on the details. They assured me it's positive."

I tried to relax after that. Optimism faded once Hal arrived, hands clenched in tension and forehead twisted with strain. He left his chair in the waiting room and shuffled toward Bubbe's kitchen propped up between Faith and the wall. Once seated, he refused all offers of refreshments. I didn't press about why. After all the effort to get in here, the last thing he'd want was needing the bathroom in the middle of this meeting.

Faith paced the room while Hal sat. Dylan opened a cabinet and brought down tea bags. The table only seated four, so I got a few extra chairs from an empty exam room. I set one each at the head and foot of the table, then glanced around, trying to figure out where the odd one ought to go.

"I'll take that one." Dylan reached for it. "Be a wallflower." He placed it between the doorway and the corner, then sat.

"Hey." Logan paused in the open doorway and nodded at us. "A car just pulled up in the driveway. Wanted to let you know."

"You coming in?" Hal asked.

"I'm about to have my hands full with baby karkinos feeding time. Good luck!" He grinned.

"Thanks."

The door chime sounded, and Bubbe left the room. She returned in moments, leading a man and a woman. The only similarities between them were their pallor and a sense that each was out of time somehow. His clothes reminded me of old movies Bubbe watched. She wore a lab coat over full skirts and a shirtwaist that could have come out of a history textbook about the Industrial Revolution, but her briefcase was decidedly twenty-first century. They sat across from Hal and Faith after Bubbe took the seat at the head of the table. I stood at the foot, leaning my hands on the back of the chair. From there, I had a view of everyone in the room, the door, and even the little window over the sink.

Why are you in defense mode?

"Please, Aliyah. Sit," Bubbe requested. "It's only polite."

"No, I understand." The man grinned. "Your granddaughter has a sense of tactics. Detective Klein, Newport Police Department."

"And I'm Doctor Klein, Director of Magical Conditions at Rhode Island Hospital." She cleared her throat. "Which is part of the reason we're here, Harold."

"My blood tests." Hal nodded. "Call me Hal. Are you related?"

"We were married, once upon a time. That's part of why we asked to meet in person instead of doing this over the phone." Doctor Klein pulled a folder from the briefcase. "With magical anemia cases, my lab also runs DNA profiles. Harold, you share a significant match with both of us."

"What?"

"We're your maternal grandparents."

Hal sat with that for a minute while pouring hot water over a sachet of chamomile. He stirred the tea he never ended up drinking, possibly a picture of calm to the Kleins, who had only just met him. The rest of us knew better. The tea was busywork for his hands. Hal's serious business had gone dire. His next words confirmed it.

"Shouldn't my mother be here, then?"

"I invited her," Bubbe admitted. "She never answered or returned my calls."

"So you knew, Bubbe."

"We asked Doctor Morgenstern to let us give you this news in person." Detective Klein gazed at Hal, his eyes filled with that same light of determination my friend often displayed. "Among other things."

"Okay." Hal nodded. "I'll hear you out."

"When Steph—" Detective Klein shook his head. "When your mother went missing, we never stopped looking. Police in other jurisdictions wouldn't talk to me once they checked my status in the registry. Vampire problems. We hired a psychic investigator, but it led to another young woman instead. Eventually, we realized law enforcement wasn't working."

"So, you went with science." The corners of Hal's mouth turned up. "Medical records."

"Exactly." Doctor Klein flipped the folder open. "It took a long time for older records to go digital. Even then, your mother must have avoided conventional doctors. Dhampyr blood isn't easy to hide."

"That's why I was born on the Hawthorn campus." Hal's mouth

dropped open. "But why? If you loved her so much, cared enough to search for decades. Why did she hide from you?"

"That's a question even we can't answer." Detective Klein sighed.

"She should be here then." His jaw tightened. "She'll hear from me. Even if I have to send Detective Ambersmith to her door again."

"Again?" Doctor Klein blinked.

Hal shook his head, hands balled into fists. Faith put an arm around him. She looked up at me, eyes narrow and nostrils flared. The silence stretched until I broke it for them.

"She managed all his health care, medical records. He had to sneak in here and get a blood test from my grandmother, just to get diagnosed."

"This was the anonymous test from twenty months ago?" Doctor Klein consulted her folder. "That's the first you knew of your condition?"

Hal looked up, eyes shining with tears, nodding.

"No." Detective Klein looked smaller somehow after that. Like he'd deflated. "We're too late."

"Too late?" Dylan blinked. "For what?"

"A license, of course." Faith clicked her tongue. "To turn him before—"

"Before I die." Hal swallowed. "If there's any chance at all, I'll fill them out with you today."

"There's not." Bubbe sighed. "The waitlist is two years long, even for emergencies. I checked right after they called."

"We thought we had more time." Doctor Klein shook her head.

"What about testing his blood?" I straightened. "Get a better idea of how far his progression is? Maybe he's got more time than you think."

"That's a good idea Miss Morgenstern, but unlikely. If he'd known, started those experimental infusions before the onset of symptoms, we'd have better odds. Still, I'll do the tests."

"A long shot's still a shot," Faith said. "Hal's a fighter."

"Not like you." Hal grinned at her. "But thanks. So, what's the other reason you're here? You talked like there was more than one."

"He's got your curiosity, Cal." Doctor Klein flipped through the papers in her folder. "My department's doing research on testing. Collecting samples from as many extrahuman types as possible. We've only got one extramagus in the bank so far and wanted to ask Miss Morgenstern and Mr. Khan if they're willing to participate."

"Is it for magic in the blood, or DNA, or maybe metabolism? Blood only, or cheek cells too? Oh! What about stem cells from teeth?"

"You must have big college plans, Miss Morgenstern." Doctor Klein raised an eyebrow. "To answer your question, we're developing a blood test to identify genetic conditions like Hal's. We're also blood typing for extrahuman ability. We're already there with common shifters and halfway with changelings, but we haven't got enough data from magi. Especially extramagi. And there's a growing demand for an alternative test, considering the news this autumn."

"My grounding lasted longer than that video's had its fifteen minutes." I sighed.

"On television, perhaps." She tilted her head. "In medicine, it's big news. A psychiatric colleague of mine is very interested. She thinks we must abolish the old way of testing. There's a path forward if my test works, but I need a bigger control group of known extramagi. Something more recent than Mr. Pierce's translations. Your grandmother's been sharing those with us and they've been a help in research, but not when it comes to registry regulations."

"Okay." I nodded.

"Sure," Dylan said.

"Have you checked with Nurse Smith at Hawthorn Academy?" Bubbe asked. "Perhaps the infirmary has a sample on file for Filberto Luciano. If you accept a hair sample, I've got some of my brother's. He was an extramagus too."

Hal, Dylan, and I went about the business of donating blood. Faith called Hawthorn's infirmary while Bubbe headed to the basement to get the box of Great Uncle Noah's things. After that, the Kleins exchanged contact information with Hal, who insisted on including Faith. We all waited around as the vampire guests left. Once they were out the door, Hal drooped, unable to rise from his seat.

In the end, Dylan carried him out to the waiting room and placed him in his magical moving chair. Logan, all finished with the now sleepy crab family, listened to Faith relate what had happened as we all bundled up for the walk back to Hawthorn campus. Frigid air pinched at my nose and cheeks. Logan and I didn't linger at the door. We had to meet Cadence down at The Point in five minutes, so there wasn't even time for coffee.

I set a brisk pace, trying to keep warm. Ember helped, snuggled inside my coat like a hot water bottle with scales. Logan carried Doris the same way. He struggled to keep up by the time we got to Harbor Street, so I slowed. Cadence beckoned to us halfway down the block from the apartment building she lived in with her parents, turning down a side street I recognized.

"Is she taking us to Noah's?" Logan asked.

"Looks like it."

Sure enough, Cadence lingered by the basement entrance. A hat and scarves covered her entire head and most of her face, not a typical look for her even in the depths of winter. Once we reached her side, she rang the bell on the door's frame.

"So, what's—"

"Shh. Inside."

I stood in the cold, blinking. The last word I'd use to describe Cadence was covert. Somehow, that's how she acted. Elanor let us in, and we all walked past her down the stairs, letting her follow us down.

Instead of sitting on the futon or one of the beanbags in the living room, my friend headed straight into the soundproofed music studio. Once we were all inside, Elanor closed the door behind us and remained outside.

"Okay, what gives, Cadence?"

"You guys, this is serious." She tossed her coat on a stool, unwound the scarf, and removed the hat, revealing red-rimmed eyes, tear-blotched cheeks, and half her hair shaved off.

"What happened?" Logan gasped. "You look like—"

"2008 Britney, I know."

"No, not her." Logan blushed. "Cyndi Lauper."

"He's right. It's more of an undercut."

"Hmm. You two don't lie about stuff like that." She sighed. "I feel more like Britney all the same."

"What did Crow do this time?" The room warmed up a little too rapidly. I drew a deep breath and banished the tiny flames around my hands.

"No, Aliyah. It's about last night." She sniffled. "My mom. She's not who I thought she was."

"What?" I blinked.

"Not her, not Dad. Not me either." Cadence wrung her hands. "Our whole family, we're not ambassadors. We're exiles. So, Mom has no strings left to pull. She's got to stay in her lane at work. Or she's out of a job, and we're out on the street."

"That's horrible!" I ran to her side and put my arms around her. "Cadence, I'm so sorry."

She cried on my shoulder for a while. I wasn't sure how long, but Logan came over and patted us both on the shoulder, holding a box of tissues. Although in other ways Cadence wasn't acting like herself, in her sadness, she remained the same friend I'd always known. Mercurial and thoughtful.

She pulled back, wiping her eyes on her sleeves.

"Triton's Beard, Aliyah. Don't apologize. It's not your fault."

"It's mine." Logan held a small globe of water and stared into it. Doris rubbed against his legs.

"No." She sniffled again. "That's not how it works."

"Wait, what's happening here?" I blinked.

"Sorry for borrowing your tears, Cadence. Water never forgets." Logan spoke at the globe. "How did I not see it before? How much did my father pay them?"

"Too little." Cadence's voice shook. "Even if it had been billions, too little."

"Probably it was a threat." He sniffled. "That's more his speed."

"What did he buy?" My voice sounded tiny, squeaky. Cadence opened her mouth to answer three times but couldn't manage.

"A kraken egg." Tears streamed down Logan's face. "He wanted me to bond with her, but she never even hatched."

"Kraken are sacred to merfolk." Cadence choked back a sob. "So, the DelMars are exiles. Forever. Down the entire family line. And we're not supposed to tell outsiders why. Or swim past the shallows."

We ended up in a hug pile on the floor in the middle of the room. Eventually, someone knocked on the door. I got up to open it and found Elanor and Izzy on the other side with more tissues and mugs of hot cocoa. Cadence and Logan walked out shortly after I did and we each took turns washing our faces in the bathroom before joining our other friends in the living room.

Cadence told them about the exile situation, how the reason was a secret. Elanor flat out accepted the fact that she'd never hear it, but Izzy drew some cards before nodding and letting it go. After we'd all calmed down, I asked the question that had been bothering me the entire time.

"Why not come to my house for this?"

"To be honest, I think all of you ought to find somewhere else to meet off-campus. Because the Morgenstern house isn't safe." Elanor sighed. "It's connected to the school, and our dad and his cronies are nothing nice."

"We can't invade your space all the time. You guys need to practice if you want to pay the rent."

"What about the extra Bishop's Row practices?" Elanor nodded. "Salem State's gym is safe enough, and I'm there if you want help."

"Oh yeah." I winced. "I was supposed to put a group together but dropped the ball."

"Dylan ran with it, so you're good." She grinned. "He asked Noah, Bar, and Brianna already. So Izzy, how about it? Extra Bishop's Row practices on Saturday mornings? Just until the week before the tourney."

"I'm in." She sighed. "Maybe one or two more teammates can make it but most have other obligations on weekends."

"I'd better captain better." My laugh came out all nervous. "Sorry."

"Can we do cheer stuff too?" Cadence jerked a thumb at Logan. "I hadn't considered extra training."

"Sure, why not?"

Noah walked through the door, hung his coat and a green apron on the coat rack, and went to change. Dylan and Arick showed up a few minutes later because Piercing Whispers had practice.

The rest of us stuck around to listen in and help them decide their next gig's setlist. Before she left, Cadence thanked everyone for helping salvage the evening.

CHAPTER TWENTY-ONE

On my first day back on campus, I sent Ember around with messages for the team, asking them to meet in the gym after lunch. Alex arrived first, and the pit of my stomach dropped. He walked right up to me and stood with his arms crossed as though he dared me to admit I'd made a mistake. To avoid embarrassing him, I dealt with his situation before everyone else showed.

I tried telling myself Coach Pickman might be wrong. Despite what I'd overheard during break, maybe his mom would let him come to extra practice. I wasn't wearing ear cuffs.

You already know the answer without asking.

I extended the invitation anyway.

"No way, Morgenstern." He tilted his chin up, trying his best to look down his nose at me. "Impossible."

"Remember, you'll be welcome if, uh, things change."

"Why don't you change the location to here, then?" He snorted.

I said nothing, just pulled the jewelry box out of my pocket and showed it to him.

"We're both shackled then." His brow furrowed. "I'm not sure which of us has the harsher jailer."

"It's not a contest." I sighed and returned the box to my blazer.

"Anyway, I can run extra drills and give you notes in the gym on a different day."

"Coach has to be there." He sniffed. "For...reasons."

"Okay, let's talk schedule, and I'll make it happen." I got out my notebook.

He rattled off his work hours, and I jotted them down. As we finished, Dylan sauntered through the door. He stopped at the bleachers, apparently tying his shoe. Alex turned his back and took a step away from me before pausing.

"Thanks, Morgenstern."

"No problem, Alex."

"My mother calls me that." He looked over his shoulder. "It's Xan."

"Xan then. See you later."

Dylan didn't approach until the door closed. I glanced down at his shoes, which were new, and noticed something interesting.

"Those are slip-on. No laces."

"Right. Christmas present. Mum's doing well here." He cleared his throat. "I remember the work-study shuffle. Is that going to hinder him, what with all the extra practices?"

"No."

"It's not work though."

"What did you see?"

"Big green miasma. What did you hear?"

"Discord. He's in trouble."

"Surely not as bad as last year, with Intemperance?"

"No. Not as bad. But different."

"Bollocks. What should we do?"

"I'm not sure. We need more information."

"I'll keep my eyes peeled if you put your ears on the walls."

"Did Noah give you a Ted Talk on snark?"

"I wish." He sighed.

"If you like him, say something."

"Noah must need something more grandiose than a plain declaration."

"I've known him most of his life, Dylan." I grinned. "Don't posture or make him think you're waiting for an answer. Just put your feelings out there. He's cautious, takes his time. But he can't choose something if he's got no idea it's even an option."

"So I'm not super obvious, then?"

"Only to the mind magus."

"Aces." He slapped his hand over his mouth. "Sorry."

"It's cool."

The rest of the team arrived, all carrying beverages. I made the announcement and gave them the schedule. Nobody asked about Xan, so I added that information at the end, including his nickname.

Might be a mistake. If his mother was right and nobody really cares what happens to him.

Someone did, though. One of my teammates lingered after everyone else had gone.

"Can I come to those extra drills?" Lee tapped one foot against the hardwood.

"Sure. Once I know exactly when they are."

"Good." He nodded, then turned on his heel and stalked out of the gymnasium, leaving me with my thoughts. I took off along the track, trying to outrun them.

I showered before dinner, of course, putting on pajamas afterward because nobody much cared what we wore in the cafeteria on Sundays. Dorian stood outside the door to my room.

"Can I come in?"

"If you don't mind me drying my hair."

"That doesn't bother me."

Grace had left a note on my desk saying her stomach couldn't wait. I put my basket of toiletries away and sat with my hairbrush on my bed, leaving the chair for Dorian. He stood blinking at me.

"What's up?"

"Don't you need a hairdryer?"

"No." I smiled and held up my hands. "I use magic for that. So what can I do for you?"

"First of all, thanks."

"Hmm?" I held the brush in one hand and put the other over it as I went over my hair, conjuring a small amount of solar energy to help it dry.

"For going out of your way to include Xan. Not holding a grudge."

"Don't thank me for being a decent human. You're the one who's really helping. Inviting him ho—"

"Shh." He swallowed. "I think the walls have ears."

"Yeah." I sighed. "Okay. You're really kind to him."

"I wanted to ask, because of the mind magic, I mean. Do you know if it's helping? Like, are things getting better for him?"

Don't say one word about them spending break together. You've got no idea who knows what. And he's right about the walls.

I closed my eyes and tried to sense my surroundings beyond what the voice said. Sure enough, a mild hum came from the wooden walls. What sort of magic energy had caused it, I couldn't tell.

He's waiting for an answer.

"He's not the same as he was last year. But Dorian, I haven't interacted with him enough to say for sure what the changes mean. I think the best thing to do is wait and let him show us."

"What about your first year?" He studied his fingers, which he'd locked together in front of him. "Because I wasn't there for that. And yeah, I've heard the rumors."

"The only things I see in him now from back then are mannerisms." My hair was dry, so I set the brush on my nightstand.

"I guess you're right." Dorian nodded. "Anyway, are you ready for dinner?"

"Sure, let's go."

The week passed much like the ones before winter break, for class and regular Bishop's Row practice anyway. The sessions with Mr.

Fairbanks were as fraught with tension. Hal sat in his magic chair instead of the couch, revealing its reclining feature. On Friday in the lounge with our to-go dinners, I mentioned it, igniting an excited discussion about enhancements and applications for an entire fleet of them.

"You don't even have to worry whether there's stairs or ramps because of the levitation," Dylan said. "Faith's idea, but Hal invented the process."

"But I didn't invent physics," Hal protested.

"I bet you can add a wood magic enchantment." Lee nodded. "So the frame has a flexible size range for navigating different doorways."

"We could make them look any which way." Grace smiled. "Glamour and umbral enchantments would do that. I've been working on a color and pattern dial with Az for shoes. I bet it'd work on that too. How cool would it be to make the frame match your outfit?"

"That's amazing!" Kitty clapped her hands. "Have you considered heating and cooling? You already have water and air in there. Why not add heating and cooling so you're comfortable no matter what?"

"Awesome ideas, folks." Hal grinned.

"Use them, then," Eston said. "Build the best chair possible."

"I'll think about it. Incidentally, the engineering design was my entry in the local magipsych fair. I'll give those a try after it's scored in February." The grin faded. Mine followed.

He knows he won't have time. Not to do all that.

"Hey," I cleared my throat. "The team and the squad have extra practice at Salem State tomorrow at eight-thirty. I talked it over with Logan, and we don't mind an audience. So, come along. The more, the merrier."

The subject shifted to cheer squad, with Kitty and Logan asking opinions on music choices through the rest of dinner. Dorian kept recommending Weird Al songs that made everyone laugh even if they all got vetoed. Eventually, the lights went off behind the café counter.

"Guess that's our cue." Dylan jerked a thumb at the darkened area. He whistled for Gale. "Come on, buddy. Upstairs time."

The dragonet didn't respond. I turned to look up at the perch he'd been sitting on with Ember and found her missing, too.

"Oh no." I jumped out of my seat, stepped around the low table, and prepared to sprint off in search of her.

"Wait." Logan put a hand on my elbow. "Shh. I'm listening."

He tilted his head, stepping carefully toward the column by the doorway. It was shaped to look like a tree trunk, with the archway made in the likeness of a coniferous branch, needles and all. After a moment of standing beneath it, Logan beamed and pointed up. We all stood there staring, unable to see what he indicated until we walked to stand beside him. That's when we finally noticed the golden tail curling around from the lobby side of the decorative embellishment.

I stepped into the open space, still looking up. Nestled in the Y made by the stylized trunk and arching branch sat a nest. The bundles of dining hall napkins and scraps of fabric from Creatives mostly obscured her hindquarters, but Ember was clearly laying eggs.

"So much for that brooding box, eh?" Grace elbowed me.

"Yeah." I nodded.

"Are you surprised?" Grace asked.

"Not really." I sighed. "How are we going to move them down?"

"I'm in this with you, Aliyah." Dylan chuckled. "No trouble for an air magus."

"It's almost lights out though," Eston pointed out. "We'll get in trouble if we're not upstairs in a few minutes. Is it safe to move a dragonet nest that quickly?"

"You shouldn't move them tonight anyway," Logan added. "She might keep laying eggs for hours and moving them in the middle stresses the whole family. Actually, moving them at all might be a bad idea. We should check with Bubbe."

"How many do you think there are?" Kitty peered up, trying to get a better look. "I see two."

"Ember doesn't know, so neither do I." I shrugged.

"Move along now. I'm closing up." Xan strode out of the café's lounge, pointing at his apron. "Scram so I can clock out already."

"Don't have to tell me twice."

Dylan led the way toward the stairs, Hal bringing up the rear in his chair. I followed them halfway across the lobby before I realized Dorian wasn't with us.

He's not okay.

Sure enough, when I turned to look, he was back by the doorway and gazing up at the nest. His shoulders shook although no sound of sniffles or sobs carried across the space between us. Julia the strix swooped down from somewhere overhead. When she landed on his shoulder, he only shrugged her off, shooing her away. Dorian's bewildered familiar came to me instead, perching on my shoulder where she fluttered and hooted her dismay. I wasn't sure what to do for her at first. Owls didn't like being petted.

Just wait for it.

I let Julia use me as a perch and gave Dorian a few moments to compose himself, unsure why Ember and Gale making a nest had him so distraught.

Gryphons hatch. And Mercy was awfully young.

My stinging eyes erupted with full-blown tears when Xan emerged from the now darkened lounge and put his arms around Dorian. The pair turned to face each other, revealing how red Dorian's face was and the tender way Xan stroked his hair as they rocked back and forth. Now I could hear them, one sobbing as the other murmured.

Feeling like an intruder, I turned and got on the stairs, whispering our floor. Logan waited at the top. He took one look at Julia, nodded, then escorted me to Dorian's room where we waited with the strix. Five minutes later, Dorian showed up alone, eyes puffy but much more composed. Julia turned her head all the way around. He murmured a few words of thanks to us, then walked behind me. Logan followed.

"Sorry, Julia." He sighed. "There's no good excuse. I know you're grieving too."

She hooted, then clicked her beak twice.

"She says you owe her ten crickets," Logan said.

He shouldn't have translated that.

"Twenty, if you want."

"Well, isn't this interesting."

I turned to face Leo Pierce, who'd walked up behind the boys as they addressed Julia. The last thing I wanted was for him to witness Logan's rare ability. Especially after what I'd learned about his sister Petra in the yearbook. So I scrambled to cover for him.

"Yeah, mind magic has loads of cool features." I put on my best intimidating grin, the one I'd used so often last year during the social skirmishes with Temperance Fairbanks. "Great for amazing and astounding your friends."

"This is why nobody trusts the Morgensterns. You're all a pack of shysters." Mr. Pierce snorted. "And you're the most flagrant liar of the bunch. I happen to know mind magic doesn't work that way."

"She's an extramagus." Dorian stepped between Logan and his father. "Are you sure it doesn't work that way for her?"

"I always suspected this." He ignored Dorian. "You can't hide from me much longer, Logan. Not even behind your most powerful friends."

"Are you threatening me?" Logan's voice cracked.

"Not at all. I only want what's best for you, son." He turned his back and sauntered away down the hall. "And the rest of the family. Enjoy what little freedom you've got while it lasts."

Once he was gone, Dorian leaned against the wall.

"Gods, Logan. I'm sorry."

"Why?"

"I got you in trouble. Because I got all emo downstairs and left you all in the lurch."

"How my father acts isn't your fault." Logan cleared his throat. "Or mine. I blurted it on an official record by accident. So it was only a matter of time before he found out."

"Yeah, Dorian." I nodded. "Grief happens."

"Thanks." He held out his arm, and Julia hopped to it. "I'd better get some sleep before anything else goes wrong tonight."

"See you tomorrow?" I asked.

"At Salem State? Yeah, I'm recording practice for Xan. Goodnight."

"Goodnight."

I walked Logan to his room, not leaving until the door latched behind him. After that, I went to mine, where Grace already slept soundly. It took me what felt like an hour of tossing and turning before I slept too.

I got up earlier than I normally did for classes. Nobody else was around in the cafeteria, not even the kitchen staff. So I had instant oatmeal and black tea using the self-service hot water dispenser. The oatmeal was always out on the counter in a metal rack, along with the tea and coffee sweeteners. It took a few minutes for the grains to soak, so I searched unsuccessfully for a spoon.

Normally, I would have relied on Ember to hunt down an item like that. But on the way in, I'd caught a glimpse of her asleep in her nest. Instead of waking the broody dragonet, I added more water to my breakfast, cold this time, until it became a slurry I could drink from the cup. Not exactly pleasant, but nourishing.

Salem State was a mile and a half from that day's Hawthorn door beside the Peabody Essex Museum. I jogged, which kept me warm enough without any magic in only my sweats, a hat, and gloves. Most of the time, I enjoyed cozy clothes on winter mornings and the company of friends around town. However, I'd never been to the gym at Salem State University before. Arriving early and on my own would give me a chance to figure out how to use the space.

Because of this, I expected to be the first person inside. Maybe even be stuck outside for a few minutes, since I got there before six. I was wrong. A chunk of brick held the door open a crack so I widened it more to step over it and inside, where all the lights were on.

Someone in a hooded sweatshirt sat on the bleachers, surrounded by books. A blond man dribbled a basketball down the court, coming to a short stop before shooting a perfect two-point basket. The hooded person sat up, revealing her face and clearing her throat. It was Lynn Frampton, who I'd met at the college fair.

The man on the court straightened, then turned to face me. I knew this fellow, too.

"Bobby Tremain?"

"Yeah." He rubbed the back of his head with one hand with a sheepish grin as he held the other out. "Aliyah, right? Captain of Hawthorn's Bishop's Row team?"

"That's right." I nodded and shook his hand.

"Nice to see you again."

"My coach said her friend was going to help me out here."

"Oh, Coach Warren isn't a morning person. She sent me to open the doors and just kind of hang out."

"You're supervising Bobby," Lynn chided. "It's part of your Mass Ed certification. Or are you having second thoughts about that Gallows Hill PE position?"

"Yeah, no." Bobby chuckled. "I kind of understate stuff sometimes. Anyway, I'll show you where the locker rooms are. What kind of equipment do you need?"

I rattled off a list as we walked. The setup was similar to Hawthorn's with a gender-neutral locker room between two gendered ones but smaller. Equipment closets were off to the left of the women's. He opened one, revealing racks and hooks with sets of ballistae, cestus, and ankyr in various sizes. I thanked him, and he headed to the other side of the gym.

At first, I expected Bobby to go back to shooting hoops. He walked right past the ball, not stopping until he reached the opposite wall and opened a small panel, the sort that covers circuit breakers. Some of the switches inside glowed. He flipped those, then toggled a few more. In a moment, I understood.

Those were controls, magipsychic ones, that customized the lines on the court. Shifter-regulation basketball lines morphed into official Bishop's Row boundaries. The baskets folded back against the wall, and wards went up along the lines between the playing area and the bleachers.

Initially, I'd worried about space for both the Bishop's Row practice and the cheer squads. I shouldn't have. The court only took up half the gym, which had sacrificed locker room size for play area. Sensible, considering they were one of the first formerly mundane public universities to have shifter regulation sports.

The tea and oatmeal breakfast plus the jog over gave me an excuse to check out the locker rooms. There wasn't a lot of space for changing, the shower and toilet stalls were cramped, and luxury features like the sauna, steam room, and whirlpool bath weren't included here. A sign informed me they were at the sports medicine office around the corner outside. However, this place didn't need to be fancy, just inclusive enough for all of us to practice using our full abilities.

I hung my hat and gloves on a hook beside the lockers. The facilities were typical of mundane spaces, nothing special. Everything worked fine. After washing my hands, I left the locker room. Before I made it halfway across the gym, the door opened again signaling new arrivals.

It was Izzy, walking with Lee and a few Bishop's Row players from Messing. They chuckled together over cups of hot chocolate I could smell from where I stood. Still nervous, my stomach didn't envy their beverages. The only reservations I had about being such an early bird were for someone else. Should I have woken Logan, brought him along? I didn't like imagining him making the trek alone.

My worries vanished a moment later when he entered and stood holding the door open for Hal's chair. Everyone else from my year at Hawthorn walked in after that. Arick Magnuson showed up as well, a handful of second years following him with Lena bringing up the rear.

"Hey, Aliyah!" Dylan waved, then jogged over. "I saw Brianna out there with her team and Cadence with her squad. They'll be here in a minute."

"Thanks."

Once everyone was inside, I showed them the locker rooms. Logan and Cadence went back to talk to Bobby, who brought them to another closet. Inside were batons, pom-poms, and ribbons on sticks. I glanced back at the door, expecting to see more students. Kitty tapped me on the shoulder.

"Jacinda's not coming." She sighed and shook her head. "I asked, and she said her squad doesn't need extra practice."

"Oh." I swallowed. "I hope everything's okay."

"It is." Izzy nodded. "Basically, she thinks it's more auspicious to rehearse in the evenings."

"Is that a thing?"

"It is to her." Izzy shrugged. "Just know that it's got nothing to do with Logan."

"Are you sure?"

"She met a guy on vacation in Disney World. Dead ringer for Flynn Ryder, judging by the pic she showed me. Anyway, let's do this."

Izzy went to round up her teammates while Lee stuck with us. Elanor showed up, then had a few words with Bobby. He went out the door to the hallway where sports medicine was and returned with Noah, who'd arrived by tunnel.

All told, we had enough players total to run four teams, and Salem State's gym was large enough to accommodate two simultaneous games and still leave room for both cheer squads to practice. While Bobby changed the court markings and wards to make two courts, Izzy, Brianna, and I sorted all the players, working out a schedule to switch opponents.

One amazing thing about the morning was getting the chance to play with and against students from the other schools. It felt more fun than regular practice, providing challenges that felt fresher than drills and disjointed plays.

The best part was how it felt, playing as I'd done since first year without the ear cuffs. Instead of that dulled-down sense of tunnel vision I'd experienced on campus lately, I felt almost hyperaware and more connected to my team in general and the overall fun of the game.

Dorian recorded everything. Not with his phone as I'd expected, either, but a set of magipsychic cameras he'd checked out from Salem State's AV center. Hal helped, filming from his chair. I heard them talking during one of my water breaks.

"This is some amazing footage." Dorian smiled. "Like, pro sports network quality. Thanks, Hal."

"Make sure you show it off, then." Hal grinned. "After edits and stuff."

"That's the plan."

We had to be out of the gym by noon, so we wrapped practice at eleven-thirty. People shook hands, exchanged high fives, and headed off to the locker rooms tired but mostly smiling. Someone tugged at my sleeve. I turned to find Lena Zanelli.

"Thanks," she mumbled.

"No problem."

"Could've been. Micello's a beast. Now I know."

"You know?"

"Strategy." She tapped the side of her head. "Counters for glamour."

"We're doing it again in two weeks."

"Good." She nodded. "Thanks again, Captain."

Before I could insist she call me Aliyah, Lena strode away to the locker room.

"Wow." Arick stood nearby blinking. "That's more than she says in class when she's called on."

"Really?"

"Pretty much." He nodded. "Cadence went to clean up, but she wanted me to ask if Hawthorn and Messing want Engine House for lunch."

"I'll let everyone know, including Izzy. Thanks, Arick."

Hal, Faith, and Dorian headed back toward campus, but everyone else went out for lunch. I ordered a pizza to go for them, and caught up half a block later. Dorian saved his share, said he wasn't hungry. Later on, I saw him pass his pizza along to Xan.

CHAPTER TWENTY-TWO

We practiced every other Saturday at Salem State after that. Our audience changed sometimes, but the players stayed the same. Hal and Faith always left together instead of meeting up for lunch either on or off-campus. The second week, I spotted them halfway up the block from me on Hawthorne Street, stepping out of the driveway between my and Izzy's houses. It became a regular occurrence.

Bubbe never mentioned their visits, not even when I asked if she'd seen them lately. They separately made the same excuse to me. Vitamins for Nin and Seth. I knew that cover story well enough, but I trusted them both. If the reason for meeting with Bubbe ever became my business, they'd tell me.

Each Sunday, I met with Dorian and Xan at the gym on campus to go over the videos. Lena ended up tagging along, watching in silence as Xan asked questions. I'd expected anger or at least bitterness over being left out. If he bore any ill will, he didn't direct it at the rest of the team or me.

Letters trickled in from colleges and universities. Faith made early acceptance at Providence Paranormal College. Kitty got an offer at Virginia Magitech, but Eston didn't. Emerson College invited Dorian to an audition, but he received an early admissions academic rejection the next day. Everybody buckled down on studying, hitting the books harder than at any time besides exams last spring. We had dinner in the lounge every night, even on weekends, wolfing down food so we'd still have time to visit the library before lights out.

Logan's guarantee at Providence Paranormal didn't make him immune. He divided his time between translating Ludovico's journals and helping all of us. I worked hard too. My college application was regular rather than early admission but that didn't make slacking a good idea.

The only one of us not scrambling was Grace. Her plans didn't include a conventional extrahuman education path. Instead, she'd applied at Salem State for a mundane business degree. They had rolling admissions, so she wouldn't get rejected there.

"Don't you want to study more magic?" I asked one night before bed. "You're so good at theory, and your lab work is awesome."

"I want to run my own business." She shrugged. "I need to learn that part as soon as possible, or I could get into legal trouble."

"You're so practical."

"And you're not? You've got a knack for coaching. If you weren't set on extraveterinary, I'd expect to see you running a team someday."

I told her about my doubts and the Coast Guard.

"You're going to rock at any of those things, but you told me years ago about taking over Bubbe's practice. And Providence Paranormal."

"I'm not so sure anymore."

"Any particular reason?"

"Logan's better with critters than I am, and look at Faith. She's going pre-med when she used to be all about poly-sci."

"You want to be a doctor then." She nodded.

"Well, maybe. If I can get in, and if people would even trust their health to an extramagus."

"They trust vampire doctors, right?" She pulled the blanket to cover her shoulder. "Anyway, there's nothing wrong with changing your major. Start with general requirements in your first semester."

"You have a point." I yawned. "I'll figure it out eventually, I guess. Thanks, Grace. Goodnight."

"Night."

The Magipsych Fair was off-campus, in the Peabody Essex Museum's Atrium, and included the other area schools. The event was packed, but not with students presenting. We weren't required to submit projects. Messing students filled most of the tables, with seven projects on display. Gallows Hill only had two. Hawthorn brought three, two from second-year students and Hal's, which involved most of the third years.

Hal asked me to help fold and stow his table. Since the very chair he sat in was his project, he didn't want to hide it. After propping it against the wall, I turned to see a group of our friends heading toward us.

"How will you display your abstract, though?" Logan scratched his head. "All the data on the enchantments you tried before getting it just right?"

"Like this." Hal grinned and pressed a button on the chair's left arm.

A magipsychic projection expanded above his head, opening like a set of curtains on a stage. The data arrayed itself neatly, with a 3-D rendered image of the chair rotating as it assembled and disassembled itself.

"Wow." I smiled. "You already won."

"If this contraption places, then everyone's a winner."

"Hey, don't call it that." Dylan frowned. "Still think he needs a proper name."

"He vetoed Ellida." Faith shrugged. "No dragons, he said."

"How about Argo?" Dorian asked. "I mean, a moving chair is sort of like a ship."

"Why not have everyone write their ideas on paper and pull one out of a hat?" Eston said.

"I like that idea." Hal nodded. "Who's got stuff to write with?"

"Me!" Logan pulled a memo pad and stub of pencil out of his blazer pocket, but the tip was broken.

"Hang on." Kitty reached into her purse and pulled out an eyeliner sharpener.

"I've got this." Grace took off her mauve cloche hat and turned it upside-down.

"Better do it fast." Lee pointed across the room. "Judges headed this way."

Everyone took a turn with the paper and pencil, scrawling their ideas, tearing paper, and dropping them into the hat. The twins hurried over to join in. Grace passed the hat to Hal, who closed his eyes and rummaged. He opened them a second before unfolding the blue and white scrap.

"Okay. Who wrote Floaty McChairface?"

Silence reigned until Faith snorted. After that, everybody laughed.

"Just kidding." Hal smiled down at the paper. "This works." He opened a panel in the right armrest and keyed the word in. "I present Neshmet."

The chair's new name appeared on the display as the judges approached.

We let Hal do most of the talking, except when one of them asked a specific question. I hung back, cleaning up paper scraps along with Hailey and Bailey.

"We didn't really do anything, Aliyah," Hailey said. "You should be up there with the rest of them."

"The only thing I contributed was moral support."

"Still more than I did." Bailey sighed. "Feels like I wasted a lot of time. Now high school's almost over."

"It's never too late." Hailey elbowed her twin. "To make up for that, I mean."

Hailey was only partly correct.

Hal's wasn't the last project the judges looked at. When they returned ten minutes later, I rejoined the group because I knew before they said a word what had happened.

"Congratulations, Team Hawthorn." A diminutive woman with freckles, laugh lines, and salt and paprika hair extended her hand. "I'm

Doctor Smith. Your Neshmet chair won. We'd like to invite you all to the state fair this spring. If you haven't applied to MIT Mr. Hawkins, please consider it. I'm in charge of the magipsychic studies department there, and the enchantments are truly impressive. I can tell your leadership and personal experience were strong elements here."

"Thank you," Hal responded. "If some of us can't be at state, is that okay?"

"As long as at least one member of your team is present and able to answer questions like the ones tonight, that's acceptable." She nodded.

"I'm there, whatever happens." Faith reached for Hal's hand.

Something flashed as their fingers intertwined. Metal. Jewelry. Rings, a pair of them. Were they engaged?

"Sounds great." Hal gazed up at her, beaming. That smile lit up his entire face.

It was almost the last time I saw him wear any sort of joyful expression.

With how busy I'd been, preparing for the Valentine's Day dance felt like almost an afterthought. Grace wasn't anywhere near as enthusiastic about it as she'd been for any of the other dances. Although she brought each of her classmates outfits again, she laid a secret on me.

"It's almost all upcycling," she confessed. "I don't have the time I used to, so I started out with pieces from the thrift store over at the Boy's and Girl's Club."

"I don't think anyone will mind, Grace." I grinned into the mirror, holding golden straps adorned with draped blue chiffon at my shoulders. The empire waist reminded me of Jane Austen novels. "It's gorgeous."

"We'll see." She jerked her thumb at the rest of the garment bags on the collapsible rack. "When everyone else gets here to pick theirs up."

Dorian showed first. He didn't stop to open the bags he took, one for him and the other for Alex.

"I totally trust your fashion sense," he said.

Similarly, Faith picked up Hal's as well as hers. She peeked. "White? Interesting choice for him."

"All Hal's accessories are red to match yours." Grace shrugged. "I didn't want him to blend in with his chair, is all."

"This is different though." Faith held up a round hammered copper disc on a comb. "I like it." She stood at the mirror, holding it up behind her head.

Kitty took one look at the beaded yellow drop-waist dress in her bag and crowed. Eston's reaction was a sedate grin as he nodded over the silver pinstripe on navy.

"We're going to look like the Roaring Twenties." Before the door closed behind them, she added, "Thanks, Grace!"

Hailey and Bailey insisted on taking theirs out of the bag. Hailey's was sunrise mauve tulle with a tea-length circle skirt in a '50s design. Bailey's was bias-cut peach satin in a draped mermaid, like a 1940s movie star.

"Rita Hayworth hairstyle, here I come." Bailey grinned. "You owe me twenty bucks, Hale."

"Worth it." Hailey beamed. "Thanks, Grace. The boat party is a casual event. I can't believe this is the last dance with one of your creations."

"Well, I'm going directly into business." She smiled back. "State of Grace dot com if you need anything at college or other occasions."

"Wow." Bailey blinked. "You've got a whole plan."

Grace only nodded as they headed out.

"What about school, though?"

"Salem State business school for me." She smiled. "I know everyone else is looking at Ivies abroad or in Rhode Island. I want to invest in my business while getting the parchment to support it. That's not in my budget, either financially or timewise."

"I hear you." I swallowed.

Logan and Dylan knocked on the door next. So much had changed since the first time we'd done the pre-dance outfitting ritual. For the better, because all of us felt so comfortable that their presence didn't derail me.

"Guys, I'm still not sure what I'm doing after graduation."

"I kind of figured." Logan patted my shoulder. "Whatever you do, I'm in your corner."

"Well, not everyone's early acceptance like Faith or Logan here. Even I don't have that all hammered down." Dylan sighed. "Whichever school gives me the biggest scholarship is where I'll end up. I'm waiting to see what I get after the big games on the common."

"It's all too much fuss if you ask me." Grace sighed. "That the adults make, I mean. The whole idea that everyone has to be a hundred percent sure what they want to do forever. There's no wrong way, Aliyah. Only the one that works best at the time."

"Yeah." I nodded. "You all have a point. Thanks, guys."

A few nights later, it was time for the dance. Hal wasn't at the top of the stairs like last time, even though we had the same formal introductions they did at Parent's Night. Instead, Faith stood alone, behind Logan and me but ahead of everyone else. Hiram Hawkins still insisted on sticking to the oldest-fashioned interpretation of school rules. I realized that there was no way around it. He had no choice but to make an exception for Hal.

His chair sat at the foot of the stairs. He rose when we got halfway down, pacing forward slowly, as though he walked on the bottom of the ocean with leaden boots instead of across a few feet of parquet in the same atmosphere as the rest of us. Hal's grin stuck to his face like festive decals on a window. The white of his suit shone like a star. She took his hand and together, they paced behind Logan and me on the dance floor.

"By request," Dorian murmured into the mic. The music started, *Never Tear Us Apart* by INXS.

Logan gazed over my shoulder, nose and eyes reddening as tears trickled down his face.

"What's wrong?" I asked.

He shook his head, unable to answer with words. Instead, he turned us and I saw everything he had.

Hal Hawkins hadn't always felt well at our dances. I'd watched him take it easy, let Faith lead, even go so far as striking poses as she moved around him. This was almost horrifyingly different.

Although he'd grown a few inches taller than her, Hal clung to Faith, leaning his head on her shoulder as if he hadn't the strength to hold it up himself. They barely even swayed. At first, I wondered why she didn't help him back to his chair and continue dancing from there. Then I saw his lips moving.

He's singing it. To Faith.

Logan and I spent the rest of the song leaning on each other's shoulders, sniffling occasionally. At the end, Faith did lead Hal back to his chair. He moved it along to the punchbowl after Grace took her arm and led her off to dance to the next song, which was *Keep Holding On* by Avril Lavigne.

"I need a minute," Logan said.

"Me too."

We started away from the punch bowl, the reason unspoken between us, how we should compose ourselves before checking on Hal.

"Turn around, Morgenstern." Coach Pickman stepped in our way, brandishing a tiny package of tissues. Coach Chen stood beside her, nodding. "Take these if you want, but don't leave him there by himself."

I nodded, taking the tissues and Logan's hand. We went back like she said and found Hal alone and in as much need of the packaged paper as we were.

"Thanks. The napkins make my skin all chapped," he managed. "I don't blame you for trying to jet."

"We were coming back," Logan said.

"Well, then." Hal managed a grin. "Would you mind getting me some punch before anything, uh, happens to it? I'm not up to getting tipsy tonight."

I ladled out three cups and passed them around.

"Don't worry." Xan stepped out of the shadows beside the DJ table. "Your liquor's at another party."

"Did you just make a Mario joke?" Logan blinked.

"Played a lot of video games over break." He turned his hand and stared at his fingernails, which were purple to match his tie. "Don't ask me where."

"I know." I nodded. "Walls and ears."

"Alexander." Mrs. Onassis stepped up beside her son, bumping into me in the process. "Come away from the rabble and dance with your old mother." She looped her arm through his, locking it into what looked more like a martial arts grip than a friendly gesture.

"Old?" Logan shook his head.

He had a point. She looked more like a college student than a woman with a recently adult son.

"Flattery will get you everywhere." She dropped Logan a wink. Then narrowed her eyes at me of course.

"Eww." Hal waved one hand in front of his nose. "Sorry, Xan."

She turned her nose up to eleven and hustled away with our favorite frenemy.

"God, I wish all the parents were like yours, Aliyah." Logan sighed.

"Even magic wishes can't do that." Andre Gauthier reached for the punch ladle. "The only way out of such trouble is through, and breaking the patterns, Mr. Pierce."

"You know an awful lot about magic wishes, Mr. Gauthier." I dropped Logan's hand and put mine on my hips. "You ought to take your advice. Like standing up to Mrs. Onassis instead of hiding from her."

"She's beyond all hope. Abandon it, ye who enter her." He chuckled. "That's uncouth, but you're all adults despite your lack of diplomas. Speaking of which." He took a metal flask out of the pocket inside his suit jacket.

"Yeah, speaking of Noah." Logan stared at Andre's nose.

"The meeting's tomorrow night. I haven't forgotten." He tipped the flask over his cup. "I will be standing up to far more substantial foes than a frustrated piggy-bank for minor Greek nobility."

Hal pointed at the wall, then his ear.

"I have my ways of dealing with that, young Hawkins." Andre grinned. "Be patient. My end of our bargain is coming to a close." He raised his cup to us as though it were made of diamond instead of plastic and sauntered off.

Logan and Hal chatted for a few moments, discussing how an undeath magus could theoretically counter both space and mind magic. I used the time to try listening on my own. So much and so many felt and sounded familiar to me. One set of vibrations stood out as strange.

I followed them, sticking to the side of the room behind the chairs for sitting and the refreshment tables. Whoever I tracked kept ahead of me, though. How they were aware, I didn't know. Unless it was another mind magus. The idea of a stranger with my barely explored ability on campus alarmed me enough to tug Professor Hawkins' sleeve.

"Sir, I, uh, sense an unfamiliar mind here."

"Thank you for telling me, Miss Morgenstern." His brow furrowed as he pressed his hand to the wall. "Please fetch Mr. Young for me."

It was easy to find Lee. He stood by the door, gazing at it because off-campus dates hadn't been approved at all this time.

"Professor Hawkins needs you."

"Why?"

"It's a security issue."

"On my way." He headed off immediately. I kept my ears open. Moments after Lee joined the headmaster, all sense of Hiram's alarm deescalated.

Logan beckoned from the edge of the dance floor. When Dorian's voice announced this was another request, I understood he'd made it. So I went directly into his arms before I even recognized *The Only Exception* by Paramore. We danced through to the first chorus, leaning with heads on each other's shoulders. He spoke.

"You deserve so much love, Aliyah," he murmured in my ear. "Like the princess finds in a fairy tale. But—" He swallowed, hands trembling against my shoulder and back. "I'm no prince. I don't know what kind of love lives in my heart because my life's mostly been a mess. But you're the first person I ever wanted to give it to."

"I love you too." I lifted my head and pulled back so he could see my face. "My life was pretty decent, but having you in it makes it a million times better."

He nodded, eyes shining.

Everything but Logan went away after that. That focus on him was almost like wearing the ear cuffs. Not only being in tune with him but attuned to each other and that song. The feeling extended to almost all the remaining music. We paused before the final song, because Hal once again rose from his chair.

Dorian played *Disenchanted* by My Chemical Romance to close out the evening. An odd choice.

Cadence had explained The Black Parade album to me ages ago since it was one of her favorites. It was about a dying young man's journey out of his life, carried away by a terminal illness. In the track *Disenchanted*, the patient looks at his life, warts and all, accepting it before laying it to rest. The lyrics fit Hal's situation so closely I wondered whether Dorian's precognitive mother had suggested he play it.

A little over halfway through, he collapsed, seizing on the floor. Dorian cut the music as of the lyrics mentioned going away, his face white as a sheet. Faith pressed her fingers to Hal's neck and her ear to his chest.

"He's not breathing!"

I joined her on the floor as we began CPR. Nurse Smith and Charles took over a moment later, but Faith never left his side. When they put him on a gurney instead of Timmy the karkinos, I knew this was the worst he'd ever been.

Minutes later, they had him out the door to meet the Emergency Medical Extrahumans at the ambulance. Mr. Fairbanks tried to stop Faith from leaving, but she held her hand up, brandishing the new ring at him. He stepped back and let her go, looking for all the world like he'd been slapped.

Maybe we all had, with an all too brutal and mundane reality.

School rules meant the rest of us had to be in our rooms with the lights out. I'm not sure any of the third-years slept.

CHAPTER TWENTY-THREE

The Trouble With Andre
Andre Gauthier

The incorrigible children had me over a barrel since October, and I wasn't sure how many of them knew it. Waiting practically all winter to finally exit such a compromising position hadn't been ideal. Although once they owed me a favor, Petra's long wait would end with a well-timed wish.

"Don't get ahead of yourself, Andre."

"Make yourself scarce, Gamila." I sighed over the collection of documents supporting the new arguments on my desk. Including one bombshell endorsement certain to ruffle feathers and tip scales. "You know the risks if they see you at the meeting."

"And you know what's at stake if you wish from afar." She shook her head. "You could get Logan's help to manage her release mundanely, you know. He's her blood kin."

"I could, but I want a sure bet." I smirked to banish the threatening sting at the corners of my eyes. "Wishes are guaranteed by the Queen herself."

"What will you do if Leo gets hold of my lamp and simply undoes it all?" She tapped her foot, reminding me of the classrooms downstairs. "Or worse, Abraham. Can you not imagine the ruin he'd cause?"

The shudder racked my body before I could hide it. The lamp's powers would have revealed my feelings to her regardless. Perhaps an empath had done a turn in it. I reached for the drawer—the small one, which most of my peers might use to store writing implements.

"You didn't need that Magifinil when you were my student." She raised an eyebrow. "And you don't now."

"I do." I sighed. "I've never gotten one over on Abe without it."

"You never faced him sober before."

"I did. Once." I closed my eyes and behind them, Petra stared at me through a van window. The kind with a wire mesh between two panes of glass.

"I wish you'd stop." She gazed down at where my fingertips met the bottle. "They're killing you."

"My work's too important to drop this crutch just yet. Sorry, Professor." I winced at the slip.

Mistakes like that could doom me and by extension the only person I ever loved in the very near future. So I pressed down and turned, shook two out, thought better of it, and added a third. The bitterness as they funneled down my gullet with water matched the vast portion of my life. Dramatic? No. More of an understatement. The pills were sweeter. So why did my hand shake as I returned the bottle to its hiding place?

I swept the documents into a folder emblazoned with the school's seal, then headed to the mirror to adjust my tie so it felt less like a noose. My old teacher had a point. I had no way of directing where her lamp went once my turn as its master ended. At least my enemies didn't know I had it.

For now. Because if the Morgenstern girl figured it out, Fairbanks might extract that information from her brain during those mandatory "training" sessions. I'd thought Logan less of a risk, which was why I'd sent Gamila to him in the library. With Hal Hawkins in the hospital, my only hope now was that shady Abe would underestimate him like he'd done with Petra ages ago.

"Shady Abe." I chuckled. "There I go, an old pot name-calling a kettle."

Silence stretched like the horizon at sea. Gamila Haddad-Hawkins was many things, but dishonest wasn't one of them. It must have galled her to her core, working for Richard Hopewell. I wasn't much of a step up in the honesty department, although she'd told me my motives were worlds above his.

As I left my quarters for the meeting that would decide Noah's educational fate for the second time, I prayed that Gamila's third and final master would be a better man than I.

I approached with caution, as one should when preparing to enter a pit of vipers. That wasn't fair to Hank Thurston and Justin Glen. Yes, I handled Georgina Dunstable with care. No ordinary Sidhe is granted an honorable discharge and return to mundanity from the Faerie Queen. Circumspection notwithstanding, standing still or even moving slowly grants advantages most overlook.

So, I found myself around the corner, eavesdropping on my enemies. Unsurprisingly, they discussed the recent nuptials of Harold Hawkins and Faith Hawkins, née Fairbanks.

"Doctor Morgenstern is a Justice of the Peace," Abe said. "She had them do all the paperwork at visits for their familiars. The ceremony, too."

"The nerve!" I could practically hear Lavinia press a hand to her breastbone.

"He must already be lawyering up to have it annulled." Leo snorted. "That's what I'd do with one of mine."

"You'll have to fight Hiram and Hector both over that." Lavinia clicked her tongue. "Because he married up."

"You're wrong as usual." Abe chuckled. "He's dying, so their future's over before it begins. If she stands to inherit this school, I'll tear the papers up. Otherwise, she's a pen stroke away from being disowned."

A scent of freshly crushed apple blossoms wafted past me in

Georgina Dunstable's wake. She noticed me but said nothing as she sailed past like a float at a homecoming parade.

"Honestly, Abraham." She stood at the corner, her back to me, fully obscuring the shadows where I stood. "They're adults. Talking annulment is rich, coming from you. Her mother hadn't even started her last year here before you had that ring on her finger, and pregnant with your eldest as she graduated besides."

"I don't recall it quite as you describe," he countered in a monotone. His attempt at denial might have worked if only Justin Glen hadn't strode right past and stepped through the opening Georgina gave him.

"I remember well enough. Let's get into the meeting and on to business that pertains to this school." He sighed. "Gossiping as though we're students is the opposite of setting a good example."

"We're still missing two," Leo protested.

"Let's wait in chambers," Georgina said. "This hallway's grown crowded, and my poor old feet can't take any more abuse."

Their grumbles receded as they shuffled away. Hank Thurston stepped out from behind the column across the hall from me. He paused before following the others through the now-closed door.

"Isn't it better to change with the times than be stuck in the past?" He didn't turn his head or give any other indication he knew I was there, although his words to an otherwise empty room told another story. Mr. Thurston might have arrived and hidden before I did. Then again, he might simply have had a senior moment.

I didn't speak until I'd counted a full minute after he'd gone in. That was no issue. The answer wasn't for him.

"Because no matter how I adapt, part of me always will be."

Abe Fairbanks rose as I entered the room, a move so out of character that I almost turned around and left. If he was on to me, all was lost. But his motivation was as mundane as the man himself. Almost.

"Finally, Gauthier's arrived. Now, who moves to adjourn?"

"Not so fast." I crossed to the empty podium and set my folder on it. "I've got business to bring before you all."

"I move to dismiss." Leo Pierce yawned.

"I move we hear it." Hank Thurston leaned forward in his seat.

"Oh, come on." Lavinia Onassis rolled her eyes. "You might not have a life outside this boardroom, but I do."

"I'm intrigued." Hank's fox familiar yipped in agreement. My interpretation, at least.

"All in favor of hearing Mr. Gauthier?" Fairbanks drawled.

Three hands rose, including mine. Justin Glen gave me a lopsided grin.

"Speak then. But keep it concise. That's a good lad." Fairbanks waved his gavel as I wished I could whack him in the teeth with it. I had four years on him, Leo two, and the other trustees even more. Abe was the most junior unless you counted Lavinia, which I tried never to do. But his family traced its association with the school back farthest. Barring a Hawkins or a Morgenstern joining the board, he'd hold that gavel.

"I address the matter of nonmagi on campus. Specifically, ones who attended in good faith while they were magi, but are no longer designated as such, for whatever reason."

"You ruled against the Morgenstern boy last year." Georgina Dunstable raised an eyebrow.

"Certain details have come to light. I think I might have made a mistake." I opened my folder. "The court ruled in *Salem v. Arnold* that both the defendant Jonah and his associate Noah Morgenstern acted under duress. It's neither young man's fault the latter got turned. Messing Academy didn't penalize Mr. Arnold, which casts Hawthorn Academy in a negative light."

"Messing Academy has no clause in their bylaws banning individuals on threat registries from the student body." Fairbanks shook his head. "You cited it last time in your statement."

"It's come to my attention, however, that both Dylan Khan and Aliyah Morgenstern are now on a similar registry. The one for extramagi. Mr. Khan's been on it for over a year. They both attend with no issue."

"I beg to differ." Lavinia Onassis snorted. "She's all but poisoned my son's mind with the wrong sort of values. If he doesn't come around, I'll have to write him out of my will."

Hank Thurston let out a papery chuckle, displaying the expression that gave him his laugh lines.

"What's so funny?" Lavinia's nostrils flared.

Fairbanks tapped his gavel. "More importantly, how is it relevant?"

"Well, the idea of a poison magus getting himself poisoned for one. And someone your age with a will, but I suppose that comes with 'old name, new money' territory." Her face went an alarming shade of crimson, but he only smiled and continued as mildly as the north wind. "As to relevance, any student will tell you she's spent most of the last two years keeping her distance from him when she wasn't busy being spirit week monarch and helping us win a championship title. So, I beg to differ."

"Where was he all winter then?" Two bright red spots bloomed high on her cheeks. The force of her words filled the air between her and me with the tang of wine. So I wasn't the only one hitting a bottle, even if mine rattled instead of sloshing.

"Your son's an adult, Lavinia. His moral choices are his own now." Georgina Dunstable shook her head. "Territory every parent must navigate someday, myself included."

"This isn't a discussion of individual character, but one of risk to the student body." I cleared my throat. "I think they, along with Noah, don't pose any. They want to get through school. Mr. Morgenstern only wants to be allowed on campus so he can study for and take final exams. Provided blood is in stock and he's verified well-fed, I believe it's in the school's best interests to make accommodations. As we do for any other student with different abilities."

Leo Pierce opened his mouth, then shut it again. He wasn't a genius like my Petra or his son. But he had half a brain under that professionally styled hair.

I outlined the logistics of blood storage and gave a list of potential testing locations, including the library as Logan had suggested, plus the auditorium and Creatives room, which could be easily isolated during exam week. I even gave them a list of accommodations used at other schools for former vampire staff, part of the selection of documents in my folder.

The last of those was the true pièce de résistance—a written agreement with my argument, penned by none other than Director-General Rockport. No sane person would expect teenagers to petition their bogeyman, so I'd done it for them. A stroke of brilliance on my part, judging by the silence in the room. Not even a paper rustled.

For one brief shining moment, I dared to believe in Camelot. Or the closest one could get to it in a boardroom full of privileged, scheming well-to-do ne'er-do-wells.

Chaos usurped, but Abe Fairbanks and his gavel guillotined its reign.

"So, what's your motion then, Gauthier?" His lip curled up in a sneer, a tell as familiar as my owl, Serapis. He'd read my intent already.

"I move we allow nonmagi, enrolled in good faith as magi before a change in registered status, to complete their educations."

"All in favor?" Abe Fairbanks gestured with the gavel. Four hands rose, and I won. But he thrust his implement forward and insisted, "All opposed?"

Lavinia, Leo, and Abe raised their hands, scowling in tandem like a series of sour freight cars. I watched Abe's knuckles whiten around the gavel and just barely refrained from blurting out everything I hated about him. Beginning with all of the literal and figurative headaches his mind magic had caused me through the years. But I rose above petty and premature stone throwing. My mission didn't end here, not by a long shot.

Justin Glen applauded like he'd seen a Broadway finale on closing night. Georgina Dunstable clapped like this was the golf course. Hank Thurston added whistles and a few hoots and hollers for good measure. Leave it to a swamp Yankee to raise a little hell. If I were his age and could have gotten away with it, I might have joined.

Thurston was life goals. If I ever made it that far.

After the door to my quarters closed, my knees buckled. Serapis hooted while flapping madly to keep me off the floor.

"Let go, old friend." I waved him away, but he didn't heed me. We'd end up on the floor together. Wiry brown arms caught me under the shoulders, carrying with them the aroma of oranges. It was Gamila lowering me to the floor safely.

"Bucket," I managed. Serapis dropped it in front of me.

The next thing out of my mouth was far more colorful but less eloquent. A side-effect I'd dealt with for the past four years as I'd homed in on my chance to rescue Petra. After I'd done that, I could quit. Once this nausea passed, I'd finish the remnants of my promise to the children and sleep the rest of Magifinil's nasty aftermath off.

Our quarters had a sitting room with a water closet off one corner. The moment my legs cooperated, I headed there, wastebasket under my arm. After washing it and myself up, I went back to the desk and jotted a note off to Noah Morgenstern, care of his sister here on campus. A formal address, a brief statement of the new policy, and a cool but firm closing.

As a Gauthier, duty required my adherence to our traditional manners. On paper, at least. If someone intercepted it, the note was unimpeachably bland.

"Now I can drop dead." I pushed the envelope through the slot leading to the pneumatic system. All my strength left with it, dropping off my body like a cast-off dressing gown.

"What about Petra?" Gamila tapped her foot against the hardwood.

I rose. Too quickly. "Sarcasm—" My knees buckled, and I swallowed the start of her name. "'Mila."

"Don't call me that." She caught me again.

"Thought I knew 'bout lamps." My face felt like rubber. "How djinn work."

"You know well enough now we're not as advertised." She got under my arm somehow.

"Hope a kid gets your lamp even if it's that Alexanax. Xandralexa." I sobbed. "You know."

"I do." A twist of her hair brushed against my cheek.

The void behind the drug yawned beneath me. I dangled from Gamila's shoulder like an empty rucksack. Before finding her lamp, I used to tumble into bed after the Magifinil wore off. Sometimes I'd miss and wake on the floor, face imprinted with the grain of whatever cheap carpet the current motel employed.

After "acquiring" the lamp via unwitting vampiric help from a certain high-security magical evidence locker, my awakenings, however rude, always occurred in a bed. Djinn had their own will to an extent. As still as I'd stood since age eighteen, as underhanded as I'd become when I overheard Hiram Hawkins mention his better half's lamp being in Rhode Island, as shipwrecked as I was in the storm of addiction and this quest, my old teacher was there.

Maybe she missed her son. Or being in the lamp, in service to a fallible queen and the man who desired her throne, had tempered her. Perhaps she was simply, at the core, kinder than I'd remembered her to be. Whatever the reason, gratitude leaked from my eyes, dropping ahead of me into the darkness of sleep.

CHAPTER TWENTY-FOUR

I tucked the envelope from my mail slot into my blazer pocket, totally preoccupied.

Faith and Hal hadn't been at breakfast Sunday morning after the dance or anywhere on campus the rest of that day. I'd expected them back on Monday morning, which was the usual course of events whenever Hal went to the hospital on the weekend in non-emergency situations.

However, the booth I usually shared with them and Logan stood empty. Before I could figure out whether to sit in it alone or join one of the other tables, a throat cleared behind me. I turned to see Professor Susan DeBeer. Dylan stood at her elbow, shifting his weight from one foot to the other.

"Miss Morgenstern, a moment of your time, please?"

"Uh, sure." I gestured at the booth. I'd made loads of good memories there since first year, despite all the chaos and pain. It couldn't hurt to have what might be an uncomfortable conversation someplace familiar. "Works for Bubbe anyway."

If Professor DeBeer noticed I'd made a disconnected comment, she took it in stride as she sat on one side of the booth. Dylan and I got on the bench across from her. I looked up, hoping to see Ember, but she hadn't come out of the nest since she'd laid her eggs. I'd have worried, but I sensed her contentedness through our bond. Gale always managed to get food for them both.

"Mr. Khan. Miss Morgenstern. I wanted to set things right between us. Until Hal's back, all of you from Professor Hawkins' class are with me for the morning lecture. Last year, I said some awful things about extramagi. I was wrong, and I'm sorry."

If I'd been alone, I'd have told her it wasn't a big deal. That was true for me, but not Dylan. I sensed something from him, a note of discord.

"You've had, hm." Dylan thrummed his fingers against the table. "Just over a year to speak up about it. And yeah, I get why now. It's an emergency. There's one thing important to me. How do you feel about what you said?"

She hung her head. "Like a total piece of shite." She looked up. "So where do we go from here? You're welcome in my classroom with the rest of the students in your section, but I understand if you're worried about unfair treatment. So, I've spoken to the headmaster and the Ashfords. They've agreed to let you have study hall at the library instead."

Dylan blinked. "No." He shook his head, then glanced at me. "Not for me, at least. I want to be with my classmates."

"Me too." I fought the impulse to reach across the table and take her hand, as Bubbe did for anyone sitting opposite her. "The third-years are a team. We've been through a lot and mostly made it by sticking together."

Professor DeBeer's nose reddened, along with her eyes. She sniffled, then nodded. Somehow, I understood she was thinking about her old frenemy, Professor Luciano.

Maybe she's born with it. Maybe it's mind magic.

"I'll see you both in class by the bell, then." She slid across the bench on her side of the booth, rose, and walked away more stiffly than I'd ever seen her move.

"Well, that was awkward." I sighed.

"But it had to happen." Dylan shook his head, got up, then gestured at the food line. "Wish it'd been sooner, but better late than never."

"You sound like Noah." I got up and followed him.

"Thanks."

"Wow." I chuckled. "You two spending a lot of time together?" It was the closest I'd gotten to asking whether he'd said anything about his feelings.

"Our practice and your practice, but it's all business." He paused at the hot bar to load scrambled eggs and sausages on his plate. "Or I should say, he's all business."

"Sounds about right for him." Cereal clinked into my bowl from the dispenser. "You, not so much."

"Well, it's not for lack of trying. I think he's avoiding me. Or the topic. Or both." He shrugged. "Whatever. Anyway, where do we sit?"

Before I could answer, Logan waved us over to where he sat with Grace, Kitty, and Eston. "We have lecture all together. And I'm coming with you this afternoon, Aliyah," he said.

"Yeah, DeBeer um, told us," I said. "Thanks."

"Does anyone know what happened?" Kitty asked. "With Hal, I mean. Faith never came home last night."

"No." I shook my head. "Beyond that it's his illness."

"This isn't like his other flares though," Eston pointed out. "Seizures. We're all worried about him."

"Well, Professor DeBeer said we're only joining you for the morning lecture," I replied. "Professor Hawkins is supposed to be back in the afternoon." I gasped when I remembered the mail I'd picked up earlier. "Wait. Maybe there's news."

Everyone waited as I ripped the envelope open. It wasn't from our absent friends or about them. No less important, but more personal than I'd expected.

"What's it say?" Grace leaned forward.

"It's from a trustee." I shook my head. "For Noah."

"Oh." Grace blinked. "I'd forgotten their meeting was last night."

"What's it say?"

"It pertains to a couple of us, so I'll read it." I cleared my throat. "To

287

Mr. Noah Morgenstern, greetings. I write to inform you that Hawthorn Academy has altered its bylaws and now allows nonmagi, enrolled in good faith as magi before a change in registered status, to complete their educations. As this decision affects your situation directly, I thought it proper to send news. Please contact the headmaster to discuss arrangements and accommodations at your earliest convenience. Regards, Andre Gauthier, Esquire."

"Wow." Dylan's mouth dropped open. "He'll be so happy."

"Why don't you take a walk off campus after Lab and deliver it to him? I'll be busy." I passed the note to him.

"Sure." He beamed.

The bell ending breakfast rang. We brought our plates to the dishwashing station and headed to lecture, which passed peacefully enough. Creatives, lunch, gym, and our hour in the library went by. Our section stood outside the lab, waiting, watching, and hoping.

The bell rang so we filed into the room without Professor Hawkins. Only Logan, Dylan, Dorian, and me.

"It's giving me the creeps." Dylan waved a hand at the front of the room.

"Yeah, major goose over grave vibes for me too." Dorian walked toward the perch Julia usually sat on, but she didn't budge from his shoulder. "What gives, lady J?"

"She doesn't like the room being so empty." Logan reached down and scooped Doris up in his arms. "Neither of them do."

"I miss Ember." I sighed.

"It's bad timing, for sure, having our critters off keeping house." Dylan shrugged. "What can we do?"

"Not much."

Someone knocked on the door, and we jumped. Before any of us could answer, it opened and revealed Georgina Dunstable.

"I'm here to audit your class."

"I'd afraid it's a bit sparse at the moment." Dorian bowed his head. "And our professor's running late."

"I'm aware." Instead of settling down in the back of the room as usual for auditing trustees, Miss Dunstable took a seat at the front although not behind the teacher's bench. "I heard you were continuing an examination of faerie artifacts, and that's my favorite subject."

"That's right." Logan nodded. "We'll have to wait for the professor. He's the one with access to the materials."

"Why not tell me what you learned last time, then?"

"Odd for a trustee." Dylan put his hand over his mouth. "Oops."

"I'll take that as a compliment, Mr. Khan, all things considered." Her pale lips turned up at the corners. "Now, what did you look at on Friday?"

Dorian rattled off a list of gnome treasures, mundane items they'd won, and brought back to the Under where they got infused with magical energy.

"The last one we saw, the gnome used as teeth." Dorian pointed at his. "Because they don't have any to begin with. They looked new and old at the same time. It was weird, and I couldn't figure out why."

"I looked that up in the library Friday night." Logan grinned. "It's gnomish time magic. They can move ahead or back, but only tiny amounts of time. It's fascinating."

"And college-level study stuff." Dylan chuckled. "Smartypants."

"What else?" Miss Dunstable asked.

"Do you mind if I draw it?" Logan stood by the magipsychic screen, hand hovering over the stylus. "There's a replica but I can't find it in the box."

"Not at all."

Logan drew an old brass oil lamp on the board. Miss Dunstable wore that slight grin the entire time, which reminded me more of *Lady with an Ermine* than the *Mona Lisa*.

"Excellent work, Mr. Pierce. Although they aren't all bronze.. Did Professor Hawkins tell you how to identify the genuine article?"

That's a leading question if I ever heard one.

"No." I shook my head. "He said they're extremely difficult to identify. Is it important for us to know?"

"Indubitably." She nodded. "I think you'd have little trouble, Miss Morgenstern. Because—"

"The lamp has a mind attached to it!" Logan dropped the stylus and waved his hands. "And she's got—"

"Exactly." Miss Dunstable put a finger over her lips, then beckoned us all closer. "One other important fact about magic lamps is this. Once a holder makes the last wish, the lamp comes unstuck in space. It's impossible for any psychic, faerie, or even a dragon to know where it is until it lands."

"What about magi?"

"It takes a rare element and an even more obscure talent amongst those to track a lamp with any degree of accuracy. Or previous mastery. But that's a moot point, because former masters are exempt from taking another round of wishes. I daresay I've got nothing else to speak of on this subject here."

"Oh." Logan put his hand to his cheek. "Wow, Miss Dunstable, that was amazing."

The rest of us nodded. Maybe the odd vibes we'd gotten on arrival had something to do with this because it seemed downright destined, like something Izzy might have read in her cards.

"Well, it looks like my class has been in good hands." Professor Hawkins walked around our little cluster, taking the long way to the business end of his lab bench.

"Your students are quite astute, Hector." She smiled. "They gave me a review of all you taught on Friday."

"Excellent." He clapped his hands, the signal for us all to get back to our benches. The guys did, but I remained.

"Professor?" I swallowed. "I'm sorry, and I don't want to waste time. But we're all worried about Hal—"

"I've got a statement from him to read before we begin."

"Thanks, Professor." I walked back to sit with Logan, hoping my knees didn't wobble too much. I reached into my bag and brought the box with the ear cuffs out, which I was supposed to wear in Lab. Professor Hawkins shook his head, and I put them back.

He pulled a piece of paper out of his jacket pocket, unfolded it, and cleared his throat.

"Hal writes, 'I miss panini and beverage roulette. Faith's badgering the nurses so they gave me the good Jell-O. I'll be back in time for dinner on Monday. Dylan, don't eat all the chicken parm. Dorian, don't drink all the root beer. Aliyah, drink a smoothie before running laps. Logan, I want more Ludovico translations so get ready. Tell Lee that Nin needs about ten playdates with Scratch. Tell Grace her blanket's way warmer than anything they've got in this hospital, and I look like a fashion god thanks to her. You all make this illness suck less than it has to. See you soon.'"

The entire room seemed to exhale, including Doris and Julia, who finally went to the familiar's area while I put my earcuffs on. For a while, all we thought about were artifacts from faerie—specifically, the feathers of the three mystical birds. One was the Alkonost, a rainbow-plumed songbird connected to the Queen. The second was the Gamayun, a gray-feathered hunter, neutral and able to act as a go-between for the monarchs in the Under and this world. Last was the Sirin, a contrary corvid in service to the King. Each feather was unique, and who could use them was extremely limited.

"You'll likely never see the Alkonost's or the Gamayun's feathers." Professor Hawkins gestured at the magipsychic screen displaying images of them in 3D. "Can any of you tell me why that is?"

"They're bonded already," I replied. "The Gamayun since before I was born, and the Alkonost more recently."

"Correct." The professor nodded. "The Sirin's feather is still somewhere in one of the worlds."

"Shouldn't the monarchs be searching for it almost constantly?" Dylan asked. "Now that they're united, I mean. It would have unbalanced power before that."

"You'd think so, Mr. Khan." Professor Hawkins nodded at Miss Dunstable. "I'm not well-versed in how the monarchs operate, but perhaps our guest can do the subject more justice than I?"

"You already gave the correct answer, Hector." She nodded. "It bears repeating. Their usage is extremely limited. The monarchs believe in patterns of coincidence, that it's impossible for the feathers to fall into the wrong hands."

The bell rang. I packed my things up, mentally steeling myself for another mind magic session with Mr. Fairbanks. I paced through the halls with Logan, wishing the whole way there that I had the Faerie Queen's faith in coincidence, that somehow I'd be in the right place at the right time. No matter how risky it seemed at the moment.

Georgina Dunstable managed it. She took her chance to drop information you've sought all year.

Now I've got to keep everything she said out of Mr. Fairbanks' head. Thanks, inside voice.

You're welcome, it sang.

I stopped before turning the corner toward the offices and faced my boyfriend.

"Logan, are you going to be safe in there?" I jerked my thumb over my shoulder.

"Don't worry." He patted his translation notebook, which he'd tucked under one arm. "Ludovico's keeping me company, but not his stuff on extramagi. He went on a tangent about merfolk. Maybe it'll cheer Cadence up at practice this weekend."

"Good idea." I nodded. "Well, let's go then."

Mr. Fairbanks was on the phone when we walked in. The smile on his face was easy, relaxed, and made me profoundly uncomfortable. He spoke to the person on the other end of the line after I put the box with my ear cuffs on his desk.

"No need for that disciplinary hearing, Hiram. She's arrived." I froze, and he chuckled. "No, I don't expect I will call again. Visit your grandson. This campus is in good hands." He hung up.

I dropped into the seat behind me as heavily as the handset on the phone's base. Behind me, the rustling sound of notebook pages shook me loose from shock's vise-grip. Anger ignited in my chest. Mr. Fairbanks had been about to set my expulsion in motion, all because I'd been less than a minute late walking through the door.

"Something wrong, Miss Morgenstern?"

"I wasn't late," I blurted.

"Ten more seconds and you would have been."

He didn't expect you to show at all. Listen and learn.

I narrowed my eyes and focused, staring at his face. I ignored everything else, even something waving on the desk near where I'd rested my hand. Paper? No. I couldn't let whatever it was distract me now. Concentration had rewards if only I could manage it.

For the first time in all our mind magic sessions, I heard something coming from his. A sing-song set of piano chords, tinny and in a minor key. Like a taunt. My anger grew, but I treated it like fire magic, using the same banishing technique as in Lab or on the Bishop's Row court but turned inward. It worked. Although I imagined something crawling over my hand.

Nice job. Go farther.

It felt unusually forceful, and direct compliments weren't usually part of its repertoire. However, I trusted my inside voice as much as any of my friends. So I kept up the work of banishing, thinking back to my first year in the lab, the day I'd banished a literal inferno. I heard something else under that music coming from Mr. Fairbanks. A sound of scattering gravel, how it flies when a bike goes out from under its rider. Knee-jerk fear and confusion. From the bogeyman trustee?

His eyes widened. Instead of rising and insisting I leave or putting on some show of feather-ruffling bravado, Mr. Fairbanks did something much worse.

He smiled. It lit his face, genuine, like a child unwrapping the biggest of his birthday gifts.

The voice spoke in its usual tone instead of the strange one from moments ago. For the first time since its arrival, I couldn't make it out.

Over-banishing with fire chilled me. Over-banishing with mind magic did something similar—a sense of being outside myself, observing this scene from an impossible vantage point. I sat straight as an arrow, back not touching the chair, eyes no longer narrowed or intense. I gazed at Mr. Fairbanks instead, as I might with a solution in Lab. Like he was an inanimate object, not a person, or even an animal, magical or otherwise. Everything in the room seemed matchstick-frail and inconsequential. Like kindling, fuel to burn. Disposable. It reminded me of something. But what?

Like Temperance with Alex last year. Except that girl only copied the father she idolized. She wasn't the genuine article, couldn't be, without mind magic. You, on the other hand... Well. He must have a motive for insisting on these sessions with you of all people.

What if I toppled like the bike I'd imagined? Lost not balance, but empathy? Connecting was easy, but caring went deeper. It was *hard*. Empathy took work. Practice. And it left me open to pain whenever someone I cared for got hurt.

Just like that, I understood. Detachment, this being above and slightly to the side of everything, felt way too comfortable.

Every extramagus stereotype I'd rebelled against, every personal truth I'd fought to affirm in my first year and struggled to keep hold of in the second, flashed before my eyes. Here I was, about to lose it all and become someone I never wanted to be, just like that.

That slight discordance coming off Mr. Fairbanks moved up and sharpened. Or maybe my frequency flattened. Either way, we began meeting in the middle.

Logan hummed, one of his habits while reading. Not just any random tune, but our song. From the dance.

It pulled me back, almost. That crawling sensation on my hand intensified.

My eyes stung, and I fought to ride the wave of emotion that surged in the heart I'd detached from. Doris leaped into my lap and lay on her side. From above and slightly to the left I watched the tip of her tail flick, sea-green eyes fixed on the desk. On my hand. I couldn't make it out from that detached vantage. I wanted to know what it was.

A familiar shriek sounded outside the door. Something familiar. *My* familiar.

Ember, who hadn't moved from her nest in months, clawed at the doorknob outside. A futile exercise for a creature without opposable thumbs.

Logan twisted the knob. Mr. Fairbanks glared at him, lip curling up as he barked out a command.

"Stop!"

"No, sir." Logan shook his head. "I won't."

"Your father will hear about this."

"Fine." He pushed the door open while glancing down and to the right.

The next moment, a skinny, stinky dragonet entangled herself in my hair. My hand touched her flank, and we connected. I connected back to myself. Then burst into tears. The insect on my hand scuttled away in a flash of metallic green and blue. I didn't have time to consider the scarab because it hurt.

People sit the wrong way and end up with a foot, hand, even an entire arm or leg falling asleep. Coming back felt like that turned up to eleven, except for brain instead of body. If that makes any sense.

Ember *peeped* and I sobbed. She needed a bath and oil for her scales, her talons trimmed and filed. Was this typical for nesting dragonets, normal as they waited for eggs to hatch? I couldn't recall, but I untangled her from my hair and cuddled her, stench and all.

"Get out." I looked up to find Mr. Fairbanks out of his seat and pointing at the door. "Find someone else to attend next time, Miss Morgenstern. Mr. Pierce is no longer welcome in my office."

I stood, Doris launching herself from my lap just in time. Logan and I left in such a hurry that I forgot the ear cuffs in their box on his desk. Doris remembered. When I turned around at the end of the hall, hellbent on walking back into the lion's den to fetch them, I saw the cat trotting after us with the box in her mouth. She dropped it at Logan's feet like it was a mouse she'd killed for him.

"Thanks." He bent to scratch her behind the ears with one hand and pick up the box with the other.

"I should thank all three of you." I wrinkled my nose. "Ember, you want a bath, girl?"

"Peep." She craned her neck, turning her head back toward her nest in the eaves of the lobby.

"Brooding box wasn't your thing, huh?" I chuckled. "I get it. I, too, am no typical nester. Go on, but I'm talking to Dorian. Maybe Julia can bring you a food basket. Thanks for the rescue." I nodded at Doris and Logan. "All three of you."

"Peep!" She rubbed her cheek against mine, then took off, winging up and away.

A moment after she entered the shadows up there, a pair of birds glided out and down. I blinked.

"Are those the Overton's pigeons?"

"Yeah." Logan nodded. "I heard Ember calling them before she got to the door. They, uh, babysat I guess."

"I'd better go thank them, and the twins too."

"Maybe wash up first." He reached toward my hair. As he withdrew his hand, something pulled. "See?"

He held a desiccated scrap of orange peel. At least, I think it came from an orange. It was a little green around the edges.

We walked to the stairs. At dinner, I asked for two slices of German chocolate cake and brought the twins their favorite dessert. Dorian said Julia would send up whatever food I brought in a basket. We sat, most of us picking at our food and watching the door.

Halfway through the meal, Hal's chair glided into the dining hall with Faith pacing slowly alongside. She looked like she hadn't slept. He seemed stretched thin, duller than Ember's scales earlier.

All the third-years got up. Once everyone else noticed, the entire room gave him the same welcome. I'm not sure who started clapping, but it wasn't important because Hal brightened up immediately.

Not for the last time, I hoped.

CHAPTER TWENTY-FIVE

Hal made it to my next meetings with Mr. Fairbanks, and I didn't have a repeat dissociative experience. After talking the whole thing over with Ms. Khan, I had a word for the feeling. I asked her if it meant I needed more help, maybe medication.

"It's hard to tell." She shook her head. "It's unlikely unless that starts happening more frequently."

"Could it have come from him, then? Like, maybe I picked up on something wrong with him with my magic? I mean, if Mr. Fairbanks needs help—"

"Then it's up to him to seek it." She cleared her throat. "And not a subject I'm at liberty to discuss."

"I get it."

Before leaving her office, I promised to contact her right away if I dissociated again. It was a relief to get back to the routine of school, even if I still felt like the worst wasn't over. How could it be, with what Logan and I overheard during winter break? Aside from my incident, the trustees hadn't done a thing besides approve Noah's return for exams. It was all too easy to get complacent. Faith remained vigilant.

"I don't buy it for a minute," she said in the baths Wednesday night. "They're waiting for the right moment."

"If only we had some way of knowing when that was." I winced. "Although it feels like I should have that figured out by now."

"I know mind magic doesn't work like telepathy, Aliyah." She sighed. "Sorry if that sounded like a blame game."

"It didn't."

"I know my father's tells. He knows I'm watching him." She shook her head. "He's in a holding pattern. Like he's waiting for something."

"There are three of them, working together. What if he's waiting for Leo or Lavinia to do something first?"

"Maybe it's Lavinia, then." Faith shrugged. "She's like a cat in a room full of rocking chairs."

"She's already ruining Xan's life though." I paddled my feet in the water. "Her plots are all about keeping a grip on him."

"And magisupremacy, don't forget that." Faith sighed. "I saw her in town last Sunday, at some sort of ladies-who-lunch affair at a cafe on the Wharf. Mrs. Merlini was there too, with Crow hovering around. So I went in and ordered a coffee."

"Did you hear something?"

"No, only saw them shake hands. Crow went for a walk with Xan's mom afterward." Faith grimaced. "On the way out, I saw a pamphlet they'd left on the table. Natural Order propaganda."

"I forget what they are."

"It's like a bigotry pyramid scheme. Magi on top, predatory shifters as enforcers, psychics and the other shifters rank-and-file. They favor enslaving mundanes."

"And vampires?"

"Slain."

"What about Faeries?"

"Sealed in the Under."

"Ugh."

"You think Mrs. Merlini buys it?

"I've got no idea." I shrugged. "She had Crow out and about last year, threatening business owners. The idea of either of them working with Lavinia isn't comforting."

"Hmm. What was that you heard Leo say again?" She snapped her fingers, trying to remember. "The lawyering up thing he's trying."

"Conservatorship."

She shivered although the water was warm.

"What is it?"

"That's big money talk for total control. Like what Lavinia's doing turned up to eleven. Basically, like having Logan declared a child for the rest of his life."

"How is that legal?"

"It's not, with how well Logan's doing here and that scholarship to PPC. So it sounds scary but pulling it off is a long shot. A doctor would have to declare him incompetent or a danger to himself. Or he'd have to admit it himself. How likely is Logan Pierce to have a mental breakdown?"

I got into the pool without answering because I didn't like the direction my mind went. Logan wasn't my rock. He was my ocean. Seas got tossed under the right conditions. For most of his life, his parents had used that against him. He'd grown and become more confident. Was it enough?

Faith let me have my silence during our swim. After we were in pajamas, she stopped me before opening the door to the hall. Light flashed off the band of metal on her left hand before she wrapped her arms around me.

"Sometimes there's nothing you can do," she said in my ear. "You can't see it coming or fight the battle for him. But it helps to believe, even if he's losing."

I hugged her back, understanding. She was talking about Hal, not just Logan. When she pulled away, the shoulder of my robe was damp with her tears.

We studied at the cafe the next night, sitting in pairs, flipping through flashcards Dorian had made.

"Thanks, these really help," Hal told him.

"That's major praise, coming from one of you geniuses."

"You're no slouch yourself." Hal waved a card. "I didn't think of this. You did. We'd be squinting at lists in our notebooks if it wasn't for you."

"I only made them because I need serious help studying." Dorian snorted. "You all fell for my evil plan. Muahaha!"

"Would you just take the compliment, already?" Faith chuckled. "You're almost as bad as I am with that stuff."

"Okay, fine." He held his hands up. "Thanks, then."

After the study session, I felt a lot better about using so much of my time on the extra Bishop's Row practice. Until an announcement over the PA gave me an enormous shock.

"Aliyah Morgenstern, Dylan Khan, and Hal Hawkins, report to the infirmary."

The guys went along, but before I left, I glanced through the café and counted all my friends. Nobody was missing. On the way into the lobby, I looked up at Ember's nest. She and Gale were present and accounted for too. I jogged ahead of Hal and Dylan, still unable to banish my sense of fear. Too much had gone wrong.

"Noah!" I gasped and ran down the ramp and into the waiting room.

He sat there, reading a magazine with a bunch of devices attached to his arms and head, grinning up at me.

"You should see the look on your face. Seriously."

"It's not funny." I put my hands on my hips.

"Or my fault. I'm getting the required medical tests I need before moving on campus for exams." He gestured at one of the treatment rooms. "The folks who called you are in there."

I walked in to find Doctor Klein and Stephanie Hawkins with Nurse Smith. They sat looking over an open file. One of the bedside tables held a box of lancets and band-aids. A stack of oversized index cards stood beside them.

"What's all this?"

"It's the Rapid Extrahuman Typing test I asked your help with months ago." Dr. Klein grinned. "I'm testing its efficacy, and since we did your typing with the longer form method, I hoped you'd all consent to take the RET."

"I'll take it, Grandma. I have to ask something before we start," Hal said. "Why are you here, Mom? Why do you care about identifying extrahumans now?"

"I saw that after the fact." She shrugged and sighed at the end. "My —um, the doctor sent letters. About her work, how life-or-death it is. I made so many mistakes. Ones that hurt you. I can't take them back. Maybe it's too little and too late. You're the only one who can decide that. But I want to do better going forward. Say the word, and I'll leave until you've finished here."

"Oh, Mom." Hal sniffled and held his arms out. "I forgive you."

They embraced like they hadn't seen each other for a hundred years. Or wouldn't meet again for twice as long. There wasn't a dry eye in that room.

Using the lancets and smearing blood from our fingertips along rows of marked circles on the cards felt like an afterthought. In minutes, the cards with the extrahuman typing had results. Dr. Klein did one herself, which came up black on the V for vampires. Stephanie's turned pink under D for dhampyr. We all came up purple in the spot marked M for magus. Hal's was a faint thistle, Dylan's royal, and mine nearly indigo.

"The darker the purple, the more magic in your blood at the time of testing," Dr. Klein advised. "Now, let's check element typing."

As expected, my card came up purple for solar, fire, and mind. Dylan's had air and ice. Hal's made everyone besides Dr. Klein gasp. The letter A had appeared beside the S for space magic. Dr. Klein consulted her folder.

"It looks like you've got space affinity, Hal."

"How?" He shook his head. "I don't understand. I thought magiglobular anemia prevented affinities. And anyway, I was never able to dowse or any of that affinity stuff."

"Possibly, this is a side effect of your infusions." Dr. Klein said. "The magic they give you is raw, neutral as far as elements go. So your blood processes it according to your magical potential. Because the Under gives form to our truest selves, this has been seen in other cases."

"It makes sense." Nurse Smith nodded. "Somewhere way back, a Hawkins must have had space affinity. Likely before the school existed. Because this campus couldn't have been built without mapping the space between worlds. Something only a magus with space affinity could do."

Hal asked no more questions. But we'd all heard of affinities. Logan's ability to understand critters was one example. Extra talents were well documented, even if they were fairly rare. Which might be why I saw Hal in the library later, reading a book about dowsing.

I almost asked him about it, curious what he meant to do with the knowledge or the talent if he managed to use it. But he yawned. After he checked the book out, I helped him back to the dorm instead.

Hal didn't come with us to the last off-campus practice before the Bishop's Row tournament at Salem Common, but he saw us off. In his lap sat a stack of notebooks, including one of Logan's. His translations from Ludovico's journal.

"Are you sure you don't want to take a walk with us?" Faith asked.

"I'm proofreading my final documentation for the chair. I want everything perfect when it goes to state after exams." He tapped the library book and Logan's notebook, which he must have borrowed. "And doing a little extra reading on a new topic of interest."

"Sounds cool." I nodded. Logan grinned.

Faith gave him a hug and a kiss goodbye, and we headed out. As soon as the door closed behind us, Logan tugged my sleeve.

"There's affinity stuff in there," Logan said. "He says he needs to learn it fast."

"Bet he has a plan for it, then."

"I'm sure we'll see. He didn't want to talk about it on campus."

As we walked down the street, I shook my head, the ghost of a smile haunting my lips. We'd all come a long way on this journey through high school. At one point, I'd imagined we'd stop learning and set aside picking up new knowledge to review for finals.

However, learning had transformed from something we had to do into an essential part of life as magi. One that would continue long after graduation.

Practice proceeded in the usual way, with Lynn studying way up in the bleachers. Bobby had a second watcher with him this time. A man, younger than Hank Thurston but older than Andre Gauthier. He wore a purple knit cap on a head that might otherwise be bald. Bushy gray eyebrows matched a goatee that framed a lopsided grin.

The two of them sat through our entire practice and watched most of it. The newcomer seemed to doze off a few times. On one of our breaks, I stood on the sidelines peering at him while scratching my head.

"You know what he's doing, right?" Izzy held a cup of water out to me.

"Thanks." I gulped some down. "No, I don't."

"Projection."

"So he's foretelling our plays?"

"No. The out of body kind."

"Oh." My mind drew blanks. Cadence trotted over.

"Hey, what's Nate Watkins doing here?"

"I don't know." I shrugged. "Is he important or something?"

"He's a pretty big deal at Providence Paranormal College."

"Maybe he's visiting Bobby then." I shrugged. "He graduated from there."

"Doesn't explain why he's projecting during our practice, though." Izzy shook her head.

"Want me to go ask, Iz?" I patted her shoulder. "Is it like a bad vibe or something?"

"No. Nothing bad. Just curiosity and my cards are in the locker room."

"Okay."

Break ended and we finished our practice. I meant to go over and introduce myself after stowing all the equipment, but by the time we'd done that, Mr. Watkins was gone. Most of the others went home or to their respective campuses. Cadence, Izzy, and I stayed out. We ordered pizza to go at Engine House. While waiting, Izzy pulled cards and said we'd hear more about Mr. Watkins soon. We headed back to Noah's apartment, where he, Elanor, Brianna, and Arick sat playing Mario Kart.

Dylan sat on a stool nearby, strumming his guitar, not even stopping for lunch like the rest of us. I raised an eyebrow at him, but he shook his head. Noah got a mug of blood from the fridge and hovered nearby as we wolfed down delicious pizza. We chatted about the upcoming tournament next week and the big party and dance afterward.

"I can't believe they had enough in the budget to charter a harbor cruise!" Cadence glanced at Arick, who blushed. "It'll be so much fun."

"Are you going to make it, Noah?" Brianna asked. "Elanor already has permission to go as my date."

"I know." He sighed and shook his head. "I'm technically a student at Hawthorn for cram and exam the week after, but not allowed until then on my own. So the headmaster said I need an escort for the cruise."

"I'll do it." Dylan plucked a string and busied himself with tuning it. "If you haven't already got someone that is."

Noah blinked. He glanced at me, and at first, I didn't understand why.

He wants permission.

Finally, it all made sense why Noah had given Dylan the cold shoulder for so long. He didn't want to hurt me. Although he knew I'd meshed with Logan, my brother understood that our relationship wasn't exactly conventional.

So I nodded, smiled, then jerked my thumb at Dylan, who still avoided looking at anyone or anything in the room besides his guitar. Noah crossed the room in three long strides.

"I'd be honored to have your company, Dylan Khan." He smiled down. "Thank you."

I glanced up, wishing Ember and Gale were there to peep and crow about it. Lotan made up for it by swaying happily on Noah's shoulder. Izzy pulled a card out of her bag and shook her head. Before I could ask about it, my phone beeped. I took one look at the message and groaned at my mistake.

"Gotta go, guys." I tucked the phone away and headed for the door. "I'm late to go over the practice recordings with Xan."

I left in a chorus of "see you later."

CHAPTER TWENTY-SIX

The next week passed less eventfully than the one before. Even with an enormous game ahead, one where there'd be scouts from colleges and universities all over the world, I felt oddly calm. As I sat in the café that Friday night, I realized I wasn't alone.

"This is like being in the eye of a storm." Lee wrapped his hands around his mug of cocoa. "Resting, waiting for the wind to pick us up again, and no idea where we'll land when it's over."

"Wow, that's poetry." I intended to chuckle but it came out almost like a sob.

"You don't know where you're going either?" He blinked.

"Not a clue." I sighed. "No offers from any schools. Maybe I'll end up in the Coast Guard like my great uncle."

"I hadn't thought of enlisting." Lee leaned his cheek on his hand. "Visa might be a problem."

"You want to stay here?" I stirred my tea. "I always imagined you going to university in Europe or something."

"If I can't stay here, I'd rather go home." He sighed. "My parents worked so hard to give me a way out. They say there's no future for a magus in rural China, but the only other place that feels like home is with Izzy."

"She's in at Providence Paranormal."

"I know, like Logan. And I'm not, like you."

"Your only chance is getting scouted at the game, huh?"

"Pretty much."

"Save a seat on the college rejection ship." Dorian sat with a green smoothie, Julia perched sleepily on his shoulder. "The drawer in my desk is stuffed full of letters that say no. Coast-to-coast tour, even."

"Ditto. Let's ask Grace to make us a commemorative quilt out of those papers."

"Sorry, I burned mine." I held my hand out, palm up, and conjured a tiny flame. "Accidentally on purpose."

We laughed because the alternative was worse. Maybe that storm Lee mentioned earlier would wash something better ashore.

The next day, I couldn't eat. However, playing on an empty stomach with my history of collapsing was madness. I got a coconut smoothie with the works from the café and took it back to my room. After drinking it, I put my uniform on. The common had a tent, wards, and special transport to shield Messing's vampire players from the sun, but nowhere for us to change clothes. I had some time to think over strategy alone since Grace was still downstairs at the dining hall.

It wouldn't matter which team won. Winning boosted prospects in most mundane sports, but Bishop's Row at the college level was so new, the scouts simply wanted to see us play. So, I'd planned everything around showcasing the players I thought needed to be seen. Until last night, I hadn't known Lee's situation.

Grace and Lena were so solid together on defense. If I sat either of them, we might lose too quickly to show off. That left Faith or me at mid. Faith already agreed to sit for Xan against Gallows Hill since strategically we'd need her against Messing's vampire players. Showing off his poison against shifters and changelings was his best shot at getting scouted.

If Lee didn't get a student visa, he'd have to leave the country. I had a place to go no matter what. I'd step out for him in that second match since his conjuring speed made up for my dual magics.

That's settled. Don't be tardy now.

I headed out onto Essex Street, ending up in a throng of students, staff, and faculty. Everyone, not only the Bishop's Row team and the cheer squad, was coming. Even the trustees, although Andre Gauthier looked green around the gills. I searched the crowd for one face in particular because I wanted to run my strategy for sitting out by Hal. I didn't find him.

The pit of my stomach dropped until I asked Faith where he was.

"He's watching on an orb with his dad. Saving his spoons for the boat cruise."

"At least he can still see you play." I told her my idea, along with why I was changing the rotation.

"You're something else. You know that?" She grinned.

"Did I hear you right?" Grace tapped my shoulder. "You're benching yourself against the hard-mode team?"

I nodded. "Keep it quiet. I want to tell the rest of the team together."

"That's our captain." Grace smiled.

After I attached my ear cuffs and we'd put on our ballistae, ankyr, and cestus, we huddled up. Dylan nodded, Xan blinked, and Lee cheered. We broke, and I ran out on the field, leaving Lee and Xan on the sidelines.

The game against Messing went better than I'd hoped. They had two vampire girls from first and second year in addition to Jonah, and their conjures were fast instead of powerful. Grace and Lena both had enough brute force to absorb their throws easily and Faith tagged them out pretty quickly. They didn't have Jonah's power, and Faith's orbs were too hefty for them to block.

Izzy was our most formidable opponent. She managed to tag me and duck behind Jonah in time to evade Dylan's massive ice orb. She'd surpassed me for sure. She got Lena too, although Jonah went down right after that under Grace's umbral throw. Grace's cestus flashed red a moment later. I stood at the side, watching with a furrowed brow. That tag came from out of nowhere. Grace didn't call time out, only grumbled as she stepped beside me.

Izzy was somehow the last Messing player standing, but only three of her teammates stood aside when there should have been four. It confused me so I counted again while scratching my head.

"Watch out!" Grace shouted to Faith. Finally, I noticed that other player. A guy I'd never seen before. "Umbral affinity three o'clock!"

Of course, Izzy's secret weapon couldn't possibly have umbral affinity. That was a magus thing. Telepaths sometimes had a similar trait. Just like that, he tagged Faith out. Dylan stood alone, staring at the telepath player because if you looked away from folks with powers like that, you'd never remember they were there in the first place.

Dylan dual conjured, a trick he'd only worked on at the gym on campus. He wasn't amazing at it but shocked both Izzy and the telepath with the play. He almost hit himself in the face with his air orb but managed to launch it along with the ice one. The telepath tried jumping in front of Izzy to absorb both tags, but he went down under the ice, leaving the air orb in play.

Dylan's air orbs dissipated slightly under normal conditions, increasing in diameter. With a dual conjure, they doubled in size.

Izzy hit the dirt too late. We won. Barely.

In the middle of the court, we took turns shaking hands with our opponents.

"Good game." Izzy smiled.

"Good game," I replied.

Dad and Bubbe came down from the bleachers to say hello.

"Nice strategy, kid," Dad said.

"We wouldn't have squeaked out that win if Grace hadn't seen their telepath."

"You're the one who put her on defense." Dad shrugged. "I've got dad-tinted glasses on." He grinned at the others. "Amazing work, everybody. You would have given my old team a run for their money."

"You were a team captain, Mr. Morgenstern?" Dylan blinked.

"Yeah, I was." He smiled. "Runs in the family I guess, because Bubbe was too."

"Why didn't you ever tell me?" I chuckled at my grandmother.

"Back in those days, Hawthorn was much bigger, with four divisions in each year. It's why you see things like Root or Berry on the older trophies." She shook her head but still grinned. "Mine was Branch, and you won't see that because we lost every match but had a blast."

After they left, we watched the Messing cheer squad's interpretation of *Natural* by Imagine Dragons. Their act was solid although once again unconventional for a cheer routine.

"Looks more like something that belongs in a Broadway musical finale," Dorian commented from his seat behind the sound equipment. "Probably on purpose." He pointed out a woman in the front row on the opposite side of the court. "She's the NYU faculty member who signed my rejection letter. Bet Jacinda gets in."

"Did you hear back since early acceptance, though?" Dylan asked. Dorian shook his head. "Don't give up hope then, mate. You're still in for regular."

Our team's break continued through the match between Messing and Gallows Hill.

"Ouch!" Lee winced as Jonah ended up on his back under one of Crow's orbs. "When did Merlini get so brutal?"

"I don't know. He never came to weekend practice." I shrugged. "Brianna says he's their MVP now."

"And you want me off reserves?"

"Well, you and Xan. Yeah."

He whistled. "You sure you still want to put me out there? I think you're the only one with the firepower to counter him."

"Absolutely." I grinned. "Don't underestimate yourself. You conjure faster than anyone else on our team, and most of theirs."

Izzy was the last woman standing and turned sideways to make a smaller target, panting as she struggled to gather enough energy for one more orb. Even the dodgy telepath got tagged out. Brianna still had Azrael on defense and Crow at mid. All three of them threw, and that was the end of Izzy's last stand. Gallows Hill won.

"I'm nervous." Lee wrung his hands.

"We all are." Dylan grimaced.

"Not me." Grace smiled.

"Good." I patted her back. "That's the kind of defense we need. Right, Lena?"

She nodded and cracked her knuckles while grinning like a wolf at Crow Merlini, who'd left the court without a single handshake for his opponents.

"What are you doing?" Xan asked.

"Getting ready to make bully toast," she murmured.

"Gods, I'm glad you're on our side." Xan let out a nervous chuckle.

"Relax." Dorian waved a hand. "Cheer time part two."

Cadence led her squad out on to the field. Dorian waited for her nod, then pressed a button. I sat there blinking, totally stunned. I shouldn't have been. Because, like at the talent show last year, Cadence used music as a weapon. This time was pop instead of punk, a dance remix of Taylor Swift's *We Are Never Ever Getting Back Together*.

Almost everyone over on the Hawthorn side cheered, and a few laughed. But not Grace.

"What?" I asked her.

"Trouble." She jerked her chin at the Gallows Hill section. "He's nothing nice, but you already know that. Acts like she's like his property or something."

Crow sat with his jaw clenched, fists too. I didn't like how his eyes glittered. They reminded me too much of Halloween when he almost attacked Hal and me. I glanced at Messing's benches, where Izzy sat staring down at something in her hand. A card. She paled.

I had no time to go over and ask her about it because once Gallows Hill's routine ended, I had to send my team out on the court for the final match of the day.

It went better than I expected after watching Messing's defeat. We lasted longer than them by a full three minutes, mostly thanks to Lee's near constant barrage of wood orbs. Lena absorbed three of Crow's uber throws by holding the most compact conjures I'd ever seen. Also, her stature and slight build made her a difficult target.

Grace took a direct hit from Brianna to save Dylan. Lee managed to bring Azrael down by tossing on the right after Lena discarded an absorbed orb to Az's left. Xan stepped up, running between the mid and defensive lines to misdirect and block, employing one of my plays from the videos.

Brianna took Xan down right after that. If she'd been used to seeing him on weekends, she might have done it sooner, but I think she underestimated him. Lena howled for all the world like a wolf shifter and threw at Brianna. She would have won us the game right then and there, but Bar took the hit for his captain and Crow followed up while Lena was vulnerable and tagged her out. She'd gotten over-confident.

It was going rough out there. Dylan started his double conjure, but Crow knocked the air orb right out of his left hand. Lee went into a sort of overdrive at that point, forcing Crow to defend himself. As they duked it out and tagged each other simultaneously, Brianna tossed a solid glamour ball at Dylan, whose ice orb was only half-formed. Direct hit. Game over.

Everybody cheered because the plays were brilliant on both sides. Gallows Hill's section of bleachers went wild. I headed out on to the court with Faith to join the line of players. I grinned at my team.

"You all rocked it out there, and I'm so proud. Thanks for being the best team ever. Hope you're not sore that we lost this one."

"Nah." Dylan grinned. "Everyone we played with today was a friend."

"Almost." Grace rolled her eyes in Crow's general direction. He'd walked right past us without stopping to shake hands.

"One bad apple." Lee shrugged.

"He'd better not spoil a single one of that bunch." Faith jerked a thumb at Bar and Az, who marched off the court with Brianna on their shoulders.

As I thought about leading my team back to our seats, Logan approached, walking a ways ahead of his squad.

"Sorry, Aliyah." He hugged me.

"It's cool." I hugged back. "You've got a routine to lead. Knock it out of the park, Logan."

"Thanks."

The players left to make room for our other classmates to show off. We weren't disappointed. Hawthorn might have lost the tournament, but we won the cheer competition. They did a practically flawless performance to *My Songs Know What You Did In The Dark* by Fallout Boy that used every participant's magic. The familiars joined in, too.

The Overtons danced like dervishes, extending their leaps into near flight with air magic, framed by their pigeons. Logan and Eston made rainbows with fine sprays of mist backlit by lights their familiars carried. Every time the lyrics mentioned fire, Kitty shot jets of it from both hands, boosted above the rainbows by Arick.

The entire crowd got on their feet, swaying in the stands.

Except for Leo Pierce. He sat sour-faced, as though his son, the routine, or even the song itself gave him personal insult. Maybe it did. Noah played that song on repeat for practically six months so I happened to know it was pretty scathing. Especially to a fire magus with tons of skeletons in his closet, like Mr. Pierce.

At the end, I removed my ballistae, ankyr, and cestus. Also my ear cuffs. I looked up to see Bobby Tremain grinning at me from across the field, both thumbs up. He pointed at another man hurrying across the field toward my team and me. Mr. Watkins. I nodded and smiled back. Before he got there, something else happened.

"Khan, is it?" A voice with an across-the-pond accent sounded behind me, much more polished than Dylan's. I turned to see a nimble-looking fellow with gray at the temples of his otherwise sandy hair. He extended his hand. "Coach Nigel Quinn. From Oxford Occult."

"Yes, sir." Dylan nodded and took it. "You played for the London Ravens. MVP five years in a row."

"Indubitably." He nodded. "You're a brilliant player, but I'm sure you're already aware. I'd very much like you on my junior team, if you haven't made a decision yet on a university, that is."

"I haven't, sir."

"We're covering tuition for our players although not room, board, books, or fees. If that's feasible for you, please do consider my offer, Mr. Khan."

"I'll talk it over with me mum. I mean, I'll discuss it with my mother, sir. Thank you, sir."

"Very good." He produced a card from his coat pocket. "Please contact me with your decision, one way or another. Good day."

He sauntered away, not across the field as I expected, but into the bleachers behind us. I turned to see who he approached, but before that happened, someone cleared their throat behind me.

"Bobby Tremain called me a million times about you and your team. Lynn, too. Said I'd have to see it to believe it."

My mouth dropped open. Had they been scouting me all that time? I remembered where I'd heard of him before.

"Um, see what? Sir."

Nate Watkins was the toughest professor at PPC. Not just academically, either. He'd endured a magical coma, out of his body for months, harmed by bad old Uncle Richard. Now here he was, dangling a future I hadn't realized I still wanted over my head.

"You're the captain here, Morgenstern." Mr. Watkins raised an eyebrow. "But you barely played. Tell me, why is that?"

Was this a test? A million different answers flew around my brain. Strategy, synergy, following classic plays from the game's history. None of those impressive-sounding answers was the truth.

Go with honesty, then.

"I wanted to give them all a chance to play because they deserved to be seen." I glanced at Xan. "They're all my friends."

"You applied at Providence Paranormal College back in September." He glanced down at his phone and frowned. "Early acceptance denied, I see."

"Yes, sir."

"Hey, you." He snapped his fingers. "Team Hawthorn. Tell me what you think of Morgenstern here. Would you play on a team for her again?"

"Definitely." Faith nodded.

"Three more years and then some." Grace smiled.

"Any time." Lee grinned.

"Yup," Lena mumbled.

I looked down at my shoes, waiting to see whether Xan would snark off about me or follow the crowd with hollow platitudes. He did neither.

"She never gives up and doesn't hang anyone out to dry. Not even me."

"What's that mean?" Mr. Watkins glanced at his jersey to check his name. "Onassis?"

"It means I was a total douche canoe for a year and a half." He cleared his throat. "She could have sat me all day here. Instead, she recorded practices I couldn't make because I work and put me in against our toughest challenger. Sir."

I looked up. Xan's face was red. Mr. Watkins chuckled, then peered down at his phone and shook his head.

"Well, you've still got another year to go at Hawthorn, Onassis, like Zanelli. Plus, I promised Nigel I wouldn't try poaching Khan. Anyway, I'm putting together the first official junior team for PPC, and I want the rest of you on it. Mendez, Collins, and Micello already said yes. Practice starts the same week as orientation."

"But we're not accepted." Lee blinked.

"Yeah." I nodded. "I even got a rejection."

"Early acceptance doesn't mean no acceptance, kiddos." Mr. Watkins chuckled. "Your letters are in the mail Monday morning."

"*If* they play." Xan crossed his arms over his chest. "That's what you mean, right? This is an ultimatum, some kind of *quid pro quo?*"

"No." He shook his head. "That happens to be when this batch goes out. There's scholarship money for anyone on this team from a former student's memorial trust."

He looked tired for a moment. I knew all too well what that look felt like. I wanted to say yes more than anything, but he hadn't come to recruit me. He said he wanted a team, including my friends in need.

"What do you say, folks?"

"Are you all mad?" Dylan blinked. "Don't you want something big to celebrate at the party tonight? Take the offer!"

He got his drafts, minus one. Grace declined, as I expected. That didn't faze Mr. Watkins.

"Yeah, Ambersmith gave me the same answer. Nigel also took Merlini." He shrugged. "Having a little room on the team is a good thing. Tryouts hype everyone up."

Noah stood with Elanor, giving me his best golf clap. Between his first and middle fingers, I saw a duplicate of the card Nigel had given to Dylan. Was Oxford Occult looking at him too? I couldn't ask until later, because he got into an enclosed transport with the students from Messing.

Finally, I knew what I'd be doing for the next four years. With my friends.

Most of them, anyway.

CHAPTER TWENTY-SEVEN

The boat cruise was a casual affair, so Grace hadn't made outfits for it. In a way, that was a relief. I'd have felt overdressed in a major way, wearing Hawthorn formal with everyone else in t-shirts. The boat didn't leave until eight, so we all had dinner before going upstairs to get ready. That was a good thing since my appetite returned with a vengeance on the way back to campus from the games.

Logan still showed up at my door wearing a sea green tie with a blue shirt and navy sport coat. His eyes sparkled like light on the ocean. I smiled because he looked happy and at ease like a weight was off his shoulders. I wasn't sure why, so I asked.

"It's hard to explain." He shook his head. "I wouldn't have thought so if you'd asked me yesterday. It's because I won a performance competition, one with critters involved. But, I did it on my terms, without anyone or their familiars feeling uncomfortable. I think that's why he wasn't happy about it."

"You took something you were raised to do and made your way with it." I nodded. "I'm proud of you."

"He's not." Logan sighed. "No matter what I do or how well it turns out, he's never satisfied. Maybe that's not as important as I thought it was. Your mom came right over after the routine. She said I exceed expectations. Maybe that sounds a little odd to most people. Not me."

"That's how Mom talks sometimes. She's right because you do." I took his hand. "If your father can't see it, that's his loss."

We headed down the stairs and off-campus, this time in a group of all the third-years, and their plus ones..

Hal's chair glided easily along Essex Street and to the Wharf, where we got on the boat. The festivities took place on a three-season deck with a solid roof overhead with columns evenly spaced along it for extra support. In foul weather, the sides would have had windows and panels up. Since it was balmy, only the windows stayed up, giving us a partially outdoor venue.

Messing was already there, and Gallows Hill arrived after we had. I looked around for Izzy, but Lee had found her first. I let them have some time together, figuring he'd want to tell her the good news about college.

Cadence squealed and dashed in my direction. I braced for impact unnecessarily since she ran right past me and embraced Arick. Romantically—I'm talking like hands in the hair and open-mouth kissing. Logan and I stood there blinking while Xan chuckled and Dorian applauded.

"Whoa." Eston reached into his pocket. "Guess I owe you twenty bucks, Dorian."

"Should have talked to Dylan before making that bet." Xan grinned. "He's known about Carick for a week straight."

"Wouldn't that be Ardence?" Eston raised an eyebrow.

"They liked Carick better."

I glanced at a stack of audio equipment, waiting to see what kind of entertainment they had planned. If it were Piercing Whispers, Dylan wouldn't have gotten the chance to ask Noah on that date. After a moment, I saw a familiar face.

"Hey, is that—"

"Uncle Paolo, yeah." Bar leaned against a nearby column. "He's a landlord, but karaoke's his real job."

"Did you say karaoke?" Dorian waved Eston's money away. "Keep that yuppie food stamp for refreshments later. I'm glad those two are at the PDA stage. Well, this just became the best party ever."

"Thanks." Eston smiled and put the bill back in his pocket. "Want to go look at that list?"

They headed off toward some tables, where Paolo had left a stack of notebooks with his selection of songs. I intended to go with them.

A sudden high-pitched whine made me wince. At first, I thought it came from Paolo Micello's equipment, but he stood holding the cord, about to plug it all in. Nobody else reacted, and it had sounded behind me. I turned.

Crow leaned against the boat's railing outside the nearest window. He had one hand in his pocket, and the other made a fist in front of his chest. With eyes narrowed and upper lip curled, he turned his back on Cadence and Arick as they chattered over the available karaoke songs. I lifted a foot, about to go over and check on him.

Don't even think about it.

I watched him stalk toward the gate, where we'd all come up the gangway. We'd already embarked so it was closed. The ramp lifted minutes ago. Instead of hanging his head or dropping his shoulders, Crow continued walking between the railing and the windows. I hoped he'd maybe find someplace private to shift and fly home. "Don't think that's happening."

"Nothing good can come from that, yeah?" Dylan said.

He and Noah stood at my shoulder. I turned while sighing.

"Best I can imagine is he goes home."

"No." Noah shook his head. "He's got some scary older siblings. Home for him means coming back with reinforcements."

"Mavis seems like a good kid, though." I raised an eyebrow.

"She's the odd duck in that house, like the apple that rolled into another orchard." Noah wrinkled his nose. "I'll hope he goes anywhere else in town besides there."

As it turned out, he did neither thing.

We'd earned that celebration, but it felt as temporary as finishing a collaborative chalk mural with thunderclouds on the horizon. Bright colors were everywhere, as were the flash of phone cameras and a sense of flying time. Almost all the students sang, except for Kitty who said she'd sound better wearing tinfoil gloves and scratching chalkboards, and Crow stuck to one of the two corners. Everybody danced when we weren't singing. Alone, in groups, and with each other. Even the faculty, staff, and trustees.

The dance floor was packed while Grace sang *Boombayah* by Blackpink. When she finished, and Noah got up to sing *Impossible Year* by Panic! At The Disco, even the friends dancing in groups stuck around. Some of them lit up their phones and waved them in the air.

Toward the end of that song, Lavinia Onassis tried to drag Xan out on the dance floor with her. Dorian grinned and stepped between them.

"Allow me, milord." He gave Xan's mother a borderline absurd theatrical flourishing bow. "Milady, if I may?"

At first, Lavinia simpered, smiling as he led her away to the dance floor. Behind her back, Dorian gave the next singer a wink. It was Cadence.

"What's she singing?" I asked Arick.

"She only told us it's from the '90s and called *Bitch*. Mrs. Onassis isn't going to like this." He winced. "Dorian knew that going in."

"I'm never letting him call himself a coward ever again." Dylan shook his head.

"Brass balls." Noah nodded sagely. "He has them."

Cadence nailed the song, singing directly at Crow, who fumed even more over by the refreshment table. His grip shattered the clear plastic cup in his hand. He dropped it, then blended into the crowd. Dorian jounced Lavinia around the dance floor, pointing at her every time the song's title came up with his goofiest grin. The best and worst thing happened.

Everybody laughed.

The sound coming off the crowd was pure release because the Hawthorn students mostly feared the trustees and our friends at the other schools knew how we felt. Our coaches and professors must have joined in for a different reason. I couldn't imagine what that was, but it felt like they meant to laugh with her. But the trustees laughed *at* Lavinia Onassis.

She didn't realize this until the song was half over, at which point she stomped off toward the ladies room, glaring at me the entire way, for some reason.

"I don't get it." I shrugged.

"You will." A low, intense voice sounded behind me.

I turned and found only Lena there.

"Did you say something?"

She shook her head. Her presence confused me for a moment. Only third years and their dates were supposed to be at this party. Dylan had brought Noah, Cadence brought Arick, and Dorian invited Xan. Who'd brought Lena?

Bar sauntered over with a bottle of water and handed it to her.

"Thanks, Bartholomew." Her voice came out a little raspy, definitely not the same as whoever had spoken before.

"Next time we face off on the court, breathe from the gut before howling." He grinned down at her.

"Not gonna say I shouldn't?" She blinked.

"No way, short, small, and ferocious." He shook his head. "Just advice. Uncle Paolo says breathing right helps save your pipes."

She put the water down. "Let's dance." They headed off and did exactly that.

Logan linked his arm through mine and raised his eyebrows. I nodded, and we followed them. Izzy was up at the mic with Lee, singing *You're My Best Friend* by Queen. For those few minutes, I forgot about all the drama and that mysterious voice, at least until the next singer got up.

Crow chose a song on the radio from back when Bubbe was our age, one a lot of people considered plaintive or even sweet. My grandmother had assured me that *Every Breath You Take* was nothing nice no matter how pretty the music sounded. People kept right on dancing, too. Logan grimaced at the lyrics and gladly sat out the rest of it with me. We found Cadence and Arick by the refreshment table, and both were put off.

"It's been six months already." Cadence wrinkled her nose.

"Yeah, what gives?" Logan shook his head.

"Be careful." I patted Cadence's arm. "He's dangerous."

"I should say the same thing to you." She gave me a half-grin. "With the way that trustee woman's been glaring at you all evening."

"She thinks Aliyah messed with Xan's mind," Logan said.

"Well, you've been a good influence on him." Arick nodded. "Which she doesn't like."

"Huh?" Logan blinked along with me because Arick didn't know what we'd overheard on winter break.

"She's been stopping by at our room all year, asking to be let in." He shrugged. "Xan always says no because he doesn't want her there. She blames Aliyah for that. So yeah, you've got something there, Logan."

"Why do parents suck so much?" Cadence sighed.

We all looked across the room, where Professor Hawkins and his ex-wife stood together in what could only be an awkward conversation. How she managed to keep her position as principal at Gallows Hill after pretending to be psychic, I didn't know. It wouldn't have flown at Hawthorn, but Gallows Hill didn't have trustees controlling everything.

Lavinia Onassis sat in a corner, nursing a bright blue cocktail. She wasn't alone in it anymore, however. Crow sat listening to her and shaking his head. She handed him something I couldn't see. I almost followed him to investigate. When he went to the bar and returned with a water, I figured it was only money and let it be.

That turned out to be a mistake.

The music changed as Paolo performed *All Star* by Smashmouth. We all got back out on the dance floor. After that, Azrael sang *Yellow Submarine* by the Beatles. Lena surprised us all with a rendition of *Volare* in Italian.

After that, Paolo set up a playlist and took a break from the karaoke for a bit.

Dylan, Elanor, and Noah chatted over one of the books while

selecting a song. Izzy stood across the room separated from me by the crowd, waving a tarot card. I couldn't hear her over the music, but she held The World reversed. Cadence's card. Not good.

The exact opposite of good, in fact.

I wasn't sure where Cadence had gone. Crow was nowhere to be seen.

My ears practically stung with discordance. Since that always seemed to mean trouble, I followed the sound past the half-open enclosure, out toward the railing on the starboard side. Halfway down from the prow I found trouble.

Cadence faced Crow with her hands on her hips, back pressed against whitewashed steel tubes, the only thing separating her from the depths of the harbor. Which we were at the edge of, judging by the tankers on the horizon's edge.

A soft hiss came from my left. I turned my head to see Logan with Doris on his shoulder, her tail up and bushed out.

"You're taking me back." Crow's voice sounded hollow, as though he read from an encyclopedia, stating facts. "Then coming to Oxford with me. End of discussion, Cadence."

"Crow." She rolled her eyes. "We're not even friends anymore."

"You'll do what I say." He reached out and grabbed her wrists before she could pull away. "Because you're mine. Forever."

"Let her go." Arick stood on the other side of them with his hands conjuring. His wood magic was there but faded somehow.

"Get lost, kid." Crow tilted his head. "A man's talking."

"Being an asshole doesn't make you a man." Arick's hands shook, and his voice cracked. But he threw.

Or at least tried. The orb fizzled out the moment it left his hands.

Crow laughed, then took one hand off Cadence and made a fist.

"Stop!" I knew that tone in Cadence's voice, but the command in it fell flat.

Arick raised his hands, holding another orb to absorb the blow. This one fizzled too, and he took the hit on the chin. He fell to the deck, knocked out. Skinner crawled out of his jacket and crooned on his chest.

Cadence opened her mouth and drew a breath, about to scream. He opened his fist and placed his palm over it.

"It's me or the ocean, bitch." Crow leaned forward, catching my friend between him and the rail. "The Boss knows about the DelMar exile. There's a new order coming to town. The only way you and your folks get to stay on land is you with me. Choose wisely." He took his hand off her mouth and tapped his foot, waiting for an answer.

"Wow." Cadence blinked. "You can't even call her your mom anymore? How pathetic."

Crow slapped her. Doris hissed.

I moved to defend my friend although magic wasn't working the way it should. Logan held my hand in a vise grip and shook his head while pointing at Arick.

"Don't, Aliyah," he breathed. "You can't win without magic."

"I can." Xan stepped out of the shadows, near where Arick still lay knocked out. "Don't make me hurt you, Merlini."

"Queers like you can't fight." Crow snorted.

Xan chuckled. "You're a shittier bully than I ever was. Let her go."

"This ain't your business."

"I've been where you are, Crow. Someday, you'll wish you never did this." Xan shook his head. "So let her go."

"Make me." Crow leered. "Your mom said you're due for a thrashing."

Xan swung at Crow, fist arcing through the air on a collision course with his face. He dodged it but had to release Cadence in the process. Enraged, Crow let out a sharp cry. A knife gleamed in his hand, not the one from the park months ago.

For some reason, it reminded me of my ear cuffs.

He slashed, and Xan ducked. Instead of a slice across the face, a lock of black hair blew away in the breeze. I waited for Xan to swing again, or maybe conjure poison and throw an orb Bishop's Row-style. He didn't. Instead, he waited.

The next time Crow slashed, Xan blocked with a kick. This time, the end of a shoelace went flying.

I beckoned to Cadence, trying to coax her away from the railing.

She stood like a statue, eyes fixed on the fight. If I'd had Ember with me, I would have sent her over. She was back at school, nesting. So I tried mind magic to get Cadence's attention.

Easier said than done. For whatever reason, I couldn't catch her gaze, no matter how much I focused on her. It wasn't going well for my former enemy, either.

"Get help," Xan panted.

Blood dripped off the side of Xan's hand although he hadn't landed a blow. I understood why when Crow's blade gleamed red in the moonlight. Logan dropped my hand and hurried away.

"Magi suck." Crow chuckled. "Can't even heal."

With Logan away, I put up my dukes and conjured. Or at least, tried to. My hands flushed briefly with heat that fizzled out almost immediately.

Even if none of my magic worked, my extra sense did. Crow's weapon was enhanced somehow.

"Magic knife!"

"He's scared of a fair fight." Xan chuckled. "Coward."

"You're dead!" Crow snarled. He slashed again, this time at his opponent's face.

Xan ducked and attempted a leg sweep, but Crow hopped aside. Toward me.

I made my move. Nothing fancy, just a slap at his wrist. It worked. I jumped back as the knife flew from his hand and skidded along the deck, past Arick, and out of range.

Xan popped up with a left hook that finally connected and knocked Crow's jaw askance with a *crack*. The green glow on impact meant he'd conjured poison. Unfortunately, even shifters of the bird variety had an advantage magi didn't.

Crow shook his head, and the side of his face straightened out again. He'd already healed the bone, and my extra sense told me his body had already handled the toxin.

I conjured fire and took a step closer, but with Cadence and Xan so close I feared hitting them. Crow knew enough about fighting to sense that, too.

With one hand, he grabbed Xan by the throat and squeezed. Not with the flat of his palm, either, but digging in with his fingers. Like he intended to tear his throat out. Asceco came to her magus's rescue, striking from her hiding place in his shirt. Crow only laughed.

"Basilisk venom? Against a shifter? Don't make me laugh."

I banished the fire and prepared to conjure solar, hoping to blind Crow long enough for Xan to break free.

Three things happened at the same time.

Logan returned, shoes squeaking on the deck as he pointed at the fighting pair.

Bar appeared from under cover of a glamour, fist smashing Crow's wrist like a sledgehammer, releasing Xan.

Cadence lost her balance and grabbed at her ex-boyfriend's trench coat. She missed and went over the side.

An instant later, Dylan skidded to a hard stop against the railing, frantically conjuring air in a last-ditch attempt to stop the banished mermaid from hitting the forbidden deep water.

He was too late.

The rest of us rushed to the side and gazed down into the water, the shock of what had just happened ending the fight. Xan and Bar couldn't possibly have known how dire this situation was for Cadence. Bar frantically searched for a float or a life vest.

Boat security arrived. Xan pointed out the knife, the wound on his hand, and Arick. The burly guard slapped cuffs on Crow. The kind that stopped shifters from changing form.

Logan, Dylan, and I knew there were worse consequences than cold water, concussions, and handcuffs. I stood, clutching my stomach because I sensed some vast and powerful force coming.

Crow did too. His reaction was the opposite of mine.

I knew from both the sickeningly excited hum of his mind and the rapt expression of fascination on his face.

Down in the water, Cadence shook her head. It was the last thing I saw her do before the depths rose beneath her. An enormous limb, spotted and covered with tentacles, obscured her face as it lifted her over the water. All we could see were the red-gold tips of her tail fins.

The rest of the creature rose, its massive bulk still mostly underwater but nearly the size of the ship we stood on. Logan and I identified it at the same time.

"Kraken," we both whispered.

Classmates, teachers, and trustees filed in behind us, all connected by a growing sense of alarm. Understandable, since the boat rocked, moved by the displaced water. Almost everyone stepped back from the railing.

It towered above us at first, then brought its head down. Atop it sat a figure, nearly as burly as Bar, wearing a crown of coral. His beard was turquoise with white streaks, and he had green scales on his tail.

"Since she entered the water on her own, the DelMar daughter will pay for her parents' crime of abducting and slaying my companion's child." He stroked the kraken's glistening skin. "You'll lift anchor and leave her with me."

"It wasn't her fault!" My hands balled into fists. "She fell in by accident."

"Was she pushed?" the merman inquired.

"She was threatened." I pointed at Crow. "He attacked her. But no, she wasn't pushed when she fell."

"My decision stands."

"She's my student." Stephanie Hawkins stepped forward. "I'm responsible for her safety. Take me instead."

"That doesn't satisfy our grievance. A dhampyr is no substitute for what the DelMars took from us. You have no connection to the incident."

"I do." Logan stood in front of us all. "The theft of that egg had everything to do with me."

"Shut your mouth!" Leo Pierce strode toward his son. "Stop talking now."

"No, Dad." Logan trembled like a leaf but held his head high. "I'll own my mistakes. Sir, I've got something to say."

"Speak your piece, magus." The merman raised one hand. Leo had no choice but to back off.

"Not to you." Logan pointed at the kraken. "To her."

I'd never heard sounds like the ones out of Logan's mouth at that moment. Maybe nobody who lived on land had ever made them. I don't think anyone other than me understood the sentiment.

Logan apologized. By the time he finished, he'd dropped to his knees with his hands raised, palms up. Tears streamed down his face.

Now, nobody could deny his talent for speaking to magical creatures. Not after he'd just had an entire conversation with something as mysterious and rare as a kraken.

"From the bottom of my heart, sir, I apologize."

"For?" The merman blinked.

"Not being good enough to bond with the hatchling. I think I could have saved her if I'd managed. So it's my fault. Let Cadence go and punish me instead."

"Young magus, please rise."

Logan did while wiping his nose on his sleeve.

"The lore you land-dwellers have on us is scarce by design, but you must know this. Kraken can only bond with merfolk. Your gifts are undeniably strong, but no magus could have managed that. Cadence DelMar is not responsible. So, we release her from punishment."

The kraken's tentacle unfurled and set Cadence on the deck.

Mermaids sometimes lost their lower garments when shifting unexpectedly. Cadence's legs remained a tail for a moment, which gave me time to remove my jacket and wrap it around her waist. Izzy did the same so she was completely covered. She leaned between us, sobbing.

"A price must be paid." Everything went silent. I looked up. "A child for a child is my thinking. That is the way of the sea."

Leo nodded, one corner of his mouth upturned.

"What?" Logan stared up at his father, eyes wide open. "Dad. No."

"You brought this on yourself," he scoffed. "I warned you."

The tentacle reached for Logan. Doris yowled and bounded in front of Leo where she hissed and spit, tail lashing. Brand the phoenix dove at the mercat, talons out and wings blazing.

"I wish for Leo to pay this price. And suffer for it."

Andre Gauthier stood in the middle of all the chaos with a brass lamp glowing in his hands. A figure shimmered into existence beside him. I recognized her from Logan's description. The woman from the library.

"I'm sorry." The handsome woman waved her hand as a tear trickled down her face.

"It seems my companion wants a different sort of justice from your family," the merman said.

The kraken's appendage hung in midair, then descended again, this time in front of Leo, where Brand did battle with Doris.

I heard a hiss, a scuffle, and a caw. Leo blocked my view of the kraken's tentacle. Logan cried out as the air around him trembled with pain. A fine mist fell on his face, tears in the rain. The tentacle lifted something off the deck—two bundles, gray and still. Finally, the massive creature and her merman sank beneath the water, slowly enough that the boat barely rocked.

Logan fell to the deck and curled up on his side. Despair came off him in waves. My breath caught in my throat. Elanor approached her father with her hands ablaze.

"What did you do?"

"What any reasonable person would have." He banished her conjure. "They were only animals."

I pulled Logan's head into my lap, where he wept in silence. I'd seen this before a year ago, with Dorian.

Doris was gone. Brand, too. Sacrificed in place of Logan himself. Leo Pierce hadn't flinched through any of it, although Andre's wish stipulated his pain.

He'll hurt. Eventually.

All our research told us that wishes always came home to roost. The voice's truth offered cold comfort.

Somewhere behind me, I heard that low intense voice again, chuckling.

CHAPTER TWENTY-EIGHT

We all sat in the infirmary the next morning with Logan asleep in one bed and Hal getting his infusion in another. Hal's chair stood in a corner, a satchel filled with the books and papers from the other day slung across the back.

"I don't get it." Dylan scratched his head. "Why the conference?"

"Everybody knows now that Gauthier had Grandma's lamp," Hal said. "That must have been his last wish."

"So where is it now?" Faith asked.

"Well, one thing's certain," Xan gazed at his bandaged hand. "The wrong people don't have it."

"How do you figure?" Grace asked.

"I know them too well." He tapped his temple. "Things wouldn't be this peaceful if they had their way. They'll find it eventually. Then, we're screwed."

"I know what we all need." Hal smiled. "Coffee and pastry."

"What?" I blinked.

"Normally, I never say no to food." Dylan shook his head. "This is a crisis. Leaving now is madness."

"Risky maybe, but not madness," Hal said. "Trust me on this. We need Witches Brew breakfast. For morale. Nurse Smith and Ian are both here. Logan will be okay."

"I don't want to leave him." I patted Logan's hand. "But Xan's right. So is Hal. We need some breakfast, fresh air, and space to breathe."

When Ian came in to disconnect Hal's infusion, I took Logan's hand and kissed his forehead.

"I'll be back in a bit, dear."

He didn't make a sound or open his eyes, but his hand squeezed mine before we let go. The trauma of losing a familiar affected each magus differently. Logan's talent probably made it harder for him.

Hal kept moving his chair right past Witches Brew and crossed Front Street without stopping, then crossed Derby, which resulted in a lot of head-scratching. Dylan looked longingly over his shoulder at Engine House, which hadn't opened yet.

The entire way, Hal held his phone in his lap, sending texts. He stopped on Washington Street until he read a response, then crossed into The Point.

"They're not going to let me into N—"

"Don't worry, Xan." Hal tucked his phone back in his pocket. "He already said it's okay."

My brother let us into his apartment, finger to his lips. Nobody spoke until we were inside the warded practice room.

"Now that we're in here, they won't know what we say, not even if they've bugged us."

"Are you honestly worried about that?" Grace raised an eyebrow. "Never mind. It's wishes."

"My father would kill to get his hands on that lamp." Faith clenched her fists. "It vanished, so that means it has no master until the next person picks it up."

"Next person who isn't Andre Gauthier or Richard Hopewell, yeah." Hal nodded. "Dad used to joke that the decorations on lamps are actually ancient djinn for no repeat business."

"So, how do we keep it away from him?"

"That lamp's directly connected to my family," Hal said. "It's barely functional, but I'm still a space magus and I'm related by blood."

"Isn't it the same for the headmaster?" Xan asked.

"Nope. He married up." Hal grinned. "Only related to the Haddads by marriage."

"What about your dad?"

"Technically, yes. But he's off-campus today, dealing with the boat charter company. It's pretty safe to assume we lost our deposit."

"You planned this." I nodded. "Since last night when you saw the lamp vanish."

"Exactly." He nodded.

"Don't you need big amplification devices to track something like a lamp though?" Noah asked.

"No, nothing like that." Hal grinned. "Turns out, I've got space affinity. I'm low on power because of my anemia, even right after this morning's infusion. But I learned a trick thanks to Logan, from that green dragon journal he's translated. Just need the wards in here and a little help from you all in the magic department."

Hal pulled an atlas out from under the blanket in his lap and turned to the table of contents. Then, he took a pendulum from his pocket and looped the end of the chain around his middle and ring fingers. He held it above the printed page and stared at it while conjuring.

Sweat beaded on his forehead. Nin sat on his shoulder and pressed her cheek against his. Faith took his free hand, then reached for Grace's with her empty one. I got the idea and laid one of my hands on his shoulder and grabbed Noah's with the other. We formed a circle, gently conjuring and passing the energy of our elements around.

It reminded me of the calming exercise Elanor taught me for Bishop's Row, but somehow, our elements channeled together despite some of them opposing each other.

Faith squeezed Hal's hand. "Go on, ask."

"What page?"

The pendulum swung, defying the laws of physics.

"Ninety." Hal let the bob rest in his lap and flipped through the atlas. "Now, where in Salem?"

The pendulum swung back and forth over Essex Street, eventually coming to rest on the spot by CVS, where the door was today. Faith was prepared. She pulled out a sketch on notebook paper, a map of campus. Hal drew a deep breath and began again.

The pendulum swung past the infirmary and the trustees' quarters, swinging back and forth between the academic wing and student housing. It slowed over the dorms, which Faith hadn't replicated to show every floor. Hal dropped his hand and leaned back in the chair, panting like he'd run wind sprints.

"Do any of the trustees have access there?" Faith asked. "I thought it was off-limits."

"It's lax enough for my mom to knock on my door whenever she's in the bottle," Xan said.

"There are restrictions, though." I chewed my lower lip while thinking. "What was it the headmaster said at the welcome speech? Something about detection wards."

Someone knocked on the door.

"What the hell?" Noah opened it to reveal Elanor.

"Brianna called. It's an emergency. We have to go back to Hawthorn. Now."

"Elanor, we're doing serious sh—"

"Shut up, Noah!" She clutched her phone to her chest. "It's Logan. My dad put him in a car outside the Essex Street Garage. He was unconscious."

"Where?" I shouldered past my brother.

"Nobody knows." She trembled. "And he was bleeding."

Most of us hurried back to campus, where I acted as Elanor's escort. Dylan asked Brianna to stay on Essex Street, so we'd have someone watching the door to message Faith and Hal, who'd stayed behind with Noah at the apartment. He was too bushed to make the trip back without rest, even in the chair. Noah had no choice but to hide from the sun.

We needed information so we split up, intending to ask everyone around what they'd seen or heard. Dylan went to the infirmary, Xan to the café, Dorian the cafeteria, and Grace the dorms. I escorted Elanor to the office, where she pounded on the headmaster's door. He opened it and stared at us with a face like stone.

"Where's my brother?"

"I suggest you ask a relative, Miss Pierce." He shook his head. "I'm unable to discuss medical matters about any Hawthorn students. Privacy, you know."

"We're estranged."

"All the more reason I can't tell you. You're a grown woman, Miss Pierce. Act like it, and handle your family business."

"Sir," I stepped in. "Logan's estranged from them. He's an adult too. So, please. We only want to know where he is, to make sure he's safe."

"He's in the care of medical professionals."

"That's not good enough." The air around Elanor heated up. "I happen to know he left in a car, not an ambulance."

"I'm sorry I can't do more, Miss Pierce. Please. Find *a relative*. It's the only way." He closed the door.

She stalked out of the hall and through the lobby, making a beeline for the exit. I jogged to get in front of her, then turned around and walked backward.

"Stop, Elanor. Think."

"About what?"

"Why was he so insistent about a relative?" I pushed the vestibule door open with my hands behind my back. "I mean, he could have said your father if that's who he meant."

"Mom's in Vegas. The only other relative I have around here is locked up." She kept walking toward the exterior door.

"Wait." I stopped so abruptly she almost ran into me. "Do you mean your aunt? Petra?"

"How did you know about her?" She blinked. "Even Logan doesn't—"

I pushed the door open and stood with her in front of CVS,

explaining about the yearbook. Including how Gamila gave it to Logan in the library.

"Don't say another word, ladies." Andre Gauthier emerged from the school door. "Not with Lavinia about to walk out for brunch. Follow me, and we can help each other."

He led us down the street to the parking garage and into the long-term section. We turned a corner to a row where only one vehicle stood. He drove an old-fashioned hearse of course, from the 1970s and in mint condition. As we approached, two people stepped out from behind the car. Bubbe and Izzy.

"Mildred Morgenstern?" Mr. Gauthier blinked.

"You don't bring Aliyah anywhere without me, Andre."

"It's not your business."

"My grandkid, my business." She crossed her arms over her chest. "I've got a Mendez soothsayer contradicting you."

"Hi." Izzy let out a nervous giggle. "My *abuela* says you ignored her warnings back in the day and that I shouldn't help you. When I said it's for Bubbe, she gave her blessing. Anyway, everything goes up in smoke if you go in a trio. You need four or more."

"Success means two more passengers later." Mr. Gauthier frowned. "It's not legal to drive with anyone in the back who isn't dead. I won't have room if I bring you all."

"Then Bubbe stays in Salem." Izzy's hands trembled.

"No, you do." Bubbe raised an eyebrow. "We discussed this already, Isabella."

"But the cards said—"

"You stay. I go."

"If you're sure."

"I am."

"Fine." Izzy swallowed. "See you, then. When I see you."

This does not bode well.

There wasn't any time to press Izzy for more information or my grandmother for that matter. Bubbe got in the passenger side. I got in the back with Elanor. The car had bench seats, so there'd be space for two more if we all squeezed. I wondered at first why one seat wasn't enough. Until Mr. Gauthier pointed the car toward Danvers and Elanor's response brought the headmaster's words into precise focus for both of us.

"The Sanitarium?" She gasped. "Aunt Petra!"

"Yes. Where the Pierces have always put their rebels. Now hold on." Mr. Gauthier stepped on the gas. "This is a race."

"I don't get it." But I did. He was as cautious as Hal and didn't want his enemies to know where he was going. I should have been more careful. There was nothing I could do now besides keep quiet about the lamp.

And hope any damage my loose lips had done stayed at a minimum.

***

The Sanitarium in Danvers was a sprawling brick building set in the middle of a bucolic green lawn. The granite steps glittered in the late morning sun, dazzling my eyes as we went up them and through sliding glass doors. The floor and walls were wide planks, bleached like driftwood. The only decor in the immediate area were long stalks of something like bamboo in alabaster planters, which both Andre and Bubbe side-eyed immediately.

I'm not sure what I'd expected the inside to look like, but the reality was nothing like what they show in the movies. No glass laced with metal, no bars, no mundane barriers of any kind that the eye could see, besides a half-wall that reminded me of the Dutch doors in Bubbe's office.

There were no apparent gates, catches, or latches in that low wall, which was painted to resemble fieldstone. I saw no desk or any attendants. People of all shapes, sizes, and ages moved on the other side, dressed in soft pastel pants and tops, reminding me of Monet's *Garden*.

They went about the business of living gently, oblivious to our presence by the entrance. When I approached the wall and tried leaning over it to catch the nearest person's attention, a ward stopped me. The patient in question, a lanky bald man older than Bubbe, moved along as though I were invisible.

I peered at them and noticed something else that didn't track with my clearly incorrect assumptions about inpatient mental health care. Nobody looked unkempt or otherwise in distress. Some sat, others paced, and a few engaged in repetitive behaviors with hands or feet. Most seemed alert and engaged in some activity or other. Reading, or artwork, or board games, or cards. One snored faintly in a reclining chair with a cozy blanket draped over her legs. Another dozed over a magazine at a small table. As I watched, the wood beneath him shifted to match the angle of the other sleeper's seat. A blanket appeared as if by magic and tucked itself under his arms as the magazine settled in his lap, page unturned.

If the people made me think of Monet, the murals put me in mind of Van Gogh. The artwork stretched from top to bottom, with magical creatures as the most frequent subjects. There was one that featured a rainbow-hued flight of dragonets, the largest one eerily similar to Ember.

I tried picking out the dominant magical energy in the room, but so many types mingled that it was next to impossible.

"Yeah, she's here all right." Mr. Gauthier chuckled at the artwork. "I should have known. Wouldn't have needed Gamila at all if it weren't for Dishonest Abe and his blasted mind magic. Which, of course, is part and parcel of how she wound up in this place."

"I thought we were here for my kin." Elanor glared.

"Oh, we are." He nodded.

"So, exactly how are you helping?" I raised an eyebrow.

"As a chauffeur, of course." He grinned like the Cheshire Cat. "Besides, young Mr. Pierce is in here. And he owes me a favor."

"What's this really about, Andre?" Bubbe had her arms crossed over her chest.

"Why, Petra of course, Mildred."

"I should have known." Bubbe seemed to deflate. "Well, go on then. Rescue her if you've finally got the means."

"You know as well as I do that's not how the Sanitarium works. First, we've got to get in."

"That takes blood." Bubbe nodded.

I rummaged in my bag for something sharp.

"No, Aliyah." Elanor put her hand on my arm. "Watch this."

She walked over to the wall and placed her hand on the top, where one of the painted stones appeared to have a sharp edge. She wrinkled her nose, and when she took her hand away, I saw a tiny drop of blood.

"Pierce?" A voice called, but nobody appeared. "One of you passed this way a short time ago."

"I'm here for my brother Logan," Elanor said. "My Aunt Petra, too."

"I'm afraid Mr. Logan's still in eval for the next while. You're welcome to visit with Miss Petra while you wait."

"Thanks." She beckoned. "Come on."

"I'm sorry, but only family is permitted entry." The voice carried a hint of sadness.

"I was Logan's legal guardian for a year." Bubbe said. "That must count for something."

"I am Miss Petra's fiancé," Andre added.

"Please hold."

A bland tune in major key played softly.

"Miss Elanor Pierce, Mr. Andre Gauthier. Miss Petra is in the lounge."

"What about my brother?"

"Your visit time with your aunt matches the remaining time in his evaluation."

They walked directly toward a stretch of wall between two planters, as though it were a door. They passed through. I tried following, hand outstretched, but my fingers met wood.

"Glamour," Bubbe said.

"How? Nobody's out here."

"Brownies." She jerked her chin at the planters. "This place is fae-run."

"Whoa." I blinked, then thought of Logan. They'd said he was still in eval. I wondered, did that mean Leo was here with him? Were decisions being made, long-term ones, at this very moment?

Yes. You need to act now.

Short of threatening mass murder by lighting up brownies, I couldn't think of a way in.

"Bubbe, what do we do?"

"First, tell me about this deal with Andre."

I did. And what we'd overheard about the conservatorship.

"Then we need to get in there immediately."

"That's what I've been saying. But how?"

"Brownies follow rules, but they use intellect to interpret them. Letting Andre in means there's wiggle room on their interpretation of family." She tapped her temple. "Convince them."

"Oh!"

Don't get me wrong. It wasn't like I forgot about having mind magic. I had the worst teacher, so I wasn't sure when to try using it. Mr. Fairbanks had turned my training to his advantage. Professor Hawkins wasn't sure how it worked or what to do with it, but my education wasn't limited to either of them, thank goodness.

I thought back to Professor Luciano. He always told us to trust the process of our magic.

When in doubt, call on it and see what happens.

With all the vulnerable patients around, even behind wards, that was a risk I almost didn't take. However, professors weren't my only teachers. I was captain of the Bishop's Row team, bound for college on a scholarship because of my skill. Mind magic was like any other energy. Conjurable.

I held my hands up and together, focused on bringing my third magic forward.

I failed.

Fire bloomed between my palms instead. I banished it and tried again. Light took its place, and I shook my head. The third time, I felt with my fingers that it worked although I couldn't see any hint of an orb. Mind energy was more difficult to see than Faith's undeath.

"What do I do with it?"

Glancing from the space between my hands to the stretch of wall between the planters, I stood stumped.

Throwing an orb, even one made from mind magic, was a direct attack on the caretakers here. From what I'd observed, the brownie staff operated with care and kindness. It wasn't their fault that some people were here under coercion from malicious family members. They didn't deserve aggression from me and acting out like this might only support Leo Pierce's arguments that his son wasn't safer with his chosen family.

I needed to focus the energy, not aim and fire it. So I had no choice but to banish the orb.

In your bag.

The ear cuffs.

I fished them out and put them on, wincing at the pinching they made in my rush. A chuckle at the irony of this situation bubbled up from my throat. Was I using my shackles to help set someone else free? Yes. Yes, I was.

Approaching one of the planters put me beside the wall, which I realized at once was made up of brownies. I beckoned to Bubbe, who joined me. We held hands. Then, I rested my palm on the surface in front of me, remembering all the years I'd spent getting to know Logan.

Bubbe came along memory lane with me, which had more than one unintended effect. She saw me at my worst in a few of them. Then she added in some of hers. Together, we made a kaleidoscope of experience, projected through the connection the ear cuffs made between the brownies and my magic.

Logan in the Hawthorn lobby, taking my breath away the first time I saw him. How he set fear of his family aside and saved Doris. The calm comfort he offered through our first year when I feared discovery as an extramagus. His face under the sodium lamp that night in Salem, trusting me when he had nowhere else to go. Bubbe signing below his signature on a paper at Salem District Court, and the handshake that became a hug.

The kindness he offered to every guest in second year. His brilliance in the classroom and in Lab. How he never left my side, even through the horror of Temperance and Luciano's death. Kindness and comfort, given to strangers at Bubbe's practice. Interceding to save Cadence, which was how he ended up here in the first place.

"Curious. That's not what his father said."

I opened my eyes with some small amount of difficulty. My lashes were laden with tears, but I saw clearly enough through them to realize I wasn't in the lobby of Danvers Sanitarium anymore.

"You did it, Aliyah." Bubbe gestured at a long table, where Logan sat beside Leo at a bench staring at a pen, a folder open in front of him.

"We." I shook my head. "Including him. All of that, what I showed them, came from his choices."

Logan didn't look up, like the fellow I'd tried interacting with when I'd first arrived there. As though he couldn't hear or see us.

"I thought we'd get to, you know, visit with him," I said to nobody in particular.

"As recent family, this is what we can do," the voice said.

"Perhaps it'd make a difference if he could see us here." Bubbe raised an eyebrow.

"Done."

The light changed, warmed somehow. Leo noticed us. Logan still didn't look up.

"Don't you see now? All those rules, everything I did. It's because I knew you couldn't manage on your own."

"I'm still top of the class, Dad." He turned his head to look at his father. "I did that all by myself."

"Academics are only more rules. When something goes wrong, who's going to bail you out?"

"Aliyah always rescues me." He swallowed, tears rolling down his cheek. "She loves me, Dad. More than you do, I think."

"Come home, and if you do everything as I say, you'll always have a roof over your head." He didn't even glance in our direction but picked the pen up and placed it in Logan's hand. "Sign it. That girl's not here for you now, when it counts."

The voice sounded in sing-song. "Falsehood detected."

"I meant to say, where is she now?"

Logan turned his head. Leo held up his hand as if he'd slap him. Instead, he cupped it, trying to stop him from seeing us. With his other hand, Leo held his son's wrist, guiding it toward the paper.

"Just sign it."

I held my hands out, pressed them against the same sort of invisible barrier that held me back.

"Logan!" I screamed his name, making fists and pounding on the wards. Sparks flew with each beat. "Don't sign!"

Finally, he saw me and his face lit up, as though he could conjure solar magic behind his eyes. He dropped the pen.

"No, Dad." He grinned and conjured water that flowed over the contract, washing away ink and soaking through the paper. "Never."

"Evaluation complete. Outpatient therapy recommended."

He rushed to us and embraced Bubbe briefly first, then me. He stood between us, one arm around my waist. Leo stood and glowered.

"I'm out too, Leo." Petra strode through another ward on the other side of the room, Andre and Elanor behind her.

"What? How?" Mr. Pierce's face went an alarming shade of red.

"It's right here in your contract." Andre chuckled and produced an almost identical paper, this one with yellowed edges. "I did my research. Release form's only valid if a blood relative signs it."

"Elanor?" He drew the name out, raising his voice as he spoke, making the end sound like a roar.

"Yeah. Aunt Petra's a free woman. You're a monster."

"You want a monster?" His hands blazed. "I'll show you a monster."

Leo Pierce conjured an inferno. This time, it was more than double the size of the one I'd banished years ago in Lab, and Ember was back at Hawthorn, on her nest.

I immediately started banishing. So did Elanor, and Fifi who rose from her shoulder. It felt like standing in front of Mr. Ambersmith's blast furnace. I even smelled hair burning. Logan and Petra conjured water, trying to extinguish what we couldn't banish. Bubbe put her hand on my shoulder, lending me strength. Andre did the same for Elanor. It wouldn't be enough.

Mr. Pierce was almost godlike in his magic, beyond imagining. Logan told me once that his entrance music on stage was *Walking on the Sun*. I'd thought it bluster, but I'd been wrong. His fire burned so hot it was blue, a color I'd never seen from my hands or anyone else's.

The ear cuffs gave me a single advantage. Banishing an element someone else conjured was almost like touching them. So I knew his intentions.

Leo Pierce would burn the entire sanitarium down before seeing his sister and son walk out of it under their power. He almost got his way.

Blue drowned out red, but white was brighter.

Bubbe pointed at Leo and flashed light in his eyes. His flames faltered and guttered. A vine-like length of charred wood rose from the table, splintered and dripping a clear sap. It reared back like a striking serpent and punctured his arm. When he lifted his hands to cast again, it was like on the boat when Crow had that knife. His hands remained empty, his magic subdued.

"Confinement in the aggression ward, stat." The voice stated, much more calmly than expected in a recently burning place made of and run by creatures of wood.

"Oranges. Barcode. Theramin," Bubbe said. Her knees buckled. A bench moved under her as she collapsed, her right arm curling against her chest.

"Calling Emergency Extrahuman Services, Law Enforcement."

In moments, we found ourselves out on the steps, where sirens sounded nearby. People piled out of the ambulance, surrounding Bubbe and hustling her onto a gurney. I tried getting in, but they stopped me. Behind us, police cars pulled up in front of the sanitarium. Elanor ushered us toward the backseat of the restored hearse, where we sat and waited as Andre chased the ambulance.

CHAPTER TWENTY-NINE

Instead of shaking, crying, or even screaming, I reacted with numbness. Was this how an ice magus felt? I wondered as I woke my phone and called my parents. Logan put his arms around me, weeping as I told Mom where we'd been, what had happened, and where we were going.

Salem Hospital's emergency room saw Bubbe immediately, while the rest of us waited. Mom and Dad walked through the door. Noah arrived later, through the stairwell to the basement. A nurse came and brought my father through a set of double doors. My phone beeped with a message from Izzy.

I'm sorry, she sent. And immediately after, the three of swords reversed.

I couldn't text back. She must have done a reading and seen that card, one of the worst in the deck. But the message explained a lot about her argument with Bubbe in the parking garage. I couldn't blame Izzy for what happened. Nobody stopped Mildred Morgenstern when she had her mind set on something. Not even an inauspicious reading from the most talented precognitive family in Salem.

Dad emerged from the double doors. He gathered Mom, me, Noah, and Logan, then took us aside.

"I'm sorry." Logan stared at the floor.

"Nobody here blames you." Dad patted his shoulder. "Bubbe's had a stroke, but they got her here in time. Doc says she's six points on THRIVE."

"Um, can you explain that, Dad?" Noah blinked back tears. "Not a medical person here."

"It means she'll have a good outcome after recovery and therapy, but it'll take time and a lot of work. Her life might be a little different even after that." He reached out and tried to put his arms around us all. We crowded in, faces all covered with tears. Logan stood still between my mom and me, shaking.

"Hey." I rubbed his back. "Hey. What's wrong?"

"She wouldn't be in there if it wasn't for—"

"Your father." Mom looked up and wiped her eyes. "If he'd left you in the infirmary as he was supposed to, everything would have been fine. You can't blame yourself. Bubbe made sure I didn't when I was your age. Her advice is timeless. Let's honor it. Now, tell us what happened."

Logan's mouth dropped open. He looked from her to me, then at Dad and Noah. Everybody nodded.

"Nurse Smith gave me Valium last night. It wore off in his car, in the sanitarium parking lot. I was bleeding." He held up one bandage-covered forearm. "The brownies asked me a lot of questions about Doris, how I felt, asking if I still wanted to hurt myself. Dad kept insisting I wasn't safe at Hawthorn. He said he saw me try to cut my wrists in the infirmary. I almost believed him, too. Then he lied about you. Said you wouldn't come because you don't care about me. I knew that was wrong. Well, you heard all that. You were there."

"We called Nurse Smith," Dad said. "He cared for Dorian just fine last year, and you were getting the same treatment. So we knew he had everything under control."

"Right." Elanor cleared her throat. "I called the infirmary, too. You were on Ms. Khan's schedule and everything. Then Dad happened because he's a malicious son of a bitch."

"Language." Mom raised an eyebrow. "But yes. He hasn't stopped trying to sabotage Logan over the last two years. You just didn't see the paperwork." She shook her head, then gazed at Logan. "Did you sign anything while at Danvers Sanitarium?"

"No, Mrs. Morgenstern." He shook his head. "He had papers and kept pushing a pen at me. Bubbe and Aliyah got there before I did."

"Well, that's a blessing." She sighed. "Where are the documents now?"

"Burned up when he went nuclear," Elanor said.

"What?" Mom's eyes widened.

"Ask Aunt Petra."

We turned toward the seat where she sat holding hands with Andre. She resembled Logan, with the same hair and the eyes that escaped meeting gazes. While Logan reminded me of the ocean, Petra put me in mind of the time we vacationed at Niagara-on-the-Lake. We sat as each of us explained our part in the whole incident. When we finished, everyone took a few moments to process it all.

"Excuse me." Dad rose. "I'm telling all of this to Bubbe's doctors. Any information about how it happened can only help them."

Andre followed, but only to get a cup of water from the cooler in the waiting area. He popped what looked like a Tylenol capsule in his mouth and washed it down before pacing back over. He rubbed the bridge of his nose.

"So, my dad did the same thing to you?" Logan asked.

"Not him." Petra shook her head. "Our father. But that's probably where he got the idea for a conservatorship."

"Why?"

"You hear them too, right?" She grinned. "The animals. All of them. I used to do a translation act. One night, I couldn't stand it. I told them how the creatures in the menagerie really felt and spoke their misery. They brought me to Danvers and made me sign."

"So how come you weren't at their compound in Vegas?"

"I refused to leave the Sanitarium. As you saw, it's a kind sort of place. I might have been behind walls, but I was free of them." She glanced up at Andre. "I wasn't as forgotten as I'd feared."

"Please excuse my unacceptable tardiness." He bowed and held out his hand. She took it.

"We'll see." She squeezed his hand. "But I think you're in the clear."

The hospital admitted Bubbe and gave us information about visiting hours. Nurse Smith arrived to bring Logan directly back to the infirmary. Noah and Elanor headed back to their apartment through the tunnel. Mom and Dad drove me back to campus.

As we walked out of Salem Hospital, my phone *beeped* with a message from Grace. Only while checking it did I realize that the cafeteria at school hadn't finished serving lunch yet. Time moved strangely in a crisis.

Police at school. Make statement, meet me in our room.

Logan headed downstairs to the infirmary. I sat with the representative from Salem PD in the lounge corner that had been cordoned off with a fancy velvet rope.

"This is the second time in as many days that you're giving a statement, Morgenstern." Detective Ambersmith raised an eyebrow. "Should I be concerned for your safety?"

"No, ma'am." I shook my head. "I'm more worried about my friends. It's Mr. Fairbanks. He's dangerous."

"With good reason, I should say." She glanced down at the statement she'd copied. "I never liked the idea of those trustees being here. If it had all gone down on campus, I'd call the school board and ask for a shutdown and full inquiry."

"Well, it didn't, but we have exams starting Monday and—"

"Aliyah." She blinked. "You always took school seriously. I remember you trying to do Noah's homework back when I used to be your babysitter, but this is ridiculous. I'm talking about life and death here, and you're thinking of grades."

"No, I'm not. There's still a—"

"It's because you're an extramagus." She sighed and nodded. "You think you're tough enough. I get it. So, help me protect your friends. What's the risk at Hawthorn? For real."

"Like I said. Lavinia Onassis gave Crow that knife. Leo Pierce was a time bomb. The knife's gone, and Leo went off at the Sanitarium. Hawthorn Academy runs on space magic, which should have made the headmaster aware. But he wasn't. So Abe Fairbanks must be helping them hide everything with mind magic."

"Leo's staying where he is pending arraignment. You don't have to worry about him at school. Mr. Merlini's waiting on a lawyer, which is his right, so accusations against Mrs. Onassis are hearsay until we know more. Is there anyone else on campus who's a threat?"

"I told you already." I blinked. I'd said the man's name twice.

"No. You didn't."

"I'm trying to tell you. They have a ringleader."

"Go on."

"Mr. Fairbanks. He's still dangerous."

She moved her pen over the statement form, but it didn't make contact. I stared, unable to believe what I was seeing. How could a seasoned detective be unaware of not taking notes? I glanced up and looked toward the lobby entrance, where Andre Gauthier had returned. His eyes fixed on a point to my left. He tensed for a moment, then relaxed and walked in the opposite direction, toward the dorms. Detective Ambersmith cleared her throat.

"Don't you have any other concerns?" She shook her head at the paper again. "Because from what you've said already, there's nothing I can do to increase safety measures."

"Detective, I don't know how to make it any clearer. Abraham Fairbanks is behind—"

There he was, standing by the cream and sugar table and grinning at me. He tapped his temple. I glanced out at the empty lobby, the unattended counter, the unoccupied seats nearby. Then, I burst into tears. Detective Ambersmith set her clipboard aside and patted my shoulder.

"I know, I know." She handed me a tissue. "You're stressed and frightened. It's okay if you can't talk about it right now. I'll be back to talk with Logan on Tuesday after dinner. So, come and meet me then once you've had a rest. Maybe it'll be easier having your boyfriend there."

"Can't I come to the station?" I blew my nose.

"Well, I'm glad you asked that." She sighed and handed me another tissue. "It's not possible. I can't act if we discuss things off-campus. Jurisdiction is weird when it comes to between worlds spaces. The entire investigation has to happen here like it did last year."

"I understand." I wiped my eyes. I did. All too well.

Abe Fairbanks had all his interests cornered, trapped in the pocket dimension that was Hawthorn Academy. He had the means, the power, and the advantage to get everything he wanted without interference.

The lamp that was Hal's last shot at saving his life was the first item on that list.

Upstairs, I filled my friends in on what happened at Danvers Sanitarium and everything that followed, up to the futile police statement. After expressions of relief that Logan was free, Bubbe on the mend, and Leo off the board, we danced along the edge of safe conversation and saying too much.

"With Leo out of the picture, the situation from this morning is even worse."

"How can we properly look if we can't even talk?" Dylan groaned his frustration and flopped back on my bed.

"We'll have to cope with redundancy." Hal sighed. "Running over the same old ground."

"Worst efficiency ever," Faith grumbled. "Zero stars."

"Hmm." Grace peered at me, then pointed at my ear. "Can I see one of those?"

"Uh, okay?" I removed the ear cuffs and handed them over. It wasn't physically possible to forget I was wearing them, but I'd certainly forgotten the fact I could take them off in all the chaos.

Grace took her time while turning the jewelry over in her hands. She rummaged in her desk drawer and brought out a monocle, which she held up to her eye as she continued the examination.

"What are you thinking?" Hal asked.

"See for yourself, magiscience whiz." She handed both items to him.

"This is awesome." After a moment, Hal nodded. "Put them back on, Aliyah."

"Okay?" I took it from him and did.

"Now we huddle up," Grace said.

Once we met in the middle of the room, she put her arms over Dylan's and Faith's shoulders. We all followed suit. A moment later, it all came clear to me.

They'd given me the cuffs to restrict mind magic. I'd learned early on that they enhanced it with contact when I touched Logan while wearing them, but I'd assumed it was partly a quirk of how close we were.

It took a dire emergency for me to deliberately try using them to commune with a stranger, the brownie in Danvers Sanitarium. Grace seized on that immediately and made her theory, that the cuffs also blocked incoming mind magic. I felt her glee when I montaged bits of all the sessions with Mr. Fairbanks, when I'd put the cuffs in their box on the desk. Then, I saw what she did—all our faces.

"It's like Aliyah-Grace-o-vision." Dylan chuckled. "Huh."

"Shh," Hal said. Then I got a cartoonish image of a mustachioed Abe Fairbanks with his forehead on the outside of a door, zig-zags of mean thoughts spiking the wood.

We all laughed.

We didn't have an actual conversation after that, more like a series of brain art. Hal's remained like sketches, while Dylan's resembled music videos complete with a soundtrack. Faith's were verbal, words forming in front of a cursor on a screen. Our thoughts moved faster than speech.

In moments, we had a plan set up to search all eight floors in the dorm for the lamp, even the unused ones. We needed more help but

353

could discuss that without the ear cuff huddle. Everybody knew I was starting to reach my limit.

"Dylan, go get Lee and Dorian. Might as well include Xan if you can find him. Just show them the picture of you know what from our lab notes"

"What about Logan?" I asked. "Should we wait for him to get out of the infirmary?"

"Go to him after we're done here," Hal said. "We can handle this without him if he needs rest."

"We're all sleeping like logs tonight." Dylan chuckled.

"Maybe that's a good thing, with exams and all." Faith shrugged. "Anyway, let's get started."

We managed to search the entire dorm although it took the whole afternoon and part of the evening, up until dinner. None of us found Gamila's lamp. Somebody must have gotten there first. The best-case scenario was one of the first years. The worst, we didn't want to consider.

Dinner was almost over by the time I left Logan in the infirmary. He'd stay overnight, and Ian had already ordered his food from Penelope. I needed to do that for myself so I headed for the cafeteria.

One glance up at the arch in the lobby told me that Ember still sat on her nest. Gale stood watch as she slept there. As I watched, Julia soared up with a bundle of food in her talons. She dropped it off, and Gale immediately opened it, crooning to wake Ember. They shared their meal, an assortment of fish heads from the kitchen.

"Fishhead roulette's not for me." Dorian nudged me with his elbow. "Let's go get the beverage variety. The last thing I want to see is you passing out."

"I miss her."

"I get it." He sighed. "Eventually, old Julia here will feather a nest."

"It's okay to miss her too. Mercy, I mean." We got in line for food.

"I do every day. Like Julia here misses Filberto. And like Logan misses Doris."

"Bubbe won't be able to help him as she did for you."

"I, uh," he tapped his temple. "Heard how she's in the hospital. I'm paying her kindness forward. As soon as Nurse Smith lets him have another visitor."

"Thanks, Dorian."

We ordered our food, pizza slices. After that, we moved to the beverage section where Dorian looked around before speaking again.

"Did Xan really come out of nowhere and fight Crow? Without magic?"

"He didn't say anything?" I watched him get beverage roulette as he spoke.

"No. Not a word, although I asked about that cut on his hand. I went with Lee to the Witch's Brew this morning. He and Izzy told me. So, was it true?"

"Yeah, he did." I gestured at a table in the corner. "Let's sit and talk."

Over lunch, I told him everything. The magic-canceling dagger, Xan's trash talk, how I'd have ended up unconscious on the deck without my magic, like Arick. Dorian leaned across the table. I met him halfway, and he whispered in my ear.

"Okay, so I might be a total idiot. I'm in love." He sat back down, his face the utter picture of serious for once.

"I kinda figured that."

"Was I that obvious?"

"Not really. But everyone talks to me about this kind of thing lately for some reason, so I've been looking for it more."

"It doesn't bother you?"

"No. Should it?"

"When I got here, you two were enemies. I watched you help him despite that. So I figured, if anyone knew whether making big declarations to Xan Onassis is a good idea, it'd be you." He swallowed. "I'm not a total coward anymore, but old habits die hard. I trust your judgment. So, should I tell him?"

"Absolutely."

He nodded, then got up to drop off his tray. I followed him, expecting we'd say see you later, and I'd go upstairs for a nap. Dorian wasn't running on the same track as me. He made a beeline for the café, where Xan was behind the counter on shift. And he did it, right then and there.

Xan blushed but nodded and said something back. I didn't need to hear what, because that connection I'd sensed between the two of them since the masquerade ball flourished like mulberries in July. Kayleigh the manager shooed Xan out from behind the counter and grinned as the pair embraced.

I stood under Ember's arch, smiling until my cheeks hurt. Then I got back on the stairs I showered and went to bed, hoping the morning would bring even more promise.

CHAPTER THIRTY

Monday birthed exam week, and nothing at all was normal about it.

Someone knocked on my door at four-thirty in the morning. I opened it in rumpled pajamas and bed head, worrying over a medical emergency for either Logan or Hal. Or Ember's eggs hatching. It wasn't any of those things.

"Hi, Aliyah."

Noah stood outside my door. I'd forgotten he was scheduled to move in until after graduation.

"Oh, hi." I shoved my feet into slippers and stepped out of the room where Grace still slept.

"I've got stuff downstairs. Can you help?"

"Um, okay." I rubbed my eyes as I followed him. Then rubbed them again at the stack of suitcases. "It's four days, Noah."

"I'm the first vampire to graduate from here. Making the best impression is an enormous burden."

"So is impressing Dylan," I mumbled.

"Gesundheit." He gave me a fish-eye. "That was a sneeze, right?"

"Anything you say." I yawned and hoisted bags up to my shoulders and snagged a third with wheels, dragging it behind me. "What floor?"

"Down to goblin town." He chuckled. "Infirmary, away!"

"When did you become a morning person?" I groaned.

"This is like after dinner for me now." He grinned. "It's going to suck taking exams at the equivalent of three AM, though."

They'd given him Zeke's old quarters, which was good because a regular dorm room might not have accommodated his wardrobe. A refrigerator stocked with bagged blood sat in the corner, beside a sink and a microwave, amenities the rest of us didn't have. It had a restroom *en suite*, too.

"I've got room envy."

"It's only four days." He winked.

"Can I go back to bed?"

"Why not pop in and see Logan first?"

"Are you kidding? He's asleep."

"Am not." Logan stood in the doorway, rubbing one eye with a knuckle. I perked up immediately.

"How are you?"

"Sleepy. And you?"

"Same." I yawned again. "Do you want a hug?"

He nodded, and I went to his side. We stood there for so long I wasn't sure whether it was real or a dream.

Noah cleared his throat, so it was real. We stepped aside and took seats in the infirmary's waiting room as Noah went to fetch whatever else he needed. Then we went straight from hugging to full cuddle mode.

An alarm woke me later in an infirmary bed. I opened my eyes and immediately saw Logan in the next bed over as he rolled toward me. We sat up and stretched.

"Are you cleared for taking exams?"

"Yeah." He glanced at the clock above the door. "You'd better head upstairs and get dressed, though. You have half an hour before breakfast ends."

We hugged again, and I rushed out to the stairs and up them to my room. I hurried through my morning routine in half the usual time. I barely managed to grab toast before the café closed.

As I headed through the doors to the academic wing, it occurred to me that I hadn't studied at all over the weekend. Or for most of the previous week either.

"Who got the bright idea to have exams right after Bishop's Row?"

"I know, right?" Faith leaned against the wall outside our class-room. "I didn't study."

"You're not alone."

Professor Hawkins let us in after that, and we had the next three hours to mark lettered circles and fill blue books silently. Except Hal finished after an hour, with Dylan ten minutes behind him. Dorian sauntered out right before the two-hour mark, and Faith with a half-hour to spare. Logan was halfway to the front of the room when the professor called time. I set my pencil down and stretched before standing, then headed out of the room and down the hall to Creatives, where everyone else was engrossed in finishing their latest projects. Almost. Grace walked in behind me.

"Thank goodness Lab practicals are tomorrow." She grinned. "My brain feels like a fried egg."

"Mine feels like a spilled smoothie."

"Let's go make something, then."

We did, all the way up to the lunch bell, where I spotted a cluster of middle-aged people arriving on campus, dragging wheeled suit-cases toward the entrance to the faculty wing. As the last one entered, I saw Andre Gauthier hustle out before the door closed. He glanced at me and nodded as he power-walked directly toward the academic wing.

Not a peep from that man's mind.

The phenomenon was so curious, I turned around and greeted him.

"Hey, Mr. Gauthier." I gave him my most adult-friendly grin. "Do you need help with anything?"

"Er, ah." He slowed his pace, seeming a bit more winded than he should have been. "No, not really. Just late to, hmm, audit a first-year lab."

"Okay, see you later." I stopped following him halfway across the lobby.

Don't buy that story for a minute.

I didn't. So I did my best to focus, trying to break through whatever wall he had up. I couldn't. The barrier, whatever it was, felt springy and flexible, not anything rigid. So, it was shatter-proof.

Fairbanks-proof too, I'd wager.

The answers to how Andre protected his thoughts and what he was doing while shielded would have to wait. My stomach grumbled, so I hurried back to my friends.

"Are parents visiting for graduation already?" I nudged Hal as we entered the cafeteria.

"Not exactly." He shook his head. "Leo's not coming back. So we're missing a trustee. That's the last of the out-of-town alumni arriving to cast votes, but it's a technicality. I already told Logan his mother arrived this morning. She's the only one qualified for the spot."

"What about my mom or dad? Couldn't one of them try for it?"

"Neither of them are the oldest alumnus in your family." He sighed. "If Bubbe weren't still recovering, she'd be eligible. Same with my grandpa, if he weren't headmaster."

"Wow. I had no idea that was part of the requirements. Are you worried?"

"I keep telling myself at least it's not Mrs. Fairbanks."

"Why not Petra? She's older than Mrs. Pierce, I thought."

"No secondary degree." Hal shrugged. "I don't like it, but there's nothing we can do. There's only one good thing about this."

"Which is?"

"The trustees will be occupied through the meeting, vote, and most of the night getting her up to speed. We'll have no trouble from them, at least."

The fact that I didn't have any more sessions scheduled with Mr. Fairbanks was an enormous relief although the idea of Logan's mother as the new trustee still galled me. After dinner, as I watched the crowd of visiting alumni leave, I felt a little better.

Hal turned out to be correct. Mr. Fairbanks gave us no trouble at all. At least, not for the remainder of Monday.

Tuesday was another story entirely.

I woke early the next morning before it would have been light out in Salem. Grace still slept, so I dressed and went to the bathroom to brush my teeth. After that, I headed downstairs and into the twilit lobby, staring at the darkened cafeteria.

"Hey, you." Noah stepped through the doors to the academic wing.

"What are you doing up?"

"Just finished the Lab practical."

"Oh, they didn't let you take it in the library?"

"They would have, but I didn't want to make the professors set the entire thing up in two places so I got it done before sunrise." He cleared his throat although vampires don't have to do that. "I'll get us both in trouble if I say more. But there's a shockingly important item in there."

"Huh?" The only important magical item I could think of on this campus was Gamila's lamp. I banished the thought the moment after it entered my mind. Noah had all but told me someone was listening.

"I can't say more." He tugged his earlobe and glanced at the wall. "Don't want anyone thinking I'm passing you answers. Or anything."

"That's nice of you." I nodded. "Hey, for accommodations, couldn't they have covered the windows and let you take it with the rest of us instead?"

"Andre Gauthier insisted." He shook his head. "He said it might have been embarrassing. I'm required to wear gloves. Something about preventing accidental use of vampire senses to identify things, but it felt like their typical brand of prejudice. Anyway, it's over now. I'm going to bed. It's tiring, keeping two sets of waking hours."

"Won't you have to do that in college?"

"Oxford Occult offers every course of study through their Night School."

"So you accepted?"

"I'm leaning that way. It's hard to say no to a full scholarship at the world's oldest English-speaking magical school." He gave me a half-smile. "Dylan's going. So, there's that."

"What *is* that, exactly?"

"I don't ask you to define things with Logan."

"That's fair." I raised an eyebrow. "I think there's a difference between defying definitions that don't fit and being cautious."

"Which is wise in both our cases."

"You sound like Bubbe. It looks good on you."

"Ditto, kiddo."

The lights came on in the cafeteria. We spoke at the same time, but not entirely over each other.

"Get your rest."

"Get those grades." Noah chuckled. "Love you."

"Love you too."

We went our separate ways for the day.

I had breakfast before everyone else, then got my gym uniform and headed off to run laps because my nerves wouldn't let me sit still. The fine spray of water in the shower washed away sweat but not anxiety. This was an enormously important day academically, but it felt like more than a difficult exam was coming.

Like everything's about to go sideways again. Just like last year.

As I dressed, the scent of wet tile and mist-blunted light ambushed me, like a thief in the dark. For a moment, memory transported me back in time.

While still bent over my shoelaces, I returned to that night. I heard Temperance's voice in the echo of dripping water. My heart pounded like it'd burst my chest and the air in my lungs burned as though underwater. I froze like a rabbit in front of a speeding car, unable to move another inch. Thanks to all those sessions with Ms. Khan, I knew what to do.

Despite the chest pain, I tried measuring my breath. That proved impossible, so I focused on forcing my fingertips to recognize the flat, rough weave of my shoelace. Something unrelated, native to the present, to ground me. In the end, none of that saved me.

Coach Pickman did.

She squatted in front of the bench I sat on and peered up at me.

Speaking softly wasn't her way, but she lowered her typical volume, offering familiar words of encouragement.

"Come on, Morgenstern. You've got this."

I nodded, senses finally returning fully to the present. My fingers fumbled, and I hadn't taken so long to tie my shoes since grade school. However, I managed. Afterward, I sat up. She got on the bench with me and sat for a spell.

"I don't know what got into me, Coach."

"This isn't a big day. It's colossal. The last test before you're done here, yeah, but you feel like the field's got some unexpected terrain. Pay attention to everything you see today, Morgenstern. Like you're playing Gallows Hill, and they finagled that crazy cloaking psychic onto the court."

"What do you mean?" I blinked. "Why?"

"People overlook me sometimes, so I hear things. Can't say much. Movers and shakers around here are, well, moving and shaking. Stay alert."

The bell rang.

"Better move along." She nodded at the clock above the doorway. "Don't want to be late."

"Thanks, Coach."

CHAPTER THIRTY-ONE

After the final bell, both classes waited in turns outside the lab. My detour to the gym meant I arrived at the end of the line. Professor Hawkins stood at the door, letting the third-years in two at a time. He made pairs with each student from a different class.

"Don't blame Professor DeBeer or me for the order or the pairs." He held up a document on school letterhead. "Trustee designation." I saw Andre Gauthier's signature alone at the bottom.

You're nervous. And you don't want to wear those magical monstrosities.

I sighed along with the inside voice and put the ear cuffs on. There was no way around it, even with Leo Pierce off the Board of Trustees for now. Maybe future students wouldn't get stuck under such draconian measures. I'd met plenty of folks who figured they'd gotten theirs, so improving the world for the ones walking after them wasn't important.

I grinned, sure I wasn't one of them. If I'd learned anything at all over the last few years, it was that kindness matters. Everyone's fighting a secret battle, and nobody wins alone.

Hal was the first one out of the lab, with Lee exiting practically on his heels. As he passed me in the hall, Hal held his hand up and gave me a fist bump.

Our hands made contact for too brief a time for him to convey much, but hope, fear, and exhaustion flooded his mind in equal measure. I got the impression that he hurtled toward a yawning chasm, unable to stop before the edge. After that came a bizarre representation of the lab's wall, covered with carvings of Abe Fairbanks's face. Words scrawled across the whiteboard. *He's watching.*

He must have used space magic to get that information. No wonder he looked exhausted.

"Head to the library, gym, or Creatives," Professor Hawkins instructed. "Or the infirmary, as needed."

Hal and Lee headed down the hall, but I didn't see where they ultimately went.

Logan went in with Bailey Overton next. She must have studied because it was only five minutes before she headed to the library. Logan nodded at me and Grace, who pressed her lips into a thin line. I wondered why.

Faith and Eston went after that, and they took half the allotted time. Kitty and Dorian stepped through the door, but not before he glanced over his shoulder and gave the rest of us waiting two thumbs up.

Hailey went in with Dylan. It felt like an eternity, waiting outside with Grace. After thirty minutes, it was finally our turn.

"After you," I said.

Inside, the benches were arranged in two rows. Professor DeBeer started Grace up front on the left and me in the back on the right. We moved along at a similar pace, looking at pictures and replicas of a range of magical items, from ancient curiosities to mergers with modern technology.

I felt confident marking down most of the answers. The only blank I drew was over the replica amulet with a moon on one side and a wolf on the other. After picking it up and turning it over in my hands a few times, I got it. An alliance amulet used to forge pacts between werewolf packs and vampires.

Grace and I reached our last stations simultaneously, which meant she stopped where I'd started, and I ended where she'd begun. I wondered how she managed to navigate that entire ordeal so calmly once I saw the item on the bench.

An old brass lamp. Familiar, too.

I blinked, hoping my hands would stop shaking as I reached for it. Director-General Rockport had assigned me the ear cuffs, which dampened ranged mind magic but intensified it through touch. Miss Dunstable had given me exactly the information I needed so I wouldn't jot the answer down without checking. Plus, there was no way Hector Hawkins hadn't recognized his mother's lamp when he added it to the practical. Had they planned this all along? Or was this another replica, fashioned in a fit of nostalgia and wishful thinking?

The only way to find out was by touching it. I was afraid. Professor DeBeer had apologized for her bias against extramagi, but she was watching. I swallowed, unsure of what to do next.

Another student must have already touched it. Rubbed it, even and become its master. Hal had been in here first, but Gamila couldn't have shown herself. If she had, the headmaster would have postponed the exam, the room overrun by staff and faculty. He probably thought it wasn't the real thing.

Maybe she was canny enough to hold back. I couldn't resist hesitating. Too much was at stake.

On the other side of the room, Grace cleared her throat and raised her hand. Professor DeBeer turned her back to help. I knew it was a cue; the only chance I was likely to get. I took it.

The moment my fingers made contact, I felt the hum of consciousness encased by magic and metal. I tucked it under my arm, then jotted the answer "djinn lamp" in the space for station number one.

Grace leaned over her paper but tilted her head up a little, brow furrowing as she stared at my arm. Then, she jerked her chin at the door. She'd cloaked it, of course.

With the lamp still tucked under my arm, I set my answer sheet on the teacher's bench and strode out the door.

Professor Hawkins nodded as I walked by but said nothing. Nearly breathless, I kept my pace steady and pedestrian down the hall. Why hadn't I turned to see where Hal had gone?

I poked my head into the library first, then the gym, and finally Creatives. He wasn't among the students I saw in any of those places. I didn't see Faith, either. With one hand, I removed my ear cuffs, trying to home in on them. After a moment, I was aware of Grace, keeping pace a few yards behind me on the opposite side of the hall. For a moment, I thought I sensed someone else too.

As if an exam wasn't stressful enough, it had to go and transform into a heist.

Hal could have been in the café, the cafeteria, or even his room. I let my feet go where they would, trusting mind magic to lead them in the right direction. That turned out to be down the ramp to the infirmary.

The desk in the waiting room was unoccupied. Muffled voices, raised more than normal, called out at regular intervals from one of the treatment rooms. I broke into a run, bursting through the door. A moment later, I stopped.

Nurse Smith and Ian were working as hard as they could. Not to save Hal, who was where I expected him to be. Andre Gauthier lay on a wheeled stretcher. He wasn't responding, not to chest compressions or rescue breaths. Nurse Smith looked up when I walked in.

"Thank the gods, someone from a medical family." He jerked his chin at the phone on the wall. "Call rescue. Magifinil overdose, adult male, Hawthorn Academy."

Magifinil blocks mind magic. That's why any attempt to read him bounced off.

It all made sense now. Andre had found the lamp and swapped it for the replica in the exam. He knew about Noah's gloves and signed our practical schedule.

Maybe Abe Fairbanks would kill to get the lamp. Andre Gauthier was prepared to die making sure he didn't.

"Not on my watch."

I called 911 and repeated the information Nurse Smith had given so he could keep working.

"Ian, keep compressions while we wheel. I'll give them the other emergency outside. Once he's in transport, we come back for our next patient."

They ushered the stretcher out, the door swinging shut behind them.

I glanced over to see Hal hooked up to tubing, like any other infusion. But something was different this time.

He sat propped up on the bed, his face an almost claylike shade of ashy brown. His eyes were open but dull somehow, like scuffed marbles.

At first, I thought the worst. But he blinked. From the bedside, Faith looked at my hands, eyes rimmed with red.

"Fumbled the play, huh?"

"No, Faith." I walked right up beside her. "I didn't, thanks to Grace."

"I don't see it." Hal breathed. "Don't see much of anything now."

"Look again." I set the lamp in Hal's lap, breaking the veil of umbral magic Grace had cast over it.

He blinked once more, squinting like he couldn't see clearly. But Faith recognized it immediately. She took his hands and placed them on the lamp.

"I need time," he said. "We don't have it."

"Why not?"

"Grandpa's off-campus, visiting Bubbe," Faith answered. "Nurse Smith went to get the man in charge. My tyrant of a father."

"Well, he's not here yet. If he wants to come in, he'll have to get through me."

I strode toward the door. Hal spoke as I pulled it open.

"He's got help. And a shield. You'll need an army."

"Dunno what for, but we've got one." Grace stood outside, but her statement confused me because she seemed to be alone.

I filled her in as I stepped out and closed the door. Behind me, Faith locked it.

"Figured he'd pull shenanigans." Grace sighed. "Thanks for coming, folks."

Grace waved a hand, and her umbral magic faded, coloring me impressed. She'd cloaked all the third-years, probably fetched them from the rooms I checked as she followed me out of the academic wing. Everyone but Dylan and Logan had their familiars with them. Arick, Lena, and Xan were there, too.

"You're skipping class?" I blinked.

Lena nodded.

"Worth it." Arick grinned.

"What can they do, hold me back another year?" Xan snorted.

"We can do far worse than that, my dear boy."

Lavinia Onassis stood at the bottom of the ramp to the infirmary. Her basilisk hissed as venom dripped from her fangs. The smile on the woman's face was pure poison.

"I've got her." I cracked my knuckles. "Burning off poison's a piece of cake."

"No." Lena pointed. "Get him."

"None of you stand a chance." He chuckled, low and intense. It'd been him then, on the cruise. "I'll block everything you throw at us until you surrender or die. Either way, I'm getting that lamp. Don't expect any help, either."

Mr. Fairbanks stepped out of the shadows. The first thing he did was set up a barrier behind us. I recognized it because I made one like it the night of the masquerade ball to hide Dorian and Xan from Lavinia. Mrs. Pierce leaned on one of his arms. On the other, he held the shield Hal had mentioned.

It wasn't shaped like any sort of conventional weapon, either. It was magical, a device that produced wards. I knew because he put an umbral one up right after the mind, so nobody would hear or see whatever they meant to do to us.

"You could be good little children and let us in." Mr. Fairbanks chuckled again. "We've already won."

"Huddle up, team."

Everyone did, not only my Bishop's Row folks.

"He's not bluffing," I said. "We need to get that device from him and have someone positioned to get around his home-grown mind barrier once the other wards go down."

"I'm not MVP for nothing," Dylan said. "I'll dodge my way past the baddies and get help."

"BS." Grace rolled her eyes. "It's me, and you know it. Umbral's the ticket out. I just need cover."

"Got that." Lee put his hand out. Lena, Xan, and Dylan stacked theirs up. I put mine on top and nodded.

"If you need a hand up, I'm here," Eston said.

"Air support," the twins said.

"Distraction detail." Kitty joined them in a three-way fist bump.

"I'm with them." Arick jerked a thumb at his squadmates. "How will Grace remember us once she's through?"

"Ear cuffs." Logan pointed at me. "They dampen mind energy. Put them on her."

We broke the huddle. I took them off and passed them to Grace. Mr. Fairbanks frowned as she put them on.

"Tiffany, keep them on their toes."

Mrs. Pierce waved a hand, looking like the magic she conjured took barely any effort. I knew from long experience that she was afflicted by resting boredom face. So maybe calling forth an ice storm out of thin air wasn't as easy as she made it look.

"Dracula's balls!" Dorian's look of horror confirmed my suspicions. "Dylan, a little help here."

They began banishing and good thing too. We might have all ended up sliding around on the tile defenseless if it iced over.

"Rush play, cover mid, go!" I called to my team.

Lena jumped out in front, hurling a poison orb at Tiffany Pierce. Lavinia raised a hand to banish it from across the room.

Xan tossed another orb right through Lavinia's line of sight and she ended up banishing that instead. Lena's orb continued on its path.

Tiffany waved her free hand and a wall of ice formed. Lena's orb bounced off. I sent a fireball streaking toward it. Abe knocked it aside with a mind blast. I had to banish it myself before it hit the nurse's desk and did more than smolder. The Overton's pigeons dove at his head but they turned aside at the last moment to avoid a poison orb from Lavinia. Julia took wing and banished it before it could land and do any more damage.

Somewhere in all that confusion, Grace must have cloaked herself. I couldn't see her or sense her presence, which meant the ear cuffs were doing their job. Despite all the banishing Dylan and Dorian did, some of Tiffany's storm hit the floor. My fireball had melted it, which meant Grace left visible footprints.

"Logan, Eston!" I pointed at the still smoldering desk, close enough to Grace's position to indicate without giving her away.

They doused it. Water flowed with enough depth and splashing to cover Grace's tracks. Eston's Labrador familiar cavorted in the puddles with Lune, further obfuscating Grace's path.

"Cut off the head," Abe said.

"Down!" Lee knocked me aside right before a purple-tinted icicle speared me in the chest. He winced in pain as it grazed his left arm. The wood orb he'd been conjuring fizzled out like Arick's on the boat. He tried conjuring again but couldn't because Lavinia was still standing. Lune dashed to his side and helped Scratch defend him from stray orbs and icicles.

"Ladies!" Logan called out. "Thread the needle. Go!"

Kitty held her hands up, fire blazing around them. The twins stood on either side, conjuring air that fed the flames. Her sphinx twined his tail around her ankle, and the fire blasted between Tiffany and Lavinia, a move I instantly felt slice through their dual conjuring. Our opponents immediately began rebuilding their link again, but it'd take time.

I had to get to Abe. If I didn't do it now, his allies would wear us out while he erected wards behind him with the shield. Grace must have been at the exit by then, or close enough that she'd arrive once I made my play.

This wasn't Bishop's Row. We had no protective ballistae, ankyr, or cestus. Coach Pickman's whistle wouldn't blow for time out. Scores were counted by incapacitation, and Lee had been lucky.

"Cover barrage!"

Xan, Lena, and Hailey conjured orbs and hurled them at Abe. He ducked them effortlessly of course. That was fine by me. I needed a distraction while moving safely between the ice and poison magi defending him. Abe wasn't in any danger at all. I knew exactly how much of an advantage mind magic gave. Lavinia didn't. Or maybe Xan's defiance was finally too much for her.

She snarled, conjuring and throwing faster than even Lee on his best day. Lena's size gave her a small target advantage plus the ability to hide behind the desk's wreckage. Hailey stopped conjuring orbs and channeled a whirlwind around herself to deflect the poison.

I pressed my advantage and took two steps toward Mr. Fairbanks, a tightly concentrated fire orb in one of my hands. He glanced at Tiffany.

She threw ice, but I melted it. She threw another, and the ice storm lost steam. She shook her head at Abe and continued with her storm-bringing. Lavinia hadn't paused her barrage, her son the focus of all her attacks now.

Xan faced them all head-on. When he had no orb to block with, he swatted her attacks back at her with empty hands. She didn't seem to run out of steam. Poison magi were immune to their toxin, but even a parent's was different enough to be dangerous.

"Stop this, Mom." If he'd been fatally dosed, Xan gave no outward indication. Still, I heard fear singing all around him. "Before someone gets hurt."

"You'll hurt before I'm through," she shrilled. "Pharmaka, don't hold back!"

Lavinia's familiar slithered and became a purple blur on the floor. Kitty saw and aimed a jet of flame, but too late. Arick tried lifting a floorboard in her way, but the basilisk scaled it like lightning. She struck at Xan's leg quicker than I thought possible.

Asceco was faster. The smaller green basilisk struck back. Fangs slashed and clashed, venom flying every which way.

"Move it, Morgenstern!" Xan called.

I moved forward again, wondering whether Mr. Fairbanks would put up a shield at the last minute. He only stood there, an unfathomably mild grin on his face.

"Move!" Dorian called while flinging ice.

It knocked Pharmaka aside as she was about to strike.

No matter what Lavinia threw at him, she couldn't bring Xan down. I'd lost count long ago of the orbs he'd deflected unarmed. Maybe he had an antidote or learned a way to transform her toxin into his. However he managed, his victory seemed assured although he hadn't delivered anything but defensive blows.

Xan made no mistakes. Not even morally in the heat of emotionally charged combat.

His familiar took a wrong turn.

"It's okay." Lavinia gave her son a gentle smile. "I'll buy you a new one."

She destroyed Xan with a single hollow stomp as her heel crushed Asceco's head. He dropped to his knees on the sleety floor, head bowed and sobbing.

Everything stopped, at least on the student side of the battle. Most of us had seen Leo give Doris to the kraken, but he'd done the same with Brand and had the excuse of paying a life debt.

Asceco's murder was sickening.

"I'm tired of all this drama." Abe brandished the shielding device. I felt a ward go up that separated familiars from their magi. "If any break through, I kill them. Unless you're ready to surrender."

"Never!" Dorian stood holding an ice orb, Julia above him, channeling poison into it. "Take that, sadistic bitch!" He launched it at Lavinia. It hit her squarely in the face and knocked her to the floor with a wet smack.

"I warned you." Abe sighed. "You should know better, Mr. Spanos."

He didn't use magic to attack. Instead, a tiny throwing dagger whipped through the air and hit the strix in the middle of her chest. Blood dripped, pattering on the floor.

I expected Julia to drop out of the air dead like Mercy. That didn't happen. She was a tougher older bird and had never forgotten her first magus's example. Julia refused to fall without a fight.

None of us humans had seen Tiffany Pierce's familiar, but I'd sensed some creature helping her create that storm. Julia knew more than I did. It was an ice dragonet with scales the hue of a polar bear's fur, hidden under her voluminous bleached blonde hair.

The dying strix controlled her descent and scratched the dragonet on the way down. It *cheeped* unhappily. The storm didn't disappear, but it abated somewhat, and Tiffany had to use more of her power to maintain it. Dylan kept banishing, countering the ice storm on his own.

Dorian scooped Julia up, then rushed to Xan's side where they sat huddled together. Lee joined them. Kitty, Eston, Arick, and the twins defended them from Lavinia's renewed attacks with a series of fire orbs, whirlwinds, and sheets of water.

"Now, Miss Morgenstern." Abe narrowed his eyes. "Let's finish this."

I strode forward this time, unhindered. Mr. Fairbanks, despite his apparent confidence, looked tired of all of this. Maybe using the shield device had sapped his energy. Perhaps Hal wished right now. Maybe luck was on my side this time.

It wasn't.

Abe's familiar flew at my face and clung to my forehead. I had no time to dodge the scarab's attack. I'd encountered it before and nearly lost myself in the process. I was only slightly less prepared that time.

I swatted at it with two conjures, solar on one side and fire on the other. I dazzled my own eyes and singed my eyebrows. Those attacks stopped short, blocked by wards.

I tried mind, but the insect only siphoned that. I couldn't remove it mundanely. Giving the scarab more points of contact with my skin would only let it into my mind faster.

A gentle breeze blew by my right cheek and brought with it a hint of sandalwood and the memory of a pair of deep brown limpid eyes. Hal had eyes like that.

He's gone.

"No." I knew that inside voice wasn't mine this time.

Yes. That must be why you thought of him just now.

I refused to believe it. When I left the room, Hal already had the lamp. Minutes had passed. There was no way he hadn't used it. Take that and choke on it, dissociation voice.

"Shields win." Abe let out that chuckle again. "I captured the queen. Check."

Behind me, my friends gasped, growled, and cried out in defiance. However, none of them besides Logan had any idea what was in store if I couldn't resist Abe and his scarab a second time.

Whatever gambit Hal had going with the lamp and his wishes, we needed it before I dissociated again and ended this battle in the most logical and definitive way possible.

Friends, foes. There's no difference. Burn them all.

That awful voice told me exactly what that was before beginning the work of separating my mind from my body. Of course, Abe would use his shield device to save his allies, their children, and whichever of my friends he thought he could break. The rest would all be victims, and me a scapegoat like every other extramagus bogeyman.

CHAPTER THIRTY-TWO

Face Your Death
Hal

I'd spent the last three years trying not to waste time but running out of it anyway. I should have known that if anyone could buy me more, it'd be Aliyah Morgenstern. I refused to squander her kindness.

I was out of more than time now. My energy was almost gone.

Rubbing the lamp felt downright Herculean. Seconds stretched out as it glowed and spewed smoke, then revealed my grandmother who I'd only ever seen in pictures—old ones.

"Hi, Nana Mila."

"Queen's Grace, Harold!" Her eyes reddened. "In my worst nightmares, I never imagined you in this state."

At first, this confused me. I remembered in time how shocking it must have seemed, seeing someone my age at death's door.

"I'd like my wishes now if you don't mind skipping formalities." I tried to grin. The look on Faith's face told me I'd managed a grimace. "I know the rules."

"Wish on, child."

"I wish for an audience with the Sidhe Queen."

"Done."

Faith blew me a kiss. The wooden walls and tiled floor of the infirmary melted like wax under a lit wick on fast-forward. I found myself in a long hallway paved in glittering dun stone. At the end stood a set of double doors, tall and gilt.

"Come along."

Grandma Mila took my hand and a step forward. Inwardly, I balked because my brain told me there was no way I'd make it even halfway to the doors.

My body had other ideas.

I strode forward, pacing right along with her. I hadn't had a day this good since I helped Aliyah shop for Logan's birthday. It made sense. I was in the Under, where I could breathe in the magic my body needed. So we made it to the door in a few moments, where my grandmother spoke to one of the guards.

"Announce us, please."

The guard hefted her staff and used it to hammer the door three times. It opened, and she turned her back on us to step through before speaking in a booming voice.

"Duchess Gamila Haddad-Hawkins, lamp-bound, accompanied by her grandson Harold Hawkins, lamp-holder and magus of space."

"Enter and state your business," a voice replied.

The guard stepped aside to reveal a room built of the same glittering stone but ornately carved. A long red carpet ran between a row of columns, which led to a dais. Atop it sat a throne flanked by knights in alabaster armor, one with a red helmet and the other blue.

The Queen herself had amber-hued hair that hung in thick waves over her shoulders almost to her waist. A crown graced her head, golden and studded with diamond, topaz, and garnet. Her robes were long, sheer fabric with a coppery metallic sheen overlaying deep sunset orange.

We paced forward until we stepped between two columns, adorned with sconces lit by solar magic. Nana Mila bowed, holding my hand tightly so I had to follow suit. I would have anyway, but she barely knew me. For all she knew I might have had horrid manners.

That made me more determined to let her know who I was because I still wasn't sure whether my plan would work. I kept my head bowed as I made my address.

"Your Majesty, thank you for allowing me the gift of your valuable time. I seek your permission before making my second and third wishes." I dared a glance up.

"Permission?" The Queen tilted her head. "Interesting. Why?"

"It requires your intervention, Majesty. Becoming a djinn."

"To what purpose? Power? Glory? Of all the people in Faerie, djinn have the least potential for these. Theirs is a life of service and sacrifice."

"I'm dying, Majesty, of a magical malady. My illness is writ in the very fiber of my being, and I already know wishes can't erase it. But my lineage is indelible too. It's the only way to save my life."

"Technically, you are correct. However, granting your request will not cure you in the mundane realm. You'll still suffer many of its hardships, although not fatally."

"I understand, Your Majesty." I nodded. "I can live with that."

"If I say yes, what will you do?"

"Pledge fealty to Your Majesty, and take my grandmother's place in her lamp after my third wish, so it continues in your service."

"That third wish, what will it be?"

"Justice. Too many I love suffer without it."

"*My* permission is yours. But know this, young magus. Bestowing a new mantle is a tandem effort between myself and His Majesty, and more from Duchess Gamila. If consent is important to you, his is as significant as mine."

I stood at the brink of despair. Somewhere in the fog of magic deprivation, I'd miscalculated.

My friends back in the mundane world were either already engaged in combat with senior magi or about to be. They needed one of my wishes to survive as surely as I did. I'd come to terms with death before holding the lamp was certain, but only as long as they continued.

Now, caught between saving my expiring life and all of theirs, the choice was clear.

"I will face my fate and do without to save my wife, my father, and my friends. Nana, I w—"

"His Majesty, King of Wood and Wild, Master of the Hunt, Husband and Peer to the Sun Court's Glory."

"Enter, Baelgreth." The Queen rose.

The air to my left stirred like an autumn breath, the one that takes the last leaf off the oldest oak in the forest at the fall of the year.

I studied the figure standing beside the queen. They were of a height, but night and day in most other respects. He wore a long black cloak with tattered edges over forest green traveling clothes. While the Queen went unarmed, he was girt with dagger and rapier.

"My love." He took her hands and kissed each of them in turn. "Forgive my hasty entrance. I couldn't ignore these strands of fate." He tilted his head at me.

"As I suspected. I agree. The fiber of his being also calls to me."

"Empathy. Forgiveness." The King grinned.

"Honor. Above all, bravery." The Queen nodded. "Perhaps this...collaboration...is practice for something else."

"Shall we, then?" He raised an eyebrow.

"We consent, young magus. Only one more thing needs doing to complete this magic."

"Go on, Harold. Make your wish."

"I wish to be a djinn, like my grandmother before me."

Nana Mila glowed. It seemed to come from within, as though every cell in her body became luminescent. Myriad colors, a shrouded rainbow, flowed out of her and toward the Monarchs on the dais. They each held out a hand, collecting the light between them. As it gathered, they each added to it, the King's contribution in swirls of green, blue, and purple and the Queen's red, orange, and yellow.

It reminded me of Bishop's Row, what I imagined would happen if everyone combined their orbs. Except the energy between them grew impossibly large, which transcended its appearance. Visually, it fit in their hands, but I sensed that its borders exceeded the walls of the throne room.

The Queen smiled down at me. Then, with the King, she aimed that massive orb at me. It didn't fly so much as roll forward.

All my hair stood on end, even the stubble on my head, which I'd shaved in November because I thought it'd be easier to manage. It hadn't grown back. A breath later, I felt it lifting and itching as it returned.

My feet left the stone-covered carpet as light, magic, and heat encased me. I remembered a lab experiment, one of Filberto Luciano's more daring ones done with a crucible. Maybe I understood it better now, from an unexpected perspective. I hung suspended in one, both my state and composition changing irrevocably.

I opened my mouth, unsure why until light and sound poured from it. I'd always been tone-deaf, but for the only time in my life, I sang perfectly. It made sense. I was in the middle of a miracle, after all.

"You deserve one, after making so many."

The Queen's voice didn't startle me. Her words did. Until scenes from my life paraded through my consciousness.

Grandpa Hiram on house arrest, eyes lighting up when I visited.

Dad in the headmaster's office, doubting his new job until I said I believed in him.

Showing Lee around Salem the day he arrived on campus.

Faith in the cafeteria, taking my hand for the first time.

Keeping Aliyah's secret.

Grace agreeing to beat me at Scrabble during that rocky first-year winter break.

Inventing devices with Logan.

Riding the train to Boston after Dylan's breakup, just to get him out of town.

Sitting with Darren after his familiar was poisoned.

Walking a nervous Eston to cheer squad tryouts.

Meeting Dorian in the bathroom to practice his stand-up routine.

Decorating the classroom door for Professor Luciano.

Proofreading Kitty's numerous college entrance essays.

Practicing with the Overtons in a mirror so we'd stop calling Xan by his old name.

Forgiving my mother when she promised to do better.

"And now, we empower you to make one more." My song, the memories, and the magic ended on the Queen's last word.

My feet came to rest on the floor. My Hawthorn Academy infirmary slippers were gone, replaced by my favorite brown loafers. I blinked, realizing that somehow the convalescent clothing I'd been stuck wearing over the last few months was replaced by the khakis, chambray button-down, bow-tie, and blazer I favored. Plus, they were comfortable again.

"Your Majesty." I took a knee, without any worry about whether I'd be able to stand later. "I pledge myself to your service, in fealty, and dedicate my service to my wife, Faith Fairbanks-Hawkins."

"Then you will remain in the Under, Harold Hawkins, doing the work of my Court as squire to Sir Frederick. Your wife will have leave to visit once your duties are established. Your term endures for one year and one day, with one exception—the moment it takes to retrieve the lamp currently occupied by your grandmother. You will transport it here immediately after," the Queen said. "You may rise and make your final wish."

"Nana, I want justice. For my family, friends, and those who would do them harm."

"As you wish."

The Queen snapped her fingers, and a portal opened. Through it, I saw the infirmary waiting room, much of it in ruins, the battle still raging. My grandmother held her hands out, brow furrowed and beaded with effort. Justice seemed to be a taller order than I'd expected.

When she lowered her hands, I felt myself move involuntarily through space, drawn into the portal, past the magi locked in combat, over Aliyah and Mr. Fairbanks as he uttered the word check.

I wanted to stop and help but couldn't. The lamp pulled me inexorably on through the door.

On the edge of the bed I'd almost died in, Faith's eyes widened. I saw myself reflected in them, not as I'd appeared in the Under, but as a plume of golden smoke flowing toward the lamp cradled in her arms. I took form.

"It worked." Faith held the lamp out to me. "Or it will once you take her place. I love you."

I leaned forward, bending to kiss her.

"I love you too. Go out now and help Aliyah. She's in serious trouble. See you soon."

The moment I touched the polished brass, I vanished with it and Nin, back to the Under.

CHAPTER THIRTY-THREE

Aliyah

"Checkmate, Dad." Faith stood in the doorway alone, hands empty. "Get your hooks off my friend."

"You're one of us, Faith. A Fairbanks. You can't erase that."

"That's Hawkins now. I'm erasing your victory, not myself."

I felt the hum of emotion from her, how it focused on her father with laser precision. Faith hadn't been present to fight her sister last year, but she was here now and done tolerating what her family did in the shadows.

"Sic him, Seth."

I never suspected Seth was the most loyal out of all our familiars, but his devotion in those moments was legendary. I knew he smelled the throwing knives up Abe's sleeve. I sensed his fear. He followed Faith's order immediately anyway, and that little dog saved my soul.

Sha are the size of chihuahuas, but they pounce like panthers. Wards might have protected the scarab from my magic, but they did nothing against the frenzy of its natural predator. Especially one bonded to a magus as righteously angry as Faith at that moment.

Seth held the scarab in his teeth without biting down. I felt indignation and fear coming off the insect and joy from Seth. This was what he was made for. He ran under a chair on the other side of the room, separating the critter from its magus. And from me.

That waking limb feeling came over me for the second time. I cried again, but I didn't let it stop me from reaching for the shield device still in Abe's hand. I winced and looked down to find my wrist impaled with one of his blades.

"Don't bring a fist to a knife fight."

Behind him, Grace made a zipping motion over her lips. She touched the device, and it vanished a second before she did.

"Don't stab fire magi." I winced, tears still streaming from my eyes as I conjured flames to stop the bleeding. "What did you say? We've already won. Be good parents and let us through?"

"The next one goes in your throat." He snorted.

"I'm an extramagus. You think I can't stop you?" I glanced at his seemingly empty hand and hoped the pain hid my bluff. "By the way, your shield's gone."

He looked for it and blinked, then opened his hand like most people who don't believe in anything they can't see.

The device wasn't missing, of course, only cloaked. It clattered to the floor and cut off the wards for real this time. He bent to retrieve it, but a wooden panel appeared out of nowhere and knocked it across the room.

"What happened here?" A pajama-clad Noah blinked blearily at the door of his borrowed apartment, surveying the damage. "Hurricane Hawthorn?"

Justice prevailed after that.

Grace's voice echoed back through the hall followed by answering footsteps a moment later. She led a crowd through, mostly faculty but also Nurse Smith, walking with Detective Ambersmith. I learned later he called her because the wards made him think Hal and Faith were missing.

Abraham Fairbanks tried covering for himself with his magic. But the Magifinil overdose was already logged, along with a journal on

Andre's person that detailed everything he'd observed as a trustee this year.

Plus, he'd forgotten who his allies were.

Xan's mother hit him with the same nullifying toxin she'd used on the dagger and Lee. She did it the moment she saw a Salem PD uniform. Because of her betrayal, he couldn't keep himself out of the police reports.

We all made statements that day, detailing crimes like assault, threats, and killing familiars. Lavinia Onassis made the confession that ended up putting him away for crimes against extrahumanity, Geneva Convention-level stuff. Two of his planned wishes involved genocide. She gave them all the details in exchange for extradition of her case to Greece where she had the protection of her title, of course.

Tiffany Pierce didn't bother lying either. Since she hadn't technically done anything illegal and denounced the familiars' killing, she was off the hook with the police. The school stripped her of her title and alumni status, then banned her from campus for life.

Leo remained at the Danvers Sanitarium in their aggression wing. Crow joined him soon after. Mavis told me he would have been in High Extrahuman Security since he already had a record. Her mom was all set to let him rot because he'd squealed on Lavinia about the knife. Paolo Micello intervened and pulled some strings to get him a chance at rehabilitation instead.

We heard about most of this during the last week on campus, but were largely uninvolved because Ember's clutch hatched the morning after the battle. I was in the infirmary having my dressings changed when it happened.

A cacophony of peeping, cheeping, cooing, and blooing sounded in the hall and grew closer by the second. It woke Xan and Dorian, who'd slept there overnight. Logan burst through the door, followed by Dylan with Gale crooning on his shoulder.

"You're never going to belie—" Dylan got interrupted by what looked like a cloud of scaly wings and tails.

They streamed into the room in a flock, wheeling overhead as they separated. Ember dived first, puffing her skinny chest out proudly. Logan laughed.

"She says, 'I'm so awesome, I made all of these.'" He blinked as something crashed into his head. "Ow."

A little teal dragonet clung to his hair. It craned its neck over Logan's forehead and peered into his face upside-down.

"Cheep?"

"Buddy? That was a big bump. Are you okay?" Logan held his forearm out in front of him at chest level, horizontally.

"Cheep!" The dragonet glided down and hopped from one foot to the other on his new perch. "Cheep cheep!"

"Right, I get it. Buddy's your name, and you're hungry."

Nurse Smith taped the bandage over my wound. "I'll get them some snacks. No fish heads allowed in here, though."

"Um, guys?" Xan sat with his hands over his head, which a green dragonet dived at repeatedly. "What do I do?"

"Let her land." I grinned. "She likes you."

He lowered his arms, and the green dragonet went right for his head, clinging in his unkempt curls and cooing contentedly.

"Uh, I guess she's Percy." Xan looked over at Dorian, who'd pulled the covers over his head.

"Not again," he sobbed. We all huddled around his bed.

"Hey." Xan rubbed his back through the sheet. "What do you need?"

"I don't even know anymore." He sniffled. "Space, I think."

"Okay." Xan nodded. "You heard the man."

We moved to the waiting room, where Nurse Smith left a tray of fish pellets on a table. The dragonets ate while we sat and watched them. Ember flapped and hissed at any who got too greedy. She wanted to make sure her children got enough. Gale strutted around the tray without eating, admiring his offspring. A pair of yellow dragonets split their pellets and shared with each other. I guessed that they were solar. A sleek gray one examined each morsel before eating it. I also saw a blue one, a different shade than Gale and with aquatic looking fins. Buddy kept trying to pass pellets to a little white dragonet, but he *cheeped* and turned his back. He hadn't had a single bite.

"No more pining." Dorian stepped out of the doorway and took a pellet from Buddy. The white dragonet accepted it from him. "I get it. You need me." He cradled him in his arms and fed him another pellet. "His name's Rime. And yeah, he's ice."

In the office, I almost called Bubbe to examine Ember's new family. Although the hospital had discharged her, she needed three weeks at Oaken Acres Rehab. Dad came to look them over. He was the Morgenstern at the extraveterinary practice now. Bubbe already said she'd retire, unsure she'd be able to handle struggling creatures with her weakened right hand.

I brought the unbonded hatchlings to visit anyway, after getting permission from the staff. Petra was visiting with Andre in the lobby at the time, so they came with me. The blue water dragonet flew backward in front of Petra, cheeping.

"Hello there, little one." She smiled. "No, I haven't had a companion in years. Yes, I'd love to." The dragonet landed on her shoulder. "Her name's Marina, by the way."

Bubbe was in her room when we got there. She bonded with one of the yellow ones right away, and it flew to and fro, fetching little items for her. His name was Sonny.

"Don't look now, Aliyah." She glanced over my head. "I think you've got a new friend."

She was right. The other half of that pair told me her name was Dawn. Bubbe said that sometimes extramagi ended up with two familiars. That explained what happened to Dylan later.

"This one won't leave me alone." He sighed over the gray dragonet sleeping on his shoulders. "Isn't one enough? Gale keeps me on my toes."

"Gust is mild, though," Logan said. "Maybe she'll be a good influence on him."

The entire third year class went to the science fair for Hal's entry. His Neshmet chair won first place, and MIT was fine with him taking a gap year. Faith carried the blue ribbon and the news to him on her first visit to the Under.

He'd always need the chair in the mundane world, and his magic would wear down without regular visits to the Under, but as a djinn he had numerous reasons to visit. He could live a full life, although Faith insisted there was no way she was giving birth to thirteen kids.

We worried about how he'd graduate. Hal's agreement with the Queen meant he couldn't leave the Under. Instead of the lobby, Gamila suggested we hold the ceremony in the auditorium. Everybody thought it was a way to accommodate Noah since the room was sunproof. On the day, while the rest of us lined up in caps and gowns, ready to walk between the seats and across the stage, a portal opened beside the podium. Apparently, there was a thin spot in the barrier between worlds up there. Hal smiled down at us from the other side.

Hiram handed his diploma through. The sound of our applause must have carried because I saw the tears on his face as he waved before the portal closed. The rest of the ceremony proceeded in alphabetical order, beginning with Kitty Byers and ending with Lee Young.

The diploma felt oddly light in my hand, as though the education it represented wasn't such a big thing. Maybe that was right. The books, labs, and exams were only a small fraction of my lessons at Hawthorn Academy.

Walking off stage, literally and figuratively between all the friends who'd been with me on this journey through school felt like a fitting end to this story of mine.

The thing about knowledge is this. It's a lot like love, which exists all around us in infinite forms. Learning is endless, as long as you're brave enough to seek it out and let it in.

The End

Read on for an epilogue.

EPILOGUE

Dear Noah,

How's everything going across the pond? As I write this, you only left a month ago, but it feels like a year and a day. So much has happened.

I went to a Piercing Whispers show. Cadence is rocking on vocals, no offense. Can you believe Arick commuted from Norway all summer to gig with them? Carick is still a thing, and it gives them some nice energy on stage. They picked up one of Azrael's cousins as their new guitarist, Winnifred. She's pretty good.

Hawthorn held a big alumnus meeting. Hiram stepped down as headmaster, so Hector's doing the job for real now. Plus, they selected three new trustees. Hiram himself, of course. Old Grandpa Ambersmith. And wait for it...

Bubbe! She's sick of retirement already, so it's good for her. She's excited because they already voted in some changes. Students have to be magi but can attend if they're also changelings, vampires, or somehow get a magic shifter item. That's happening way more often now for some reason. All the vampires they let go last year got offers to come back. Zeke asked me to thank you for fixing that desk lamp in his apartment. The solar energy was on the fritz for decades.

Logan's mom said she wanted nothing to do with the Menagerie anymore so she sold it and moved to Hawaii. Petra flew us all out with a lawyer and got Logan and Elanor their fair share of the proceeds. Petra ended up with a share too. Dad made sure the more docile critters were adopted, but there were a whole bunch that were too big or traumatized to find homes. Petra and Logan used their shares to buy a farm in Methuen and moved them there. Dad's got visiting privileges. We'll have to go up there next time you're in town. It's beautiful.

Grace is engaged. She asked Azrael, and they're getting married next year. State Of Grace has taken off too, gone international already. You probably already knew that. I helped her pack up a suit for shipping. The label had your address in Oxford. Most of her sales outside the US are from the UK.

Dorian's coming to PPC with the rest of us. He said it was his last choice, but he looked way too happy when he got his acceptance letter. He's majoring in Extrahuman Law if you can believe that. I met his parents again on a campus tour. They're almost as funny as he is, and great people too. Xan was with them. Reminds me of how our folks were with Logan. So it turns out we're not the only magi with decent parents.

I decided on Alternative Therapies for my major, like Faith. We're already planning our schedules so we can be lab partners. Doctor Klein's an adjunct so we'll be taking her classes next year for sure. Logan's in Extraveterinary. He got all twelve of his textbooks last week and read them already. Brianna's in Social Work. Bar's in Law and Contracts. Lee's undecided but leaning toward Ecology. Izzy's in Psychic Professional Studies. Kitty and Eston ended up in Germany at Black Forest University for Magipsychic Chemistry.

The Overtons took a gap year to travel internationally, and their first stop is a visit to the Black Forest for Oktoberfest. You'll probably see them around eventually, too. They're making a travel blog for magi based on major events. College-level Bishop's Row championship games are near the top of their list. I expect you and Dylan to make it that far, so don't slack at practice. I hope he's been showing you a good time. If not, tell him to call me, and I'll badger him until he does.

In your last message, you asked if I'd heard from Hal. That's a delicate subject, and it comes with a small request. The Queen's had him on some type *of scouting mission with a knight you might remember from a few years back. Fred Redford. They're looking for an item, something extremely important to the King. Faith says he can't tell anyone more than that. Even with his space affinity and all the dowsing, he's not making any progress.*

So, he's asked all of us to keep an eye out, wherever we are. He says the graduation ceremony's giving us a connection for a while, even through the barrier between worlds. So, he'll be able to pinpoint it if we've seen the item. Whatever it is. Unfortunately, he's under a ban and can't say what.

Logan's got some ideas. Since it's for the King and an artifact, he deduced that it must have big Unseelie energy. He guesses the Queen might already have the Seelie equivalent. Also, either the item is dangerous, or dangerous folk want it. Her Majesty wouldn't send a seasoned redcap knight along when his squire could have done all the work on his own unless she thought Hal needed muscle.

I guess it's never a bad idea to go through life with our eyes wide open anyway.

All my love,
Aliyah

AUTHOR'S NOTES

Hello for the third time, Dear Reader.

I'm writing this with that tight sensation around my eyes. The one that always comes with leaky eyes. I'll be okay, this happens every time I write The End on a series. Still, saying goodbye to a main character is never easy.

Authors put characters through unforgiving paces, plotting obstacles at their feet every time we sit down at our keyboards. For the past eleven months, I've wondered whether some cosmic author out in the ether sits at their desk wincing at what they've typed. The way things have gone, I imagine his name is Chuck Shurley. If you're also a *Supernatural* fan, you might agree.

Aliyah's 2020 wasn't the same as ours, but it was the roughest ride I've sent her on so far. Some of her friends still have things to do in future books. You'll see at least one in Gallows Hill, which is the next series in the Revealed World. But for now, Aliyah Morgenstern is contented, and off being her best self.

I wish the same for you.

With gratitude,

D.R. Perry

GLOSSARY

People

- **Changeling**- A mortal child of either one or two faerie parents. Most changelings choose a monarch sometime in their twenties, although some do it earlier than they have to.
- **Dampyr**- The mortal offspring of two vampires. They aren't as rare as many suspect, although because their blood is exceptionally sustaining to vampires, they keep their status secret. Dampyr sometimes have magic or psychic powers that work unreliably.
- **Faerie**- A term used to describe either a changeling who has tithed to a monarch and spent a year and a day in the Under or the pure creatures such as Gnomes and Pixies who were created by the king and queen.
- **Ghost**- A dead person with unfinished business becomes a ghost. If a mortal makes a contract before death, that gives them unfinished business and lets them linger. When ghosts finish their business, they move on, but no one knows where they go from here.

- **Magus**- A mortal who can use magic. Magic comes from energy in the world. Most magi can only use one type of magic. However, a rare few can do more than one kind. Those are called extramagi.
- **Merfolk**- People who can live on land with legs or in the sea with fins and tails. They only emerged from the ocean after the Big Reveal and are still extremely rare outside of harbor towns.
- **Psychic**- A mortal with psychic power. Psychic ability comes from a person's own body and mind.
- **Vampire**- An unliving person who drinks blood to survive and enhance their abilities. Only regular mortals, psychics, and magi can get turned into vampires. Shifters, changelings, and faeries won't turn, and most of those won't survive an attempt.
- **Shifter**- A mortal who can take an animal's shape. Shifters have one form, with coloring similar to what they have while human. They usually have an enhanced sense while human-shaped, which goes along with their animal. For example, an owl shifter might have keen eyesight and a wolf shifter, a great sense of smell.

Shifter Varieties

- **Dragon**- The only shifters who can see both magic and psychic abilities, though only while shifted. The most powerful ones can partially shapeshift. Dragons are immortal and reproduce infrequently. There are so few of them since the Reveal that they've started taking other magical shifters as mates.
- **Kelpie**- A magical shifter who gets their abilities from an enchanted faerie pelt that bonds with their soul. The Kelpie pelts were created by the Goblin King, so they have Unseelie energy and restrictions. A Kelpie's animal form is a horse. Families pass the pelts down through generations,

and part of each ancestor lives on to help their descendants. The ancestors can get distracting, however.

- **Selkie**- A magical shifter who gets their abilities from an enchanted faerie pelt that bonds with their soul. The Selkie pelts were created by the Sidhe queen, so they have Seelie energy and restrictions. A Selkie's animal form is a seal or sometimes a sea otter. They can use water magic as long as they wear the pelt. Families pass the pelts down through the generations, and part of each ancestor lives on to help their descendants. The ancestors can get distracting, however.
- **Tanuki**- A magical shifter with enhanced speed and the ability to see all types of magic while shifted. They are also the only creatures who can manipulate luck, causing it to turn from good to bad or the other way around. They stop aging if they own a charm infused with luck from humans. Very few of those charms exist, having been either used up during the Reveal or locked away.

Powers

- **Air magic**- The power to conjure, control, and banish wind or air.
- **Earth magic**- The power to conjure, control, and banish earth, sand, or rock.
- **Empathy**- A psychic power to sense and influence emotions in other people.
- **Fire magic**- The power to conjure, control, and banish flames.
- **Ice magic**- The power to conjure, control, and banish ice.
- **Lightning magic**- The power to conjure, control, and banish lightning.
- **Poison magic**- The power to conjure, control, and banish poison. Each magus has a slightly different type of toxin they produce. Some are even antidotes to others.
- **Precognitive**- A psychic power to foretell future events.

- **Spectral magic**- the power to conjure, control, and banish light.
- **Spectral Affinity**- A trait some spectral magi have that makes them charismatic and believable.
- **Summoner**- A psychic power that lets the user make contracts with pure faeries, letting the summoner call them in times of need. Each creature has an anchor, some item symbolizing the bond. Mastery of summoning takes decades of study, which is why the most powerful are either vampires or past middle age.
- **Seelie**- The Sidhe queen's court. The Seelie way is about following the letter of the law, even when it's hard or cruel. They have a hard time reconciling faerie rules with the new mortal laws since the Big Reveal.
- **Solar Magic**- The power to conjure, control, or banish sunlight. Some of the most powerful practitioners can find hidden objects or discover long-kept secrets.
- **Solar Affinity**- A trait some solar magi have that makes them beacons for coincidence.
- **Space magic**- The power to move the self or objects instantly across distances. Some can even move other people.
- **Space Affinity**- This space power comes with an ability to locate people or things important to the magus.
- **Telekinesis**- A psychic power that moves objects.
- **Telepathy**- A psychic power to read minds.
- **Tithe**- The process of pledging to either the queen or king, making a changeling choose to be either Seelie or Unseelie.
- **Umbral magic**- The power to conjure, control, and banish shadows and veil or camouflage objects or people.
- **Umbral Affinity**- A trait some umbral magi have that makes them difficult to remember without psychic ability, faerie magic, or a shifter pack bond.
- **Undeath magic**- The power to conjure, control, and banish unliving energy.

- **Unseelie**- The Goblin king's court. The Unseelies bend the rules and often navigate mortal society more easily than their Seelie counterparts.
- **Water magic**- The power to conjure, banish, and control water.
- **Wood magic**- The power to conjure, banish, and control wood. It takes extreme power to influencing a living plant.

Creatures

- **Basilisk**- A venomous serpent that also has poison magic.
- **Dragonet**- A tiny dragon-like creature, always associated with one or more element which powers their breath attacks later in life. They have scales but are warm-blooded like birds. Most don't get much bigger than a small cat.
- **Familiar**- A magical or mythical creature who makes a bond with a magus.
- **Gryphon**- A chimera which has the head of a bird and hindquarters of a predatory mammal. They come in several combinations of base species, and habitat influences their choice in magi to bond with.
- **Karkus**- A crab that can change its shape. They're said to be the offspring of the crab that pinched Hercules as he battled the Hydra.
- **Lightning Bird**- A familiar from South Africa with an affinity for lightning. Its beak can jump-start a car.
- **Mercat**- A shapeshifting feline with fur for land and scales in the water. They can live in lakes, rivers, or in the sea as well as on land. They must never completely dry out, or they will die.
- **Moon Hare**- A magical rabbit that gets power from its particular moon phase. They commonly bond with umbral magi.
- **Pharaoh's Rat**- These natural predators of dragon shifters are the size of ferrets and resemble a mongoose with more

fur. They have an affinity for space magic and can use it on occasion.

- **Pigeon**- Not as mundane as most think, some pigeons have an uncanny sense of direction due to their affinity for air magic.
- **Pricus**- An aquatic goat said to be descended from Capricorn. They can warp time even better than Gnomes.
- **Pure Faeries**- Creatures who spring to life from magical sources in the Under. They are genderless, and their type and ability depend on place of origin. They're associated with only one court, although they will work together to defeat a common enemy.
- **Sand Cat**- A feline that lives in the desert, able to go for weeks without water. Earth magic lets them do this.
- **Sha**- A magical desert dog from Egypt. Sha are the size of mundane toy breeds with short hair and small pointy ears. They could pass for mundane except for their blue tongues. They are attracted to anything undead.
- **Sphinx**- A magic cat with an affinity for fire. The reason they're hairless is that they're resistant to flames.
- **Strix**- A venomous owl with an affinity for poison. Female striges have rounded tufts on their heads, while males have pointed ones.
- **Sumxu**- A lop-eared cat found only in northern China. They are masters of camouflage and have an affinity for several kinds of magic.

Places

- **The Academy**—Something between a community college and a military academy for extrahumans, the Academy is geared toward helping extrahumans who don't play well with mortals get ready to join a blended society. It's got divisions for learners of all ages, though they are housed separately.

- **Cherry Blossom School**- A dojo geared toward teaching extrahumans self-restraint, meditation, and how to temper their enhanced physical abilities with more mundane skills. It's been around for close to a hundred years, run by the Ichiro family. Mundane classes used to be offered as a front but now are a separate division.
- **Ellicot City Magitechnic**- A prep school for magi and psychics specializing in magipsychic technology. It's located outside Baltimore.
- **Gallows Hill School**- Traditionally for shifters, this prep school in Salem recently opened its doors to changelings and other extrahumans not categorized as magi or psychics.
- **Hawthorn Academy**- A preparatory school for magi in Salem. Its campus is in the space between the mortal realm and the Under, giving it unrivaled privacy. They specialize in teaching familiar magic.
- **Providence Paranormal College**- A school founded just one year after Brown University and located right in its shadow. Providence Paranormal used to admit only magi and psychics, but it's been accepting all types of extrahumans ever since Henrietta Thurston became headmistress. There has been trouble since then for students and faculty, leading people to believe dissenters are sabotaging the school.
- **Trout Academy**- A prestigious preparatory school for changelings with magic, recently open to magi and magical shifters. Its campus is located in South County and has been operating in some form or another since Rhode Island Colony was founded.
- **The Under**- The faerie realm. It's been divided into two parts ever since the Sidhe Queen and the Goblin king split up thousands of years ago. Mortals don't age in the Under, but it's a dangerous place for them to be. Getting lost means never being seen again, and it's easy to get indebted to

something nasty while trying to get through or out of the Under.

- **Wolf Messing Prep**- An institute for psychics to learn to control their skills before heading to college.

Events

- **The Big Reveal**- The term used for the 1990s, when the world discovered magic was real and extrahumans existed. The decade was marked with fear as everyone adjusted to the changes. Since the 21st Century, law and technology work for both humans and extrahumans.
- **Boston Internment**- A reaction by Boston government officials to the disappearance and suspected trafficking in extrahumans, especially shifters. All registered extrahumans in Boston lived on barges for close to a month under guard by the Boston Police. The traffickers got their hands on some magical gadgets, rendering the protection useless. Few survived.

PROVIDENCE PARANORMAL COLLEGE

At Providence Paranormal College, class is about to start.

Who's enrolled? Students who are a bit different: vampires, were-wolves, changelings, shifters, psychics, and magi.

For one-hundred years, the college has taught and trained only psychics or magi, and for the first time, it's opening the doors to those not different: regular humans.

At this Ivy-League school, the students are expected to learn their powers and keep high grades.

Unfortunately, grades are slipping, but that's what happens when a mysterious villain is hunting you down...

Because someone is angry about this new admissions policy and they'll kill to stop integration. To defeat this rising evil, the students must band together and master their strange powers – because if they don't..

Well, it's pretty hard to graduate when you're dead.

Includes the first five books plus four brand new short stories inside the college.

"I spent more than a couple of late nights reading through these stories to find out what was going to happen to my new friends!" – Michael Anderle, Best-Selling Author of The Kurtherian Gambit

This series is for fans of Harry Potter, Jaymin Eve, and all academy books.

Get it today at Amazon and through Kindle Unlimited

THANK YOU!

Thank you for reading! If you loved this book, please leave a review. You can find my other work by clicking the links below, going to **my website** or visiting my **Author Central page**.

Providence Paranormal College Volume 1
Providence Paranormal College Volume 2
A Change In Crime
Wiser Guys
The Longest Night Watch
Stardust, Always
Supernatural Vigilante Society
Challenge of Vircon
Poetry Collections

CONNECT WITH THE AUTHOR

Website: https://www.drperryauthor.com/

Join her newsletter!

Find more of D.R. Perry's books on Amazon.

OTHER LMBPN PUBLISHING BOOKS

To be notified of new releases and special promotions from LMBPN publishing, please join our email list:

http://lmbpn.com/email/

For a complete list of books published by LMBPN please visit the following pages:

https://lmbpn.com/books-by-lmbpn-publishing/

All LMBPN Audiobooks are Available at Audible.com and iTunes. For a complete list of audiobooks visit:

www.lmbpn.com/audible

www.ingramcontent.com/pod-product-compliance
Lightning Source LLC
Chambersburg PA
CBHW020237110726
47898CB00004B/1291